*Praise for I...*

'Sweeping powers of description transport her readers to another place
and time'
*Rosanna Ley, bestselling author of*
Return to Mandalay *and* The Villa

'A most engaging story . . . the past always catches up with the future'
*Image Magazine*

'Oh, lucky reader, here is a really super book . . . riveting,
moving and utterly feel-good'
*Daily Mail*

'Willett's romantic and bewitching novels are always delightfully
satisfying'
*Lancashire Evening Post*

'Marcia's writing is, as always, lyrical and immensely readable . . . An
excellent and uplifting read'
*Western Morning News*

'Willett portrays the pleasures of life and the joy of simple things,
while remembering the sadness that comes with ageing and
the complex nature of family relationships'
*Good Book Guide*

'Echoes of carefree childhood summers resonate throughout
Marcia Willett's beguiling story of family relationships'
*Yorkshire Evening Post*

'A warm read about friendship, loyalty and just how far
people will go to protect the ones they love'
*Candis*

'Willett captures the sights, sounds and smells of Devon superbly . . . A
must for women's fiction readers'
*Booklist*

www.penguin.co.uk

Marcia Willett's early life was devoted to the ballet, but her dreams of becoming a ballerina ended when she grew out of the classical proportions required. She had always loved books, and a family crisis made her take up a new career as a novelist – a decision she has never regretted. She lives in a beautiful and wild part of Devon.

Find out more about Marcia Willett and her novels at
www.marciawillett.co.uk

### By Marcia Willett

and published by Corgi Books

# SUMMER ON THE RIVER

### MARCIA WILLETT

## CORGI BOOKS

TRANSWORLD PUBLISHERS
61–63 Uxbridge Road, London W5 5SA
www.penguin.co.uk

Transworld is part of the Penguin Random House group of companies
whose addresses can be found at global.penguinrandomhouse.com

First published in Great Britain in 2015 by Bantam Press
an imprint of Transworld Publishers
Corgi edition published 2016

Copyright © Marcia Willett 2015

Marcia Willett has asserted her right under the Copyright,
Designs and Patents Act 1988 to be identified as the author of this work.

This book is a work of fiction and, except in the case of historical fact, any resemblance
to actual persons living or dead, is purely coincidental.

Every effort has been made to obtain the necessary permissions
with reference to copyright material, both illustrative and quoted. We
apologize for any omissions in this respect and will be pleased
to make the appropriate acknowledgements in any future edition.

A CIP catalogue record for this book
is available from the British Library.

ISBN
9780552171441

Typeset in 13/15 pt Fournier MT by Jouve (UK), Milton Keynes
Printed and bound in Great Britain by Clays Ltd, St Ives Plc

Penguin Random House is committed to a sustainable
future for our business, our readers and our planet. This book
is made from Forest Stewardship Council® certified paper.

7 9 10 8 6

To Miriam

# PART ONE

# CHAPTER ONE

The loganberries are nearly over. As she picks the soft crimson fruit, sun-warmed and so easily crushed between her stained fingers, Evie can hear the warning 'tck-tck-tck' of the blackbird half hidden in the ivy on the wall. She glances up at him, just able to spy a flicker of black wing and a flash of golden beak.

'I know you're there,' she says. 'You've been helping yourself, haven't you?'

She drops the berries into a wine glass, which also contains a few sweet peas, straightens up and looks out across the roof tops towards the harbour entrance where two tiny white boats seem to be slipping and sliding across the shiny blue silk of the sea, tacking this way and that in an attempt to catch the fitful breeze. The steep garden that rises up behind the old Merchant's House is built in a series of terraces, surrounded by high stone walls, warm and sheltered from strong winds. On this highest level a white-painted wrought-iron table and four chairs stand on slate flags, half screened by a low lavender hedge: a small formal area set above a watercolour wilderness of flowers and shrubs.

Evie sits down at the table, smiling with pleasure, reaching to run her fingers through the tall spikes of purple-blue lavender, breathing in its scent. Tommy loved it here, sitting with a bottle of wine open on the table, watching the traffic on the river streaming between the wooded cliffs out to sea. Privately, between themselves, she called him Tommy. Thomas David Fortescue: TDF. The Darling Fellow. His aunts always called him that: the darling fellow. They'd raised him, between the three of them, when his mother died young of cancer and his father was busy in London running the family wine import business. 'Is it my turn for the darling fellow this exeat . . . half term . . . holiday?' As time passed, two of the aunts − one a widow, the other unmarried − moved into the Merchant's House, so that the darling fellow's life should be as undisturbed as possible, and he grew up as his nature dictated: calm, optimistic, generous. His peers called him TDF though some, remembering with fondness the aunts and happy school holidays in Dartmouth, still referred to him as 'the darling fellow'. He didn't mind − enjoyed the joke − though his first wife, Marianne, occasionally found it irritating when this had to be explained to her own friends or to newcomers to their circle. She called him Thomas. Marianne always preferred London to Dartmouth, though it was convenient to be able to invite friends down to the Merchant's

House for a weekend party, for regatta, very occasionally for Christmas. With its elegant rooms, sweeping views of the river, the luminous quality of light and sense of spaciousness, it was the perfect house for celebrations.

As their son, Charlie, was growing up Marianne became busier than ever, organizing his social life, entertaining his friends. More and more Tommy found that he was travelling down to Dartmouth alone.

Sitting at the table on the terrace on this late August evening, Evie thinks of him: tall, lean, black hair, brown eyes. She first met him in the road outside the house as she climbed up the steep flights of steps from the converted boathouse that she was planning to buy. She reached the pavement, paused to catch her breath, and saw him coming out of the elegant townhouse opposite. He dropped his keys into his pocket, turned round, saw her standing there and smiled at her.

Nearly twenty-five years later, Evie begins to laugh: that smile had wreaked its very own kind of havoc. It was friendly, almost amused, as if he somehow guessed that she was in a state of great excitement. Eyebrows raised, he seemed to be challenging her to tell him about it – and so she did.

'Look,' she said, beckoning him across the street, leaning over the wall so as to point down to where the small, newly converted boathouse stood at the river's edge, poised above it, full of water-light and sunshine. 'Isn't it lovely? I'm going to buy it!'

'Gosh!' he said, eager as a boy – the darling

fellow – entering into her joy. 'Good for you! So we'll be neighbours.'

'Do you live there?' She nodded across the road towards the Merchant's House, impressed and, more than that, heart-thumpingly hopeful. He was rather nice.

'In London mostly,' he said ruefully. 'Dartmouth whenever I can. My wife gets bored very quickly here, and she's not a sailor. I love it, though.'

Oh, damn, she thought. A wife. Oh, well . . .

She found that she was walking with him down the hill towards Fairfax Place.

'So what about you?' he was asking. 'I haven't seen you in the town, have I? Are you local?'

'No, not a local,' she said. 'I've been renting a house near Totnes for the last five years. I taught History at Bristol University. The Civil War was my speciality. And then I began to write a novel about it and . . .'

She hesitated, unwilling to say too much – about how successful the books were, how she'd decided to give up her job so as to concentrate on her writing – but he was looking at her even more keenly.

'Don't tell me you're Evelyn Drake?'

She laughed at his excitement. 'I am. But don't tell anyone.'

'But I love your Civil War books,' he said. 'I've read every one of them. And what's this I've heard about a television series?'

She nodded, thrilled and embarrassed in equal parts. 'It's unbelievable luck. And now an American publisher has offered me a contract for the first two books, so that's why I can afford to buy the boathouse. To be honest, I don't quite know whether I'm dreaming the whole thing.'

He studied her more closely. 'Husband?' he enquired lightly. She shook her head. 'Anyone special?' Another shake of the head. 'So I shan't be treading on anyone's toes if I offer to buy you a drink?'

'I must take the keys back to the estate agent and then I'd love it,' she said – and that was the beginning.

Evie raises her glass, full of loganberries and sweet peas, and silently toasts him and their years together: ten as his mistress, twelve as his wife after Marianne died. During that time they'd continued to live between the Merchant's House and the boathouse but, when the darling fellow died in Dartmouth Hospital two days after an aortic aneurysm, she'd moved back into the boathouse and let out the Merchant's House to friends who were relocating and between houses.

Now, she puts the glass on the table and looks down across the terraced garden to the house from which a figure emerges. The tenants have gone and Ben is living here whilst he is recovering from the recent breakdown of his marriage. Ben's father and Tommy were cousins and it is with Ben that she's been sharing the bottle of wine that stands on the table. He and Charlie are so alike they could be brothers: spare, tall and dark, just like Tommy. She loves them both equally.

What am I to do? she wonders, not for the first time.

Ben, who has come up through the garden to rejoin

her, looks at her glass, raises his eyebrows. 'Not much room for wine.'

She shakes her head and gets up. 'No more for me, darling. Will you come over to the boathouse for supper?'

'Not tonight, I've got an assignment to finish off, but thanks.' He indicates the loganberries and the sweet peas. 'Do you want something to put those in?'

'I'll find something in the kitchen as I go through.'

He stoops to kiss her and she goes carefully down the zigzag of steps through the garden and into the kitchen.

The Merchant's House has never truly been home to Evie. Even when she was living there with Tommy she was too conscious of the family tradition, too aware that her tenure was merely temporary, to be able to relax and enjoy it properly. The Fortescues had always lived between Dartmouth and London but, once the aunts had died and Tommy married Marianne, the Merchant's House became less and less a family home and more and more a bolt hole. Marianne sometimes brought friends and clients down to impress them and, as boys, Charlie and Ben spent a few weeks each summer in Dartmouth, so it was at the boathouse that Evie and Tommy talked, and laughed, and learned each other's history. It wasn't an affair in the usual sense of the word, though the sex when it happened was good; there was none of the illicit thrill of it being secret to fan the flames of attraction. It was much simpler: as if they'd each found someone necessary, who filled an aching gap and made sense of life. It was something quite separate from Tommy's life

14

in London. They were discreet, and if any of the locals guessed, nobody was telling. There had been Fortescues in Dartmouth for generations, and affection for the aunts and Tommy was still very strong and very loyal.

All the same, thinks Evie, as she puts the sweet peas and the loganberries into a little pottery bowl, it was wrong, I suppose. It's just that I can't regret it. He was so grounded. Though, given that was true, I wonder why he needed me. There was something we both lacked, I suppose, that we gave each other. We were so completely on the same wavelength – books, music, films – it was extraordinary; almost as if we had been brought up together and had a whole shared reference of knowledge and experience. It was so easy, being with him.

She suspected that Charlie guessed afterwards – once she and Tommy were married – that there was already a long-standing romantic relationship. Much later Evie was able to talk to him about it, but during those early years she kept well out of the way on the few occasions when the family were in Dartmouth.

'It's a pity,' Tommy said once. 'Marianne's a terrific scalp-hunter. She'd be utterly thrilled to have you at one of her weekend parties.'

But Evie shook her head. 'No chance. I couldn't play the part. Nor could you. And it's not fair on her or Charlie. Especially Charlie. I like the sound of Charlie.'

Charlie, like his mother, prefers London. He is happily settled there now in the family house in Kensington, running the wine import business. He was delighted when

Evie and his father got married; not long married himself, a proud father, and generously disposed for everyone to be happy. He and Evie quickly adopted an easy, lighthearted relationship. Charlie would roar with laughter at her jokes and his wife would smile tightly, baffled by Evie's casual approach to life and her indifference to people's opinions or criticism.

'I can't help wondering,' Evie said to Tommy, 'whether Angela is quite the right girl for your Charlie.'

'Oh, Ange is OK,' he said tolerantly. 'Very sensible. She's an asset where the business is concerned. Very switched on and efficient.'

Evie made a face. 'He could get a PA with those qualifications.'

He looked thoughtful. 'Funny chap, Charlie. He's got his head well and truly screwed on but he's not always quite as confident as he looks. His mother had great influence over him. Marianne thoroughly approved of Ange – we've known the family for years – and I think he's simply grown used to her. He could see that she'd be good at making sure everything runs smoothly.'

And so she did. Like Marianne before her, she knew the right people, made the right kind of friends and was good with the clients, though she lacked Marianne's generosity. Nevertheless, the business continued to flourish, and Charlie's prospects with it.

So what did I know? Evie asks herself, closing the front door behind her and crossing the road. Tommy was right and it was none of my business.

But it is her business now: Tommy has made it her business. Charlie has inherited the house in Kensington, the wine import business, the assets; but the Merchant's House has been left to Evie. Charlie is puzzled but courteous; Ange is furious.

'Rather unusual,' she said to Evie after the will was read. 'The house has been in the family for generations.'

'Evie is family,' Charlie reminded her gently, and Ange flushed that unbecoming red that flows up from her chest and over her face each time she is annoyed.

'You know what I mean,' she muttered.

Evie wanted to agree but was obliged to remain silent: she was as shocked as Ange. It never occurred to her that Tommy would do such a thing.

Clutching the bowl, Evie descends the steep flights of steps that lead down to the shared paved area behind the boathouse and lets herself in. River-light flows across the polished wood floor, trembles on the white walls, washes up into the high-raftered roof of this huge living space. She sets the bowl down beside the Belfast sink, crosses the length of the room to the big glass doors, which open on to the wooden balcony, and steps outside. If she turns her back on the river and looks up she can see the Merchant's House standing in its elegant row across the road high above her. All around her are other converted boathouses, jumbled amongst fishermen's cottages built below the level of the road, backed into the rock and huddled above the river. Some have ports with heavy wooden doors that can be closed against the tide and

17

where small boats can be kept. A few owners have built tall stone columns into which lifts have been installed to avoid climbing steep steps to the road above. Some of the cottages have tiny courtyards surrounded by high stone walls. These walls are bright with flowers: valerian, feverfew, mallows, lacecap hydrangeas spring from the crevices in these stones and flourish in the salty air.

If she looks across the river Evie can see Kingswear with its tier upon tier of houses stacked on the hill above the marina: narrow terraced houses the colour of ice cream: mint, vanilla, bubblegum, coffee.

The sun has slipped away behind the hill and the balcony is in shadow. This is when she misses Tommy most: early evening when work is done and it's time to light the candles, to prepare supper, to talk over the events of the day. In the winter she will pull down the pretty hand-painted blinds over the windows that face northwards upriver and south to the sea, and close the curtains across the big glass doors. She will go through the connecting door from the utility room behind the kitchen, into the small adjoining fisherman's cottage where she works and where there is the den, cosy and warm, sheltered from winter storms and the high spring tides that race in from the sea. The bedrooms are here, too: not very big but quite adequate. The contrast is extraordinary: the higgledy-piggledy cottage with twists and turns and unexpected steps, and the huge light-filled space that feels like an extension of the river.

Evie opens a cupboard and finds a vase for the sweet peas;

she empties the loganberries into a smaller dish. The bowl must be returned to the Merchant's House. She is always most particular that there should never be any muddle.

'It's yours too, now,' Tommy would say after they were married, but she'd shake her head.

'It belongs to your family, not to me.'

'But you are my family,' he'd protest. 'This is our home, darling Evie. Relax into it. Don't be so independent. You are happy, aren't you? I know you love your boathouse but you like this old place, too, don't you?'

And she did love it: the Merchant's House was graceful, elegant, and yet warm and friendly. She loved the big comfortable breakfast room, which led off from the kitchen, and the bright, sunny drawing-room on the first floor with its big sash windows looking across the river. She loved the sheltered terraced garden, with its amazing views, the fruit trees growing against the high stone walls, and the scent of the lavender hedge at the end of a hot day. It was a family house, but it wasn't *her* family, as Ange always made sure to underline. Whenever she and Charlie visited, with Alice as a tiny baby – and later with Millie, too – Ange took opportunities to assert her position as Tommy's daughter-in-law, wife of his beloved son, mother of his adorable granddaughters. She'd visited Dartmouth when Marianne was still alive, knew the house intimately, and never missed the chance to make Evie feel that she was an outsider. Not in front of Charlie or Tommy – she was too clever for that – but by subtle hints and actions Ange indicated her rights of possession.

Of course, she never dreamed that Tommy would leave the house to Evie.

Now, as if she is casting off the problem – or running away from it – Evie picks up her bag and goes out again. She crosses the paved area, which her neighbour has made delightful with terracotta pots full of bedding plants, and climbs the flight of steps to the road above. She will go down to the Embankment, watch the boats and the people, maybe have something to eat in the Royal Castle Hotel. This evening she doesn't want to be alone. Tomorrow Claude will be back: Tommy's oldest, dearest friend. Boys together at boarding school, holidays at the Merchant's House with the aunts, jaunts in London – throughout their lives their friendship remained strong, surviving marriage, babies, distance. Claude has been a widower for nearly four years and now he spends a great deal of time with Evie in Dartmouth. A retired naval commander, he likes to be here in the town, remembering his days as a cadet at the Britannia Royal Naval College, watching the new young intake out on the river.

Evie feels a special affection for Claude. He was the only one of Tommy's friends who knew about their affair. He never judged, never criticized, welcoming her warmly into the relationship he shared with his oldest friend.

'He doesn't get on very well with Marianne,' was all Tommy said. 'I'd like you to be friends.'

And so they are; and tomorrow morning she will go to fetch him from the train at Totnes. Claude is always here for regatta.

She wanders along the Embankment where visitors linger by the river, then turns into the town, past the Boat Float where small boats are moored. She crosses the road and pushes open the door of the Royal Castle Hotel. It's quiet in the long, low bar with its large oak beams, rather too early for visitors or locals, and she is able to bag her favourite table by the window. She leaves her jacket on the chair and goes to the bar to order some supper and a glass of Pinot Grigio. A group of cheerful, noisy people come crowding in and she smiles at them as she squeezes by, carrying her wine back to her table.

Evie relaxes in her chair, gazing out at the Boat Float, wondering how often she has sat here with cups of coffee or glasses of wine and thought about the current novel.

'Do you get lonely?' Tommy would ask just occasionally, his arms tightly around her, his voice anxious lest she should say 'Yes', and accuse him of leaving her alone, of using her.

She'd laugh, mocking his fear. 'With my head full of all my people?' she'd ask. 'Are you joking?'

And it was partly true: fragments of conversation, threads of plots, odd connections crisscrossing the relationships of the characters, continually jostled her thoughts.

Here, in the Royal Castle, she's watched people eating, drinking, laughing, talking; she's observed expressions, gestures, body language, and while she's making mental notes she's also conscious of long-gone generations inhabiting this old medieval port, from which merchant-venturers sailed out to find their fortunes and where the

Pilgrim Fathers anchored for a while on their way to America.

As she sips her wine, she gradually becomes aware that this time it is she who is under observation: someone is watching her. An odd sensation, like a light current of cold air, seems to brush against her skin. She glances round quite casually and sees a thin, fair man in the far corner at the table by the door. He is watching her with a cool stare, his face inscrutable but certainly not friendly. She has grown used to a certain amount of attention. People recognize her from the photographs on the dust covers of her books, from literary festivals, from local television – she often encounters a 'Don't I know you from somewhere?' glance – but what is not familiar is this sense of hostility; of active dislike.

She looks back at him, tries a little friendly smile, but the inimical stare doesn't change and she turns again to look out of the window. Oddly, she feels unsettled. People are friendly in this small town, locals and visitors alike, and she is unnerved. She wonders if he might be a descendant of one the great West Country families that she has written about and that has appeared in an unfavourable light.

Her supper arrives and the jolly group of people come to sit at the tables near by, shielding her from her observer. She eats quickly, prey to foolish fears. Supposing he should follow her when she leaves? Perhaps she should return to the Merchant's House and find company with Ben? But when she's finished her supper, and glances into the corner with a nicely simulated mix of friendly indifference, she sees that the watcher is gone.

Her relief is shot through with fantastic and fearful ideas – she is, after all, a novelist – which she thrusts impatiently aside. However, she doesn't stroll around the Boat Float or along the Embankment but walks straight home, through Fairfax Place to Southtown, glancing from time to time behind her.

Once inside the boathouse, she laughs at her fears. Nevertheless she is glad that Claude will be here in the morning.

## CHAPTER TWO

Everything looks different from the train. Secret places far from roads and villages; glimpses of other worlds. Scrubby trees crowding round a dark pool, their feet in the brackish oily water, and a heron standing watchful in the reeds. Swans, breast to breast with their pale elegant reflections, drifting across flooded lowland. An unexpected rectangle of allotments, productive and untidy, and a brightly painted narrowboat called *Bess* moored alongside a canal path. And now, in the distance, there are the round small hills of Devon and neat little fields – emerald green, corn gold, dusty pink – looking like crumpled rugs laid out to dry in the sun.

Claude loves this train journey to the west, so familiar from his childhood, still retaining its sense of magic and promise. Going to Dartmouth for school holidays with TDF, returning to the Naval College from leave, travelling down from Hampshire annually for regatta, he feels that this journey marks the stages in his life. He'd loved TDF, and envied him. He was everything Claude was not: tall, good-looking, socially at ease, popular. Claude was a short, chunky, red-headed boy who looked — in his own eyes — as if he'd been taken apart and reassembled in a hurry and who, as he grew older, felt defensive in the presence of girls. Yet he never resented TDF for all these gifts with which he was endowed. The darling fellow had drawn Claude into his magic circle. He'd sprinkled the glitter of his own popularity over his friend and lent him grace. Claude misses him but is grateful for Evie, who made TDF so happy.

As the train leaves Exeter Claude leans forward ready to gaze out at the estuary, where boats rest on the shining mud and egrets strut long-legged behind the receding tide; and then he turns to look inland, to the parkland of Powderham Castle, to glimpse the shadowy shapes of deer grazing in the dappled shade of the trees.

He settles back in his seat as the train travels onwards to Dawlish and Teignmouth. If he's honest, he never liked Marianne much, though he tried not to show it. She was too organized, too sensible. TDF guessed, of course, and saw to it that the Merchant's House was where he and Claude would meet for an occasional weekend when Marianne was busy with her endless social engagements or her plans for Charlie's advancement. Claude's own wife, Jilly — generous, warm-hearted, used to the separations and vagaries of naval life — was perfectly content to see him off to Dartmouth for an occasional run ashore with TDF, though even she didn't know about Evie. To be honest, Claude had enjoyed his position of privilege; the only one taken into their confidence. Despite the huge success of the television series and her books, Evie kept a very low profile and they both welcomed him as the one friend with whom they could share the happiness of their unusual relationship. He liked her at once; she was amusing, laid-back, independent. He could see the point of Evie. Even after she and TDF were married, Claude remained special to them. Jilly, busy with her family, had been surprised and interested that TDF should remarry – and especially the well-known writer – and delighted that Claude should retain his friendship with his childhood friend, but was much more focused on their new grandson and her garden. When their son-in-law got a teaching post in Winchester, and their daughter was expecting their third child, it was Jilly who suggested that the growing family should move into the main house whilst she and Claude took up residence in the annexe. It had always been the plan but now, Jilly said, the time was right and so the move was made. Five years later Jilly was dead and, as Claude combats his grief and loneliness, he is glad and grateful to be close to his family whilst retaining a measure of independence. Nevertheless, these trips to Dartmouth are a treat. Here he sheds his responsibilities as father and grandfather and is simply Claude.

The train passes above a smooth sandy beach where a dog runs, scattering the gulls that perch on the rotting wooden groins that stride out into the sea; it dives through rocky tunnels formed by red sandstone, stops at Newton Abbot, then heads off again towards Totnes.

Claude stands up, lifts down his bag, makes his way

along the carriage. He never brings the car to Dartmouth. Parking is difficult and, anyway, he enjoys the train journey, always taken very early – and always first class. This is a very special perk he allows himself as part of the treat. Evie keeps her own car in the garage that belongs to the Merchant's House and with it, tucked well out of the way, is Claude's small motorbike. He loves his little red and white Peugeot scooter. He uses it to potter round the town or for sorties out along the coast. Sometimes Evie will come with him, clinging on like a monkey, roaring with laughter as he negotiates the steep hills and narrow bends through Strete and Stoke Fleming. They'll stop at the beach café at Strete Gate, enjoying the surprised glances when he takes off his helmet and reveals his grey hair. He likes to whizz along Torcross Line on their way to Stokeley Farm Shop for a cream tea, and then back again to Slapton Ley to park up and go for a walk.

As the train slows down he peers through the window to look for Evie. He catches sight of her waiting by the gate. She's in her usual rig: jeans, a loose shirt with the sleeves rolled up, deck shoes. Her thick greying fair hair, slightly curly and rumpled, is clipped back at the temples and she is deeply tanned. She looks more like a sailor than a writer – and nothing like her sixty-odd years.

He smiles and raises a hand, though he knows she can't see him, and he's suddenly filled with the usual mix of emotions – of relaxation and anticipation; of peace and excitement; of homecoming.

*

They climb into Evie's small car and drive out of the station yard, up the hill and away to Dartmouth.

'So how's the family?' asks Evie.

'The kids have friends staying,' he answers, 'with small children and babies of their own so that the place is filled with young. Lovely, great fun and all that, but very nice to get away from for a bit of peace and quiet.'

'Well, Dartmouth is filling up,' warns Evie. 'But at least we have a bird's-eye view without having to leave the house.'

'You could rent the Merchant's House out for regatta. You'd get a small fortune for it.'

'But Ben is staying there,' she protests, 'and now Charlie's talking of coming down. Ange wants to bring some friends, apparently.'

He stares out of the car window. 'Still treats it like her own, doesn't she?'

'Well, in a way it is, isn't it?'

'You mean she expects you to leave it to them?'

'Well, after all, who else would I leave it to? I have no family of my own. Even so, it's not quite that simple . . .'

He is aware of tension and he backs off. He was slightly puzzled when TDF left the house to Evie, given the strong family tradition and given that Evie was very well off in her own right, but he hasn't spared it much thought.

'How's Ben?' he asks. 'What's this about his marriage breaking up?'

'It appears that Kirsty has grown tired of living in a small garden flat without the prospect of ever moving up and on. But, much more to the point, on one of her visits to Scotland to see her parents she met up with an ex-boyfriend and is now seriously involved with him.'

'Good grief,' says Claude. 'So it's really over?'

Evie shrugs. 'The flat in London is up for sale and she's going back to Edinburgh as soon as it's sold.'

'Well, that's sad news. What about Laura?'

'Darling Laura got a First, which was terrific. I told you, didn't I? Ben is so proud. She came down to see us all a few weeks ago and then went off backpacking with some friends.'

'And how has she taken all this?'

'When she came down to stay she and Ben had a long session. You can see that she's gutted but she's trying to be very sensible about it. We all had supper together.'

'I'm glad Ben's here in Dartmouth. At least he's got some moral support.'

'He doesn't seem to blame Kirsty — I think he must have seen it coming for quite a while now — but the ex-boyfriend was a bit of a shock. Ben has that optimistic, easy-going Fortescue streak but even he's having to face that it's really over.'

'Ben's always worked hard. I'm glad he stuck to his art and his photography,' says Claude. 'He's very talented and he's made a good living at it.'

'Mmm. Not ever quite good enough for Kirsty.'

'Does Charlie know?'

'I'm sure he does. Ben's probably looking forward to talking it over with him.'

'Will they be coming by car?'

Cars always cause problems during regatta. The funfair will take up the whole of Mayor's Avenue car park, the 'No parking in the town' signs will be posted beside the entrances to all the approach roads, and Park and Ride is the only means of getting into the town. Garages and driveways, or any space where a car can be squeezed in, will be at a premium. Evie has a friend who lets her use her driveway when Charlie comes down for regatta, but this year there's Ben's car, too.

'Ange wouldn't dream of coming on the train,' says Evie. 'Charlie does sometimes when he's on his own but not with Ange. You know that.'

'But then Ben hasn't been living there before, has he? How does he feel about them turning up? After all, the house is yours and you're letting Ben use it. Does Ange still feel they have the divine right to stay whenever they want to and turn your car out of the garage?'

'Well, she does actually. She rather insisted that our old bedroom with the en suite should always be kept for them and the other one across the landing for the girls or for guests.'

'That's a bit rich, isn't it?'

Evie shrugs, turning off the main road at Halwell. 'Ben is very happy up on the second floor. He's got fantastic views and there's the little hobbies room next door to his bedroom where he keeps his computer and all his artist's materials. He's been making some lovely greetings cards, which he's had a bit of success with locally, and he has his photographic work, of course. He can muck in with us if he feels *de trop* occasionally, but I don't think Charlie will allow that to happen.'

Claude snorts. 'I still think she's out of order.'

Evie looks sideways at him. 'That's because you don't like Ange. We'll sort it somehow. We've got nearly another week yet.'

They travel through the familiar countryside for a while in companionable silence. He's always found it easy to be quiet with Evie; no necessity for banal chatter. He knows that she will drive him through the town though it isn't her usual route to the boathouse. It's become a custom, on his arrival, to drive down College Way, along the Embankment, turning right into Oxford Street and up to Southtown, so that he can experience a true sense of homecoming. Memories crowd in: crab-fishing off the Embankment with TDF during school holidays; out on the river as a new cadet with his oppos in a picket boat; the final Passing-out Parade and Summer Ball as a midshipman – more than fifty years ago, he reminds himself – full of pride, with Jilly in her pretty ball gown.

In the town, busy as a hive of bees, there are already signs of the preparation for regatta. Bunting is strung across the streets and a few houses are draped with huge Union flags. Evie drives slowly so that Claude can see the small boats out on the river, visitors wandering happily along the Embankment in the sunshine, children fishing watched by noisy vigilant gulls. There is an empty parking space almost opposite the Merchant's House and Evie darts into it with a whoop of triumph.

Claude climbs out and stands, leaning on the wall, gazing down-river and out to sea. The lower ferry edges out from the slip at Kingswear, nudged by the tug hooting to warn the other river traffic, performing its graceful turn midstream as it meets its fellow coming out from Bayard's Cove so that they seem to be executing a slow, elegant dance.

'Coffee?' Evie suggests, as she opens the hatchback.

This is another little custom. They will have coffee and *pains au chocolat* in the boathouse – on the balcony if the weather allows – and then he will go for a walk around the town on his own. Because of his early start he's always hungry when he arrives. He takes his bag from the car and slams the door.

'It's good to be back,' he says.

He roams about while Evie makes the coffee. His room isn't very big but he's used to cabins, wardrooms, living on warships, and it's quite comfortable enough for him. Evie has had the third bedroom converted into an en suite and small dressing room off her own room, so he is able to use the bathroom without any anxiety. He unpacks quickly, tidies everything away into the appropriate spaces; he travels light.

Back in the kitchen Claude is drawn to the great glass doors open to the sunlight and the river. He steps out on to the balcony. It is as if he is in the prow of a boat sailing down-river amongst the smaller craft: a fleet of little din-ghies with brown sails; the blue-painted passenger ferry – the old pilot boat *Achieve* – ploughing out to the Castle; one of the College yachts, *Martlet*, heading out to sea.

As he turns round to look up at the Merchant's House he hears the ring of the doorbell.

'Might be Ben,' calls Evie. 'I suggested he came over to say hello.'

And it is Ben, coming in through the great light-washed spaces all dappled with sunshine, looking so like TDF that Claude almost wants to weep.

'Ben.' Their hands meet in a strong warm clasp. 'Good to see you.'

Claude remembers what Evie has told him and can't quite think what to say. Each conversational gambit seems loaded with what might cause Ben embarrassment.

'Great to see you back,' says Ben. He is calm; no stress here. 'Did Evie tell you that Charlie's coming down for regatta?'

'She did. And I told her that I think they're out of order still using the house as if it's theirs.'

Ben bursts out laughing and Evie, arriving with the tray of coffee, shakes her head at Claude.

'Not that it's any of his business,' she says to Ben. 'I've told him, it's a family house.'

Claude grunts his disapproval, sits down at the wooden table.

'And,' adds Evie, filling his mug with coffee, passing it

to him, 'you will be polite to Ange. This is not a subject for negotiation.'

Claude makes a face. 'I can't get on with her. Makes me feel I'm back at school.'

'Ange is all right,' says Ben tolerantly. 'She just needs to be in control. It's only for a weekend, after all, and I've had a text from Charlie saying that the friends can't come after all. I think he and Ange are going on down to Ange's mother in Polzeath. The girls are there already.'

In the face of Ben's good humour Claude's irascibility fades. It was the same with TDF, his calm optimism defusing Claude's wrathful outbursts. He sips his coffee, accepts a *pain au chocolat* and relaxes, stretching in the warm sunshine.

'God, it's good to be here,' he says.

Suddenly he feels immensely tired. The early start, the journey, and then this magic place always have this effect, as if his taut strings have been cut. In a moment he'll go out and walk around the town and his energy will surge back, but just now it's utter bliss to sit here at the river's edge with Evie and Ben drinking coffee in the sun.

# CHAPTER THREE

'He's looking good, isn't he?' says Ben as Claude goes striding away, down the hill and into the town.

He's very fond of Claude. He and Charlie regard him as a kind of uncle but without the constraints that are bound up in the relationship with someone who is actually a blood relative. Claude wouldn't dream of remonstrating with them or giving them advice but there is a comfortable familiarity, a sense of security, in his company. It's much the same with Evie. Ben knows that Charlie doesn't in the least regard her as his stepmother but there is a close, easy relationship between them that he, Ben, has benefited from almost as much as Charlie has.

He and Charlie are good mates. His own mother died when he was fifteen and Charlie's mum always made sure that Ben was included: invited to parties and at Christmas, taken to Dartmouth for nearly all of his holidays. His own father was a photojournalist, living on the edge but happy, and he bore no grudge that Charlie's father – the darling fellow – had inherited a thriving wine import business, the Merchant's House, a house in Kensington and all the comfort that went with it.

'It would have been wasted on me,' he'd say. 'I'm no businessman. Our side of the family was always artistic. And anyway, TDF is always ready to help out if the chips are really down.'

Ben has inherited his father's artistic talent. He is well known for his work in the glossy 'gardens and interiors' magazines, but he has never earned enough to pay the mortgage on the kind of house Kirsty aspires to and, once Laura was born, the need to contribute became even more critical. Recently he's borrowed from Charlie so as to update some of his photographic equipment.

'For God's sake don't tell Ange,' Charlie said. 'We'll sort it out somehow.'

Well, now it seems that some of his one-third share of the flat in London – not very much once the huge mortgage is paid off – will belong to Charlie. Thank God for Evie and the Merchant's House, a regular trickle of photoshoots, and his new project. He loves a new project.

Ben glances at Evie and sees that she is watching him.

'So what's the plan?' she asks cheerfully.

It is his theory that she can read his mind as easily as the screen of her laptop, and he grins at her.

'I've got a few new outlets lined up for the cards. Some art shops and galleries I haven't tried yet. I imagine you won't want to come along? Not with Claude here.'

Sometimes she goes with him for the ride when he

visits the bookshops and galleries that are beginning to display his cards. She chats with the booksellers who know her very well, though it is five years now since she's had a book published.

'All written out,' she says, when they press her to produce a new one. 'Nothing left to say.'

Ben doesn't believe it. Maybe she's exhausted the Civil War as a subject but he feels that Evie still has something to say.

'No, I shan't come today,' she answers. 'But good luck.'

He nods. 'See you later.'

By lunchtime he is at Stokeley Farm Shop. The shop is busy but he checks the card displays and sees only one of his cards remaining: Start Point Lighthouse taken from one of his own photographs. Ben is seized with a thrill of pleasure. He has some more packs in his bag just in case and he is confident that he'll be able to persuade them to take more. It's too busy just at the moment to make his number so he orders an Americano and flops down on the long grey cord-covered sofa that faces the big open glass doors on to the patio area where people are sitting in the sunshine. He loves it here in the farm shop café, with its high pine roof and big pizza oven. The café is almost empty and he relaxes, leaning back against the red cord cushions, aware of this new and very odd sensation of extreme wellbeing shot through with moments of terrible sadness.

It was a huge shock when Kirsty told him that their marriage was over, though it had been limping along for quite some time. The real shock, of course, was that she'd found someone else; a man she'd known from childhood, and then at university in London, who caught up with her on Friends Reunited. Ben suffers a brief stab of jealousy at the thought of this man who knows Kirsty from way back. He feels a fool that she's been cheating on him for the last year.

He stretches out his legs, remembering those early years and how happy they were. Kirsty stayed in London after university and she and Ben met at a party and fell in love. She was working in IT with an American company; his own career was just beginning to take shape and he'd been lucky enough to land a big commission that might well have inflated Kirsty's hopes. They rented a small garden flat in Chiswick, which they were able to buy with the help of Kirsty's parents when Laura arrived. Twenty-two years on they were still there. He can't quite remember at what point money worries, the cares of parenthood, the simple daily grind, began to wear down that early passionate love. He is aware, however, that after Laura went off to university there was an emptiness, a lack of purpose. Perhaps she was the glue of familiar necessity still holding them together: without her there was a kind of pointlessness to the daily round. Kirsty began to go regularly to Edinburgh to see her parents – or that was the story – whilst he took more and more assignments that brought him down into the West Country where he loved to be.

He's always been happy to spend time alone. Only then is he most truly himself, free for a while from the responsibility for other people who rely upon him. His innate sense of guilt makes it impossible to relax completely whilst any-one who has a claim upon him is within his orbit.

Intertwined with his great love for Kirsty and Laura was always this anxiety that he might fail them, which – however hard he tried to rationalize it – coloured his relationships with them. Neither of them could possibly have guessed at the sense of deep peace that engulfed him whenever he climbed into his car to go on an assignment that required him to be away from home alone for a few precious days. These brief respites enabled him to return refreshed, ready to resume his duties as husband and father. Because he worked so much at home he was able to look after Laura when she was small, to take her to and fetch her from school, to attend plays and sports days, and they formed a strong, close bond.

As he sits waiting for his coffee he remembers their last meeting. He picked her up from the train in Totnes and drove her back to the Merchant's House. It was an odd journey, neither of them quite ready to discuss what was uppermost in their minds. Instead, they talked about her plan to go backpacking and then work in Switzerland as a chalet-girl, but all the while he could sense Laura's tension as she sat beside him. She pushed back her short dark hair with quick, nervous fingers, or clenched her hands between her long legs clad in denim jeans.

Once they were inside, in the hall, she dropped her bag on the floor and let out a huge sigh of relief.

'I love this place,' she said, looking around. 'It always feels so welcoming. I'm glad you're here, Dad.'

'So am I,' he said cheerfully. 'I don't know why it feels like home but it does. All those summer holidays here with Charlie when we were kids, I suppose, though I spent just as much time with him in London. Dartmouth is very special to me.'

They looked at one another, smiling, and then her expression changed and he held out his arms and she rushed into them, pushing her head into his shoulder.

'Mum's explained things,' she said, muffled. 'She's told me about Iain. It was a real shock, I can tell you. How are you with that?'

She leaned back and looked up at him woefully, her brown eyes anxious, full of tears, and he held her tightly for a moment longer and then let her go.

'Let's have a drink,' he said, leading the way into the kitchen. 'Coffee? Tea? Something stronger?'

'Do you have a fruit tea?' she asked. 'I've got some in my bag if you haven't.'

'Hang on.' He swung open a cupboard door and took out a cardboard carton. 'There you are. Take your pick.'

She chose one, dropped the teabag into a mug, and asked hopefully, 'Any honey?'

Just for a moment he was transported back in time: honey toast, honey sandwiches – Laura had always loved honey. He reached down the jar from the shelf and pushed it across, gave her a spoon, and then led the way through the arch into the breakfast room. They sat together at the big table and he wondered how to frame his words so that they might lessen her hurt.

'I think your mum and I had been drifting for a while,' he said at last. 'You'd probably noticed that. It's sad but it happens.'

'Mmm,' she said, stirring the honey into her tea, not looking at him. 'I'd seen that you were each kind of doing your own thing. You'd got a bit semi-detached.' She looks up at him, disbelief in her eyes. 'But, I mean, another man? I can hardly believe it. Actually it was a bit embarrassing when she told me. All excited like she was a teenager or something and expecting me to be pleased about it. I think Mum's being very selfish, actually. Like it's only her life that's important and that's it. Marriage over. End of. What about us? What about you? Just suddenly given your marching orders because she's met someone else?'

Ben could see then how very easy it would be to engage Laura's sympathy, to draw on the partisanship that exists between them. Her love for him and her disapproval of her mother, the hurt she has caused her daughter, could so easily bring Laura on to his side. He could play the martyr, show his wounds, and allow her to comfort him. Or he could be noble, brave, and win her admiration. He hadn't realized how dangerous such a situation could be or how hard it was not to manipulate it to his own advantage.

'I think we could both see the end coming,' he said gently. 'But we hadn't bothered to do anything about it. You could say that it's a good thing to make us face up to it rather than just drift endlessly on. You're right about us becoming semi-detached, but I'm OK with it, sweetheart, as long you can handle it, too. It's just as tough for you.'

'I'm very sad about it. Of course I am,' she said miserably. 'I don't quite know how it works any more. OK, I'm not a kid and I know that these last few years, since I went to uni, you and mum have spent quite a lot of time apart. But it's broken us up, hasn't it? We don't have a home together any more. Obviously Mum will be OK. She'll be going back to Edinburgh once the flat sells, to a new life. She's got this new flat, new man, as well as Granny and Grandpa not far away. What about us?'

'You've always got a home with me here. You know that, sweetheart.'

She nods, still slightly tearful. 'Actually, Mum's got a small spare room in her flat she's said I can use, and Granny's keeping some of my stuff in store, but anyway I shall be abroad for the best part of a year with my chalet job. Then I'm hoping to go to teacher-training college.'

'Well then, I'm sure we shall work it out between us. And don't be too tough on your mum. She and I were very happy, she worked hard to keep us going, and we all had some really good times. It hasn't been all jam for her, you know, and I don't grudge her another chance. Yes, Iain came as a shock, and he's wounded my pride, but I'll get over it. You're an adult now, Laura. You're up and running and doing so well that I will admit that I'm enjoying myself doing my own thing. And I love it here.'

His cool assessment calmed her.

'As long as you're OK,' she said, still slightly doubtfully but wanting to be convinced. 'And you've got Evie across the road.'

'I have indeed. She's invited us over to supper later so you can tell her how you're doing and all about this chalet job.'

Now, as his coffee arrives and he smiles a thank you, draws in his long legs and sits up straighter, he is aware of being watched. A small girl is standing at the open doors staring intently at him. In her hand she holds a lead, at the end of which is a black Labrador.

'No, Otto,' the child says firmly to the dog. 'You're not allowed in. Stop pulling.'

The dog sits down suddenly, floppy ears pricked forward as he watches someone inside, and Ben glances at the counter to see what has attracted its attention. A woman is standing there with her back to him. Between choosing and ordering she glances out at the girl and the dog and smiles encouragingly. Ben assesses that she's probably early forties; thick blond hair wound into a casual knot, pretty profile, a long flowery skirt. The order completed, she goes outside, taking Otto's lead and leading them towards a table under an umbrella.

The child breaks away from them and comes back; waiting at the door, staring at Ben with an eager wistfulness that puzzles him. He smiles at her but makes no effort to encourage her. From the shop behind him another woman appears carrying a canvas bag full of groceries and vegetables. She stops, bending to speak to the child, who still looks at Ben. The woman glances round; her expression changing from a smiling motherly tenderness to irritation. She gives Ben an almost apologetic little smile, seizes the child's hand and marches her away to the blonde woman and the dog, who wait for them at the table under the umbrella.

It's an odd little scene and Ben finishes his coffee watching them, glad that none of them is his responsibility, enjoying the luxury of being alone.

Jemima Spencer puts the bowl of water, always available for visiting dogs, beside the table for Otto and sits down again with her friend Miranda beneath the umbrella. Maisie has taken a piece of cake and is sitting under the table with Otto, who watches each bite with close attention.

'Maisie's driving me mad,' mutters Miranda, 'and now Dave's dumped me. Honestly, Mimes, I am feeling completely bloody.'

Jemima waits, sipping her coffee: it's always a mistake to rush in where Miranda is concerned. If she is sympathetic Miranda will feel she is being patronized; if she is bracing, then Miranda will be aggrieved. It's best simply to allow her to talk and get it out of her system. She met Miranda through a mutual friend, who has since moved away, and they've grown much closer with the friend's departure but, just lately, Miranda has become rather needy; rather demanding. Nevertheless, Jemima has grown fond of her and of small Maisie. She respects Miranda's commitment to her nursing work at the hospital, and she continues to attempt to support them with her friendship. She shifts so that she can concentrate, so that Miranda knows she has her whole attention.

'Of course, he and Maisie simply didn't hit it off. I

44

thought she might be pleased now that she's got so fixated on this idea about her father turning up out of the blue. I wonder if I was right to tell her that he simply abandoned me when I told him I was pregnant. Did you see how she was staring at that poor chap in there? He looked rather nice, actually. Anyway, poor Dave simply couldn't cope . . .'

Jemima makes encouraging and sympathetic noises as the drama unfolds. There have been several Daves in the six years since Maisie's father left but privately she wonders if it's Miranda's tendency to cling that frightens them off rather than Maisie's behaviour. Miranda clings to her mother, to Maisie, to Jemima – and, when she meets a man that she really likes, she tends to come on a bit too strong too quickly. There is a neediness that is off-putting, combined with the slightly claustrophobic world that she has built around the two of them, which Maisie is beginning to challenge. Of course, Miranda's nursing work keeps her busy, but her social life suffers because she is working shifts at the hospital, finding child-care for Maisie, running their home and suffering an ongoing exhaustion from juggling all these aspects of her life.

'Did you really like him?' Jemima asks gently. 'Are you really gutted? I didn't feel you were absolutely, you know, in love with him.'

'Well, I wasn't,' says Miranda, rather discontentedly. 'But it's just nice to have a man around, isn't it? Someone you can rely on for a change. And it might have developed into something more . . .'

Jemima listens, glad that she's contented with her own single state, with her job as a manager in the holiday-let company she's worked with for twelve years now; with her little team who clean the cottages and carry out the changeovers between visitors. She loves her work, and her tiny cottage at Torcross, and dear old Otto sitting with Maisie under the table. Her own love life is rather hit and miss but that's much more to do with her reluctance to commit. She prefers to love them and leave them.

She relaxes a little, just a little, so that Miranda doesn't notice. It's warm and comfortable beneath the umbrella, the little garden centre is filled with rows of plants and shrubs and flowers, and there is a delicious hot scent of earth and blossoms. If she screws up her eyes and peers in through the big glass doors she can just see the tall dark man sitting on the sofa, legs outstretched. She can't see him properly but he looks at ease there by himself: comfortable and relaxed.

She wonders if he is watching them, if he were in the least put out by Maisie's intent regard. Of course it's difficult for Miranda now that Maisie is convinced that her father will come back to find them. Jemima feels sorry for her friend and wonders how she can help her, apart from the occasional stints she puts in looking after Maisie when Miranda is working and her mother can't cope.

She and Maisie and Otto get on very well together and Jemima enjoys those sleepovers. The child brings another dimension to her life so that there's a different dynamic in her little cottage when Maisie is present.

Miranda sighs as if she is aware that Jemima's attention has been distracted.

'And then there's Mum,' she says, 'going on about the boys in Australia. Did I tell you she's suggesting that we go out for Christmas? It's rather a tempting thought, actually. It's just so expensive.'

Jemima nods sympathetically. She knows that they all miss Miranda's brothers, who both live with their families in Melbourne. They miss the regular contact, and especially now that both wives have had babies within the last few months.

'It would be wonderful,' Jemima says encouragingly. 'Fantastic for Maisie. Worth every penny, I should say. You might meet someone rather nice out there and it would give Maisie something else to think about.'

Miranda looks more cheerful, she sits up straighter, and Jemima breathes a silent sigh of relief. The awkward moment has passed. They collect their belongings, and Otto and Maisie, and make their way back to the car park. Jemima gives a last glance through the big glass doors but the tall dark man is no longer there.

Miranda follows behind Jemima, envious of her friend's placidity. Nothing seems to faze Jemima: she is so independent, so self-sufficient. She has no idea what it is like to know fear, to have the sole responsibility of a child. At the same time, Miranda knows, if she's honest, she only has herself to blame. She let herself get pregnant thinking it was the way to make Maisie's father commit after a long relationship that never seemed to be quite as secure as she longed for it to be. She needed to feel sure of him; to bind him to her. Well, that certainly backfired. She was left to manage alone, with all the pain and humiliation of rejection – and, in due course, with Maisie. No one will know how much she longs for security: for someone else to take the strain. Maisie is a darling but as she grows older she's beginning to push the boundaries, to challenge authority and argue about even the smallest things. She used to be so easy, so sweet and such a wonderful companion. Of course, she's angelic with Jemima which is irritating in one way but gratifying in another. At least it shows that Maisie does know how to behave.

Even now, she's swinging along on Jemima's hand, chattering and laughing whilst Jemima strolls at the child's pace, listening to her, Otto on his lead in her other hand. Onlookers might think that she was Maisie's mother, so comfortable do they look together. This thought might bring a bitter taste, send a tiny shaft of jealousy to the heart, yet it is such a relief to watch somebody else taking charge that Miranda simply feels grateful.

Maisie glances back and beams at her and Miranda's heart twists with a painful mix of love and anxiety.

'Come on, Mummy,' Maisie cries. 'We're going to take Otto for a walk along the ley.'

They climb into Jemima's car and drive away towards Torcross, and Miranda begins to gird herself up for the trip back to Torquay and the night shift at the hospital.

# CHAPTER FOUR

Claude sits on a bench on the Embankment in the sunshine watching the busy holiday scene. At little octagonal wooden kiosks, painted like beach huts, river trips are advertised; plastic pails containing bait for sale stand in a row outside the station café; people disembark from the Castle ferry, climbing the steep stone steps to the Embankment. Out on a mooring a young couple is making ready to go to sea in a small yacht. Loaded with provisions, they clamber from their little dinghy on to the deck and disappear below to stow things away.

The excitement and anticipation of regatta buzzes all around Claude: the flare and explosion of fireworks high above the town, the air-shattering roar of the Red Arrows slicing up the river; races and competitions; rowing and sailing; the raucous shriek and thump of the fairground. There is nothing quite like regatta.

A thin fair man sits down at the other end of the bench and as Claude glances at him he is shocked by the expression of misery on the man's face. It is an expression of loss, of loneliness, and Claude guesses that this man has lost someone very dear to him and he knows exactly how that feels. It is a few years now since Jilly died but the pain still strikes fresh; nothing ever quite fills the emptiness.

Even as he glances at the thin fair man Claude sees his face change, as if he is willing down his grief so as to smile at a boy standing nearby at the edge of the Embankment where children lie peering over the edge into the water, their fishing lines hanging down weighted with bait, waiting for crabs to bite. The boy – Claude guesses that he is about twelve – smiles back, clearly enjoying the contest, looking as if he might like to join in whilst conscious that he's rather too old for such games. Parents are at hand lest the younger ones become too excited and in danger of falling in or getting their fingers nipped. Seagulls sometimes make opportunistic forays on the exposed bait lying beside the young fishermen, and a very small boy screams with terror as a herring-gull swoops in and snatches at the piece of out-of-date bacon. As the great bird carries its trophy away it is immediately mobbed by a group of gulls who drive it down towards the dazzling water where they fight and quarrel noisily as they snatch for the prize.

Claude watches sympathetically as the little fellow sobs, shocked by the noise of the shrieks from vicious yellow beaks and the violence of the beating of powerful white wings; his father, almost as scared as his child by the sudden attack, puts an arm around him.

'I didn't think they'd dare to come in so close,' he says, bewildered, to sympathetic onlookers. He glances around anxiously, probably expecting to see the child's mother rushing up to see what the trouble is all about; telling him off for not exercising more care.

Claude experiences a twinge of fellow feeling: he often gets into trouble with his daughter for allowing the children too much freedom.

The older boy comes across to the bench, looking shocked but excited, too.

'Did you see that, Dad?' he asks the thin fair man, sitting down beside him. 'That was really scary.'

His father puts an arm around the boy's shoulders. 'Remember that, Mikey, next time you have an ice cream,' he says, 'or you could be sharing it with one of those brutes.'

'Are you OK, Dad?' the boy asks, rather as if it is he who is the adult; as if he is used to checking up on his father.

'Yeah, yeah. Sure. Just one of those moments, you know.'

The boy, Mikey, nods. Yes, he knows.

Claude is struck by a sense of their private suffering: he feels that he is eavesdropping on them. He stands up and walks away from the scene, around the Boat Float, where small boats lie at their moorings along the wall, into the town. He tries not to dwell on how much it has changed since he was a young sub-lieutenant up at the College and instead concentrates on the preparations for regatta: marquees being erected around the bandstand in Royal Avenue Gardens, burger stalls, the fair, traffic notices. He turns into Anzac Street and passes beneath the churchyard wall, with its overhanging canopy of feverfew and valerian, the east window of St Saviour's towering above him. It's getting on towards lunchtime but he's probably got time for a quick pint before he goes back to the boathouse. He crosses Fairfax Place, passes the cars queuing for the lower ferry, heads for the Dartmouth Arms and disappears into the bar.

When Claude arrives back at the boathouse Evie is waiting for him. She has a purposeful look, as if she has taken a decision, and she is holding a glass of wine.

'Have you had a drink?' she asks, indicating the glass.

'Had a pint,' he answers. 'Not for me, thanks. What's up?'

'There's something I want to tell you,' she says, and makes a little gesture behind her.

On the big oak table are some small framed sketches and he bends to look at them. They are almost cartoons: an elephant with a howdah full of astonished-looking dignitaries; a blimpish-looking colonel; an Indian rajah. In each of these is a small dog: a Cairn terrier, whisking round a corner, sitting up to beg, nipping someone's ankle. The drawings are full of character and charm, and down in the right-hand corner are the initials DF.

'I recognize these,' Claude says. 'They used to hang in one of the bedrooms in the Merchant's House.'

'I want to tell you about them,' Evie says, sitting down.

'It's a way of clearing my mind. It's quite a story. I'm not going to tell it to you the way TDF pieced it together but as his final conclusion. I've got to share it with somebody, Claude, and you are the only person I can totally trust. I'm telling you in complete confidence.'

He sits down, flattered but rather puzzled, and also slightly nervous.

'I shan't say a word, of course.' He looks again at the cartoons. 'Who was DF? He was a relation, wasn't he?'

Evic picks up the sketch of the elephant. She stares at it as if she is getting things organized in her mind and then begins.

'The Fortescue estate was always entailed on the eldest son. TDF's great-great-grandfather had two sons, Thomas and David. The younger, David, married first and had a son called George. David was an artist, he worked for the *Illustrated London News* and he did these cartoons.'

She puts the sketch down again and clasps her hands together. Claude waits.

'David was given an income from the estate and was generally looked after but it was nothing compared to his older brother, Thomas's, inheritance: the wine import business, property, investments. Thomas married later and there was only one child, Charles, TDF's grandfather. OK so far?'

Claude nods. 'All clear.'

'So we fast-forward through three generations. Cousins, second cousins, until we get to Charlie and Ben. Now just before he died, TDF found two very beautiful little

53

etchings in Totnes market. He brought them back as a present for my birthday and, because he didn't have much time to get them framed, he decided to use two frames from the cartoons. They are all different and they aren't very valuable but there were two exactly the right size and colour for the etchings. When TDF took them apart he found that in the back of one of them was a piece of paper.'

Evie sits back and takes a breath.

'A letter?' asks Claude.

She frowns and shakes her head. 'Not as such. It was a piece of paper that looked as if it had been torn from a notebook. The family history relates that the cartoons were sent to TDF's grandfather, Charles, each birthday when he was a small boy from his uncle David. Charles had a Cairn terrier and there is a little sketch of the dog in each of the cartoons.'

She pushes one across the table.

'David sent sketches to his own son, George, and to other members of his family when he was working abroad but only Charles's cartoons had the dog. It was like a signature, a code between them.'

Claude draws the cartoon towards him. There is the dog: eyes bright, ears cocked. In one sketch he is lifting his leg and a small puddle is forming. Claude gives an amused snort.

'They are very charming.'

'Yes. Delightful. Except that the implication is that David is writing to his son and not his nephew. He writes that it is very hard not to admit the truth and that he hadn't imagined how difficult it would be not to be able to acknowledge Charles as his son. TDF was intrigued. He checked all the cartoons and found several other pieces of paper. On one of them David writes that they are like letters in a bottle cast into the sea hoping that someone will find them and discover the truth; that he, not his brother, Thomas, was Charles's father and that some kind of restitution be made.'

'But nobody had found them? Not before TDF?'

Evie shakes her head. 'If the papers had been found they would almost certainly have been destroyed.'

Claude is puzzled. 'But why? Surely there's no great harm even if it's true, is there? It was all a long time ago. So David, apparently, had an affair with his sister-in-law. It's not unknown. What does he mean by restitution?'

Evie leans forward. 'Think about it, Claude. Apart from the scandal it would have caused at the time it means that, if it's true, then Charles shouldn't have inherited when his father died. He was illegitimate. The estate should have gone to Thomas's brother, David, if he were still alive, or to David's own son, George, who was older than Charles.'

'Good God! You mean that technically . . . Bloody hell.'

'The estate should have come down on David's side to George. Thomas had no other children. TDF checked back through the family records. David died first of some disease he picked up abroad. At that point his son,

George, was the legitimate heir. But when Thomas died everything was left to Charles.'

'But how serious is this stuff? I mean, can you really believe these letters? Maybe he was just a bitter younger brother.'

'TDF believed them to be genuine. And he believed that it was true that Charles was David's son. Thomas was often abroad on business and there was a kind of family rumour that his wife was much too friendly with his younger brother. Later, one of the papers shows that David had begun to feel resentful that his elder son, George, would inherit nothing whilst Charles – who was technically illegitimate – would get the lot, but he was clearly anxious about making things difficult for his sister-in-law. He wrote about the love they had for each other.'

'Poor devil.'

Evie looks sad for a moment; then she shrugs. 'TDF's only comfort was that if George had inherited there would probably be nothing left now. He was a wild young man, a gambler, and he went out to America to try his luck in the gold rush. He was killed in some kind of shoot-out, leaving his wife and children more or less destitute. His cousin – well, half-brother – Charles looked after them. Even so, TDF was gutted. He didn't know if he should try to put things right but he could think of no way of making restitution without telling Ben the truth and he feared that it might cause huge problems.'

'But what could Ben do? It's hardly hard evidence, is it? A few flimsy letters? Nothing to back them up.'

'TDF was afraid that Kirsty might think it was worth a legal try. They were very hard up at the time. But it wasn't just that. He thought that it would destroy the family. Ben and Charlie are very close and he was afraid that this news might cause a lot of misery. Let's face it, Ben would never be able to run the business. He has no head for figures and he wouldn't want to. TDF and Charlie worked very hard to keep it so successful, and TDF feared it might all be broken up. Yet he still wanted to make some kind of restitution.'

'Hang on a minute,' says Claude. 'Just to be clear. Ben's great-great-grandfather, David – who already has a son, George – has an affair with his sister-in-law, Charlie's great-great-grandmother, who becomes pregnant and bears David's child, and calls him Charles. So Ben and Charlie's great-grandfathers, George and Charles, were half-brothers not cousins. And, because the estate was entailed, George, being the elder and legitimate, should have inherited, which means that everything would have come down to Ben and not to Charlie.' He begins to smile. 'Ah, I begin to see. So you think that's why TDF left the Merchant's House to you?'

She nods. 'It was a huge shock but I've wondered if that might be the reason. He couldn't leave it to Ben without some kind of explanation but now that the laws of entail no longer apply he could leave it to me as his wife even though it might raise a few eyebrows.'

'As it did. And you leave it to Ben?'

She is silent for a moment. 'Possibly. Clearly TDF still

couldn't decide how to make restitution or he'd have made it clear in his will. Maybe he thought I'd have a better idea.'

'That's a bit tough on you, isn't it? I mean, how can you possibly know the future?'

'Well, I still haven't come to a decision and I'd welcome any ideas. Meanwhile, Ange is furious that the house is mine. It all came off the boil when I let the house to those friends. Ange and Charlie didn't come down for a while so it went a bit quiet but I'm rather dreading regatta.'

'And where are the letters?'

Evie sighs. 'In a sealed envelope in my desk.'

'And what will you do with them?'

She shrugs. 'What would you do, chum?'

He thinks about it. 'Have you made a will?'

'Of course I have. The Merchant's House is left equally between Charlie and Ben at the moment, though neither of them knows that. It's not the right answer but what else could I do? I had no idea when I made the will that Ben would need somewhere to live and would move in, so I have to think again now. I certainly wouldn't want him chucked out if anything happened to me, and Ange wanted their share of the money.'

'Would Charlie let her do that?'

'How do I know? Left to himself Charlie would probably just let Ben carry on there but who can say what anyone inside a marriage might do? I suspect that Ange would make his life very difficult.'

'So why are you telling me now?'

'Since the house was let after TDF died I've hardly seen Ange. Charlie has been down and stayed here with me but we haven't talked about the Merchant's House. Now they'll both be down next weekend for regatta and I'm pretty certain that the subject will crop up. Ange is very unhappy about Ben being there. Perhaps she's afraid it might give him tenant's rights or something. It's a bit pathetic but I wanted someone whom I can trust and is on my side to know the truth. I'm sorry to involve you, Claude, but I need some moral support. I know TDF would agree with what I'm doing.'

Claude is still taking it in. 'No wonder you've been a bit odd about it. I guessed that you were trying to decide how it should be left – and I was slightly surprised that TDF didn't leave it to Charlie – but I couldn't have dreamed of the other complications.'

"There's a moral dilemma. If the truth had been known back in the eighteen seventies Charlie would have none of the things he has now. But, if we can believe the rumours from the past, nobody else would either because it would have all been gambled away. I suppose you could say that if Ben needs money, sells the Merchant's House, loses it all, then so what? It doesn't affect what Charlie still has. I hate the thought, though, of leaving it to Ben without Charlie knowing why. I love both those boys very much. I know I wouldn't be around to see Charlie being hurt but I still can't quite bring myself to take that decision. And I can't tell him why without causing even more problems. How would Ben take it knowing his great-grandfather had been done out of a huge inheritance from which Charlie is benefiting? Of course, there was much more to the estate back then.'

'I take your point,' says Claude thoughtfully. 'It would change the relationship between them completely.'

'Of course it would. They're not brothers so there's none of that kind of sibling rivalry; they each respect what the other does without feeling the least bit envious. Charlie works very hard, has a lot of pressure and great rewards. Ben is very artistic, very laid-back and likes a quiet life. Charlie recognizes that Ben doesn't have a business head and doesn't panic when he comes unstuck. But he doesn't patronize him either. They tease each other and bicker but there's no ill will. I'd hate to spoil that.'

'It would be very sad,' agrees Claude. 'To be honest, I simply cannot see a really good solution.'

'No,' says Evie sadly. 'Neither can I. I love Ben being there. I can use the garden and the garage and it's fun having him around. I'm very happy for it to stay that way. And if it's left to them both and they sell up I suppose that's OK too. At least Ben would have enough money out of it to buy a small property and nobody would be any wiser.'

Claude holds up a cartoon. 'Except that you know the truth and, as you said, there's a kind of moral dimension to it now.'

She nods. 'And Ben utterly loves the Merchant's House. He is so happy there.'

'And Charlie has a house.'

'Yes, but it's the breaking with centuries of tradition. And Ben isn't even his brother. He's a fourth cousin. It's a big break. I know Charlie is puzzled and even rather hurt that TDF left the house to me. I think he thinks that it's a kind of protection for me and that it will be naturally left to him anyway, so it was just TDF making a generous gesture to me. Though normally it would have been put in trust for my use or something, wouldn't it? Anyway, it's a muddle. Luckily, Charlie and I have a very strong relationship and I have no intention of spoiling it.'

'Quite,' says Claude. He thinks of the coming regatta; the arrival of Charlie and Angela. 'You know, I think I might have that drink after all. Anything else you want to tell me? Any more shocks? Don't hold back.'

She stands up to fetch the wine and another glass. 'Nothing I can think of. Oh, well, only a rather odd man watching me in the Castle last night.'

'Watching?'

'Sitting in a corner, just watching me.'

'Well, you're used to that. Was it a fan?'

She shook her head. 'He didn't speak. Just stared in a grim kind of way as if he didn't like me. It was a bit unnerving, actually.'

Claude grins. 'Probably a failed novelist. So what happened?'

'Nothing. He got up and left.'

'What sort of age?'

Evie thinks about it. 'Mid-forties.'

'Not an old lover, then?'

'Hardly,' she says – but suddenly some memory stirs; just a flicker then it's gone.

Claude sees the tremor cross her face but decides to leave the subject alone. There has been enough drama for one morning. He talks about Ben's work and whilst Evie prepares some lunch he moves out on to the balcony to watch the river-life; to think about all that has been said about the Merchant's House. About Evie's watcher he doesn't think at all.

The tiny flat is hidden away in one of the narrow alleys behind St Saviour's. He lets himself into the vestibule, which leads directly up the flight of stairs to the front door. The sitting-dining room looks across the alley at the house opposite but there's a glimpse of St Saviour's tower from the small kitchen. Upstairs, two bedrooms and a shower-room and loo.

'It's a bolt hole, Jay,' his sister-in-law said. 'Somewhere you go out from. It's not luxurious or anything, but it's big enough for you and Mikey. Go down for regatta week. It'll take your mind off things and give Mikey a break. It's not just you that's lost Helena. He's lost his mum.'

Jason drops his rucksack on the sitting-room floor. Mikey's still out in the town; he's loving it.

'It's great here, Dad,' he said. 'Really cool.' He stared round at the river, the boats and the preparation for regatta, and his eyes shone. He looked like any twelve-year-old on holiday; for that moment he'd forgotten his mother died six months ago.

Jason sits down on the neat little sofa and buries his head in his hands. He wants to howl like a dog; to scream and rage against the world, against life, against the unfairness of it all. Helena was his lodestar, his linchpin; she grounded him, kept him centred. How can he possibly manage without her?

'Stay calm, Jay-bird,' she'd say. 'You can do it. Breathe. Keep those demons at bay. No, you don't need a drink . . .'

He draws up his knees, wraps his arms about them, trying not to think about the bottle of water he keeps at hand now, ever since she died, with its shot of vodka; just a little shot, hardly anything, just enough to keep him balanced. At least it would be if he hadn't seen that bloody woman Evelyn Drake in the Royal Castle last evening. He shouldn't have been there really. He'd popped in for a quick glass of wine — no harm in one small glass — on his way to pick up fish and chips while Mikey was unpacking and there she was, the bitch. He recognized her from newspaper reviews, from television interviews; she was like a burr under the skin. How his mother hated Evelyn Drake. She and his father were colleagues: History was their subject: Cromwell his father's special interest. That's where it started: her affair with his father, his mother's distress, his own problems. Everything started back there when he was seven and Evelyn Drake came into their lives. And here she is in bloody Dartmouth just when he was hoping to have a break, a little holiday with Mikey. In a town this small, she'll be popping up everywhere. He'll be watching, waiting, continually reminded of the past, instead of feeling free and relaxed. It's the story of his life: always something to make him angry, depressed, unable to cope. Just lately it's become even more difficult to control unexpected bursts of violence: smashing a mug, punching a door. That's why he lost his job in the bookshop; small things get under his skin, and now there's no Helena to listen to him, to talk him down, to keep him balanced.

The door below opens and he hears Mikey's feet on the stairs. Time for a quick swig, just the one; a very quick one to help him. There, that's much better. He'll be fine now. He puts the bottle in the front pocket of the rucksack, stands up, and carries it into the kitchen.

'Hi, Mikey,' he calls. 'Great timing. Just unpacking the shopping. Cake for tea. So how was it?'

'It's epic,' Mikey replies.


For the first time since Mum died Mikey feels peaceful. All the cruel knots that tangle like barbed wire so painfully around his heart, squeezing and dragging at his insides, are smoothing out just a bit. Not that he isn't still missing her, or doesn't feel he might suddenly burst into tears or anything, it's just that here in this place the pain has dulled a bit.

'I wish we could live here,' he says.

Dad comes out of the kitchen, which is so small it's like a galley on a boat.

'Wouldn't get all your stuff in here,' he says jokingly.

He puts two mugs of tea on the low table by the sofa. Mikey likes that Dad makes him tea. Though he doesn't much care for the taste of it, it makes him feel grown up. And now without Mum he has to feel grown up; he has to watch out for Dad's funny moods the way Mum used to. Sometimes Dad's hands shake and sometimes he has this really weird spaced-out look and when he goes off on one it can be really scary.

Not that he often loses it with me, Mikey reminds himself, taking a cake. Quite the contrary; most of the time he's very loving, lots of hugs and assurances that he'll make up for Mum not being there, that he'll find another job soon, that things will be great. He cries a lot, too, which makes it difficult for Mikey to hold back his own tears.

'It's OK,' Dad says. 'We can mourn together. It's good.'

Mikey doesn't argue but sometimes it doesn't feel right just to cry and cry, like they're egging each other on; he doesn't feel comfortable with it. But he doesn't like to make a fuss either.

'Where would you keep your bike, for a start?' Dad's saying.

'Down in the hall,' says Mikey. 'There's just room.'

Dad smiles at him. 'I'm sure your aunt Liz will let us use it quite often out of season.'

'I'd be here all the time if it was mine,' says Mikey enviously.

'They've bought it as an investment. To let it out and make some money from it. Lucky they haven't started yet or we wouldn't be here now. Liz says she'll reserve a few weeks for us out of season in future. We could come down for half term. Anyway, you're back to school straight after the regatta.'

Mikey groans, finishes his tea, licks his fingers. He wants to go into the town again, to watch the stalls being set up, the rowing gigs out on the river, to be part of all the excitement. He assesses his father; looking for familiar signs that might lead to depression or an outburst against something or somebody, but Dad looks OK, not too twitchy. Mikey gives an inward sigh of relief.

'Can I go out?' he asks. He can hardly bear to sit still knowing all that is happening just beyond the door.

'We'll go together,' Dad says, which is a bit disappointing; Mikey really liked being in the town by himself but he doesn't argue.

Dad goes into the kitchen to fetch his rucksack. These days he never goes anywhere without his rucksack and his bottle of water tucked in its front pocket. The rucksack and the bottle are new; since Mikey got back from school for the summer holidays. Dad says he has this problem with a dry mouth and throat and needs frequent little sips, but he'll never let Mikey touch the bottle.

'Don't want you catching anything,' he says. 'You can never tell with throats.'

Mikey can hear water running, so he's probably topping it up, and then Dad comes out and grins at him and it's such a relief that he's OK that Mikey feels a happiness that he's almost forgotten about. He feels guilty, too, because it seems terrible to be happy with Mum dead, but just this minute he can't help it.

'Ready?' Dad asks, and Mikey nods and leads the way downstairs.

Evie sees them walking towards her as she makes her way home. Instinctively she hesitates, recognizing her watcher, and then stares curiously at the striking-looking boy beside him. He looks up at the thin fair man beside him and then turns away, laughing, and pointing at something out on the river. That little streak of memory she experienced with Claude shifts slightly and she is thrust back thirty years or more to a crowded study in a different town and Russell Dean laughing and gesticulating at something beyond the window.

Russ: how she loved Russ. He was one of the first of the 'history men'; those forerunners of Schama and his like, striding across our television screens, talking on hilltops, expounding at gravesides, theorizing on cliffs. Russ had won hearts and minds. He was exciting, amusing, intelligent and he put sex into dull old history. The nation loved him.

He and Evie worked together at the university, sharing their passion for that particular period of English history: the Civil War. They'd talk for hours, laugh together, as Russ put forward ideas to encourage the great British public to love Cromwell, warts and all.

Half hidden behind a newly erected stall, Evie stares at the boy, seeing Russ in the shape of his brow and the set of his eyes. Then she looks at the man. There is another tug of memory, a twinge of guilt, reminding her of Russ's wife, suffering from MS, already confined to a wheelchair. Pat was a pretty, pale woman; slightly whiny, her suffering so nobly borne that it was rather like another person in the room. She adored the boy, her hand always reaching to smooth his head where he stood beside her chair; a small, watchful, wary boy of seven or eight. What was his name? James? Jake? Jason, that was it. She called him Jay and he'd nestle into her, his pale eyes – his mother's eyes – fixed mistrustfully on Evie.

Jason and his son are coming closer. Abruptly Evie turns and walks away, but the past goes with her. She remembers Russ's study, the piles and shelves of books, half-folded maps, the smell of his Gauloise cigarettes and the scent of his aftershave. Their shared passion drove the relationship forward. He loved Pat, made sure she was looked after, watched over Jason – but his vitality, his energy, was always seeking after something new and exciting. For a short while Evie fitted into that space. They snatched opportunities to be alone together, precious moments to make love in her small room, and now, as she walks quickly through the streets, she feels guilt that she allowed it to happen; that back then she didn't think much about Pat, confined and hedged about, but simply accepted everything Russ had to give – the love, the sharing, the passion – before they moved apart.

Thinking about it now, it seems that Pat hardly entered into that scholarly part of Russ's life. It was as if she had her own private, separate, inviolable existence – Russ's wife and the mother of his son – that was never discussed, certainly never to be questioned or threatened. It didn't occur to Evie that she might be a threat to Pat. In her late twenties, ten years Russ's junior, sharing ideas, research, Evie knew very well that she was just one in a line of young women that Russ attracted. She began to write novels in her spare time, he encouraged her, and, after her early success, she left the university. He pursued his television career but at some point it lost that first impact, was crowded out by the competition. Then, nearly ten years after their affair, she had the letter from him.

Evie stops to lean on the wall opposite the Merchant's House where she first met Tommy. It was Tommy who told her to have nothing to do with it. They were still in the early stages of their relationship and she'd told him about Russ. There were similarities between the two men: Tommy was nearly ten years older than she was; he had the same ability to inspire enthusiasm, to enter into the world of her imagination.

'My darling girl,' he said, 'you can't possibly commit to something like that. Five years' public school fees? It's madness. OK, so you've done well, but you've invested nearly all your money in your house and you've still got a mortgage, which you're relying on the sales of future books to pay. It's much too risky and he has no right to ask, no matter how much help he gave you with your research.' He paused. '*Did* he help you that much?'

Evie considered the question. 'It's impossible to answer that truthfully,' she said at last. 'Who can actually define what has informed someone's work? We are all inspired by the great artists in our field; we read books, or listen to music, or look at great art. We absorb it, digest it, live with it. Who can accurately say what is directly attributable? Russ never gave me specific ideas or information but he inspired me with his love of his work. How can I evaluate that?'

'It's your decision,' Tommy said gently, 'but you asked me for my opinion and I'm telling you what I think. It's too risky and not fair on the boy. If you had to stop half-way through it would be a disaster.'

So she'd written back to Russ, explaining, saying how sorry she was, and a few weeks later she had another letter, beseeching her, telling her that Jason had set his heart on Winchester, that it would mean so much to Pat, who was now very ill, and then a stronger hint this time about how much Evie owed him for his help in her research.

In this letter she recognized another voice – Pat's? – and her reply this time was more forceful and after that there was silence. Evie stares across the roof-tops: no wonder Jason had been watching her with such dislike. Clearly he recognized her and he was remembering her refusal to help. Perhaps he blamed her for his missed opportunity, though it was possible that his parents had found the money from another source. Perhaps he guessed at her relationship with his father and was resentful on his mother's behalf. It certainly explained that sense of hostility.

Nevertheless, she would like to speak to the boy: Jason's son; Russ's grandson. She feels sad that her relationship

70

with Russ was spoiled at the end; that she must have seemed so uncaring – selfish, even – in refusing to help. Looking back, she wonders how much she was influenced by Tommy; whether left to herself she might have agreed to pay out, though she knows in her heart that Tommy was right and the request was out of order. Still, she wonders how hurt Russ must have been and she feels an odd, foolish desire to reconnect with him, to make up in some way for that earlier decision.

The boy looked so much like his grandfather, his eager brightness contrasting with the inimical stare and cold, pale eyes of his father. Perhaps, if she hadn't run away, she could have mended a few fences. She wonders if they are here for regatta; if there is a wife somewhere. Dartmouth is a very small town whose life centres around the few streets just off the Embankment and around the Boat Float, especially during regatta. If they are staying it would be almost impossible to avoid them. Yet an irrational fear remains; it was an instinctive reaction to avoid Jason but she can't think why. What could he possibly do to harm her?

# CHAPTER FIVE

Jemima sits at a table in Café Alf Resco, close to the door under the big awning, finishing her breakfast. She likes taking the occasional unscheduled break in the middle of the morning for one of Alf's breakfasts, but it's busy today. All the tables outside are crammed with holidaymakers and even inside there are very few spaces left. She's managed to get the only unoccupied table for two, with the black Lab, Otto, curled in under her feet.

A tall, dark-haired man turns in off the road, pauses at the door and glances round, and she feels a little shock of recognition. He looks at her and she sees that he is having the same reaction: he raises his eyebrows, smiling a little, and she smiles back at him. He makes a little gesture at the packed café and another at the empty chair at her table and she nods. He goes into the cavernous interior to order and presently reappears beside her.

'Thanks,' he says, sitting down. He looks down at Otto and back at Jemima. 'At the risk of sounding corny, I think I've seen you before. At Stokeley Farm Shop, wasn't it? I remember this fellow. You were with another woman and a little girl.'

She remembers now; she'd been with Miranda and Maisie. Maisie had been having one of her difficult moments, staring at this man sitting on the sofa, and Miranda had been cross with her. She remembers, too, that she liked the look of him.

He's watching her; his expression is friendly, alert. 'I'm Ben Fortescue,' he says.

'I remember seeing you,' Jemima says. 'I'm Jemima Spencer. Do you live locally?'

'Just up in Southtown. I moved down from London at Easter. It's been a family house for generations so I know the area very well. It's great to be actually living here rather than just coming for holidays.'

'I know those houses,' she says. 'I work for a company who lets out holiday cottages. We've got one in Southtown on our books. Very nice it is too. Is your house beautiful?'

He nods. 'It is very beautiful. I've always coveted it but sadly it doesn't belong to my side of the family. Never mind. I can rent it for as long as I need to, so I can pretend.'

She smiles at him, liking him. 'I know how you feel. I rented a flat once in Salcombe right on the harbour. Gosh, I loved it. Then I moved to Kingsbridge for a few years but I realized that I am unhappy unless I can see water so now I rent a tiny bit of a cottage at Torcross.'

'Ah, so you can look at the sea?'

She shakes her head. 'I couldn't afford the sea view. I look the other way, at Slapton Ley. My cottage is built on the back of one of those lovely big houses on the sea wall. But at least I don't have visitors walking up and down outside my windows all day and I'm safe from the high tides.'

He laughs. 'And you haven't got far to walk to look at the sea.'

'Not far. And the ley is wonderful.'

'And the fellow here?' Ben jogs the Lab gently with his foot. 'Otto, isn't it? He doesn't chase the waterfowl?'

The dog raises his head and looks up at him with an expression that is at once reproachful and expectant. 'Just tell me what you want me to do,' he seems to say, 'and I'll try to oblige.'

'Certainly not. He's very well trained. He's a rescue dog. His elderly owner died and I took him on. She was a client, an absolute sweetie, and I always promised her I'd look after Otto if anything happened to her. His proper name is Othello.'

Ben leans down to smooth Otto's head; his hand is gentle, long-fingered. She wonders if he's married; attached.

Before she can speak, one of the waitresses calls out, 'Ben?' and he raises his hand in acknowledgement. She brings his coffee to him and he nods his thanks as she puts it on the table and dashes away.

'And the little girl?' he asks casually. 'She seemed to think she knew me.'

'Ah, Maisie.' Jemima pushes her plate aside, picks up her mug of coffee. 'Well, poor little Maisie has a problem. Her father abandoned her and her mother just before she was born. Said he wasn't ready for the responsibility and upped and left them to it. Miranda's been a very protective mum, very "you and me against the world", but recently Maisie's begun to ask serious questions about her father. She's started primary school and loves it, and Miranda decided that she should know the truth.'

Jemima hesitates, uncertain whether she should be telling this stranger these intimate details and then decides to go on. After all, it isn't a secret.

'Poor Maisie,' Ben is saying. 'And poor Miranda. That's a very difficult situation.'

'Mmm. Maisie's taken it rather badly, behaving as if it must have been Miranda's fault that he went, and now she looks for him everywhere. It's driving poor Miranda round the bend.'

'I can imagine.'

His ready sympathy warms her heart. She summons up her courage and asks casually: 'Do you have children?'

He answers easily, with no embarrassment. 'I have a daughter, Laura. She's twenty-two. She just got a languages degree and she's off backpacking with friends. Her mother and I are splitting up, which is why I've come back to Dartmouth. I'm a freelance photographer so I can work almost anywhere.'

His directness silences her for a moment. She is confused by her feelings, by her attraction to this man.

'Well, I have no experience of marriage or children,' she says after a short pause, 'apart from my half-sister's two, so I don't know how to help with Maisie at the moment.'

'Small girls can be incredibly complicated,' says Ben. He shows no reaction to the information she's deliberately given him. 'But then so can big ones. I suppose they're getting on each other's nerves.'

'Yes,' says Jemima, surprised by his intuitiveness. 'That's exactly right. Miranda is hurt that Maisie has not immediately rejected her father because of his behaviour to her mother – and to her – and Maisie is upset that her mother wasn't able to keep hold of her father for her. It's very odd.'

'And very destructive. It's all to do with loyalty, isn't it?'

'Yes. Look, this is really weird. Why am I telling you this five minutes after I've met you? It seems a bit disloyal to Miranda really.'

Ben shrugs. 'How long does it take to feel you can trust someone?'

She snorts derisively. 'And have you never made a mistake about that?'

'Of course. But it doesn't stop you being optimistic about it.'

Jemima laughs. 'OK. But I must go. We're taking on a cottage at Dittisham and I've got to check it out.'

'And I was hoping you might come and see my beautiful house and that you'd invite me to see your bit of a cottage.'

She stands up, reaching for her bag and Otto's lead, smiling a little.

'It's not impossible, I suppose.'

He takes out his wallet and hands her a card. 'Just in case,' he says.

She takes it, hesitating, still smiling. 'Thanks,' she says, and hurries out, wondering if he is looking after her. She hopes that he is – but she doesn't look back.

Ben watches her go. He feels very much at ease; delighted to have seen her again but very calm about the outcome. This strange sense of peacefulness, of wellbeing, contains him. There is no stress; no anxiety. He can't quite understand it, sometimes even testing it with a series of negative reactions about his failed marriage, but the feeling persists. He can't believe his luck that his life should have fallen into such a pleasant pattern – enough work, the Merchant's House, his card project – and Jemima Spencer, on top of all this, seems rather too much to add to it all.

He drinks his coffee and thinks about the little girl, Maisie. He can imagine the kind of 'you and me against the world' scenario in which she and her mother have lived, happily dependent on each other, until Maisie was old enough to begin to discover that she quite liked the world. How difficult, then, for her mother to step back and allow her to enter into it. How hurtful to discover that, far from being angry with her father for abandoning them, Maisie blames her mother for allowing him to go.

Ben thinks about Laura. She, too, is feeling resentful that Kirsty has chosen Iain, announced that the marriage is at an end and the family home must be sold. Part of Ben feels sorry for Kirsty. Theirs has not been a relationship ending in quarrels, shouting, arguments: it has been a quiet descent into a kind of indifference. He can't blame Kirsty for being attracted to this man whom she's known in another life and obviously likes enough to cause such a rift. Perhaps Iain has brought a new excitement to her life; a different dimension. But how is she to explain it to Laura in a way so that her daughter won't be hurt, diminished and resentful on her father's behalf?

He and Laura didn't inhabit the 'you and me against the world' scenario of Miranda and Maisie, but he was very present during her growing up: taking and fetching her from school, attending assemblies and plays, amusing her, bathing her, putting her to bed. His beautiful photographs in the well-known glossy magazines were far more easily appreciated than Kirsty's long hours in the office and the added responsibility when she was promoted.

When was it that Kirsty began to be jealous of his and Laura's easy camaraderie, her natural instinct to turn to him first; to ask for his help, to tell him about her childish victories and disasters? When did bitterness begin to creep into decisions to do with home improvements, new clothes, foreign holidays? At what point did his own irritation with Kirsty's subtle – and not so subtle – implications that without her hard work such luxuries wouldn't be possible begin to turn into resentment? Increasingly her air of martyrdom began to colour her attitude towards him, though he still worked hard, shopped, did most of the cooking.

It was a slow process. There were still happy moments, periods of contentment, but the spaces between them grew longer, and by the time Laura went to university there was not much left. Nevertheless, it was a shock to discover that Kirsty had been seeing Iain: that this unknown man had revived in her the love and passion that had been lost in their own relationship. When she'd told Ben that it was over, that she was going back to Edinburgh and the flat must be sold, he'd experienced a terrible sadness, jealousy, an overwhelming sense of loss – but also, deep down, this sense of relief, of peace.

It was odd that in his moment of crisis, wondering where he would go, what he would do, it had been to Evie that he turned, hoping he might stay with her at the boathouse until he sorted himself out. He knew that here there would be no judgement, no criticism; there would be none of that salacious, dreadful glee that is so often present even in the best of people when such a disaster happens. Amongst his and Kirsty's friends there was a degree of that lip-licking, eye-glittering voyeurism, that eager neck-craning to get a glimpse into the pain of somebody else's failure, that was barely disguised by sympathy.

Well, he'd agreed to Kirsty's terms: no arguments, no quibbling about the divorce. The flat to be sold and split three ways – between him, Kirsty and Laura – after the mortgage was paid, and the inference that he was lucky to be getting his share. Perhaps he was. He'd always contributed what he could, though his earnings were irregular and it was her salary that kept the mortgage paid. He'd have enough to pay Charlie back and some left over – but where to go while he sorted himself out?

That's when he telephoned Evie.

'Of course you can come,' she said. 'It will be lovely to have some company.'

A week later, his old VW Golf packed with his belongings, he was on his way to Dartmouth. It was so good to be going back, going home: that's how he always felt about returning to the West Country, to Dartmouth.

Evie welcomed him as she always did; not as a guest, or a visitor, but as someone returning to the place where he belonged. He sat on her huge sofa, with its back resting against the long wide oak table, and stared out at the river. It was as if he were supported and embraced by the dazzling light, his spirit lifted and carried by the rising tide.

When she offered him the Merchant's House he was silent with surprise.

'Why not?' she asked. 'The tenants are going in a few weeks. It will be empty. I'd rather you were there than someone I don't know.' And again she asked, 'Why not?'

He was confused. 'Well, it seems a bit cheeky, I suppose. I probably can't afford the rent you'd get for it and . . . what about Charlie?'

'What about him?'

'Well, I suppose I feel that he might not like it.'

'You mean Ange might not like it.'

He laughed then. 'Yes, I suppose I do.'

'Well, TDF left the house to me so I shall do as I please with it and I'd love to have you there if you'd like it.'

He was overwhelmed with such joy that he felt he might burst into tears. Nobody had ever guessed how much he loved the elegant, graceful house overlooking the river.

'Never mind about the rent for the time being. We'll come to some arrangement about that later. Just think how nice for me to have you there, and there's room for Laura when she needs a bolt hole,' Evie was saying. 'If it means that we shall see more of darling Laura it will be an added bonus. I can use the garden and the garage, those are my conditions, though you'll have to share with Charlie and Ange when they come down. Not that it happens very often. Will you mind that?'

Ben shook his head. 'There's plenty of room.' He was already planning that he'd have the two rooms on the second floor for his own quarters. 'It would be amazing, Evie. If you're really sure?'

He was slightly surprised by her own delight at the scheme; as if it had solved a problem. Perhaps it had. Perhaps she didn't want any more tenants though it was a big house to leave empty for most of the year. It was a relief to think that he might be helping her out, paying some rent, paying the utility bills, whilst realizing his own private dream.

'The last of the really good pieces went to London

when TDF died,' she was saying, 'but it's more than adequately furnished. Quite comfortable.'

'I can't wait to see it again,' he said.

'I'm afraid you'll have to. It won't be empty for another few weeks but you'll have all the fun of anticipation.'

Now, Ben finishes his coffee, gets up and goes out. He's been at the Merchant's House for four months, and in a few days Charlie and Ange will be down for regatta. How will it work out?

# CHAPTER SIX

Maisie loves Jemima's little cottage. There's a tiny room at the top of the house where Maisie sleeps when Mummy is on a night or weekend shift at the hospital and Granny is away. It's her own special place; nobody else sleeps in the small camp bed and a few special toys are always kept there. There's another bedroom next to Jemima's where Maisie can be if she wants to, but she likes to be in the little loft room. Granny's house is nice, and it has a garden with a swing and a slide and a trampoline, but Jemima's cottage is very nearly on the beach. She loves being with Jemima in the car and going for walks with Otto — and Jemima doesn't get cross when Maisie talks about her father.

All the time, now, she's looking for him. Ever since Mummy told her about how he left them, she's been watching: it could be the man at the check-out, or someone in the farm shop, or at the garage.

'No,' Mummy says. 'No, it doesn't work like that. I'd

recognize him. He'd recognize me. You've got to stop this, Maisie.'

But Maisie can't stop. It's nearly six years since he left them and he might have changed. Mummy's changed. Her hair is shorter and darker than it is in the photographs taken when Maisie was a baby. And she's much thinner. He might not know her straight away, and so Maisie has to keep watching.

She doesn't look at fathers with children – if her father didn't want her then he wouldn't want anyone else – and she knows she mustn't talk to strangers or wander off alone, but she can't stop herself watching. She's stopped asking Mummy about him because she gets a funny look on her face: part of it as if she is angry and part of it is like she might cry.

Sometimes Mummy makes friends with men who don't live with their families: they live on their own. When one of these men comes round to the flat Mummy is different. She's like a person that Maisie doesn't know, which can be a bit frightening. She gets a bit giggly, and talks very quickly, like she's a little girl. She hugs Maisie: her cheeks get very pink and she fiddles with her hair whilst looking at this other man. Then Maisie gets uncomfortable and pulls away and then Mummy gets cross and the man looks uncomfortable, too. It's much better when these other men aren't there.

Maisie climbs carefully down the little wooden staircase to the landing where Jemima is waiting for her.

'All settled in?' Jemima asks. 'Unpacked?'

Maisie nods. She likes it that Jemima doesn't fuss. She

feels comfortable and happy with Jemima like she used to feel with Mummy. Now, though, Mummy seems to be a bit upset when Maisie wants to be with her friends or go to clubs after school, and then she feels sad because Mummy is on her own. If her father were to come back then Mummy needn't be alone, but she got upset when Maisie said that so now she has to be very careful. It's good to be with Jemima and not to have to think about what she's saying all the time.

'So,' Jemima says. 'Otto needs a walk before supper. Are you OK with that?'

Maisie nods happily, she's very OK with that, and they go downstairs together. Maisie thinks the cottage is like a doll's house. The sitting room is upstairs and really small, and the kitchen has a glass room leading off it that is called a conservatory. This is Jemima's favourite room: she can see the ley from the windows and she can watch the ducks and the swans. All along the windowsills are painted pots with flowers in them.

'This is my garden,' Jemima tells people. 'Good, isn't it?'

And Maisie thinks it's really good. And so does Otto. He has a basket under one of the windows and he stretches out in it with his paws hanging over the edge. He's waiting for them now; he looks excited like that, with his ears pricked up and his tongue hanging out and his tail wagging. Jemima puts his lead on and gives Maisie a blue cotton bag, in case she finds a precious stone or some pretty glass, and they all go out through the little yard.

Maisie carefully closes the gate behind them and they

turn down the narrow passage between the houses to the beach. She loves this beach, which stretches so far she can't see the end of it. It's not sand, though; she can't build sandcastles but she doesn't want to do that anyway. She likes to see what the tide has washed up: strange smooth lumps of coloured glass, oddly marked pebbles, pieces of wood bleached white as bones. She collects these things and makes patterns in Jemima's yard or on the windowsill beside the flowerpots. Their own flat doesn't have a garden, and her collection grew too big for her bedroom, so now she leaves some of them with Jemima and takes some to Granny, who has given her a special box for the best pieces.

Otto is running towards the sea, his tail going round and round in circles, his galloping paws sending up showers of shingle, which makes her laugh. She turns to look up at Jemima, who is laughing too, and Maisie seizes her hand and they run together after him over the shingle down to the sea.

When Maisie starts to hunt for treasure, Jemima strolls behind her keeping one eye on Otto, who is splashing at the water's edge. Most of the families have packed up and gone back to their hotels or B & Bs or camp sites.

It's been a hot day and a sea mist is rising. The distant headland, humped and grey as an elephant, is vanishing as the mist rolls inland; soft and gentle as a muslin curtain, it sweeps across the sea, across the patchwork of cliff-top fields and small white cottages. The sea birds rise up from the smooth pearly surface of the water, breasting the air-waves, turning towards the shore.

Jemima watches Maisie searching for treasure. Once she found a pound coin and they eventually decided, after serious discussion, that since the owner couldn't possibly be traced it could go into the ice-cream fund. At nearly six, Maisie can be expected to make her bed tidy, dress herself, lay the table, and if she is good and quick then fifty pence or maybe a pound goes into the ice-cream fund. Jemima knows that Miranda only slightly approves but this is because she has to fight a little against the idea of anyone having any kind of control over Maisie other than herself. She is grateful that Jemima steps in when a childcare crisis occurs but, at the same time, she is very slightly jealous of the easy companionship between them.

The small figure in flowered boots and pink shorts and T-shirt crouches to examine something amongst the shingle. Otto joins her, curious and friendly, swiping her cheek with his tongue. She shrieks in protest, throws a pebble for him, and he goes pounding away after it. Maisie stands up, looks around for Jemima and waves excitedly.

'Look what I've found,' she cries. 'Come and see, Jemima.'

It is a quartz stone, glittering with tiny specks of silver; it looks magical.

'Is it treasure?' asks Maisie, her voice hushed with awe. 'Is it a magic stone?'

How to answer? The real treasure, the true magic, is being here with this child and the dog on the long empty beach, listening to the hush of the waves along the shore and the cries of the sea birds. She looks into the child's face and sees the longing and the wonder – and her heart is touched.

'It's a very special stone,' she answers. 'Let's put it into the bag. Oh, and here's Otto with his pebble. Good boy!'

He lays the big pebble very carefully at Maisie's feet and backs away a little, watching it anxiously, glancing up hopefully at her. To Jemima's relief Maisie begins to laugh. She puts her stone into the bag and then picks up Otto's pebble and hurls it as far as she can. He's off like a rocket and Maisie runs after him, splashing down into the shallows, calling to Otto, her voice as high and piercing as the shrieks of the gulls wheeling above her head.

Following them, Jemima tries to imagine how she would feel if Maisie were her own child; if she had the responsibility of this small, vivid person. She's always feared this kind of commitment: the weight of another person's happiness, and the expectation.

'I'm too selfish,' she said to Miranda once. 'I've been in love. I know what it's like but it never quite gels. Anyway, I like my life the way it is.'

'But don't you get lonely?' Miranda asked. 'I couldn't begin to imagine my life without Maisie.'

'Nothing's perfect,' Jemima answered. 'And one day Maisie will grow up and leave home. What then?'

'Don't,' said Miranda, shaking her head. 'I can't think about that. We'll always be close. Nothing can change that.'

But Jemima can see other things at work here. Young though Maisie is, Jemima can see her beginning to grow beyond this tight, protective trinity of child, mother and granny. She's a social, grounded child who reaches out for friends and new challenges, embraces change. Maisie feels stifled by all this care and control whilst Miranda is dismayed at the speed with which her daughter is ready to experiment, to leave her behind.

'It's good,' Jemima says encouragingly. 'Fantastic. Imagine how awful if she were a lonely, no-mates, insecure little girl. You've done a great job with her. And it gives you some time for yourself. That's good, too, isn't it?'

But Miranda seems to have lost the trick of how to be on her own, or with friends – unless, like Jemima, they are unattached.

Jemima can't help thinking that the recently proposed visit to Australia at Christmas, to connect again with their family, would be very beneficial for both Miranda and Maisie.

Maisie and Otto are racing back towards her. Maisie jumps and twirls and points behind her up towards the road. Jemima can see the source of all the excitement. The ice-cream van is still there in the car park. Jemima fishes in the pocket of her jeans – she keeps a five-pound note available on these walks for just such an emergency – and waves it in the air.

'Yay!' shouts Maisie. 'Cool!' She puts her arms around Otto's neck and hugs him. 'Ice cream, Otto.'

'As long as you eat all your supper,' says Jemima sternly. 'No fussing. Promise? OK, then. Come on.'

# CHAPTER SEVEN

In the car park on Torcross Line Evie climbs from the back of Claude's scooter and shakes her hair free of her helmet. It's still warm here despite the rising mist. The sun is dropping behind the hills to the west, flooding the bay with warm golden light; no breath of wind. Start Point Lighthouse has been blotted out by banks of softly rolling cloud from which small boats appear, ghostly and mysterious.

'Do we need an ice cream?' asks Claude, emerging from his helmet.

'Oh, I think we do,' she answers. 'Better hurry. Looks like he's packing up.'

'Got a few more punters, by the look of it,' says Claude, fishing for his wallet, nodding towards a woman with a small child and a dog, who are climbing up from the sea.

Evie watches them. The woman is bending to put the dog on its lead while the girl hurries ahead, clearly anxious that the ice-cream van might vanish as easily as the light-house or the cliffs have been swallowed by the mist.

'You can order two small cones, Maisie,' the woman shouts. 'Small ones, mind!'

Evie looks at Maisie as she scrambles up the shingle bank. She's a slender, striking-looking child, with honey-brown eyes and red-brown hair wound into a thick plait. She glances at Evie but her attention is on Claude at the van window and she waves to the ice-cream man so as to get his attention.

'Two small cones, please,' she cries breathlessly, as Claude pockets his change and turns away. 'Jemima's coming with the money.'

Jemima: not Mummy. Evie looks at Jemima who smiles as she approaches, rolls her eyes at Maisie's impatience, and pays for the ice cream. They are certainly not alike. Jemima is fair-haired, blue-eyed, shapely.

Because she cannot help herself, Evie begins to weave a little history about the child, the woman, and the dog who are now sitting in a row at the top of the shingle bank, looking out to sea, eating ice cream. The dog watches, alert, hopeful.

'I shall save the last bit of cone for him,' Maisie is saying. 'Will you save yours, Jemima?'

'Oh, yes,' agrees Jemima. 'Poor Otto. He has to have a share. Don't you, old fellow?'

Otto wags his tail expectantly, glancing briefly at Claude who strolls out on to the beach, ice cream in one hand, binoculars in the other. He smiles at them.

'Keeping an eye out for the guardship for regatta,' he tells them, indicating the binoculars. 'Due any time. Though I doubt I'll see it with this mist closing in. Are you down on holiday?'

'We're locals,' Jemima says. 'I live in the village,' she points along the beach towards Torcross, 'and Maisie lives in Torquay. Her mum is a nurse at Torbay Hospital and she's got extra shifts for the next couple of days so Maisie's staying with me and Otto. We're hoping to see a few of the events. Maisie wants to go to the funfair.'

Evie wanders closer. This is typical of Claude; he'll strike up a conversation with anyone who looks friendly and Jemima seems to be a kindred spirit.

'The town's filling up,' Evie says. 'What do you do? Park and Ride?'

Jemima smiles up at her. 'It's the only way. We don't mind.'

'But Otto has to stay at home,' says Maisie. 'He doesn't like it on the bus.'

'Don't blame him,' says Claude, finishing his ice cream.

Maisie watches him reproachfully. 'We usually give Otto the last bit of cone,' she says pointedly.

'Oh, gosh.' Claude looks guilty. 'Sorry, old chap. Didn't know the house rules.'

Jemima laughs. 'He gets quite enough treats, believe me. He'll get Maisie's and mine.'

'And mine,' says Evie, offering the end of her cone to Otto who receives it gratefully. 'It must be great fun, living on the beach.'

'I love it,' says Jemima. 'It's a tiny bit of cottage, about as big as a rabbit hutch, but it's worth it just to look out at the ley. I can't quite afford a sea view yet but I'm working on it.'

'Evie lives right down on the river in Dartmouth,' says Claude, surveying the horizon keenly. 'In one of the old boathouses.'

'Wow!' says Jemima. 'That must be really something.'

'It's only a small one,' says Evie quickly. 'But yes, it's rather special. Particularly during regatta. Front-row seat.'

She wonders if she should make some sort of invitation, for coffee or a cup of tea, but she hesitates.

'I'm down for regatta,' says Claude. 'It's an annual event for me. And Evie's kind enough to put me up. Perhaps we'll see you in the town.'

'That would be good.' Jemima feeds her piece of cone to Otto and stands up. 'Is that your bike?'

'It is,' says Claude proudly. 'Only way to get around during regatta.'

'It's cool,' says Maisie. 'I wish we had a bike like that, Jemima.'

'It might surprise you to know I used to have a little scooter once,' says Jemima. 'But not any more. These days I'd rather cope with Park and Ride. Time for tea, Maisie.'

Maisie waves and dashes away, Jemima unclips Otto's lead, smiles goodbye and sets off after them across the beach. Evie watches them go, oddly attracted to the little trio, wishing she'd invited them to the boathouse.

'Rather fun,' she says. 'Maisie's sweet and I've a feeling I've seen Jemima around in the town.'

'Home?' asks Claude.

She nods, though rather reluctantly. Charlie and Ange arrive tomorrow and she is not looking forward to it.

'It's crazy, isn't it?' she says. 'I feel really nervous about the weekend. But actually nothing has changed.'

'Oh, but it has,' he answers. 'At least it has for me. I know things now that I didn't know the last time I saw them. It's tricky, knowing secrets.'

'Perhaps I shouldn't have told you. But you can't imagine the relief it is to share it. I look at Ben, who is so grateful to be at the Merchant's House, and I think that if justice were done he would have inherited it. After all, we can't know that his great-grandfather would have gambled everything away. Perhaps he would have been quite different if everything had come down on his side of the family. And then I look at Charlie, who shouldn't have any of it but who has worked so hard to preserve what TDF passed on to him through his own efforts.'

'Well, at least you have the conviction that, whatever Ange thinks, Ben has a perfect right to be there. That'll help if she starts getting bitchy. How long is it since you saw her?'

'I've seen her in London a few times but this is the first time she's been to Dartmouth since TDF died. I just know there's going to be some kind of confrontation.'

Evie stands for a moment, postponing her return, steadying herself. All the while there were tenants in the house the final decision seemed less urgent: the temporary, easy option to leave the house jointly to Ben and Charlie solved the immediate problem. Now that she's shared the discovery of the letters with Claude, her dilemma is back in the forefront of her mind.

'It's crazy,' she says. 'On the strength of these pieces of paper we've let it grow out of proportion. Nobody will be any wiser if I leave the house between the two boys. They might wonder why, but who cares?'

'That's not quite the point, is it? TDF believed the papers to be an accurate record of what happened. Charlie shouldn't have his big house in Kensington, a thriving wine import business, and lots of shares and investments. Whether or not it would still be intact if Ben's great-grandfather inherited isn't the point. You know very well that if you leave the house to them both, Ange will insist that Ben buys Charlie out if he wants to keep it – which he can't afford.'

'The trouble is that the Merchant's House has been part of the inheritance for generations. Why, suddenly, would TDF leave it to Ben who, close though they were, is only a third or fourth cousin? He didn't want to have to confront Charlie with that. Nor do I. He hated to think of Charlie realizing that actually he wasn't entitled to any of it. It was quite a shock to TDF to learn that he wasn't who he thought he was, if you see what I mean. He wanted to protect Charlie from all of that but his sense of fair play confused the issue. I keep thinking that some miracle is going to happen to sort it out for me.'

'Well, it won't.' Claude hands her the helmet. 'But we might think of something between us.'

# CHAPTER EIGHT

Mikey is sitting on a bench outside the pub at Bayard's Cove when Evie sees him the next morning. He's alone, no sign of Jason, and on an impulse she sits down at the other end of the seat. She knows she has to be careful, that he might be frightened at her approach, that he's probably been brought up in the modern climate of 'stranger danger'.

He glances at her and she's struck by his resemblance to Russ: those sparkling dark blue eyes, black hair that seems to crisp and curl with an energy all of its own. She smiles at him; takes the plunge.

'Don't be anxious,' she says, 'but I think I know your grandparents, Russell and Patricia Dean. I worked with Russell at Bristol University. My name's Evelyn Fortescue.'

He looks at her, an intent look, open and friendly, and her heart warms towards him.

'I'm afraid they're dead,' he says regretfully. 'I never

knew my grandmother – she died before I was born – but Grampy was really cool.'

So Russ is dead: a cloud of sadness engulfs her but dissolves in the bright regard of this boy, his grandson.

'Your father,' she says cautiously, 'was just a little boy when I last saw him. Probably seven or eight.'

The boy instinctively glances behind him, as if Jason might be standing at his back, and then looks at her.

'He's just dashed into the pub to the loo,' he says. 'He's a bit . . . like, edgy, just now. My mum died six months ago and we're . . .'

He swallows, his eyes suddenly flood with tears, which he blinks away, and Evie is filled with compassion. She, the least maternal of women, longs to gather him into her arms.

'I am so sorry,' she says quietly. 'How very terrible.'

He nods; it is unspeakably terrible.

'Will you tell me your name?' she asks gently.

'It's Mikey,' he says, swiping his bare brown arm across his eyes. 'Mikey Dean.'

'Well, Mikey,' she says, 'it's very good to meet you. I live across there. See those houses down along the river? They're converted boathouses. That's where I am.'

She doesn't quite know why she's telling him; Jason would never bring him to see her.

'That's really cool,' he says, shielding his eyes from the sun and staring across to where the boathouse stands. 'Your view must be epic.'

'It's pretty special,' she says, smiling. 'Is this your first time in Dartmouth?'

'Uh-huh. My aunt and uncle have just bought a little flat by the church for holiday lets. They're letting me and Dad use it for a holiday.'

'It's a great week for your first visit to Dartmouth. Regatta week.'

Mikey lets out a great sigh. 'I just love it. I can't wait to see the fireworks and the Red Arrows. I want to stay. I want to live here for ever.'

'But you have to go back to school?'

He nods, makes a face.

'Do you still live in Bristol?'

'We've got a flat in Tyndall's Park Road,' he tells her. 'We lived in Grampy's house for a while after he died but then we had to sell it and get something smaller.'

'Where do you go to school?'

She wonders if she's being too inquisitive but he answers readily.

'I'm at Wells Cathedral School. I'm a chorister.'

'That's wonderful,' she says warmly, and he smiles at her enthusiasm.

'It's OK,' he says nonchalantly.

Silence falls between them. He glances anxiously behind him again, and she gets up reluctantly. 'I must go. Good to meet you, Mikey. See you around.'

She walks quickly away, up the hill to Southtown and down the steps to the boathouse where Claude is reading on the balcony, waiting for Charlie and Ange to arrive.

*

Driving into Dartmouth past the old Pottery, through Warfleet down to the Merchant's House, Charlie struggles with a growing sense of unease. Ange's friends have cried off the visit to regatta – some family crisis, apparently – and Charlie is beginning to wonder if indeed there was ever any intention of their coming. After all, Ange has never been down for regatta without friends in tow – she sees no point in it – and he suspects that Ange wants to see for herself just how well Ben is dug in at the Merchant's House without it being too obvious.

'Evie will never get him out if she's not careful,' she said when she heard of Evie's gesture. 'I think it's very unwise of her.'

'You make him sound like a squatter,' Charlie said, quite lightly. He didn't want to make a big deal of it; he's still coming to terms with the fact that his father didn't leave the house to him. 'Ben's not some ne'er-do-well looking for an easy option. He's always got work and he's very well known in his field.'

Ange shrugged this aside. Until the Merchant's House had been left to Evie she'd been quite fond of Ben; leaving the magazines that published his work on show around the house, boasting about his latest shoot if it were at a grand enough house. Now she's nervous: Evie is very fond of Ben, his marriage is breaking up, and he has his foot in the door. Ange has a strong sense of ownership and, in her view, the Merchant's House belongs to Charlie and his family, not to Evie – and certainly not to Ben.

All the way from London, Ange has been making little comments that reflect her anxiety and irritation.

'I don't know what your father was thinking about. He could have simply put the house into some kind of trust for Evie to use in her lifetime if she needed it, though I can't see why she should. She's got her own house. She must have influenced him in some way.'

'Rubbish,' he says irritably. He doesn't believe that Evie influenced his father but this constant need to defend TDF's rather hurtful decision and pretend that he doesn't mind is beginning to wear him down. 'That's not at all Evie's style. Why shouldn't he leave her the house? She was his wife.'

'His second wife,' she corrects him quickly. 'Not the same at all. We have the girls to think about. It's breaking with family tradition. I'm just saying that it's unwise of Evie to give Ben any ideas about it.'

'Well, at least he loves the place,' Charlie says. 'Which is more than you do. Even the girls prefer to stay with your mother down at Polzeath than come to Dartmouth.'

'That's because their school-friends are there in the summer,' she answers. 'It will be different when they're older. Anyway, that's not the point.'

He doesn't ask what the point is: he's weary of skating around the problem. Personally, he's delighted that old Benj is staying at the Merchant's House; better than tenants wrecking the place or a succession of holidaymakers coming and going. And it's nice for Evie to have him just across the road.

'I suppose Claude will be here,' Angie says, resigned, as they drive down into Southtown. 'An extraordinary relationship, I always think. He and Evie behave like a couple of undergraduates, dashing about on that silly scooter. Your father was just as bad once Marianne died.'

Charlie resists the urge to defend Evie and Claude; he simply hasn't got the energy. Lately, however, he's become more and more sympathetic to his father's marital disloyalty. Having someone like Evie to spend time with, to relax with, must have been utter heaven. He loves Ange – and he totally respects her drive and ambition and devotion to the family business – but, oh goodness, what he wouldn't give for a few weeks of behaving like an undergraduate again.

He peers ahead. 'Great,' he says. 'Benj has opened the garage door. I can reverse in.'

'No,' Ange says at once. 'No you can't. It makes it much more difficult to unload the car. Drive straight in.'

'But reversing out on to this road is very tricky,' he argues. 'Much better to back in.'

'Don't be silly,' she says. 'There's hardly any traffic down this road during regatta. Just do it, Charlie.'

And so he does, but he experiences an almost overwhelming desire to perform some violent action: crash his hand down on the horn, drive the car into the back wall of the garage, something to stop the frustration of being obedient to Ange's relentless will.

Instead he switches off the engine, gets out and tries the interconnecting door to the house. It opens and he goes into the hall and shouts, 'We're here,' and Benj comes out of the kitchen and they stand and grin at each other as if they are children again. Charlie remembers that his cousin's marriage has come apart, that he's homeless, and he holds out his arms to him.

'Good to see you, Benj,' he says, and they hug, while Ange's voice, raised in irritation, can be heard from the garage.

'Hi. Where are you? Is anyone going to come and help me with this luggage?'

Ben is surprised and touched at the warmth of Charlie's greeting. He senses some stress here, and he can make a pretty good guess at what's causing it. Ange appears at the door; her quite pretty face is marred by an almost habitual harassed frown. It is the expression of someone who needs to be in control; to be watchful lest her instructions are misunderstood or, worse, disobeyed.

How awful it must be, thinks Ben, to be Ange. Pretty awful for poor old Charlie, too.

'Can nobody hear me?' she cries. 'Oh, there you are.'

He raises his hand in greeting. 'Hi, Ange,' he says, but she's already turned away with a quick wave of her hand, instructions still trailing behind her.

Charlie shrugs, follows her out to help, and Ben waits at the door wondering how to play this rather odd scene. It seems strange to be welcoming Charlie and Ange to the Merchant's House.

'Shall I take that up for you?' he asks, as Ange reappears

with a large holdall. 'You're in the room on the left at the top of the stairs.'

'I know where our bedroom is, thank you, Ben,' she says brightly. 'I can manage.'

He watches her small figure stomping up the stairs; her bottom is rather too big in her unflatteringly loose linen trousers and her back view is not particularly attractive. He feels another wash of sympathy for Charlie, who has now appeared with two suitcases. Ben raises his eyebrows at the amount of luggage and Charlie shakes his head defensively.

'I know. I know. Don't worry. We've only come for the weekend, honestly. God, what a journey.'

'Want a drink?' he asks.

'Don't tempt me,' says Charlie. 'It's too early.'

'Is it? The sun must be over the yardarm somewhere. It wouldn't have worried you once.'

'Shut up and put the kettle on. Ange will appreciate a cup of tea.'

He turns away, begins to climb the stairs, and Ben goes into the kitchen. The kitchen and the breakfast room, divided only by a graceful arch, occupy most of the ground floor since the sitting-room was converted into a garage. Ben likes this mix of space and cosiness. The kitchen's sash window looks into the garden; the break-fast room's windows look out on the street. In common with most of these houses, the drawing-room is on the first floor so as to take advantage of the views of the river but Ben likes this long, light room with its high ceilings, deep skirting boards and beautiful timber floor. This is where he spends most of his time when he isn't working. In recent years the house has been used only for holidays and the original Regency furniture has been replaced with more durable pieces. The long, rather battered, refectory table is very useful to work at, to read at – as well as to eat at – and Ben has been busy tidying up. There is a sofa along one wall and built-in bookshelves on either side of the window, and now he glances through the arch into the breakfast room to satisfy himself that it is as tidy as Ange will expect it to be.

When she does appear, however, she says, 'Oh, I thought we'd have tea in the drawing-room,' and, 'Have you got any Earl Grey?' which makes him feel like a rather inadequate footman. But Charlie says, 'Oh, for goodness' sake, we don't want to cart it upstairs. In fact I might go out into the garden. I need some fresh air.'

With relief Ben follows him outside, leaving Ange to agonize over Earl Grey or a fruit tea, and Charlie says: 'This probably sounds really crass, Benj, given what you've been through, but just at the moment I rather envy you.'

As soon as they've gone Ange slips back upstairs. A quick glance around the drawing-room shows that there is very little change: some books and magazines on the floor by an armchair but not much else. The spare bedrooms are clearly unused, the beds stripped, cupboards bare, and the little dressing-room that leads off one of the rooms is empty, but in the two rooms up on the second floor the reality of Ben's occupation is very clear. The bedroom is untidy, the bed unmade: quilt rumpled, pillows piled up, clothes tossed over chairs. The study is now a workroom filled with photographic equipment, painting equipment, piles of paper, card; there is barely room to walk.

Her worst fears are realized as she stares in through the doorway: Ben is clearly very much at home. Her mind darts to and fro: a sharp needle flying in and out of the tough fabric of her anxiety. She wonders what the tax implications are regarding Ben working here and whether Evie has thought about it.

Through a window she can see Ben and Charlie sitting at the table at the top of the garden with their mugs of tea. Ben is talking, gesticulating, and suddenly Charlie throws back his head and roars with laughter. She watches them for a moment, resenting their camaraderie, fearing it – Charlie can be so foolishly soft-hearted, it still irritates her to hear him using that childish name for Ben – and then she slips back downstairs. She reboils the kettle, puts a teabag into a mug and all the while there is something nagging at the back of her mind; something different, something she's missed. Her instinct tells her that it's important but, before she can go back for another check around, Ben appears.

'We wondered if you were OK?' he asks. 'And I remembered that Evie brought some stuff over. Cakes and things.'

The kettle boils and Ange makes her tea. 'Not for me, thanks,' she says. 'This will do me fine.'

He smiles at her, steps aside so that she is obliged to precede him outside, and she has no alternative but to climb up through the garden to join Charlie. And all the time that they are talking, drinking tea, her thoughts are doubling to and fro, trying to remember what it is that she has missed.

Now that the moment is upon her, Evie is rather regretting inviting Charlie, Ange and Ben to supper. She is still fearful about how Ange will be reacting to Ben's presence in the Merchant's House. She says so to Claude.

'I knew you'd feel like that,' says Claude rather gloomily. He's wondering how he's going to cope with seeing Charlie now he has inside information. He feels uneasy, hoping he can carry it off, and he wonders how Evie has coped with it for the last two years.

'I suppose it was silly of me,' she says. 'But what could I do? Dartmouth will be packed and they'll be tired after the journey. I had to offer. I was half hoping Ben might phone and say they weren't coming. I half expected Ange to cry off. She'll have brought provisions. She always does.'

'It's odd,' he says. 'The prospect of seeing them. Now that I know about Charlie, I mean.'

'I can imagine how you're feeling. I was the same. I've got slightly used to it now but it's unsettling knowing things about people that they don't know themselves. You keep wondering how they'd react if you told them. I'm sorry, Claude, it's unfair to involve you, but I just needed someone else to know.'

'I still think it was wrong of TDF to leave you with it. It was his decision to make, not yours.'

Before she can answer there's a knock on the door, which opens, and Charlie shouts, 'Hi. Are you there, Evie?' and comes into the big room where she and Claude are sitting at the table.

'Charlie.' She gets up and goes to hug him, moved as always by his resemblance to her darling Tommy. She hates it that Claude is judging his old friend so harshly, though it's difficult to defend Tommy: it was his property, his son, his decision. However, she can remember his distress, his desire to make amends without causing too much destruction, her own readiness to relieve him of some of the stress without quite knowing how. Nevertheless, Claude's ready sympathy and understanding have eased her anxiety a little and she is grateful to him.

As she hugs Charlie she tries to imagine telling him the truth – that all he has should by rights belong to Ben – and she simply can't envisage having the courage. Instead she smiles up at him with genuine pleasure at seeing him and stands back to watch him embrace Claude.

'It's great to be here,' he's saying. 'And thanks, Evie, for letting us use the garage. I see you've managed to get a space outside, but it's a real problem during regatta, isn't it?'

'Ben and I are coxing and boxing with the space,' she answers. 'My old friend lets me use her driveway for one of the cars so if I have to go out Ben moves his car down here to keep the space. It's not ideal but it's only for a few days while you're here.'

Charlie strolls to the balcony and wanders out, staring down-river, hands in his jeans pockets. Claude watches him. It might be TDF standing there: long, lean legs, broad shoulders, dark head slightly bent. How wonderful it must be to be tall and elegant; to be able to attract women without even trying. He remembers how he used to envy TDF his grace, and Charlie and Ben have inherited those same qualities. They have no idea what it's like to be short and stocky and unremarkable, with gingery hair that curls like a tonsure around a prematurely bald head.

Charlie is turning back now, his face peaceful, and Claude wonders how he would react if he were to tell him the truth; imagines that calm expression changing to disbelief and shock.

'I should get down more often,' Charlie says. 'I forget how good it is here. It's a different world after London.'

'Not at regatta,' says Evie. 'The town is heaving and the noise is unbelievable. The funfair, pop music belting out from each stall . . .'

'Not to mention the smell of beefburgers,' says Claude.

'Even so,' says Charlie. 'We're going down to Polzeath on Monday to meet up with the girls for a week but perhaps I'll come down on my own after the holidays and spend some time with old Benj. He's looking good.'

'That's a brilliant idea,' says Evie. 'He's managing very well but I'm sure it would do him good. Are they coming over for supper?'

'Yes. He and Ange will be over soon. I just wanted to have a few minutes on my own with you.'

'Checking us out,' asks Evie, amused, 'before we put on our party faces?'

'Something like that,' he answers. He sits down again at the table. 'I'm still hoping that you're going to tell me that you're writing again, Evie. It's been much too long.'

She shakes her head. 'I've told you. I've finished with all that.'

'The Civil War, yes,' he says. 'I can see that. But there are other things to write about.'

Claude listens to the familiar argument, agreeing with Charlie but saying nothing.

It isn't long before Evie says, 'Enough, Charlie. I'm not writing another book. It's finished. Done with. Now, tell me about the girls. It's ages since I saw them.'

As she and Claude prepare the supper – Claude is very handy in the kitchen – Evie concentrates on the coming evening, on Ange's attitude to Ben and how it will affect them all.

And here they are: Ben and Ange coming in together. Ange greets them, an air-kiss near both cheeks, and Claude offers them a drink, talks about regatta, how they might wander round the town tomorrow and enjoy the fun.

'I always forget,' Ange says, walking to the big windows, 'how early you lose the sun here. It's quite gloomy, isn't it, even on such a bright evening?'

There is a tiny silence and Evie can't help but chuckle to herself: it's so Ange, this kind of remark. A little put-down, an implied criticism, that slightly wrong-foots people and fractures the jolly atmosphere.

Ben and Charlie are silent; they look embarrassed, Claude looks cross. Evie steps in. She smiles at Ben, gives him a tiny wink.

'It is, Ange,' she says, 'and, you know, it's something you really notice as you grow older. The sun and light become so important. I've been seriously considering letting out the boathouse or even selling it and moving across the road. It's so much higher, gets more sunshine, and I wouldn't have to climb up all those steps to the road each time I go out. Of course, that's if Ben thinks he could cope with me.'

Ben has turned aside to hide his grin but Ange is completely taken aback.

'Well,' she says, after a moment, 'if you want my opinion I've never heard anything so foolish.'

'But why?' asks Evie, taking her glass from Claude. 'I thought about it quite a lot last winter. Then, when spring arrived, I began to have second thoughts and then Ben needed a place to catch his breath so I rather put it on hold, but you're quite right. It *can* be rather gloomy here and, now I'm on my own again and getting old, I'm beginning to think about it seriously.'

This is indeed carrying the war into the enemy's camp and for once Ange is silenced. Evie feels she might explode with suppressed mirth and she can see that Claude feels the same.

'But you love it here,' says Ange rather feebly. She

glances at Charlie who looks away, still feeling uncomfortable by her earlier remark.

'I do,' agrees Evie. 'But maybe it's time for a change. Come and help me with the supper, Claude.'

And she turns away, still fizzing with a sense of triumph and amusement.


Mikey piles up the cartons from the Chinese takeaway and puts them in the bin. Dad's slumped in front of the telly, channel-hopping. He's in one of his moods this evening and Mikey's being careful, just like Mum taught him to be.

'Daddy can't help his moods,' she used to tell him. 'It's just the way he is. He loves you, don't ever forget that, but we just have to stay very calm and not let it upset us.'

It's hard, though, tiptoeing around him, especially now Mum's not here. Mikey puts the plates in the little dishwasher. He gets a bit frightened, sometimes, and a bit tired making sure that Dad doesn't lose it or have one of his real downers.

'Life's shit,' he says when he's having a downer. His face goes all grim, like a light's gone out behind his eyes, and Mikey's heart always races with anxiety. 'Really shit. I never had a proper chance. It was terrible, Mikey, having a mother in a wheelchair, in pain all the time. God, Mikey, you can't imagine how she suffered and she was so brave.'

He never knows what to say, so he just nods and tries to look sympathetic. Now he switches on the dishwasher, trying to concentrate on good things: being here in Dartmouth and meeting that woman, Evelyn Fortescue. He liked her;

she was really cool. He hasn't told Dad about her. He doesn't quite know why but something tells him to keep quiet. Probably because she was Grampy's friend. Dad can be a bit funny about Grampy, like he's jealous of him; angry with him. It's Grandma he adored – and Mum.

Mikey struggles against a black wave of misery: he feels terribly alone. He wishes he could be back at school with some of his mates, or with his aunt Liz in Taunton, or perhaps see Evelyn Fortescue again. She was nice and normal.

'Want some coffee?' he calls through the doorway.

Dad's still slumped there, spaced out, like he's not seeing what's on the screen. He looks round, seems to come to, nods.

'Yeah. Thanks, Mikey.'

Mikey sighs, fills the kettle and switches it on. He must be strong for Mum. That terrible cancer had eaten her up and done for her so quickly.

'Aunt Liz will look out for you,' she told him, gripping his hand, her face all ravaged. She looked a hundred. 'Take care of Dad. Liz will be there.'

But Aunt Liz lives in Taunton and isn't there most of the time, and he must do the best he can. The trouble is, Dad is his own worst enemy. He can be such fun, but then somebody says something that he takes against and that's the end of it. He's seized by a terrible rage, he shouts and shakes, but when it's over he weeps with remorse and swears it won't happen again.

Mikey peeps in at him. Dad's having a little swig at the

water bottle. He does it quite often and Mikey's frightened that there's something really wrong with Dad; that he might have throat cancer or something. Dad says it's to do with the medication he takes for his depression, his happy pills, which makes his throat dry. He wishes Dad would have another check-up with the doctor but he gets surly when it's mentioned.

Mikey cranes sideways so he can see the little slice of the church tower out of the window. He'll go on Sunday to see if they have a choir. Singing lifts him, carries him away from all his troubles. He loves school and the choir and his mates. He's really, really grateful that he's got a scholarship so that they won't have to worry about fees, even when his voice breaks and he gets older. Anyway, Mum took out some kind of insurance for school fees when he was just a baby. She said she did it because of Dad not being able to go to Winchester, though he passed the entrance exam, because Grampy couldn't afford the fees and that Dad never got over it; that it was the root of all his problems and that it was Grampy's fault, though Mikey can't quite see why. Not everyone can afford expensive school fees.

The kettle boils and he makes coffee in a mug, carries it through and puts it on the little table. Dad's asleep, head tipped sideways, snoring. He's still there when Mikey goes to bed.

Jason wakes suddenly, heart pounding, staring round him. His throat is rough and sore from snoring and his head aches. The television is switched off and there's no sign of Mikey. Jason groans, hauls himself upright, peers at his watch. Christ! It's a quarter to bloody three. Mikey must have gone to bed long since. Well, no harm done.

He gets up, goes into the kitchen and fills a glass with tap water, gulping it back. His throat is on fire and he fills the glass again and drinks the water down. He leans against the sink, his eyes closed, trying to stop the panic that churns his gut. He can hear Helena telling him to breathe and he tries to do it, hauling air in through his nose, willing down the fear.

'Try to rationalize it,' she says to him. 'What's the worst that can happen?'

He thinks about it, what it is that's nagging at the back of his mind, and then remembers: Evelyn bloody Drake sitting on a bench outside the pub with Mikey. He'd really had to control himself; restrain his wild desire to run forward and simply grab her and drag her away from his son.

He remembers now that he went into the pub to have a leak, and then a very quick shot of whisky at the bar on the way back – well, you can't just use the loo without buying a drink – and then he'd come out and there she was, cool as you like, sitting there talking to Mikey. He nearly lost it but something held him back. For one thing, the place was heaving with people and even he could see that it would be asking for trouble to slap her about a bit in front of a crowd. For another, there was Mikey. He needs to keep Mikey on side; needs to show him that it's she who is the root of all their troubles. Her affair with his father that caused darling Mama so much pain, her refusal to help in the slightest way with the school fees, even though by then she was rolling in it, all thanks to his father's own research and all the help he'd given her.

'She owes you,' Mama said, way back then, staring at his father. Her face was so brittle, so white, it looked like it might shatter into pieces. 'She owes us all. She nearly destroyed our marriage and without you she'd be nothing. You must write to her again but for God's sake make your point. Don't pussyfoot about this time. Jay's whole future is at stake here.'

He'd been just outside the door, watching and listening; he was good at that, making himself small, invisible, listening to the rows, the arguments.

'It wasn't like that,' his father replied wearily. 'You know it wasn't. My affair with Evie never threatened our marriage and she didn't steal my research. You're being utterly irrational.'

But she'd given him no peace. Jason smiles to himself. You had to admit that darling Mama never gave up: she was implacable. His father had written to Evelyn Drake again but the answer was still 'no'. Even now he can remember the wrenching shock when Mama told him that he couldn't go to Winchester; that he must go to the local grammar school.

He got over it, of course – or he thought he had until he saw Evelyn Drake in the Royal Castle. He can see now that all the little failures and disappointments lead directly back to her refusal to help: the bullying at school, his low self-esteem, which affects his interpersonal skills, the terrible depression. Watching her in the bar at the Royal Castle, and then earlier outside the pub, his hatred for her crystallized into a desire to do something violent: to make her pay for ruining his life. She has success, money, an international reputation, whilst he has so little in comparison: no wife, no job, a little flat that he might lose at any time. He'd like to break her neck — but not tonight.

Jason runs the cold tap, laves his face with cold water, dries it on some kitchen towel and creeps quietly up the stairs to bed.

# CHAPTER NINE

Charlie gets up early the next morning, sliding out of bed, picking up his towelling robe, which he pulls on as he goes quietly downstairs. He makes himself a cup of coffee and then unlocks the kitchen door and climbs up through the garden. On the top terrace he puts his mug on the table and stands looking out to sea. His love for this place always comes as a little shock; each time he visits he promises himself he will visit Dartmouth more often and then, once he's back in London, his life resumes its usual shape and the memory fades. He's glad that Benj was here to welcome them; it seemed even more like a home-coming, and he realizes that this is the first time he's stayed in the Merchant's House since his father died. Last time there were tenants here and he stayed with Evie – and they had great fun.

'I just can't quite see how you can be so besotted with her,' Ange said once, a long time ago. 'After all, she was your father's mistress. Don't you feel disloyal to your mother, being so affectionate to her?'

He'd loved his mother, valued her advice, sought her good opinion and was grateful for everything she'd done for him. Yet alongside his love ran a current of anxiety lest he should disappoint her, let her down, incur that cool emotional withdrawal of which she was capable each time he challenged her authority. Evie was so much easier to be with; ready to joke, treat him as an equal, give him space.

'Well, of course she is,' cried Ange, when he tried to explain this to her. 'She has no responsibility for you. She doesn't care. Your mother loved you. She wanted the best for you.'

Charlie didn't disagree, but after that he avoided conversations about Evie. He knew that his father had known Evie for some time before his mother's death – that they'd had a relationship – but deep down he couldn't quite condemn TDF. The temptation to be able to relax, to be free from his mother's watchfulness, must have been overwhelming. Yet he can see that, like his father before him, he benefits from the same kind of relentless power that drives Ange in pursuit of the best for her family.

The town is waking up to regatta, preparing for the fête: the guardship lies at her mooring. Charlie wipes the dew from the chair with the hem of his towelling robe and sits down at the table. His father loved it up here, sitting watching the river, joshing with Claude – who called this top terrace the poop deck – and with Evie. He made the steps through the garden more accessible, levelling them so that they were easier to climb. During the last five years, after he retired and rarely went to London, he and Evie lived here at the Merchant's House and Evie kept the boathouse for visiting friends and family and for working, though she'd begun to do less of that.

It's odd, thinks Charlie, that there are no real memories of his mother here. Like Ange, she preferred to be in London or to jet off to some luxurious hotel and sunshine. Self-catering in the damp West Country didn't appeal to her.

'Terribly dull, darling,' she'd say. 'I simply don't know what people do all day. It's rather fun for an occasional weekend, but two days are about my limit, I'm afraid.'

He'd come down in the summer holidays with his father and Benj, just for two weeks. He and Benj would go out into the town, play with the local children, go swimming at the nearby beaches, sail on the river. They still have friends in the town, working in the tourist industry: one owns a chandlery, another a small restaurant.

'I suppose I ought to let the old place,' his father would say, standing in the drawing-room, gazing from the window, 'but I can't quite bring myself to do it. It's good to know that I can come down here when the mood takes me; remembrance of things past and all that.'

Other people used the house for holidays; friends and relations were glad to take the opportunity to spend time there. Claude brought his family once or twice. Marianne's older sister and her family spent Easter at the Merchant's

House for a few years when the children were small. Then TDF married Evie and began spending more and more time in Dartmouth, until he finally passed the reins to Charlie and moved down permanently.

'Do you mind?' Charlie asked Evie once. 'Leaving your boathouse and living here?'

'I haven't really left it,' she answered. 'I still work there. This is a beautiful house, and I adore the garden, it's just that I can't quite think of it as mine. It belongs to your family so I feel very slightly like a guest in it.'

He could see what she meant. Because it was fully furnished, fully equipped, there was no point in changing things. Evie had no opportunity to imprint her own personality except in very small ways, nor did she attempt it. He accepted her implication that once his father died it would be left to him, and so she had no true sense of belonging, yet he was upset that she felt that way and tried to assure her that it was her home.

She gave him a hug. 'Thanks, Charlie. It's fine, honestly. I'm very happy here.'

Nobody guessed for a moment that TDF would leave the house to her.

Charlie leans back in his chair, stretching his legs out under the table. What he can't understand is why his father didn't warn him: explain why, for the first time in five generations, the Merchant's House should be left away from the rest of the estate. Although he won't enter into Ange's discussions about it, he too is puzzled as to why it wasn't simply left in trust for Evie's lifetime so as to keep it in the family. He feels oddly hurt that his father didn't take him into his confidence and explain his reasons.

The top terrace is warm in the early morning sunshine; Charlie can smell the lavender. He breathes deeply, expels anxiety, and decides that he will walk into the town after breakfast. Part of him hopes that Ange won't want to come with him. He finishes his coffee, wanders back down the steps and into the kitchen. Ben is there, yawning over a fresh-made cafetiere.

'Morning,' he says. 'Is Ange up?'

Charlie shakes his head. 'I'll take her some coffee. She might like a bit of a lie-in.'

Ben's raised eyebrows suggest that this is unlikely; that Ange is more likely to be down organizing breakfast. Charlie shrugs, takes a mug of coffee and goes upstairs. Ange is sitting up in bed, checking her iPhone, tapping out a text. She gestures with her head towards the bedside table and continues tapping. He sets the coffee down.

'Thanks,' she says. 'You can shower first. I brought croissants with me but I doubt Ben will have thought about lunch so I shall go and forage. Thank God there's a Marks and Spencer's in the town now. Don't be long.'

It's mid-morning by the time Charlie closes the front door behind him, crosses the road, and strides down Bayard's Hill. He pauses outside the Dartmouth Arms, wanders over to stand at the wall and look across to

Kingswear. The river is full of small craft, some of which jostle round the guardship like goslings paddling around a stately grey goose.

He turns away, heading for the Embankment, enjoying being alone: knowing that he is a local amongst the crowds of holidaymakers and visitors. There is music blaring from stalls, echoing from the funfair; an atmosphere of carnival, of gaiety. He remembers how, when his girls were younger, they loved regatta; clinging to his hands lest they should be separated by the crowds, screaming in the bumper car and on the big wheel, begging for ice creams. Now, at thirteen and fifteen, they are frighteningly sophisticated, plugged into iPods, endlessly texting, preferring to be with their friends down at Polzeath than with their parents. He misses them; misses their small warm hands holding his, their dependency, the way they used to laugh at his jokes.

A woman is coming towards him, holding a little girl by the hand, laughing down at her. The child looks up with a trusting, happy smile, giving a little skip of anticipation as if at some promised treat, and just for a moment Charlie experiences a sharp pang of loss; a longing for times past. Then, as he watches them, the woman glances at him and her face opens into an expression of pleasure, of recognition. Even the child seems to know who he is – and, as they move towards him through the throng of people, he finds himself smiling back at them, his heart beating more quickly as if something momentous is happening.

The woman — she is beautiful, warm, vivid with the joy of simply being here — cries out: 'Hello. Isn't this great? We came in on the Park and Ride.'

And, despite the fact that he has no idea who she is, he knows nothing will ever be quite the same again.

Even as she calls out to him, Jemima is suddenly filled with disquiet. The man who now approaches them is so like Ben — his height and grace, his dark hair and smiling brown eyes — and yet it isn't Ben. Not quite. She stares at him, her smile fading a little, feeling a bit crazy.

At her side, Maisie jumps with excitement, swinging on her hand, as if she remembers the man from Stokeley Farm Shop, and shouts, 'Hello!'

Jemima stares at him; and as he stretches out his hand, and she automatically takes it in her own, she knows that nothing will ever be quite the same again. They stand still, the crowds surging and barging around them and the music playing, linked, staring at each other.

Jemima gathers her wits, smiles quickly, and lets go of his hand.

'This is crazy,' she says. 'I actually thought for a moment that you were Ben Fortescue but you're not.' A tiny hesitation. 'Are you?'

The question makes him laugh, and she laughs with him, and the tension flows out of the situation.

'I really wish I were,' he says. 'I'm his cousin, Charlie.'

'Gosh,' she says. 'Well, at least I'm not quite crazy. That was totally surreal. I'm Jemima Spencer and this is

Maisie. Her mum has to work so she's staying with me for the weekend.'

'Hello, Maisie,' he says.

'Otto couldn't come,' Maisie tells him seriously. 'He has to stay at home because he doesn't like the bus.'

'Otto?' Charlie raises an eyebrow at Jemima.

'My Labrador,' she says quickly. 'He's not bus-trained and he whines all the time. Look, I'm sorry about rushing at you like that. You are so alike. You must have thought I was out of my mind.'

He shrugs, shakes his head. 'So what's on the agenda? Coffee? An ice cream?'

'Ice cream!' shouts Maisie. 'Jemima said I could have one. Please, Jemima.'

She doesn't quite know how to handle it: whether to let him come along simply because he's Ben's cousin; whether it would look petty to refuse. He's looking at her as if he's trying to feel his way forward and she simply can't bear the thought of watching him walk away.

'There's a stall selling coffee and ice cream,' she says. 'Let's slum it, shall we?'

She sees his look of relief, of pleasure, and she is filled with such joy that she can barely stop herself from jumping up and down like Maisie is; from beaming at him. Instead, she takes hold of Maisie's hand more firmly.

'Come on, then. The treat's on me. It's regatta.'

'So how do you know old Benj?' asks Charlie, taking the polystyrene cup, tasting the coffee cautiously; actually, it's not too bad. He watches Jemima passing Maisie her ice cream.

'We seem to frequent the same cafés,' she says. 'We saw him first at Stokeley and then I met him again at Alf's and we had coffee together. He loves being up there in Southtown, doesn't he?'

'Yes,' says Charlie. He has a childish desire to be competitive: to say, 'But it's my house not his' – and then remembers that, actually, it's Evie's. 'Have you been there?'

She shakes her head. 'Oh, no. I don't really know him all that well.'

He remembers her expression of pleasure when she first saw him, thinking he was Benj, and feels a little jab of envy.

'Though,' she adds, glancing away from him, 'he did invite me to see the house. I work for a company that does holiday lets and we've got one in Southtown. It's beautiful.'

'Do you live in the town?' He'd been on the verge of inviting her back there and then, but suddenly he sees the foolishness of it: Benj's surprise, not to mention Ange's.

'I live at Torcross.' Suddenly she laughs. 'This is a bit like déjà vu. I had a very similar conversation with Ben and the fact that you look so alike makes this seriously weird. Did you double for each other when you were children?'

'Just occasionally we helped each other out.' He grins, reminiscently. 'Not any more, though.'

'So are you on holiday or just down for regatta? Ben

mentioned that some of his family live in London but that he's renting the house from them because his marriage is over.'

Charlie raises his eyebrows. Clearly Benj and Jemima got quite a long way on just one cup of coffee. 'That's right. Well, more or less. Ange and I are down for the weekend staying with Benj.'

How hard it is to mention Ange's name; impossible not to.

'Ange?'

'My wife.' Their eyes meet briefly, acknowledge the barrier, glance away. 'She prefers London. Usually I come down on my own. We have two teenage daughters but they like to go down to Polzeath to stay with Ange's mother in the holidays. They've got lots of school-friends they meet up with. And you? Are you . . . attached?'

'No, no. I've never managed to commit.' She takes a tissue from her shoulder bag and begins to wipe Maisie's fingers.

'And are you and Benj . . .?' He has to ask the question.

'No,' she answers quickly. Then 'What d'you mean?' She looks at him; her face is creased with confusion. 'I like him. He's easy to talk to.' A little pause. 'Why d'you call him Benj?'

'Oh, well, that's what his mother always called him. She died when he was quite young, about eleven, and I kept it up. I hoped it would be . . . comforting, I suppose.'

She stares at him, the confusion smoothed away, smiling a little.

126

'That's sweet,' she says.

Maisie, who has been examining the next stall, comes hopping back. 'Is it time for the dog show, Jemima?' she asks eagerly.

'Dog show?' Charlie looks blank.

Jemima bursts out laughing. 'Any minute now in the Royal Avenue Gardens.'

Maisie looks intently at Charlie. 'Are you coming with us?' she asks hopefully.

'I'd love to,' he says at once, casting all sanity and discretion to the winds, and she seizes his hand and hops along beside him.

'Are you my daddy?' she asks him, quite naturally, and he receives his second shock of the day.

'No,' he says, staring down at her wistful, hopeful face. 'No, Maisie. I'm not. I've got two girls of my own. Much bigger than you are.'

She looks regretful, makes a little grimace of disappointment, and then Jemima catches her hand from the other side and they plunge into the crowds in the Royal Avenue Gardens.

# CHAPTER TEN

Claude watches them go. He sees what, at a casual glance, seems to be a perfectly normal-looking little family enjoying regatta, but he knows that this is not the case. He cannot imagine what the woman and the little girl he and Evie saw at Torcross the day before yesterday are doing with Charlie and he tries, without success, to conjure up various scenarios in which they might have met and become so friendly.

When he first saw them at the coffee stall he was struck by a sense of such intimacy between them that he assumed it was Ben. It's quite possible that Ben and Jemima have met somewhere locally and been attracted to each other. As soon as he realized that it was Charlie, Claude was filled with misgiving: it's not Charlie's style to chat up pretty women and drink coffee at a stall with them. And what if Ange should arrive on the scene?

Even as he thinks this, he sees her approaching along the Embankment. Ange never strolls or saunters: she walks as if there is a train to catch; short quick steps, head slightly jutting forward. In a few moments she will be passing the stall. Claude hurries towards them. Perhaps it is all quite innocent but, just in case, he will join the little party; reacquaint himself with Jemima, muddy the waters somehow to make it all seem quite natural. But, even as he approaches, Maisie seizes Charlie's hand and the three of them disappear into the crowd of holidaymakers.

Quickly Claude steps behind a booth as Ange draws level and stomps by, shopping bag over her shoulder, intent on her mission. He watches her go, relieved that she didn't see Charlie. Claude is still feeling cross with her for nearly disrupting the mood of last night's little party.

'What a tiresome woman she can be,' he said to Evie when the three of them had gone. 'You really spiked her guns, though. You could see her brain working overtime, wondering if you were really serious. Poor old Charlie.'

'She's a very good wife and mother,' Evie answered thoughtfully. 'Very focused on what the family needs.'

He very nearly said that it was like Marianne and TDF all over again.

'Women are so damned sensible,' TDF said to him once in the pub. 'They can never let go just for a moment and be silly. They're so afraid they might lose control. I suppose they get all the stress out of their systems with their girlfriends and we're supposed to be doing it over this pint we're having, Claude. But wouldn't it be good just to actually have some fun with one's wife? Let off steam and just be silly and happy together for a few hours.'

It was quite a speech for TDF, who was such a placid fellow. Claude was surprised and, oddly, rather touched by TDF's intensity. His reaction was to try to make him laugh.

'You mean like that song from *My Fair Lady*? "Why Can't a Woman Be More Like a Man?"' He began to sing it, being first Rex Harrison and then Wilfrid Hyde-White. Jilly loved musicals – she'd been brought up on them, and knew so many songs by heart – and this was one of her favourites. He sang it to TDF – quietly but guying it up, acting it out – until they were both laughing so much he couldn't sing any more and the other people in the bar were laughing with them and joining in.

It was not long afterwards, Claude remembers, that TDF met Evie. They certainly had fun together; it wasn't so much a steamy passionate affair as simply two people of like minds who enjoyed the other's company.

Now, standing on the Embankment, with the throng of happy visitors enjoying regatta sweeping around him, Claude anxiously wonders if history might be about to repeat itself and if he should mention it to Evie. On reflection he decides not to. She was very quiet after supper, thinking about TDF.

'You can't imagine how much I miss him,' she said.

'Oh, I can,' he answered. 'I miss him too. He could always make me laugh, diffuse tension, give me a sense of perspective.'

'And there was you, too, Claude,' she said. 'I was so lucky. Thank God for you.'

She put an arm round his shoulders and hugged him, and he felt foolish and emotional and didn't know how to react.

'Well,' he said lightly, 'I can't think of a better moment to ask a huge favour. Well, two, actually.'

She looked at him, amused, eyebrows raised. 'Go on then.'

'First one. The family are going skiing for Christmas. I could go but I don't particularly want to, and they don't really want me tagging along, so I was wondering . . .'

'If you could come here?' Evie's face was bright with pleasure. 'But that would be wonderful, Claude. I'd love it. It's usually such a dreary time for me on my own but with you here and Ben across the road it'll be worth making plans for.'

He took courage from her delight to make his second request.

'There's more.'

She laughed at his expression. 'Whatever can it be?'

'It's a really huge ask, this one.'

'Spit it out.'

'They've decided the annexe needs extending. They want to build a room above it to give them more space so it means I have to move out for a few weeks. I can go into the house with them in the little spare room but, to be honest, I can see it'll be a big upheaval for everyone. I've been screwing up my courage to ask if I could come to stay.'

'You daft old bugger,' she said affectionately. 'Of course you can come. You know I'd love it.'

'I was thinking that if you got tired of me I could go over and stay with Ben. Get out of your hair.'

She put both arms round him then, holding him tightly.

'Shut up. You're staying with me. That's settled.'

They stood together for a moment, sharing the affection and security of their long friendship, and then drew apart, smiling at each other.

'So when do you want to come?'

'It sounds as if it might be the middle of October,' he answered. 'Once I get back I'll be able to give you a date. Thanks, Evie.'

Now, he feels an almost overwhelming desire to go back and tell her about Charlie but he can't decide whether it is disloyal to drop Charlie in it. After all, what was he actually doing? Simply having a cup of coffee at a stall and chatting to a woman isn't a crime. And the little girl was with them: it was hardly a secret assignation.

Nevertheless, he instinctively knows that there is more to it than that. He remembers the way they stood, looked at each other, as if they were enclosed in a shiny bubble of their own devising: secret and separate and inviolable. Even the child accepted it; she'd taken Charlie's hand so naturally, as if he belonged to them. And then, as if protected by a magic cloak in a fairy story, they disappeared just as Ange came stomping by.

As he stands watching a skiff flying over the water he wonders where they are now; whether they might blunder into Ange on her way back from the shops. He feels an odd instinct to protect them though he knows he shouldn't be encouraging them. His problem is that he doesn't like Ange any more than he liked Marianne. He liked seeing TDF off the hook, relaxing and having fun, rather than being harried and controlled and treated rather like a wayward schoolboy. TDF grafted, he loved his son, was a great host – but there was so little real joy and, once Charlie began boarding school, very little fun.

'Laughter's addictive, Claude,' TDF once said. 'Once you start laughing you just want more of it.'

Claude wonders how he will react when he next meets Charlie. Will he be able to pretend that he hasn't seen Charlie and Jemima together? He feels he's witnessed something intensely private – which is ridiculous in the circumstances. Perhaps he should follow them and casually bump into them so as to see Charlie's reaction. Even as Claude considers it, Charlie emerges from the Royal Avenue Gardens and wanders across the road, hands in pockets. Claude hurries towards him and steps in front of him.

'Hi, Claude,' Charlie says.

Claude stares curiously at him. Charlie's eyes are bright, wide and amazed, as if he has just seen something infinitely precious. He smiles at Claude, evidently trying to contain some strong emotion, only just preventing himself from bursting into joyful laughter.

'Charlie.' Claude puts a hand on the younger man's arm. How strong and warm and vital it feels, tensed beneath the thin cotton of his shirt. 'I see you've made some new friends.' He speaks out with reluctance yet he is unable to pretend he doesn't know.

Charlie's eyes focus on him, his eyebrows rise – and he laughs. No guilt here, then; no awkwardness.

'Yes,' he agrees, still laughing, inviting Claude to share his happiness. 'What an amazing pair. Do you know them?'

Claude shakes his head. 'Only met them once, on Torcross Line, eating ice cream.'

'Yes, Jemima said that's where she lives. She knows Benj.'

'*Does* she?'

'Mmm. Not very well. She mistook me for him.'

'How extraordinary.'

Charlie shrugs. 'It's happened to me and Benj before but not quite like this. Never like this. Look,' he lays his hand briefly on the older man's shoulder, 'I must get back. See you later, Claude.'

Claude watches him go, smiles and raises his hand. Yet, as he turns away and gazes across the river to the guardship, with its attendants of much smaller craft, he knows that things will never be quite the same again.

## CHAPTER ELEVEN

Jemima holds tightly to Maisie's hand as they wait for the Park and Ride bus to take them back up through the town to the car park. Maisie chatters to her about the dogs they've just seen but she hardly hears her though she answers, 'Yes, the Labrador looked just like Otto. He was my favourite,' and, 'I liked the little fluffy one, too,' whilst her thoughts leap and flash like fish in a waterfall. She simply can't concentrate her mind.

'I wish we could've stayed longer,' Maisie says.

'But we must get back for Otto,' says Jemima. She is surprised that her voice sounds quite normal. 'Poor old Otto. He'll be wondering where we are.'

Inside her head other voices speak: *Are you mad? He's married. I want to see him again.*

'Shall I see you again?' Charlie asked when she said that they must go.

'I don't see how,' she answered. 'I mean . . . well, how can we?'

'But you want to?'

She stared at him and then burst out laughing because that's how he made her feel: joyful, light, happy.

'You know I do. Go away, Charlie,' and she turned and walked away from him, not quite seeing where she was going but clinging to Maisie's hand. Once, she glanced back. He was still standing there, watching them leave, and he raised his hand. Still laughing, feeling quite mad, she took her scarf from around her neck and waved it wildly so that he should see it above the heads of the visitors.

Now, as the bus carries them up the hill, she can't quite repress the bubble of excitement that still fizzes inside her. It's impossible, wrong, unthinkable – yet she is so happy. How strange that he should look so like Ben and yet be so different. But what exactly is the difference? How to describe it? She is drawn to Ben; he is intuitive, laid-back, unthreatening. Charlie shares those qualities but there's an extra element: some indefinable alchemy that worked like strong magic.

Jemima unlocks the car, helps Maisie on to her child seat and clips on her seat belt. She has won a toy – a small dolly – at the fair and she takes it out of the little rucksack she wears to examine it, showing it again to Jemima, who nods and smiles at the child's earnest expression. She's glad Maisie was with her. It made it all so much easier though she can't exactly think why; perhaps Maisie's presence protected her from behaving foolishly. The prospect of seeing Charlie alone is both exhilarating and terrifying.

The car is hot and stuffy and Jemima puts down the

windows before she drives away. Never has the familiar coastal drive been more beautiful: she notices everything as if she hasn't really seen it before. Smooth yellow beaches tucked in neatly at the feet of steep granite cliffs; a roadside edging of wild flowers – papery red poppies, shiny yellow buttercups, elegant pink campion; the distant dazzle of the sea curving in a sweep along Torcross Line and on towards Start Point. The whole landscape is brighter, more defined, infinitely precious to her.

'What's for lunch?' asks Maisie prosaically, and Jemima begins to laugh again, relishing this injection of normality.

'Fish and chips,' she says. 'We'll give Otto a walk and then we'll go to the Torcross Boathouse for a special treat. How about that?'

Maisie cheers and holds the dolly to the car window so that it can share in the glory of the day. She feels happy; it's good being with Jemima today and she liked Charlie. She thinks that she remembers him from the farm shop and how she watched him, wondering if he could be her father come back to them. It's a bit sad that he isn't, but somehow she doesn't mind. She liked the way he and Jemima talked about the dogs and that Jemima wasn't silly with him like Mummy was with Dave. They didn't make her feel that prickly feeling she gets when she thinks grown-ups are showing off.

'I don't know what to call her,' she says, holding the dolly up so that Jemima can glance at her.

'Agrappina,' Jemima says. 'Hermione. Winifred.'

And Maisie laughs because the names sound so funny.

'Those aren't real names,' she says.

'They certainly are,' Jemima says indignantly. 'I've got a nice little box at home that will make a lovely bed for her. You'll have to take her on the plane to Australia to meet your cousins at Christmas. Wait till Otto sees her.'

'But he mustn't carry her about like he does his teddy,' Maisie says anxiously.

'Of course he won't,' Jemima says. 'Anyway, she wouldn't taste very nice in that net dress. He'd spit her out at once.'

They both laugh, and Maisie is so happy that she wants to shout and run and sing.

Leaving Ange to deal with the shopping, Charlie seeks out Ben in his studio on the top floor. He's sitting at his computer, concentrating on digitally enhancing a photograph of the guardship. He doesn't take his eyes from the screen and Charlie pushes aside the muddle of cameras and photographic equipment and perches on the end of the table.

'I've just met a friend of yours,' he says. 'Jemima Spencer.'

It's a kind of madness but he can't resist: he wants to talk about her, speak her name, and gauge Ben's reaction – which is one of surprise.

'Really?' He saves his work and turns to look at Charlie. 'How did you manage that? I've only met her once myself – well, twice I suppose, though you couldn't really count the first time – so I'm not sure I could call her a friend.'

'She thought I was you.' Charlie laughs. 'And by the time she realized I wasn't we'd got talking. She had a little girl with her. Maisie.'

'Ah, yes. Maisie.'

'Jemima was looking after her while her mum was at work. We had a cup of coffee together at one of the stalls.'

'Really?' Ben's eyebrows shoot up; he looks amused. 'That was quick work.'

Charlie grins back at him, relieved that Ben is remaining very calm. There is no hint of jealousy.

'She said that's how you met. At Alf's.'

Ben nods. 'We'd sort of seen each other at Stokeley Farm Shop. She had her dog with her, as well as Maisie and Maisie's mum. So when I went into Alf's and she was sitting there with Otto, I joined her.'

'And?'

Ben shrugs. 'And nothing. We talked about houses. She works for a holiday letting company and they have a house in Southtown. I invited her to come and see the Merchant's House and gave her my mobile number but nothing yet.' He gives Charlie a puzzled, questioning look. 'So what's all this about?'

Charlie wanders over to the open window through which the distant noise of regatta is filtering: the drumming of music, the thumping of machinery, the shrieking of children. He stands staring down and when he speaks it's very quietly, as if he's talking to himself.

'I think I've just fallen in love, Benj.'

'Christ, Charlie.' Ben pushes back his chair and gets up.

Charlie looks at him. 'I know. It's utterly weird. Do you mind?'

'If you mean do I have an interest, well, not in that way, no. I like her. She's beautiful and unusual and I hoped we'd be friends, but nothing more than that.'

Charlie lets out his breath with relief. 'That's something.'

'Why?' asks Ben, almost crossly. 'You're not thinking of pursuing this, Charlie, for God's sake? I mean, come on. How would it work? What about Ange, for a start?'

Charlie shakes his head. 'I don't know, Benj. I feel I've been poleaxed.'

'So how did you leave it? Have you arranged to see her again?'

Charlie begins to laugh. 'She told me to go away.'

'Well, then . . .'

'But then she looked back and waved her scarf. She was laughing.'

He looks at his cousin as if he expects him to understand, and then Ange begins to call from the landing below and his expression changes.

'Claude knows, too. He saw us.'

'*Claude?* How on earth . . .?'

'He said he met them on Torcross Line having ice cream. Jemima lives at Torcross.'

'Yes, I know that.'

140

Ange shouts again that lunch is ready and Charlie calls back, 'OK. We're on our way.' Then, 'Come on,' he says to Ben. 'We'll talk later,' and they go downstairs together.

Much later, as they sit on the beach whilst Maisie constructs odd shapes with the pebbles, Jemima roots about in her bag and finds the card Ben gave her. She looks at his name, at his telephone number, and then she carefully enters it into her mobile.

'I'm building a castle,' says Maisie. 'No, it's not. It's a palace for Princess Poppy.'

This is the name of the new dolly, decided upon at lunch where the princess sat on the table presiding over the fish and chips. Now she sits on Maisie's rucksack so that she might observe the construction of her new home.

'Only,' says Maisie, flinging herself down in despair, 'I can't do windows.'

'It's difficult with these pebbles,' agrees Jemima, getting on to her knees. 'You need a few very big flat stones. Have a look around and see if you can find some.'

She tries to remodel Maisie's construction, which looks more like a roofless igloo than a palace. Behind her Otto stretches out in the shade of the seawall: he is deep in sleep but his paws twitch from time to time as if he is dreaming about his earlier walk by the ley. It is hot; no breeze disturbs the tranquil surface of the sea. Families seek the shade of their windbreaks, or little pop-up tents, cramming sunhats on to the heads of small children, slathering sunblock on to bare arms and legs. Maisie returns with some larger stones and Jemima attempts to help create the palace for Princess Poppy but all the time she is thinking about Charlie, wondering if he will tell Ben he met her and what he might say about her. She remembers how Maisie asked Charlie if he were her father and his straightforward answer. There was no opportunity to explain; Maisie continued to hold his hand as if she'd known him all her life and he was completely at ease with her.

'I'm tired,' she says now, collapsing suddenly on to her side and putting her thumb into her mouth. 'What shall we do, Jemima?'

Jemima slightly dreads these moments when Maisie is seized with boredom, needing entertaining, and inclined to whine. It is too hot to go for a walk along the beach and she prefers to take Maisie swimming unaccompanied by Otto, who is always uncharacteristically overexcitable at the prospect of a paddle. She falls back on her usual distraction: refreshment. To go back home for tea is rather dull, and she hasn't bothered to bring a picnic, but a little treat at the Seabreeze Café just a few yards away generally revives Maisie's good temper. They can sit outside with Otto and plan what to do during the hours before bedtime. Otto's walk beside the ley will be a must, then perhaps a DVD, or Lego.

Maisie is already running ahead with Princess Poppy whilst Jemima strolls behind with Otto. She wonders idly what she would do if Charlie were to appear. She envisages several little scenarios in which they meet again unexpectedly. She still feels foolishly excited, unbearably happy: it seems inconceivable that nothing will come of it.

'I often come to Dartmouth on my own,' he said. 'I can come and stay with Benj. We've arranged to go down to Polzeath tomorrow but I'll be back.'

She loved the way he called his cousin 'Benj' because his mother had; loved the concentration of his gaze and the way they'd connected. He was exciting, different, yet oddly familiar and comfortable to be with: how weird was that?

Maisie is already scrambling on to a chair at an outside table, putting Princess Poppy down, beaming with anticipation. It's time for tea.

# CHAPTER TWELVE

'I need a cup of tea,' Evie says to Claude. 'How about you? Shall I put the kettle on?'

'But on sunny days you always like to go up into the garden around this time to catch the last of the sunshine,' he says, throwing his book aside. 'Just because Ange is around doesn't mean you shouldn't be able to do as you always do.'

Evie wants to put her arms around him to hug him and, at the same time, she wants to give him a shake.

'I know, but it's only for two days. For heaven's sake, Claude, I shan't die of it.'

'That's not the point,' he grumbles. 'It's your house. Your garden.'

'Yes,' says Evie thoughtfully. 'It is, isn't it? I'm really beginning to take that on board.'

She can feel him studying her as she stands beside him on the balcony, watching the tide making. The boathouse is already in the shadows as the sun sinks behind the hill and she feels suddenly glad that Claude will be here with her this autumn and for Christmas. Last winter, without Tommy and with tenants in the Merchant's House, she'd felt alone for the first time in her life. She tried to reason it away: to rationalize it. After all, she'd lived alone before she met Tommy, and during those first ten years before they were married he spent most of his time in London. Ah, she reminds herself, but back then she'd had her writing. Her extensive research into those families and their friends and servants who were caught up in the Civil War had taken up so much of her time; the construction of each book, the interweaving of the people and events, the planning and plotting, possessed her. Even once she and Tommy were married she still spent a large portion of each day at work here in the boathouse whilst Tommy relandscaped the garden and oversaw the modernization of the Merchant's House. After twelve years of snatching precious hours together it seemed a luxury to have so much freedom. It's odd, though, that this time of the afternoon is still the most poignant time: when she misses him most, longs for his company – and now she can't help thinking about Russ, too, though she hasn't thought of him for many years. Both these men whom she loved are dead.

Earlier she'd seen Mikey in Marks and Spencer and was struck again by the elusive resemblance he has to his grandfather. How strange – almost bizarre – it was to see Russ's grandson in her little local branch of Marks and Spencer. He was friendly, pleased to see her; his father, he said, was back at the flat with a bad headache so he'd dashed out to buy some provisions for supper.

'If you and your father would like to come for coffee or a cup of tea . . .' she began cautiously, but at once he looked uncomfortable and she wondered what to do, what to say, that might put him at ease.

'I'd like to,' he said awkwardly, 'it's just that Dad's not terribly well right now. Since Mum died . . . you know?'

He looked so wretched, so burdened with grief and responsibility that once again she longed simply to put her arms around him and hug him tightly. She wondered how she might strengthen him, or whether her interference might simply weaken him; cause him more difficulties than he was already bearing.

'Yes,' she said. 'I am so sorry, Mikey. Look.' She opened her purse and took out one of her cards. 'This is just in case you should ever need any help or if at any point either or both of you ever wanted to find me. Put it somewhere safe, Mikey.'

He took the card and studied it.

'It says your name is Evelyn Drake,' he said. 'You told me it was something else.'

'Yes, that's my business card. I'm a writer and that's my professional name. But my married name is Fortescue. My husband died a few years ago.'

He looked at her as if he was measuring the grief of an old woman against his own raw experience.

'I knew your grandfather very well,' she told him. 'We were very good friends. So that makes us friends in a kind of way, too, doesn't it? He would be so pleased to know that I've met you. You're very like him.'

He nods rather ruefully, as if this is not always an advantage.

'Dad and Grampy didn't always hit it off,' he said. He puts the card in the back pocket of his jeans. 'Thanks, Mrs Fortescue. I promise I won't lose it.'

'You could call me Evie,' she suggested. 'I'd like that.'

His sudden smile lit his face and touched her heart.

'OK,' he said. 'That's cool. Thanks, Evie.'

She wanted to suggest that they walk part-way home together but had the wisdom to say goodbye to him.

Now, staring out at the river, thinking of Russ and Mikey, and of TDF, she feels Claude's compassionate gaze but doesn't look at him lest she should break down and howl with grief. Mentally, as she stares across the river at Kingswear basking in sunshine, she pictures Claude: his kindly, squarish face; the little curling tonsure of gingery-grey hair, small pebble-grey eyes beneath tufty brows, a wide full-lipped mouth.

'If Claude were a stick of Brighton rock,' Tommy said, 'he'd have the word "loyalty" stamped all the way through him.'

She knows how lucky she is to have his friendship and his loyalty. Claude has never judged her or Tommy and, since she's been alone, he's given his support every way he knows how. It's been a huge relief to take him into her confidence over the discovery of the papers in the cartoons. She's still convinced that there's something

147

else – something not yet revealed – though she can't imagine what it is. She wonders if she should tell him about her affair with Russ, the guilt she feels about her youthful, selfish indifference to Pat, but, even as she wonders whether she should attempt it, they hear a knocking on the door, which opens, and Ben is calling, 'Hi. Anyone in? Are you coming over for a drink?'

She turns with relief, smiling at Claude, lifted out of her grief and anxiety by Ben's suggestion. He appears in the kitchen.

'Hi,' he says again. 'I just wondered if you were being polite or something. You usually like a cuppa in the garden on a day like this. And I've got a nice bottle of Sauvi B chilling in the fridge for later. So what about it?'

'It sounds like heaven,' Evie admits, 'but I wasn't quite sure whether Charlie and Ange might have other plans.'

He shrugs. 'Kettle's on. They can join in or not. See you in a minute then.'

He exchanges a glance with Claude, who beams approvingly at him, and goes out.

'Excellent,' says Claude with great satisfaction. 'He's a good lad, is Ben.'

'It's just so heart-rending sometimes,' she admits, 'when I see him or Charlie these days. They look so much like TDF when I first met him. God, he was gorgeous. Love at first sight. Do you believe in all that stuff, Claude? Can you imagine it happening to Ben, for instance?' She snorts with amusement. 'Or Charlie?'

He doesn't answer, following her out and waiting

whilst she locks the door. Glancing at him, she sees that he looks almost anxious, rather secretive, as if he is remembering something. She climbs the first steep flight of stone steps that leads up to the road above, pausing at the turn before she embarks on the second flight, hearing Claude coming up slowly behind her. They cross the road together and go in at the front door, calling to Ben, who shouts that he is in the kitchen. Charlie is there, too, assembling the tea things on to two trays.

There is no sign of Ange. Evie suppresses a sense of guilt and prepares to enjoy the moment. it's time for tea.

From halfway down the stairs Ange listens to their voices as they go into the garden carrying the trays and then she slips back upstairs. This little thing is still niggling her; the sense of something missing. It's difficult, with Ben continually appearing unexpectedly, to have a good snoop round but from the landing window she can see them all on the terrace at the top of the garden, pouring tea, handing round plates, which gives her a moment to herself to check the rooms again.

The drawing-room is unchanged: two comfortable sofas; glass-fronted cupboards built into the alcoves on each side of the timber-surrounded fire; two big sash windows looking across the uneven roofscapes to the river and Kingswear. The china in the cupboards, the paintings, are all in their familiar places, but anyway she knows that what she is missing is something odd; something quirky that has gone from its usual place.

The big attic room on the third floor has never held anything of value, though she has another quick glance. Back on the second floor she checks out Ben's quarters again and then runs down to the first floor. She ignores the master bedroom, which she and Charlie are using, and looks again into the other bedrooms. These are the rooms she and Charlie used when the children were very small. One had once been a dining-room and off this room was the pantry; big enough to convert into a little dressing-room, with a tiny window on to the garden, and where the girls had slept as babies on those rare visits when TDF and Evie were first married. It's a pretty little room, with a small painted chest against one wall, a book-shelf with the old childhood favourites stacked along it and a Lloyd Loom chair with an embroidered cushion in its lap. As she stands at the door, glancing in, she sud-denly remembers what is missing from the room: the cartoons. On the wall above the cot seven small framed cartoons had hung: beautifully sketched and rather amus-ing. Someone told her they'd been drawn by Ben's great-great-grandfather and, on light summer nights when Millie or Alice was not sleeping, Ange would stand by the cot, murmuring to her, or rocking her in her arms, whilst she studied the little drawings. Now the wall is bare and the cartoons have gone.

Ange stands quite still. The cartoons would never have been sold. They are loved and valued family possessions and, as such, they belong to her and Charlie — and to Ben, of course. Perhaps they were moved because of the tenants, though it's unlikely. The tenants were old friends and the house was let fully furnished. She will ask Evie the question: politely but firmly. The house might be Evie's, though obviously it should be left to Charlie when she dies, but the cartoons are not. Ange considers the idea of Ben claiming them; after all, they were drawn by his great-grandfather. At the same time, he was Charlie's great-great-uncle, which means Charlie has a claim, too. Of course, it would be a pity to split them up . . .

A rather horrid idea occurs to Ange. Supposing Evie has already given them to Ben? Ange is rather surprised at the strength of her anger. It really upsets her to think of Evie disposing of any of the family belongings. She has to control a desire to rush downstairs and up through the garden to confront Evie with the question of the whereabouts of the cartoons. Ange takes a deep breath, willing herself to be calm. There might be a perfectly rational answer and she doesn't want to look a fool. She knows that Charlie isn't totally on her side in these matters and she must proceed carefully. Charlie is so laid-back, so easy-going. He has no idea of the dangers of allowing the affection between Ben and Evie to grow even stronger. Evie loves both Charlie and Ben – after all, they are the nearest she'll get to sons of her own – but it is necessary for Charlie to continue to hold his own place in Evie's affections. Ange is dismayed by the way Ben has settled in, the easy coming and going between the two households, and she wishes that she and Charlie were staying longer. In a thousand tiny ways she is able to make sure that Ben knows his status as a temporary lodger; she is able to keep him on the back foot by establishing her and Charlie's rights in the house.

As she makes her way slowly down the stairs she plays with the idea of suggesting to Charlie that he might stay on here in Dartmouth rather than accompanying her to Polzeath. He wouldn't object to that. Holidays with his mother-in-law and two rebellious teenage girls aren't exactly his idea of relaxation, but it's difficult to know exactly how to put the suggestion to him. She can hardly explain that its purpose is subtly to maintain and underline his future role as the owner of the Merchant's House. And how and when is she to bring up the matter of the cartoons?

As she reaches the hall her mobile phone begins to ring. She runs back upstairs to her bedroom and fishes the phone out of her bag.

'Mummy. Hi. Everything OK?'

She listens whilst her mother tells her that Millie has twisted her ankle and hurt her wrist in a rather nasty fall and that she's making rather a fuss about it, though she's perfectly all right really. When Ange can get a word in, she tells her mother that she will come down first thing in the morning; that Charlie can stay on with Ben for a bit longer, and should she have a quick word with the girls?

Millie is grumpy and whiny – 'it's simply so un*fair*' – and Alice is out on the beach with the gang, so Ange promises to set off after breakfast and then she goes downstairs and out into the garden.

*

Charlie watches her approach up through the garden with a faintly sinking heart. He feels he is caught between his loyalty to her and to Benj, and it's very uncomfortable. At the same time, he still hasn't recovered from his meeting with Jemima, which had the same effect as drinking several glasses of champagne. He can see that Claude has his eye on him but he doesn't fear Claude: the old boy is on his side – up to a point, anyway.

Charlie braces himself to prepare for Ange: another little snub to Evie, perhaps, or a barbed remark to Benj? But Ange is smiling an almost rueful, conciliatory smile. It indicates a kind of amused irritation that somehow involves an explanation or change of plan in which he will be involved and expected to comply.

'A bit of a drama,' she says, as she reaches the terrace and sinks down on to a chair. 'Millie's managed to twist her ankle. No, no,' she nods reassuringly at Charlie, 'she's fine, really, but I've promised to get off to Polzeath first thing after breakfast.'

His second reaction, after his relief that Millie is OK, is disappointment that he definitely won't be seeing Jemima again. The tiny hope that they might meet accidentally in the town tomorrow is crushed and he is surprised at the depth of his feelings. He watches Ange accepting a cup of tea from Benj and tries to get a grip on his emotions.

'Actually,' Ange is saying, almost casually, 'I'm wondering, Charlie, if it isn't best if you stay here. After all, there won't be much you can do, and Millie will probably be in a strop so it might be best if Granny and I manage it together. You'll probably be bored stiff and you've hardly had any time here. I can pick you up on our way back next weekend.'

Charlie's own delight and relief at her suggestion are mixed with an awareness of the reaction of the others around the table. It is clear to him that this magnanimity, Ange's recognition that he might like to spend time with Benj and Evie and Claude, is rather out of character and he can feel them all registering it in their different ways. He guesses at her ulterior motive but the prospect of a week in Dartmouth is too good an opportunity to turn down and he seizes it, although with carefully suppressed eagerness.

'Well, it's certainly a bit of a shame to dash off when we've only just got here but won't poor old Millie think it's a bit heartless if I don't come too?'

'Oh, no.' Ange shrugs off any need to consider Millie's wounded feelings. 'She's not ill, after all. She's just cross and feeling sorry for herself. And Alice won't mind. After all, they've been home for the last six weeks so it's not as if you haven't seen anything of them. I just feel that playing nursemaid isn't your scene and you might as well be enjoying yourself here.'

'Well, if you're sure . . .' he pretends reluctance a little longer. 'Yes, it would be fun to spend a bit of time exploring the old haunts.'

The joy fizzes up in him again – he can drive out to Torcross, maybe see her walking the dog – and sinks a little as he remembers that he won't have a car. Claude is watching him, his eyes crinkling a little, as if the old bugger knows just what he's thinking, and Charlie grins back at him. He simply can't help himself.

'Oh, by the way,' Ange is saying, leaning across the table towards Evie, 'I was looking for a book – that old edition of *The Wind in the Willows* – to read last night, just for old times' sake, and I see that those lovely cartoons have gone from the little dressing-room.'

Charlie feels his insides curl and shrivel. How he hates these confrontations, these veiled accusations. Ange hasn't been looking for a book; she's been prying. He is aware of tension around the table. Claude is very wary; he watches Evie who sits up straight, chin lifted, her smile fading. Only Benj seems unconcerned and faintly curious.

'The cartoons?' he asks. 'Great-great-grandfather's drawings?'

'Yes,' Ange says, turning to him quickly. 'Have you got them?'

'I have them,' says Evie calmly. 'They're in my study over in the boathouse.'

'Oh?' Ange manages to make it a question. 'They've always hung in the little dressing-room. All the children loved them. It was a kind of tradition, wasn't it, Charlie? That's what your mother told me. My girls love them.'

Charlie feels hot with embarrassment and anger. 'Rather a waste, though,' he says, attempting a casual note, 'seeing that there aren't any young to use the dressing-room any more.'

155

'But there will be,' Ange persists, though she pretends to be jolly; light-hearted, almost amused at the prospect of grandchildren. 'Our girls will have children one day, and Laura. Family traditions are so important.' She gives a little artificial laugh. 'But then I'm very hot in the matter of inheritance. You need to be scrupulously fair.'

To his amazement, Evie begins to laugh. 'You're absolutely right, Ange,' she says. 'You do, indeed.'

Charlie sees that Ange looks taken aback and Claude quickly puts out a hand as if to restrain Evie, who smiles at him.

It's Benj who saves the day by standing up and saying: 'So how about a fresh pot?'

Charlie gets up too and says: 'I'll refill the milk jug,' and, filled with relief, follows him down through the garden.

# CHAPTER THIRTEEN

Once Ange has gone, driving away up the hill, Charlie closes the garage door and strolls across the road to lean on the wall. It's still early and the town is not yet in full regatta mood. He looks down at the steep granite staircases below, through narrow alleys that topple down towards the river and disappear between high stone walls where clumps of feverfew and valerian precariously cling to crumbling mortar.

Just for this moment he feels utterly at peace. He envies old Benj living here, able to do this whenever he chooses, free to wander into the town and along the Embankment: to have coffee with Evie in the boathouse or tea in the garden, and to be utterly free to pursue Jemima Spencer. This prospect should be filling him with anxiety, jealousy, but it doesn't. He suspects that his cousin has no desire to embark on another complicated relationship just yet or he would have made a push to see her again. And it's interesting that

Jemima hasn't made a move either, despite having Benj's mobile number.

Charlie turns his back on the river, rests his elbows on the wall and gazes up at the Merchant's House: at its cool, clean lines and elegant façade. It's nice to think of old Benj living in it, that it's part of the family again. He found it really odd when the tenants were in, and he'd be staying with Evie, not to be able to fling open the front door and just walk into his own house.

Of course, it belongs to Evie now, but Evie is part of the family. He thinks about Evie's role: she's certainly not like a stepmother, nor is she like an aunt or some older relative. In an odd way, the crucial root of his relationship with Evie is a similar kind of sensation that triggered his response to Jemima: a sense of recognition, of knowing and belonging. It's as if he knew them both way back and then – after some kind of separation and in different ways – they've come back into his life.

Charlie shakes his head; it's all quite crazy. He levers himself upright, hears footsteps below and peers over the wall. Claude is climbing up, pausing to take a breath, and coming on again.

'Hi,' Charlie calls down to him. 'Where are you off to so early in the morning?'

'Alf's,' says Claude, reaching the pavement and pretending that he isn't breathing heavily. 'I fancy a nice old-fashioned full English breakfast and Evie hasn't surfaced yet. Want to join me?'

'Love to,' says Charlie promptly. 'No sign of Benj yet, either. I was just seeing Ange off.'

'Ah,' says Claude. 'Week of freedom, eh?'

Charlie grins at him. 'You said it. And what a way to start it! I haven't had one of Alf's breakfasts for years. Just think what I'm missing! God, I feel like a kid again.'

'My heart bleeds for you,' says Claude. 'All those tiresome visits to foreign vineyards, wretched wine-tastings, boring dinners with rich clients, when you could be living here in Dartmouth, having breakfast at Alf's whenever you feel like it. You poor deprived boy. Come on. The treat's on me and afterwards, if you're good, I'll take you for a ride on the big dipper and then buy you an ice cream.'


'But we could be really quick,' Maisie is pleading, perched at the kitchen table, holding up Princess Poppy as if to aid her request. 'And then we'd still be in time to meet Mummy at Dartington.'

Jemima stacks the dishwasher, fighting the desire to agree; to dash into Dartmouth for an hour to let Maisie experience the joys of regatta again whilst hoping to bump into Charlie before he goes off to Cornwall.

'We can't manage it on the bus,' she explains. 'There just isn't enough time to get there and back again and then drive to Dartington. I've promised to meet Mummy in Cranks by one o'clock. She's coming straight on after her shift. We'd have to take the car to the Park and Ride and I can't leave Otto in a hot car for a couple of hours.'

'But Otto could stay here,' wheedles Maisie. 'He wouldn't really mind. He'll be asleep for most of the time anyway.'

Jemima knows that this is true. Otto's already had a good walk, and will be perfectly happy stretched out in his basket, but she still fights the proposition simply because she wants to agree to it so much.

'I probably wouldn't be back until three o'clock,' she begins reluctantly, but Maisie senses victory is imminent, slides off her chair and comes to hug her.

'*Pleeeze*, Jemima,' she begs. 'Maybe *you'll* win something this time.'

'OK,' says Jemima. 'But we shan't be able to stay very long. Let's clean those teeth and get you packed up.'

Maisie cheers and runs out and up the stairs whilst Jemima follows more slowly, determined not to change her clothes or make any great effort with her appearance. She's wearing one of her favourite long skirts, made of pale turquoise floral cotton, with a loose white cotton over-shirt. Her hair is loosely tied back with a long narrow scarf. Yesterday she was wearing jeans, her hair bundled into a knot, and very little make-up. She wondered if he'd noticed.

She oversees the teeth-cleaning, checks Maisie's room, and packs her small case whilst discussing which toys or books she wants to carry in her little rucksack. Back downstairs, Jemima fills Otto's water bowl and tells him to stay when he prepares to climb out of his bed to come with them. He watches reproachfully but with resignation for a moment, then settles down again, and finally they are ready to go.

When Evie comes out of her bedroom she knows at once that Claude is not there. His bedroom door is slightly ajar and even before she arrives in the kitchen she guesses that he's gone out to Alf's for breakfast: one of his holiday treats. It's odd how different a house feels when there are other people around: the sense of presence, of other life. She fills the kettle, switches it on and goes to slide open the doors to the balcony. The sunshine pours in and she stands at the rail, her eyes closed, her face turned towards its warmth as she listens to the river sounds. She still feels on edge after Ange's attack about the cartoons.

'I thought for a minute you were going to blurt it all out,' Claude said when they got back to the boathouse.

'I nearly did,' she admitted, 'except that it would have been very unfair to Ben and Charlie. But gosh! I longed to see her expression if I'd taken her up on the question of inheritance.'

'It was only then,' he said, 'that I realized I've never asked you whether the contents of the house were left to you with the building itself.'

'Well, they were actually. By the time TDF and I were married, and living there, Marianne had long since taken anything really valuable to London. The cartoons hardly came into that class. They were just a bit of charming family history, along with a few small pieces of old china. But now, legally, they belong to me. I keep them in my study simply because I wanted to be on the safe side. It's typical that Ange should settle on the one thing that could actually be a threat to her.'

'Thank God she's off tomorrow,' he said. 'I can't see her dropping it, can you?'

No, thinks Evie, now. I can't see her dropping it.

It occurs to her that two of the cartoons have remained unframed ever since Tommy used their frames for the small etchings he gave her. This was when he'd first discovered those long-hidden pieces of paper – and then taken all the cartoons apart – but he'd refused to replace those two cartoons in their original frames and had put them into plastic folders until other frames could be found; but they never were.

Maybe now is the time to find new frames for her etchings and restore the two cartoons to the originals. Ange is certain to want to see them; and maybe they should all be rehung in the little dressing-room. Whatever the decision, Evie knows that an important crossroads has been reached.

She turns, leaning back against the rail, looking up at the Merchant's House washed with morning sunshine, and she thinks of Tommy.

*What shall I do?* she asks him silently. *What's the plan?*

That was one of their phrases: Tommy always had a plan, a project, a new idea. The cartoons are vivid in her mind and, alongside them, the etchings he'd chosen and framed for her. She remembers how he watched as she unwrapped them on her birthday: intent, almost as if he were willing her to discover something very special. They were beautiful and very simple: a dipper balancing on a stone midriver, and a wren perching on a holly branch.

That was the last birthday she had with him. She always opened her presents at tea-time up on the top terrace if the weather allowed. It was a hot July afternoon, tea had been carried up, and the table was strewn with cards and presents. She always kept Tommy's until last.

'They're beautiful,' she said. 'How amazing that you should find my two favourite birds. I love them. But I still wonder if you should have used these frames.'

Knowing now what they both did, about the cartoons and the secret they'd hidden for so long, she felt slightly anxious about the frames.

'I wanted you to have them today,' he said, 'but the time might come when you want to change them, find new frames, and put the cartoons back. You'll know when it's right.'

It's as if she can smell the lavender again, taste hot tea in the thin china cup: she remembers the warmth of his hug, the scent of his aftershave.

*OK*, she says to him, still silently. *I'll get them reframed. Find new ones for the etchings. That's the plan, then.*

Suddenly she feels calmer, as if this is the right decision, the next step. She makes coffee and toast and carries it out to the balcony. A skiff shoots downstream, the rowers bent low to their oars; a white ketch motors out to the sea; a cormorant flies upriver, skimming the surface of the water, black wings outstretched.

Evie watches the little scene beyond her balcony, thinking of Tommy; missing him. Later she will go out, wander round, enjoy regatta. She wonders if she will see Mikey again, or Jason. It would be wonderful if some kind of reconciliation could be effected. She would like it so much if she and Mikey could be friends.

Jemima spots her among the crowds on the Embankment and waves. Evie's face lights up with recognition and they all meet together with delight.

'I was hoping we'd see each other again,' says Evie, and Jemima feels a warmth at the older woman's genuine pleasure. 'I wanted to invite you to see my boathouse but it seemed a bit pushy when we'd only met so briefly.'

Jemima knows exactly what she means. There are some people who, however long you know them, never become close; whilst others you recognize at once as friends who will be very special. When she met them at Torcross she felt this about Evie and Claude – she wanted to hold on to them – but, like Evie, she felt it would be rather odd to say so.

Now she beams at Evie. 'I'd love to see it,' she says. 'Thank you.'

'Well, why not now?' asks Evie, smiling down at Maisie. 'Come back and have coffee. I'm sure I can find something for Maisie. I've got orange juice and apple juice.'

'Oh, I wish we could,' says Jemima regretfully. 'There just isn't time this morning. I've got to get Maisie to

Dartington to meet her mum and we've still got a few more treats to get through.'

This is true, but also she doesn't want to miss her last chance of seeing Charlie. And anyway, part of her would like to visit Evie without the responsibility of Maisie. She feels that it's something she would like to do alone. Maisie clearly agrees with this: she doesn't want to waste her precious morning visiting someone's house. She tugs at Jemima's hand.

'Come on, Jemima,' she says. 'We need to get to the funfair.'

Evie smiles at Jemima. 'Come and see me next week,' she suggests. 'Or tomorrow for coffee?'

'I'd love it,' says Jemima. 'Coffee would be good. Where exactly are you?'

Evie gives her directions, whilst Maisie hops up and down impatiently, and then they part. Jemima, watching out for Charlie, hurries with Maisie towards the noise of the funfair. She's on edge, alert; everything seems to be brighter, noisier, more vivid. At any moment he might appear, familiar yet mysterious; light-hearted but so important. She simply cannot believe that she won't see him again.

# CHAPTER FOURTEEN

'I saw Jemima and Maisie in the town,' Evie tells Claude later. 'She's coming in for coffee tomorrow. It's odd but I feel very drawn to her, as if she were a favourite child or a niece or something. Do you know what I mean?'

'Mmm,' says Claude noncommittally, trying to hide his initial dismay. Evie has been up in the garden, picking roses, and she is rooting in a cupboard for a vase whilst he sits at the big table reading the newspaper. He wonders if he should tell Evie that Charlie has met Jemima, how they looked together, but he can't quite think of the words to describe it or how to begin. After all, Evie is hardly likely to criticize. This was exactly how she and TDF began their long relationship. He tries to analyse his feelings: he always supported Evie and TDF so why should this new revelation be any different?

He enjoyed his breakfast at Alf's with Charlie, which they sat over for quite a long time drinking several cups of coffee. It amused him to watch Charlie tucking in with such frank pleasure, eating all the toast, looking around him with the delight of someone who has returned home after a long absence.

Claude was rather moved: he remembered times past – Charlie home from school, down on holiday with TDF and Ben – and suddenly he felt sad and very old.

'Do you ever think,' he asked Charlie, 'that you might retire to Dartmouth when the time comes, like TDF?'

Charlie smiled a little, raised his eyebrows, as if imagining this delightful possibility.

'*I* might,' he said, 'but Ange wouldn't begin to consider it. She's a Londoner, Ange is. She likes to be where it's all going on.'

'Rather like your mum was?'

'Yes, you could say that. But Dad always enjoyed his jaunts to Dartmouth, same as I do. It's great now old Benj is here. I shall come and stay with him.'

'You don't mind him being there, then?'

Charlie pushed aside his plate. 'Why should I?'

'Well,' Claude pursed his lips, gave a little shrug, 'Ange doesn't seem to be too happy about it.'

A cloud passed over Charlie's happiness. 'She's got a bit of a thing about it, to be honest. Afraid that he'll dig in and get squatter's rights or whatever. Crazy. To be honest, it's wearing me down just a tad. After all, it's Evie's house and it's not as if Ange has ever been particularly keen on it.'

Claude noticed that from time to time Charlie glanced towards the door; he did it again now.

'Expecting someone?' Claude asked.

Charlie looked taken aback and then he grinned. 'Not specially. But you never know your luck.'

Now, as he watches Evie arranging the roses, cutting the stems, stripping off leaves, Claude remembers that look on Charlie's face – part shamefaced, part hopeful, part pure joy – and his heart contracts with anxiety. He tells himself that he's an old fool. He wants Charlie to be happy, to have what he wants, as if he's a little boy again.

'How did it work for you?' he asks Evie suddenly. 'All those years when TDF was in London?'

Evie's hands are stilled; she stares down at the roses in them. 'When I was his mistress, you mean?'

'Yes,' he says. 'How did you feel?'

She arranges the roses in the vase with quick decisive jabs and then sits down at the table, folding her hands together as if she is praying.

'I'd never been so happy,' she says. 'I had it all. Someone to love who loved me, my work, this house. I mean, what's not to like?'

'But he was married,' Claude persists. 'You had no rights, no security. You were always alone at Christmas. He wasn't around for most of the time. You must have been lonely? Jealous, sometimes? Resentful?'

Evie frowns at her hands as if she is struggling to remember exactly how she felt; to be completely truthful.

'It's difficult to explain it exactly,' she says slowly. 'To begin with, I am not a naturally maternal woman. I never longed to be a nurturer or to be a wifely person. I loved my job at the university and then, when I began to write, it totally absorbed me. Researching the Civil War and all those old Devon families, adding a few extra relations and retainers from my imagination, this was almost all I needed. I had one or two relationships that were, to be honest, mostly physical, but TDF was . . .' she hesitates, '. . . he was utterly different. He never promised anything, you know. He was never going to leave Marianne but I didn't want him to. I'm very happy on my own. I'm very independent and I always worked antisocial hours. Our time together was a bonus. It refreshed us. And if you're wondering if I felt guilty about Marianne then I'm afraid the answer is that I didn't. TDF was old enough to know what he was doing and so was I. I played by the rules and it worked. I don't think she ever knew . . .' She tails off and looks at him, frowning. 'Why are you asking this now?'

He shakes his head, not wanting to talk about Charlie and Jemima. 'It just occurred to me that it must have been a bit tough, sometimes.'

'It probably sounds odd,' Evie says, after a moment, 'but it was the friendship we valued. People always think that any extramarital relationship has got to be about steamy sex but actually there are lots of people having perfectly satisfying physical contact with their spouses who are lonely in their marriages. They aren't mentally compatible; they don't laugh at the same things or have the same interests. Sex blinds them to begin with, then children keep the family involved through mutual needs and interests, but as the children grow up the real emptiness is revealed. It's the meeting of minds that's the real turn-on; sex is a bonus. An optional extra. But the sense of being known, understood, without having to explain – it's magical.'

Claude remembers how Charlie and Jemima stood together; the expression on Charlie's face as he came out of the Royal Avenue Gardens. He feels dread and delight both at once. He longs for Charlie to know this joy but he cannot see how it can possibly work. Should he warn him that Jemima is coming for coffee? Would that make him stay away or encourage him to turn up?

'What is it?' Evie is staring at him, puzzled.

'Nothing,' he says. 'At least not . . . no, nothing.'

'Are you thinking of taking a mistress, Claude?'

He bursts out laughing. 'I should be so lucky.'

'Then why the third degree this late in the day?'

'No, no,' he says, distressed that she should think that he is criticizing her. 'It isn't that. It's just I wondered, that's all, how hard it must have been for you.'

'Anything I say has got to sound specious, hasn't it? "Marianne didn't know so it didn't hurt her." "I made TDF happy so he was nicer to his wife." That kind of crap. Perhaps if I'd hoped he would leave her, or if I'd lived in London, I might have suffered more but we were very semi-detached. Even so, we cheated. I asked Charlie about it once.'

'*Did* you?'

She shrugs. 'He guessed. One or two things were

mentioned by accident after we were married and it seemed silly for us always to be skirting round it. So I asked him if he or Marianne had ever suspected anything. He said that he once joked to her that Dad always came back very happy and relaxed from Dartmouth and did she think it was more than the sea air that spiced him up. She answered that she didn't mind much as long as he came back in good form, and if there were a woman involved then she was getting a very poor deal out of it. Something like that. He was very laid-back about it.'

Claude can't decide whether this makes him feel better or worse: whether he should warn Evie about Jemima or tell Charlie to keep clear in the morning. The dread is beginning to outweigh the delight and he wishes that Charlie had gone to Polzeath with Ange after all.


Maisie has been safely delivered to her mother and Jemima is walking Otto beside the ley.

The meeting with Miranda was more difficult than she imagined, trying to keep her emotions under control, hiding her disappointment at not seeing Charlie.

'Are you OK, Mimes?' Miranda asked, staring at her curiously. 'You look kind of . . . het up.'

Jemima protested that she was fine, that she and Maisie had been having fun, but then Maisie had chimed in with how they met Charlie and had an ice cream and went to the dog show.

'Really?' Miranda arched her brows in a particularly irritating way. 'This sounds interesting.'

Jemima cursed under her breath and began a very light-hearted version of the story: how she'd mistaken him for someone else and it was just so typical of regatta. It was doubly embarrassing because she hadn't yet told Miranda about her meeting with Ben in Alf's and now it seemed too late. So she tried to play it down but Maisie made much of it, so that by the time the story was finished Miranda was fascinated.

'He sounds rather nice,' she said slightly enviously. 'Are you going to be seeing him again?'

Jemima had wanted to shout, 'No, I shall probably never see him again,' and instead was obliged to laugh and tell her not to be so silly.

'Only you,' said Miranda, amused, but with a faint note of bitterness in her voice, 'would let yourself be picked up like that.'

Surprisingly, the comment hurt, though it was perfectly reasonable.

'Maisie was our chaperone,' Jemima said lightly, 'and it wasn't like that at all. So how are things? Have you booked up that Australian trip yet?'

Luckily this question distracted Miranda: not only had the trip been booked, she told Jemima, but now her mother was considering the idea that they might – she, Miranda and Maisie – all move to Australia.

'With the boys out there it would be easy,' Miranda said. 'And of course I'd get a nursing job in a flash. What d'you think?'

Jemima had to prevent herself from sounding too

enthusiastic. Just at that moment she wouldn't have minded at all if Miranda had vanished away to Australia right then: lately she's been so prickly, so stressed. Jemima controlled herself, however, reminded herself of past, happier times, discussed the pros and cons, and at last they said their goodbyes and she was able to set off on the journey home.

Now, back at Torcross, there is time for some quiet reflection. She follows the track beside the reed beds, listening to the noisy squeaking of a family of coots who swim amongst the tall rushes. Spikes of purple loosestrife and dark pink willowherb lean across the path; pale convolvulus clings to bramble bushes where blackberries ripen in the sunshine. The water at this end of the ley is covered with a muddy-brown weed at the edge of which coots are feeding; a swan, with two cygnets paddling in her wake, glides on her leisurely way towards the stretch of distant, clearer water. The rushes grow so tall that the road across the Line is hidden, though the sea can be seen beyond their feathery tops, so that the roofs of cars, glimpsed intermittently, flash in the sunshine like silver-backed dolphins and the double-decker bus, gliding out of the village, is a majestic showboat sailing between the ley and the sea.

Jemima stands aside to let a party of walkers pass, smiles at them, nods in agreement with their remarks about the beauty of the scene and the wonderful weather. Otto sits obligingly, waiting for them to squeeze past on the narrow path.

'Such a good dog,' one of the party says, patting him, and Jemima nods again. Yes, Otto is a very well-behaved and obliging dog and she feels very lucky to have him, especially just at the moment. It was good to come back home from Dartington to his loyal, unquestioning devotion after a car journey fraught with odd swings between elation and despair. Charlie will have left for Polzeath and what seemed to be the most wonderful thing that had ever happened to her was nothing but a fleeting moment: a brief illusion of joy. She hadn't realized how much she'd been counting on seeing him again, though to what end is not clear. She said goodbye to him, told him to go away, but then, when she turned and waved her scarf, she saw his face illumined with joy. There, all amongst the madness and noise and excitement of regatta, it seemed impossible that they should be kept apart. Just for them, there would be a miracle: a space for their love in which nobody would be hurt.

'You are a complete fool,' Jemima tells herself. She stares out across the ley, struggling between a terrible sense of loss and a lurking conviction that it could not have been for nothing. Oh, there have been other loves, other passions, but never before this strange, deep-down sense of knowing; of belonging.

Otto waits on the path, head on one side, watching her. She crouches down, taking his head between her hands, and he licks her cheek encouragingly and wags his tail.

'What shall I do?' she asks him – and suddenly she thinks of Ben. She remembers how Charlie spoke of him with such affection and called him Benj. She wonders if Charlie told him that they met; what he said.

She stands up, turns back with Otto at her heels, and tries to decide how to contact Ben and what to say to him. Will he think she's contacting him now simply because of Charlie? That he's a kind of consolation prize?

Jemima swears under her breath: she likes Ben and she hopes they can still be friends. She'll text him, she decides; be open about meeting Charlie and take it from there. She'll invite him out to see the cottage and buy him a pint in the pub. After all, she tells herself, she has nothing to lose.

'She hasn't been in touch then?' asks Charlie for the third or fourth time and Ben puts the lasagne back in the oven, drops the cloth and reaches out to check his mobile. He shakes his head and sits down again at the table in the breakfast room where Charlie is relaxing with a gin and tonic.

If it were not so painful it would be quite amusing to see Charlie's obsession. It's like he's sixteen again – except that he's a married man of forty-three – and Ben doesn't quite know how to handle it.

'It's a damn nuisance not having a car,' Charlie says, 'or I'd drive out there. You know. Just on the off-chance. We could both go.'

Ben is silent. He simply can't imagine how Jemima might react if they both were to turn up unexpectedly.

'You could bring your car back down now from

wherever it is you keep it, couldn't you?' wheedles Charlie. 'You can put it in the garage.'

'Evie uses the garage,' Ben says. 'That's the deal.'

'OK then. You can use her space. She's parked just across the road. You bring your car down, she hops into the garage and you go into her space.' He looks happy, eager for some action. 'After all, it's silly not to have your car back again.'

Ben watches him, wondering how to distract him.

'You know that money I owe you?' he says.

Charlie stares at him, as if he is trying to bring him into focus. 'Money? Oh, that. Yes. Look, don't worry about that, Benj. That's just between us.'

'I know it is. It's only that when the flat sells I'll be able to pay it back.'

Charlie turns his chair so as to look more directly at him.

'We haven't really talked about all that properly yet, have we? You must be gutted.'

Ben thinks about what he might say; how he might perhaps draw comparisons between what has happened to him and what might happen to Charlie if he should pursue Jemima. He doesn't want to sound preachy but he wonders if this might be an opportunity he should take – for Charlie's sake. At the same time, honesty compels him to tell the truth about his feelings.

'We'd been drifting,' he says. 'Once Laura left home the cracks were more obvious. Nothing was said. I took more assignments away from home, Kirsty seemed to be visiting her family more often, and then I discovered that she was actually seeing this ex-boyfriend. That was a bit of a shock. I suppose I was prepared to put up with the lack of real closeness but I never thought she'd cheat on me. I was angry and hurt.'

Charlie looks shocked and Ben can see that he's relating this to his own experience with Jemima. His face is easy to read: *This is quite different*, Charlie is telling himself. *Whatever might happen between me and Jemima is completely separate from anything else.*

'Anyway,' Ben says, 'Kirsty wants out so we're selling the flat. We're splitting it three ways so that Laura gets her share now. What's left will come to me and then I can pay you back.'

'And what about you?' Charlie seems to be making an effort to bring his concentration back. 'How do you really feel about being alone?'

Ben knows that he must be truthful now, which will undermine what he said earlier, but he can't lie to Charlie.

'I have a weird kind of sense of relief,' he admits. 'I feel free of anxiety and responsibility. Laura is up and running, and more or less independent. She and I will continue as we always have done, and I can live how I want to live.'

Charlie's face has cleared; he looks hopeful. 'So you believe, in the long run, that it was all for the best?'

Ben searches for the right words. 'I suppose it can't be right to cheat on someone,' he says reluctantly, 'but it's very difficult to judge people, isn't it? Perhaps Kirsty was lonely within our marriage and needed something, or someone, to fill the gap. I can't blame her for it. I'd let things drift. At least she was honest about it.'

He watches Charlie filing away his words, weighing them, deciding how they might apply to him in the future.

'It worked for my father and Evie,' he says.

Before Ben can speak his mobile rings two notes: a text message. He seizes it whilst Charlie sits forward eagerly.

'A message from Jemima,' he says. 'She's suggesting I go out to see her cottage and she'll buy me a pint. Seems like an offer I can't refuse. Oh, and she mentions meeting you.'

'Does she?' Charlie can't help himself from grinning broadly. 'Does she say anything else?'

Ben shakes his head. 'And she doesn't say when.'

'She thinks I've gone,' Charlie says. 'What shall we say to her?'

'What d'you mean, "we"?' Ben counters. 'I shall accept and ask her to give me a time.'

'But soon,' pleads Charlie. 'I've only got a week. Tell her I'm still here and we'll all meet up together. Come on, Benj. No harm in that.'

Ben sighs. 'OK. I'll suggest we have dinner at the Torcross Boathouse tomorrow evening. Then it's up to her.'

He taps out the message, sends the text, gets up to check the lasagne. He's mixed a salad and there are the remains of some nice cheese. He gets the plates ready, takes a bottle of Pinot Grigio from the fridge. His mobile rings its two tones and instinctively they both reach for it.

'Sorry,' Charlie says. He draws back his hand and crosses his arms as if he is defending himself from rejection. 'What does she say?'

Ben reads the text and smiles. 'She says it's on. Six thirty-ish so as to give us time to see the cottage first. Says she'll book a table.'

'Phew,' says Charlie. He looks as if he's been winded. 'Fantastic.'

Ben takes the lasagne from the oven. He feels anxious but exhilarated: he wants to see Jemima again and he wants Charlie to be happy – but he is fearful of the outcome. Now, there is no going back.

# CHAPTER FIFTEEN

Jason wakes early in the morning and immediately has a panic attack; the clenched fist in the gut, the sick churning and terrible fear. He reaches out across the empty bed for Helena and is stricken anew with the sense of loss that is fresh each morning and must be dealt with over and over again.

He curls on his side, hands over his eyes, and weeps silently so that Mikey doesn't hear him. Something good must happen soon or he really won't be able to carry on; something positive to change the direction of his life and fill him with hope. Money is becoming a real problem. His meagre savings are vanishing quickly now that he has no job, and the mortgage must be paid or he'll have to sell the flat.

He remembers that last night, before he fell asleep, he'd been hatching a new idea about Evelyn Drake. From down amongst the darkness of his anger and his hatred, a worm of a plan had wriggled up into the light. Suppose he were to screw her for money for Mikey? Not immediately, of course, but by first cunningly allowing her to become friendly with the boy. Watching them together on that bench it was clear that she was drawn to Mikey – no doubt because he is very much like his grandfather – so why not encourage it? Then, perhaps, he could remind her of her obligations; allow her to make amends for her disgraceful behaviour thirty-five years ago.

Jason stretches himself and swings his legs over the side of the bed. He feels slightly calmer, distracted by this new plan. Last night, after a quick double whisky – as a special treat he'd taken Mikey to supper in the Royal Castle – it seemed a brilliant idea, but this morning he can see flaws. There isn't much time, for a start, and how is he to effect a meeting with her? The familiar sense of despair, of disablement, begins to blot out his weak grasp on optimism and he drags on his old towelling robe and goes quietly into the kitchen to make coffee and take his medication.

Sometimes he wonders if his medication is messing with his brain, and he knows he ought to make an appointment to see his GP, but now that Helena isn't here to make him go he keeps putting it off. His doctor asks too many questions. He's fine; he's absolutely fine as long as people leave him alone and he keeps taking the happy pills. And today he should hear about the library job at the university. Russell Dean is still revered in Bristol and Jason had no compunction in using his connections. The interview went well – though it was the least bit tricky explaining why his job in the bookshop had come to a rather sudden end without saying that it wasn't his fault that the manager there was a complete loser – and he was fairly confident that he was in with a chance. He explained that he would be away for a week, and they agreed to phone his mobile, so he must be ready for the call. The signal in the flat is poor so after breakfast he and Mikey will go out into the town.

Jason breathes deeply: he feels sure that his luck is turning. He knows that he shouldn't be drinking, that Helena would be gutted, but he'll be fine. This isn't serious stuff and, anyway, he can handle it now. It won't be like it used to be; he's changed. It's just that he needs a little treat now and then and, hell, he deserves it, doesn't he? After all he's been through? With Helena gone and Mikey away at school, what's he supposed to do? Life's so bloody empty, so pointless, without that little drink to lift his spirits; to make him feel good. He needs something to look forward to; everyone does.

Jason swallows his tablets and drinks his coffee. He thinks about his plan for Evelyn Drake, his spirits rise again, and the black dog draws back a little into the shadows.

After a rather uncommunicative breakfast at the boathouse, Evie is beginning to get quite worried about Claude. He seems edgy, almost irritable, at the prospect of meeting Jemima again and when Evie asks him if there's a problem he gets quite cross.

'Of course not,' he snaps. 'Why should there be?'

'You tell me,' she answers pacifically. 'I thought you'd like to see her again. You don't have to be here, you know, if you're not in the mood.'

He looks so anxious that she wonders if he's feeling well; or it might be that he's been cast down by one of his little grieving bouts. She's always prepared for that; for moments when memories of his and Jilly's earliest days here in Dartmouth come back to haunt him. This isn't quite the same, however: this is less like grief and more like fear.

He decides to walk out to the Castle, saying that he might call in on the boys on the way back, and Evie is relieved to see him go. She glances at her watch: it's not much after nine and the walk will probably take an hour and a half. Plenty of time to prepare for Jemima's arrival.

She clears the table on the balcony ready for coffee, tidies away newspapers, piles up books, and looks around to see that all is in order. It's always a delight when people visit the boathouse for the first time. She loves to see their expressions when they walk into the big room, pausing to exclaim before being ineluctably drawn out on to the balcony. This room is at its best on a sunny morning like this: full of brilliant, refracted light and watery reflections. She wishes that Mikey could see it; he was clearly loving Dartmouth so much. It's so strange to meet him here – Russ's grandson – and to be reminded of that earlier part of her life. She would like to talk to Mikey about his grandfather, about his pioneering television work, his great success in making dry-as-dust history fascinating. She's honest enough to know that it's not a purely altruistic desire. She's quite aware that it would make her feel better about her own role in Russ's life; that it would bring a kind of healing.

Ben texts: he and Charlie are off on a jaunt to Totnes and is it OK to use the garage when they get back, just for today. Parking is at a premium in the town so Evie texts suggesting that he can use the garage for the rest of the week.

When Claude comes back still looking preoccupied, saying that the boys aren't at home, and she tells him that they've gone off to fetch the car and have a morning in Totnes, he looks so relieved that she thinks he might actually be about to pass out.

'Are you sure you're OK?' she asks curiously.

'I'm fine,' he says. 'Honestly. I think I'll just stroll down to Pillar's and get the newspaper. Don't worry about me.'

'Right,' she says. 'Take it slowly, Claude. That's quite a walk you've just had.'

He grimaces, acknowledging the truth of this, but before he can answer there's a ring at the doorbell and Jemima comes in through the open door calling, 'Hi. Anyone at home?'

Evie hurries to meet her, drawing her in, exclaiming with pleasure. Jemima smiles warmly at Claude and then looks beyond him and says: 'Oh, gosh! Wow! This is . . . Wow!' She walks forward into the room, gazing around her, the flowers she has brought for Evie still clasped in her hand.

Evie beams at Claude, who seems to relax at last, taking a deep breath and letting his shoulders drop. It's as if he's suddenly given in to something, accepted the inevitable, though Evie still can't guess what it might be. Jemima has walked through to the balcony and stands at its rail, leaning forward, still exclaiming with delight.

'God! This is just amazing,' she says, turning back to them. 'Sorry. Gosh! Sorry, I was completely blown away. Look, these are for you.' She hands over the flowers, her face bright with the pleasure of the moment, and Evie feels touched by her warmth.

'Coffee?' she asks. 'Or do you prefer tea?'

Jemima shakes her head. 'Coffee will be great. Thanks. Gosh! I thought my old flat in Salcombe was pretty good when it came to views but this beats it hollow.'

She wanders back out on to the balcony and whilst Evie finds a vase for the flowers, makes coffee, it is Claude who goes out to join their guest.

Now that Jemima is here all his anxieties have faded away, dissolved in her warmth. He watches her face — such a lovely, sweet face — as she looks with delight at the river scene.

'You lived in Salcombe?' he asks, hardly able to take his eyes from her. There is an aura of joy about Jemima that fascinates him. He can utterly see why Charlie has become entranced.

'I rented a flat there for a while,' she is telling him. 'Right on the water like this. It belonged to the RNLI and then they needed it for their staff so I had to go. I lived in Kingsbridge for a bit but I missed living by the water so much that when the little bit of cottage came up in Torcross I went for it.'

'Do you rent it?'

'Goodness, yes! I couldn't hope to afford a house in Torcross. Even one as small as mine.'

She turns as Evie comes out with the tray of coffee, a plate of *pains au chocolat*, and gives a sigh of pleasure. 'How wonderful to sit here and have your coffee and watch the river. Have you lived here very long?'

'Twenty-five years,' Evie tells her. 'I've been very lucky. But I'm wondering if it might be time to move on.'

Claude stares at her in astonishment but Evie pours the coffee quite calmly. Jemima is exclaiming in sympathetic dismay at the prospect.

'Oh, but why? How could you bear to leave it?'

'I suppose it might depend on where I might go,' Evie says. 'I'm getting a bit creaky, you know. You came down those steps, didn't you?'

'They are the least bit ankle-twisting,' admits Jemima, 'but even so . . .'

'And we lose the sun early,' Evie is continuing. 'I'm beginning to find the winters rather long and dark.'

Claude continues to gaze at Evie, taken aback by these admissions to someone she barely knows. The boathouse is Evie's safe harbour, her beloved home. He can hardly believe she is sitting there saying these things so calmly.

'I'm the other way round,' Jemima is saying, accepting

a *pain au chocolat*. 'I get all the afternoon sun. It does help in the winter, I must admit. But where might you go?'

Evie sips her coffee; she gazes rather dreamily across the river towards Kingswear.

'Actually,' she answers, 'I might go just across the road.'

'Oh!' exclaims Jemima. 'One of those wonderful houses. I don't feel nearly so sorry for you, then. I work for a holiday letting company and we have one on our books. They are pretty amazing and the views are spectacular. Actually, I met someone who is living in one of them, though he says it doesn't belong to him. His name's Ben Fortescue. Do you know him?'

'You could say so,' answers Evie serenely. 'My late husband was his cousin and the house is mine.'

Claude sets down his cup: he feels shaky and unsettled. He no longer fancies his *pain au chocolat*. He was hoping to avoid all mention of Ben and Charlie, relieved that there was no chance of their arriving unexpectedly, but now it seems that everything is to be revealed. Jemima, too, looks slightly nonplussed.

'Well,' she says, and gives a little snort of amusement. 'That certainly answers my question very comprehensively.'

Evie smiles at her. 'Fancy you knowing Ben. And why hasn't he mentioned you to us?'

'It was only two casual meetings. Once at Stokeley Farm Shop and once in Alf's. But, since you mention it, we're all going to the Torcross Boathouse this evening for supper.'

'All?' asks Claude rather faintly.

She looks at him with that same luminous joy. 'Yes. Me and Ben and Charlie.'

Evie looks surprised; pleased. 'You've met Charlie, too?'

Just for a moment Jemima looks slightly discomfited; a bright flush washes her cheeks. She looks away from them, out to the river. 'Just once,' she says. 'He's so like Ben, isn't he?'

'Extraordinarily alike,' says Evie. 'They might be brothers.'

Claude glances at her. She looks interested, alert, but slightly amused.

'How amazing,' says Jemima, recovering her composure, 'that you should be his . . . their . . .' She hesitates over the exact word for Evie's relationship to Ben and Charlie.

'I'm Charlie's stepmother,' says Evie.

Jemima stares at her; her smile has faded and she looks wary. 'Stepmother?'

'Mmm.' Evie nods. 'But it's not quite like it sounds. I didn't marry his father until Charlie was nearly thirty. We were married for only twelve years, though I was his mistress for ten years before that.'

Claude can't decide whether to laugh or cry. All his terrors of this meeting have now very nearly been fully realized. It only needs for Jemima to admit that she and Charlie have fallen madly in love to cap Evie's revelations.

Jemima is staring at Evie with an expression in which awe, amusement and respect are nicely blended.

'Gosh!' she says. 'That's ... well, that sounds fascinating.'

'Does it?' Evie bursts out laughing. 'It's not a particularly unusual story. Would you like some more coffee?'

'Yes, please,' says Jemima enthusiastically. She leans forward. 'So where did you meet Charlie's father?'

Claude gives a tiny groan and pushes back his chair. They glance up at him questioningly, very slightly impatiently, as if he is distracting them from their conversation.

'Going to get the newspaper,' he says. 'No more coffee, thanks. Good to meet you again, Jemima. See you later, perhaps.'

He hurries away from them, stops for a quick dash to the loo, and goes out into the sunshine. As he climbs the steep steps to the road above – heart pounding, legs aching – he thinks of what Evie has said about these steps; about the lack of sunshine in the winter. All true, of course, but even so, just blurting it out like that to a stranger – and telling her she was TDF's mistress! After all his anxiety, he thinks bitterly, lest Evie should discover Charlie's meeting with Jemima and his entrancement with her, or Jemima should be taken aback by the boys bursting in unexpectedly, and then they just blurt it all out and settle down for a gossip.

'Women!' he exclaims aloud, as he gains the road.

He turns down Bayard's Hill, making for the Dartmouth Arms. Damn the paper: what he needs is a stiff drink.

*

189

After Claude has gone, Jemima settles more comfortably. She's been aware that Claude was a little on edge once they started discussing the house and Ben and Charlie. She can understand that: he is more reserved, less able to let it all hang out. She likes Claude: likes him a lot. There's something stable about him; something reassuring.

'Don't worry about Claude bolting like that,' Evie is saying. 'He always bolts when things get a bit emotional.'

Jemima laughs. 'Sorry. It's just that word always makes me think about my dear old late-lamented mum,' she says. 'My sister always called her the Bolter. She left Brigid with her father and bolted off with mine, then she bolted again, taking me with her, though. Her last bolt was to Portugal when she was in her seventies. She had a lot of fun.'

Evie smiles at her. 'Perhaps that's why you weren't shocked when I said I'd been Tommy's mistress.'

Jemima shrugs. 'Why would I be shocked? So his name was Tommy.'

'Mmm.' Evie seems surprised at herself. 'I usually don't use it except to myself. That was just between him and me. His wife called him Thomas and his family called him TDF.'

Jemima is fascinated. 'TDF?'

'They were his initials. Thomas David Fortescue. His aunts and very old friends called him The Darling Fellow.'

Jemima laughs with delight. 'I love it. Is Claude one of those friends?'

'Yes.' Evie nods. 'He was the only friend who knew

190

about us. The family live in London, they're wine importers, but Tommy always enjoyed a visit alone to Dartmouth. I met him just up there at the top of the steps. He was coming out of his house and I'd just finished viewing this one. We went off and had a drink together and that was that.'

Jemima is entranced, almost fearful; her meeting with Charlie resonates in her head.

'Did he look like Charlie?' she asks.

'Incredibly like,' says Evie. 'And about the same age.'

'Then I can understand why,' says Jemima frankly. 'Pretty devastating, aren't they? And did his wife never find out?'

'Not as far as we knew. I never went to London and Marianne rarely came to Dartmouth except with a little house party for regatta. I stayed well clear.'

'Did Charlie know?' Jemima can't help herself; she wants to know everything. It's so weird that she should be sitting here with Charlie's stepmother, and Evie is nice, so open and warm and fun.

'I asked him later. Once Marianne had died and Tommy and I were married. He was a grown man, married with children of his own. Things were said, accidentally, that must have made him suspect. I decided to be honest with him. He said he'd guessed but he was quite comfortable with it.'

'She died,' Jemima says slowly.

'Mmm. About ten years after I met him. There was never any question of divorce.'

191

Her look is very clear, very direct, and Jemima stares back at her. It is as if Evie is warning her, preparing her.

'Did that bother you?'

'Not particularly. I had my own work, this house, friends. I was very happy with things the way they were. I never really considered myself marriage material.'

Jemima gives a little cry. 'God, this is surreal. It might be me saying that. I always say I'm mistress material.'

'And you've never been married?'

'No. There was once when I might have been tempted, but he went back to his girlfriend. I was glad afterwards. I like to be independent. Perhaps I'm just too selfish.'

'And you're all having supper together?'

Jemima nods. 'Safety in numbers.'

Her light remark sounds very slightly bitter and she glances quickly at Evie, who watches her compassionately.

'What a pity it isn't Ben,' she says gently.

'I like Ben,' Jemima says quickly. 'I really like him.'

'Mmm,' says Evie. 'Not quite the same, though, is it?'

Jemima suddenly feels immeasurably sad. She wants to be comforted and reassured and strengthened. It's an odd reaction to the woman sitting opposite. After all, it would never have crossed her mind to feel like that about her own mother. Frummie was the last person to show any maternal feelings, and Evie doesn't seem to be in the least motherly either. Yet there is something here, some odd kind of recognition that is almost tangible between them; a connection at some deep level.

Jemima sighs and sits up straighter. 'Not quite the

same,' she agrees. 'I know this sounds really strange but I rather think I need them both.'

And suddenly the atmosphere is light again, Evie bursts out laughing and says, 'Well, good luck with that, darling,' and Jemima feels ready to cope with anything that might lie in the future.

When she leaves they hug each other and Evie says, 'Come again soon.'

Jemima nods, and then hurries away to catch the bus back to the car; to prepare for the evening ahead.

When Claude gets back Evie has lunch ready for him. She feels guilty that she spoke so openly with Jemima about things that previously she has only shared with Claude and she realizes that it must have been a shock to him when she talked of moving to the Merchant's House.

'I don't quite know why it all came out like that,' she says as they sit down together. She can see that he's still hurt, though he's been mellowed by a pint of beer, and she decides to be quite honest. 'It rather surprised me, too, but I feel so at ease with her. I really like her, don't you?'

He nods, his mouth full of cold beef, and gesticulates impatiently with his fork, indicating that that has never been in question.

'Of course I like her,' he says at last. 'You couldn't not. She's so genuine.'

'That's exactly it,' agrees Evie, relieved. 'You feel you've known her for ever. And it was such a surprise when she said she'd met the boys.'

'Not to me,' says Claude gloomily.

'Not?'

He shakes his head. 'I saw her with Charlie in the town. Just standing there together like they were in a world all of their own. Then they all disappeared into the crowd seconds before Ange came by.'

Evie stares at him in amazement. 'When was this? You didn't tell me. And when you say "all" . . .?'

'It was on Saturday morning. She had Maisie with her. They were having coffee and ice creams at one of the stalls. Jemima and Charlie were just completely wrapped up in each other. And then I saw Ange coming. I thought if I got there in time I could pretend we were all meeting by chance, if you see what I mean, but they suddenly just vanished into Royal Avenue Gardens.'

'But why didn't you tell me?' She allows herself to sound just the slightest bit aggrieved.

Claude shifts uncomfortably. 'I didn't quite know how to put it. He said that first of all she'd mistaken him for Ben.'

'You *talked* to Charlie about it?'

'He reappeared on his own, you see, looking like he'd been hit by a brick. I decided to be open about it, that I'd seen them together, but it was like speaking to a man under a spell and then Ange turned up and that was that. And later there was all that business about the cartoons up on the terrace.'

He looks so anxious, so miserable, that she puts out a hand to him.

'It's all a bit of a muddle, isn't it?' she admits. 'I'm

sorry I blurted out all those things without warning, Claude. Especially my idea about moving across the road. To be honest, it's only a tiny idea at the moment and I don't quite know whether it's complete madness. That's why I haven't mentioned it to you.'

He looks a little happier; they're on level ground again.

'The thing that shook me,' he says, still slightly indignantly, 'was that you were so open with her about you and TDF on such short acquaintance. I suppose that having seen her with Charlie it was a bit like déjà vu. It was almost like you were encouraging her.'

Evie begins to laugh. 'Perhaps I was. Nice for Charlie to have a bit of fun for a change. What a pity it isn't Ben.'

'And now they're all going out this evening together.' He still sounds glum.

'Safety in numbers,' she says.

'We shouldn't be encouraging them, though, should we?'

She looks at him, smiling a little. 'You didn't say that about me and TDF.'

He snorts. 'It was too late by the time I knew about it. Anyway, Charlie isn't TDF and Jemima isn't you. And Ange isn't Marianne.'

'Meaning?'

He takes a deep breath, giving himself time to marshal his thoughts. 'Marianne was a very up-together woman. She had projects, charities, Charlie to organize, the business to keep tabs on. Her life was never just TDF. She was busy, fulfilled, and actually very generous. Look at the way she took Ben under her wing when his mother died.'

'Are you trying to make me feel guilty?'

'Of course not,' he answers impatiently. 'Don't for God's sake start behaving like a woman and taking this personally. All I'm saying is that even if Marianne suspected, I doubt she'd have been the sort to throw a hissy fit. After all, you never took him away from her for very long, did you? A few days here and there throughout the year? And that's what I mean about TDF. He compartmentalized his life. You were in the Dartmouth file. He adored you, you know that, but you were his life here and you never interfered with his family or his business. And you were rather the same, Evie, weren't you? You said so yourself. You weren't jealous or resentful or lonely. You were writing. For most of your life you were totally immersed in another world and a whole cast of characters from which you were quite content to emerge occasionally and have fun with TDF. You were always completely absorbed by your work, almost longing to get back to it. It was your reality and TDF was part of your down time; little jollies before you got back to the real thing. I don't think Jemima would be like that. If they were to become lovers I think she would want much more of Charlie than a few days here and there, and I'm damned sure Ange wouldn't be philosophical about it if she ever found out.'

'And Charlie?' She's taken aback by Claude's speech; slightly unnerved by his insight. 'What about Charlie?'

Claude is silent for a moment. His gaze is inward as if he is thinking about Charlie; imagining him in this situation.

'TDF was a very confident man,' he says at last. 'He

was laid-back, always optimistic, but he was tough, too. He was used to being loved and approved. All the dear old aunts bringing him up to believe in himself but without spoiling him; the security he lived in, his inheritance, gave him total confidence. He was grounded, generous to his friends. He embraced it all: you, Marianne, Charlie, his friends, the business. He had it all. It must have been a colossal shock when he discovered that he wasn't entitled to his inheritance but deep down it wouldn't have made any difference to the essential TDF.'

He falls silent and Evie waits, moved by what he has said.

'Charlie doesn't have quite the same genetic brew,' he continues, 'and he was brought up in a much more protective way. Marianne watched over him like a hawk, guided him, told him what to think, approved his friends – or not. He kicked over the traces once or twice but generally his default mode was to listen to her. To trust her judgement. He's known Ange from childhood, Marianne loved her, showed him how right Ange was for him.' Claude shakes his head, as if to get his thoughts clear. 'I'm not sure that Charlie would be able to sideline all of that. Do you see what I'm saying? He's very loyal to Ange and his girls. He might think he can live two lives, he'll certainly imagine that he wants to give it a go, but I'm afraid that it might destroy him in the end.'

There is a silence.

'I hear what you say,' says Evie slowly, 'but I wonder if you're right.'

He raises his eyebrows. 'I'll be very glad if you prove me wrong, I promise you.'

'I agree with you in part, of course I do, when you talk about his upbringing, his deference to his mother, his loyalty to Ange and his girls. But I think there's an awful lot of TDF in Charlie – look at the way he runs the business – and it just needs something to trigger a different aspect of it. Jemima might be just that trigger. I'm not saying that he would enter into a relationship lightly or easily but I think Charlie has glimpsed something very special, which he'll be reluctant to ignore.'

Claude rubs his head, frowning confusedly, almost as if he is startled by his own outburst.

'I love Charlie like he is my own boy,' he says. 'I want him to have it all. I just don't want him to be hurt but . . .' He shrugs, makes a face, pulls down his mouth. 'It's not up to us. They're grown-up people. All we can do is to stand by to pick up the pieces if it should go wrong.'

'I'm not sure I find that very comforting,' Evie says lightly. 'I tell you what, Claude. I'm really glad that you're going to be around. Do you actually have to go back at all?'

He laughs, and she can see he feels better.

'I only packed for a week,' he says. 'I think I shall need a little more than a few summer things as winter comes on.'

Nevertheless, she feels comforted by the prospect of his presence. And, after all, perhaps little will come of it. Regatta madness: nothing more.

*

Mikey bites into his beefburger, swipes the ketchup from his chin, one eye on his father, who is standing a little distance away talking to Aunt Liz on his mobile. His free hand gesticulates, balls into a fist and pumps the air; Dad has got the job, he is victorious, he is happy.

Mum wouldn't have let Mikey have the beefburger from the stall – poison burgers, she called them – but Dad isn't into stuff like that. As long as it's quick and easy he doesn't care too much. Mikey tries to think of all the things Mum taught him so as to guide the shopping list when he's home for the holidays, to make sure they both eat lots of fruit and veggies, but it's quite a responsibility. Sometimes it feels like he's the grown-up and Dad's the child.

That's why he's really glad Dad's got the job at the university and that he's happy. It's a bit embarrassing when he's full-on; Mikey wishes that when he's happy Dad wouldn't get quite so over the top, but that's the way he is.

'No halfway measures with your father,' Mum used to say. 'He's up or he's down.'

Before – that's how he phrases it now to himself, just 'before' – he was able to get out of the way, when he wasn't at school. He'd stay in his room or go out into the garden, slip off to see one of his friends. Now, he isn't able just to walk away; it seems selfish and unkind to leave Dad on his own, having a strop or feeling mis. Even so, he'll be really glad to get back to school though it does mean leaving Dartmouth, but Dad has promised that they can come down for half term.

Mikey finishes his beefburger, wipes his fingers on the

paper napkin and throws it in the bin. Should he push his luck and ask for a Coke? He's wondering, now that Dad is back on top, whether he should mention meeting Evie. He doesn't like having secrets, and he's afraid Dad might find the card, so it might be better if he were to mention, just casually, that he saw her.

Dad's finishing his call, coming towards him. 'She's really pleased,' he calls out. 'That's great, isn't it? Don't we love your aunt Liz?'

Mikey nods, feeling a bit silly with people looking, then takes a chance.

'Could I have a Coke, please, Dad? Just for once?'

'Sure,' he says immediately. 'Sure you can. We'll both have one and then how about a visit to the funfair? You enjoyed that, didn't you?'

They stroll along together, swigging from the cans, and Mikey takes another chance.

'I met someone who knows Grampy the other day,' he says, glancing sideways to watch for any negative reaction. Dad can be funny about Grampy. 'She's a writer. Evelyn Drake.' He can't remember her other name just for the moment. 'Then I saw her in M&S and she told me she knew you when you were a little boy.'

To his surprise Dad is looking amazed but in a good way, like it's something he wanted to happen. He doesn't ask about the meeting, he just begins to laugh.

'I don't believe it,' he says. 'Fate works in a mysterious way.'

Mikey doesn't understand but he doesn't push it.

'Anyway, she said to say "hello". She gave me her card in case you wanted to meet her or anything.'

Dad bursts out laughing again, shakes his can at the sky and shouts, 'There is a God.'

Mikey feels like he might die of shame the way people are staring at him, but he's also just so relieved that Dad's OK with it and that it needn't be a secret any more.

'Why didn't you tell me?' Dad asks.

'Oh . . .' He shrugs; some instinct warns him to be cool about it. He won't say that Evie thought he looked just like Grampy. 'I forgot, I suppose. Didn't think it mattered. So do you remember her?'

'Oh, yes,' says Dad. He smiles a secret, satisfied smile that makes Mikey feel anxious. 'Oh, yes, I remember Evelyn Drake very well indeed. And I intend to know her even better. And so will you, my son. Come on. I think this calls for a ride on the big dipper to celebrate.'

Driving with Ben to Torcross in the early evening Charlie wonders if he is living in a dream from which he might wake at any moment: to be here in Dartmouth during regatta week with no family commitments and old Benj to keep him company; Evie and Claude wandering over for tea or a drink; the sounds and smells and the whole atmosphere of regatta. And on top of it the prospect of seeing Jemima again. His conscience reminds him that simply because Jemima texted Ben, that Ben has made the arrangements to see her, it doesn't mean that it's all perfectly innocent. It warns him that it is specious to pretend that this is an ordinary, friendly meeting. At the moment, however, he isn't listening to his conscience. He is persuading himself that just for this one magical week he and Jemima are beyond the conventions; the rules and regs by which other people live. It's like some kind of fairy story, or a film; he can almost imagine the soundtrack. A tiny miracle has come to pass. One minute he is at Ange's beck and call, and now here he is driving with Benj along the coast road to Torcross: to Jemima.

'This is all so weird, Benj, isn't it?' he murmurs, gazing at the wide scoop of the bay shimmering in the hazy early evening light. 'God, it's beautiful. I always forget how beautiful it is. You are so lucky to be living here.'

And then he remembers that poor old Benj's marriage has just broken up, he has no home, no money and no security.

'Sorry,' he mutters. 'That was tactless.'

Ben grins sideways at him. 'That's OK. I told you, I'm fine with it.'

Charlie wrenches his mind away from Jemima and thinks about how Benj is really feeling. He drives his little VW Golf with great confidence, backing up for nervous tourists in the narrow village street of Stoke Fleming, whizzing down the hills. After his own very smart Audi, the battered, elderly Golf leaves a bit to be desired in the comfort stakes but somehow Charlie rather envies his cousin the sense of freedom; of fun and independence.

'Will you stay in Dartmouth?' he asks.

'For the winter, at least,' answers Ben. 'As long as Evie

is prepared to let me stay. She could get a huge rent for the house next summer. I might look for somewhere else.'

'I think she likes having you there. She can use the garden and the garage, and the place isn't getting damp and cold. Do you find it a bit big, all on your own?'

'I don't really use the first floor at all.' Ben changes gear as they start up the winding hill from Blackpool Sands. 'I suppose I might use the drawing-room in the winter, but it's slightly imposing. I tend to live in the breakfast room when I'm not working. It would be quite nice to have someone sharing. Someone to chat to in the evenings, especially when winter draws in.'

'I'll come and stay,' Charlie promises, but even as he says it he wonders how it might be achieved. Maybe Ange will encourage it so as to keep tabs on Benj.

They swoop down the hill by Strete Gate and on to Torcross Line, and Charlie is clenched again with excitement and terror. It's pathetic but he's really glad that Benj is with him. Rather like having Maisie there, Benj's presence prevents the whole thing from toppling out of control. He's not quite ready for that yet. Jemima seemed so strong and confident; so amusing and fascinating. Being with her was like entering into another sphere; a completely magical experience that he longs to repeat.

His mobile beeps and he digs it out of his pocket and checks it. It's a text from Ange and immediately his stomach sinks and knots into a kind of leaden lump: he feels guilty and remorseful, yet he cannot turn back: not now; not yet.

'Ange,' he says briefly. 'Just to say everyone's OK.'

He sends a text, switches the phone off – it could be embarrassing if she rings during the next few hours – and stares ahead. The last thing he needs at the moment is a reminder of his family: how uncomfortable it is to be disloyal. Benj is turning into the car park, manoeuvring into a space, digging in his pocket for change for the parking meter.

'I'll get it,' says Charlie.

He gets out and stands for a moment gazing out to sea, stretching and relaxing and concentrating on the evening ahead: on Jemima. Just at this moment, nothing else matters.

Jemima is watching for them. Standing at the window of her sitting-room she sees them leave the car and stroll along the path beside the ley. At this distance she can barely tell them apart though she guesses that it is Ben who leads the way, pointing out the activities of the ducks on the water, pausing to study the scene as if he might be sizing it up for a photograph. Charlie waits, hands in the pockets of his jeans, scanning the houses as if he is looking for her.

She runs down the stairs, through the kitchen and the conservatory, and goes out to meet them. Charlie sees her come out of the gate and his serious expression is transformed with delight. He takes his hands from his pockets and starts forward as if he might cross the road to embrace her. She takes several deep breaths but can't prevent herself from beaming back at him, though she stays where she is.

Ben is turning and now he is smiling too so that they both arrive together and, to her relief, this prevents any kind of formal or emotional greeting. Everyone has something to say, which all gets muddled up together, and she goes back into her little yard, where Otto is waiting, and ushers them into the house.

The men both stop to speak to Otto, to smooth his head and pull his ears, so that any kind of awkwardness is over very quickly.

'I did warn you that it's only a little bit of house,' she says. She feels breathless, slightly overwhelmed, as they come into the conservatory. 'Three is definitely a crowd in here.' Fearing that this might be misconstrued she hastens on: 'This is my garden.' She indicates the wide windowledge with all the pretty pots of flowers. 'You can see the ley and pretend you're outside.'

'It's lovely,' Ben says warmly, 'especially with the evening sun pouring in. And the kitchen is through here?'

He goes ahead and Jemima glances at Charlie, who smiles at her so intimately that her heart bangs about as if it is trying to escape from her breast. She hurries after Ben who is now examining the kitchen.

'I see so many people's houses,' he says. 'They never cease to fascinate me.'

'But not little ones like this,' counters Jemima. 'You only do big, posh places.'

'Not true,' he protests. 'I sometimes do holiday lets. Cottages, barn complexes, that sort of thing.'

'Do you?' She's momentarily distracted. 'Our photographer's moving upcountry. Wouldn't like some work, would you?'

He looks at her quickly. 'I would,' he says. 'Are you serious?'

'Well, he's definitely going. And I don't think we've advertised yet.'

'Could you ask them? It would be great just at the moment.'

'With your portfolio, or whatever you call it,' says Charlie, 'I should think they'll bite your arm off.'

He looks delighted at the prospect and Jemima is touched by his partisanship.

'Of course I will,' she says. 'I'm back to work tomorrow so I'll have a word. Go on upstairs and have a look at the sitting-room and then we'll have a drink. We can have it up there if you like, or in the conservatory.'

They both opt for the conservatory and she takes a bottle of white Bordeaux from the fridge and puts a plate of nibbles on the glass-topped table. Otto cocks his head hopefully and she says, 'Leave,' very firmly. His ears flatten but his tail wags once or twice as if in acknowledgement of her instruction. She'd seen Charlie's quick look of disappointment when she mentioned going back to work after the Bank Holiday and she wonders how long he will be in Dartmouth without his family. She can hear them coming back downstairs and she takes three glasses from the cupboard.

'I love your little bit of house,' Ben says. 'I see what

you mean about the view. You know, I think if I had to choose, I'd rather have a view of the ley than the sea. There's more going on and you must be able to see the changes of the seasons much better from this side. We'll have to do a return match, won't we, Charlie, and show her the Merchant's House?'

'Definitely,' says Charlie.

Jemima can feel his relief that Ben is taking charge, turning it into something manageable and easy and fun. She feels the same and she relaxes, holding up the bottle.

'Shall we have a drink?'

'Small one for me,' says Ben. 'I'm driving.' He crouches down to talk to Otto, who struggles up gratefully in his basket and picks up a very battered teddy to offer to Ben. 'Thanks, old boy,' he murmurs. 'Just what I've always wanted.'

Charlie and Jemima stand smiling at each other, separate again just for a moment. He holds out his glass to touch it briefly against hers as if he is pledging something, and she feels quite weak and foolish – and terribly happy.

# CHAPTER SIXTEEN

Regatta: the fun of the bungee rowing in the Boat Float; two spectacular firework displays; the hauntingly beautiful illuminated river procession; a review of classic craft with its wonderfully informed commentary; the heart-stopping Red Arrows. Ben takes photographs, wanders amongst the happy visitors and provides a safe anchorage from which Jemima and Charlie sail out from time to time to conduct an odd, unlikely love affair. They contrive never to be alone yet there are moments when they can draw apart and enter into their magical, private world: holding hands as they watch the flare and drama of the fireworks; Charlie's arm protectively around her as the Red Arrows scream up the valley, turning and twisting just feet above the masts of the moored yachts; laughing together as they cheer on the tug of war in Coronation Park.

Ben watches them with a queer mixture of envy and compassion. Jemima is so open, so funny, so easy to be with, and between the three of them runs a cheerful, jokey familiarity as if they have always known each other.

Claude and Evie seem to have entered into this strange conspiracy. The garden is the place where they all congregate each afternoon and where Jemima joins them, having come down on the Park and Ride or walked over from the office after work. She wanders amongst the sweet-smelling shrubs, asking Evie the names of the plants, drawing her fingers through the lavender, teasing Claude about his knowing the Latin names.

Ben pours tea, and later wine; sometimes they have supper there, on the top terrace. Behind the laughter and the jokes he sees the memories that shadow Evie's eyes, the anxiety that lingers at the edge of Claude's smile, the pain of Charlie's undeclared love. And at some point Jemima will push back her chair and say: 'I must get back to poor old Otto,' and there are always protests of dismay, a plan for tomorrow, but it is always Ben who goes with her down through the garden, through the house.

'I love your house, Benj,' she says to him, looking around the hall and up the elegant staircase.

'Not mine, alas,' he says. 'Evie's house. Charlie's one day. Not mine.'

She reaches up to kiss him goodbye and he sees that suddenly her eyes are full of tears and he just as suddenly hates it that she cannot be openly and happily with Charlie.

'Dear Benj,' she says.

He likes it that she calls him Benj; as if she has known him from a child.

'I'm driving you up to the Park and Ride,' he says. 'No, it's no use being stubborn and independent. It's later than we usually are. Come on. Don't argue.'

Suddenly he feels angry with Charlie, who seems content to let things drift like this; who makes no move to push things to some conclusion. In silence he drives up Crowther's Hill, trying to conquer this resentment, knowing that part of it is rooted in jealousy. How easy it would be to fall in love with Jemima, to detach her gently from his cousin.

She sits beside him quietly, her blond hair falling down over her shoulders, her hands loosely clasped in her lap. She's wearing one of her pretty long skirts and a loose shirt with the sleeves pushed up over her rounded, creamy-brown arms.

'Don't, Benj,' she murmurs.

He doesn't look at her. 'Don't what?'

'Be angry.'

He gives a little gasp of despair, of irritation, and she turns her head, studying him.

'It's such a short time being all together like this,' she says. 'It's so precious, Benj. So strange and magical. You and me and Charlie. Evie and Claude. It might never happen again quite like this. We must be happy while we can.'

'And will that be enough for you?' he asks.

She is silent for a moment.

'It might have to be,' she answers him at last. 'It's not

just to do with Charlie and me, it's to do with all of us. It works so wonderfully well; as if we're a real family. Oh, I know you and Charlie are cousins but there's such an odd bond between us all, isn't there? It's precious, Benj. Any kind of love is precious. We mustn't waste it by grabbing and snatching and smashing things. It's much too important for that. We'll all remember this regatta, when you were here with Charlie, and Claude was with Evie, and I happened along and got drawn into the magic circle. It's like that thing in Ecclesiastes, isn't it? "A time to weep, and a time to laugh; a time to mourn, and a time to dance." Between us I suspect we've all been doing a bit of mourning and weeping one way and another, but just this week, well, this is our time to laugh, Benj, and to dance.'

He feels a bit choked up. 'If you say so,' he says.

He pulls into the car park, sits staring out across the steering wheel, and she leans across and kisses him on the cheek. She smells of lavender.

'See you tomorrow?'

He nods wordlessly and she hesitates, begins to get out of the car and suddenly stops.

'I completely forgot. I've told Jane about you. My boss. She says she'd love to meet you and have a chat.'

'Really?' He's shocked out of his emotional silence.

She nods. 'Mm-hm. *Very* impressed she was when I told her about you. You know where the office is in Foss Street? Well, she said tomorrow morning after ten and before midday, if you're free.'

'I certainly shall be. Will you be there?'

'If you'd like me to be there to make the introductions I can do that.'

He thinks about it. 'It might be rather good, if it's OK, but I can manage if you're busy.'

'I'll be there first thing but I've got to go out to a cottage in Dittisham before lunch so the earlier the better. Ten thirty?'

He nods. 'I'll be there.'

'Good.' She slides out, waves a hand.

As he drives back home, gradually his resentment towards Charlie fades. Perhaps, like Jemima, Charlie is simply seizing his moment to laugh, to dance, without snatching and grabbing and smashing things up. Ben puts the car in the garage and goes inside. Charlie is in the kitchen making coffee, putting mugs on to a tray.

'Hi,' Ben says. 'I decided to drive her up to the car park. She's got an interview for me with her boss tomorrow morning. Pretty good, eh?'

Charlie looks at him with such pleasure that Ben is filled with all the old familiar affection for him. He picks up the tray and they make their way up through the garden to break the good news to Evie and Claude.


This is always the difficult bit: driving home on her own. Almost at once she is missing the heart-warming quality of deep affection that passes between them all and that, by some small miracle, has extended to include her. Jemima switches on the radio. Nina Simone is singing 'Mr Bojangles' and in her mind's eye Jemima sees the melancholy clown-like figure, dancing, spinning, leaping to a background of county shows and fairgrounds, and she is seized with a nostalgic longing for childhood: for her younger self who could embark on relationships without worrying too much about the outcome. This attraction to Charlie is outside her experience: this sense of knowing and being known.

As she drives through the gathering dusk she tries to decide what the difference is between him and Benj. They are so alike, the ease of companionship is present with both of them, the ready humour, but as she listens to the haunting music she knows that it is Charlie's sense of joy that speaks so directly to her; his secret longing for the magical world beyond the everyday grind, and his readiness to believe that it still exists despite all the evidence to the contrary. It finds an echo in her: in her own determination to live alone in her odd little bit of a cottage because of its position; to take on Otto despite the inconvenience because she hates to be without the comfort and companionship of a pet; to refuse promotion or to relocate because the particular quality of how she lives is more important than money or prestige.

The difference between them is that Charlie will never be able to seize his dream. He is committed to his wife and children and she knows he will never leave them. His tragedy is that he's glimpsed the reality of the dream but either way he believes he can't win. It seems to him that if he grabs it the guilt might soon destroy him and if he turns his back on it he'll never get over losing it. Just for this week of regatta he has been offered an opportunity to enter into that magical world and revel in the freedom and joy of it and, because it is in his nature, Charlie has decided to seize the joy and make the most of it.

Jemima remembers how she first saw him, thinking he was Ben, and the way his face lit with delight as she approached him. It wasn't calculated – 'This could be my lucky day' – or wary – 'Who the hell does she think she's smiling at?' – it was the open, happy reaction of someone to whom a new experience, a smiling gesture, was welcome: it was serendipity. There was no awkwardness or embarrassment: just this weird sense of joy which has spread out during regatta week to include Benj and Evie and Claude.

Jemima parks in the little space beside her yard gate and lets herself into the conservatory. Otto comes wagging joyfully to meet her and she goes down on one knee to embrace him, allowing herself to be passionately licked. She drops her bag in the kitchen, slips her feet into sand shoes, grabs his lead and goes back out with him, through the little alleyway that leads down to the beach.

At once, the immensity of the shining seascape, the rhythmical hush and suck of the tide across the shingle, a solitary star in the western sky, all these calm her spirit, reignite optimism and restore peace. Tomorrow can look after itself.

'What I want to know,' Claude says, as he and Evie descend the steep steps, unlock the door and let themselves in, 'is what is going on? *Is* anything going on?'

Evie laughs at him, dropping her cashmere shawl on a chair, kicking off her shoes.

'If you mean Jemima and Charlie, well, yes, a great deal is going on but not necessarily in the way you mean. Nothing clandestine is going on. They're not sneaking into bed together.'

Claude looks exasperated. 'But what's going to happen, do you think?'

'Very little, I suspect. Jemima makes him happy. He can be himself with her and she with him. They're two of a kind, soul mates, and they're just taking the opportunity to be happy together. I don't think bed is the main objective at the moment. And even if it were, well . . . I mean, it would be a bit tricky for Charlie, wouldn't it, with Ben in the same house and you and me across the road? We might report back to Ange.'

Claude snorts. 'As if we would. Good grief, what does he take us for?'

'Even so, it's not quite the normal set-up. And, anyway, I'm not sure that's an issue for them. I think they're just having fun.'

'If you say so. And what happens after regatta?'

'Ah, well, that remains to be seen. I'm probably being infected by regatta madness but I find I'm incapable of doing anything except encouraging them to enjoy this week of freedom.'

'And then that will be the end of it?'

Evie sinks down on her big sofa and looks up at him.

'You're still worried?'

'Of course I am.' He sits down beside her, throws out a cushion – he hates cushions – and half turns towards her. 'They remind me of you and TDF.'

She looks beyond him, into the past, smiling a little.

'I suppose it is the same, in a way. It was the luck of meeting that really special person to whom you could say absolutely anything, who would completely understand, who got all those foolish lifetime references to books and films without saying "What do you *mean*?" all the time. It was as if we'd been brought up together and then separated for years and suddenly met up again. Oh, I can't explain it, Claude.'

He remembers how Jemima and Charlie stood together, as if separate from the crowd that swirled about them, and he feels infinitely sad.

'And do you think that's how it will be for Charlie and Jemima?'

'It might be, if Jemima is happy with it and if Charlie can compartmentalize his life in the same way TDF did.'

'Why did you bother to get married?'

'Once Marianne had died and he'd moved back to Dartmouth it seemed silly not to, and it was better for Charlie and Ange and the children and our friends, more conventional, but I'm not certain that we really felt we needed to emotionally.'

He slumps on the sofa. 'Why can't I see it being so simple for Charlie and Jemima?'

'For all those reasons you mentioned before. It's rather

childish and pathetic but I just want them to enjoy this week before Ange stomps back into all our lives.'

'Why do you think she suggested Charlie should stay here?'

'I think she wanted someone reporting back; someone on the ground keeping a watching brief. Probably so that we still remember that Charlie has as much right in the house as Ben. Who can tell with Ange?'

'I wonder what he's been telling her?'

Evie leans her head back on the cushions and closes her eyes. 'Suddenly I feel very ancient, Claude. And melancholic. I want to cry a lot.'

He looks at her compassionately. With her head flung back and her thin hands clasped in her lap, she looks old and vulnerable and frail, and he is moved with love for her and fear for himself. He loves them all: Evie and Ben and Charlie. He loves them and needs them.

'I'll make us some supper,' he says, getting up, 'and then we'll go out on the balcony and watch the fireworks. Just relax and think about that next book you're going to write.'

She smiles, eyes still closed, but at once she looks young again, amused and viable: the old Evie.

'Don't you start,' she says. 'For me the War is over. Civil or otherwise.'

She doesn't tell him what they should eat or how to prepare it; she simply edges off her shoes, folds her legs up on the sofa, and relaxes into his care.

\*

Ange phones whilst Charlie and Ben are getting ready to go down on to the Embankment to watch that night's fireworks. They've decided to get some fish and chips or something from one of the stalls; they can't be bothered to get supper for themselves.

'Two lots of fireworks are quite a treat,' Benj tells Charlie. 'We must make sure that Jemima comes in on Saturday night for the second display. We can give her some supper and run her home afterwards. Unless, you'd rather . . .?'

He hesitates, eyebrows raised and Charlie feels emotional again. He's grateful for the way old Benj is handling this and he can't help imagining what might have happened if he and Ange hadn't come down for regatta. Whether Benj and Jemima might have had a chance of getting together. He wonders how much Benj resents him.

'To be honest,' he says, 'I think we're both happier doing it this way. It's probably the cowards' way but we can just have this without doing damage. That's probably specious, of course. Just because we haven't been to bed doesn't mean that I haven't cheated, does it? I feel a bit badly, Benj, that I might have prevented you from . . . well, you know.'

But Benj gives him a little biff on the shoulder and says, 'Don't be a twit. I'm not ready for any involvement right now. I'm in the middle of a divorce, remember, and I'm actually enjoying my freedom.'

And then Ange phones and Charlie makes a face at Benj and goes out into the garden.

'Hi,' he says. 'How's everything? How's poor old Millie?'

'She's much better,' Ange says. 'A bit whingey and grumpy. She's getting really good with the crutch. How's everything with you?'

'It's good. Fine.'

'So what's been happening?'

'Well, nothing in particular. Just regatta. You know?'

'And Evie? Did she dig out those cartoons?'

'Well, no, not yet. But I don't see that's a problem.'

'No, you wouldn't. And Ben?'

'He's fine. Well, actually he's very pleased. A . . . a friend has got him an interview for a job.'

'A job? What? Not in Dartmouth?'

'Well, yes. Well, not a job exactly but taking all the photographs for a holiday-let company's brochures and so on. Is that a problem?'

'Well, of course it is. Or it could be. Just as long as he doesn't think it gives him the right to stay indefinitely in the Merchant's House, that's all.'

'Well, that's rather up to Evie, isn't it?'

'Listen, Charlie. I've just had an idea. Could you tell Evie that we'd like to come down for half term? All four of us. It would be rather nice for us to be together there again. Will you do that?'

'But why now? We haven't done that since the girls were small.'

'Well, it's about time we did it again. Dartmouth is part of their heritage, remember. Just tell Evie, could you?'

'I can suggest it.'

'OK. Suggest it. You do that. Tell her I'll send the dates as soon as we're home. End of October, anyway. Look, I must go. Mummy and the girls send their love. Don't forget to ask about the cartoons. 'Bye.'

'Love to everyone,' he says. 'Give the girls a hug. Tell them I love them. 'Bye. 'Bye then.'

He switches off the phone and stands quite still. Ange's voice, her questions and demands, shatter this atmosphere of happiness and tranquillity. How can he tell Evie that they all want to stay for half term when it has been years since Ange has shown any inclination to come to Dartmouth with the children? Evie isn't a fool, and neither is Ben. They are both very well aware that Ange has her sights fixed on the Merchant's House and that she will go to any lengths to see that it stays within the family: her family. She thinks by this casual assertion of rights that Ben and Evie will be influenced.

'What's wrong?' Benj asks as Charlie comes back into the house.

'Nothing,' he says ruefully. Might as well get it over with straight away. 'Just Ange saying that it would be nice for us all to come back for half term. With the girls.'

'What here? Well. Why not?'

'You wouldn't mind?'

Benj shrugs. 'Why would I? It's a big house. A family house. You'd need to check with Evie, though.'

'Of course.' His first reaction is relief. Then he thinks of Jemima. That first crazy meeting was one thing but now, to know that she was around while his wife and girls were here too, how would that be?

'Come on,' says Benj. 'I'm starving.'

Charlie follows Benj out through the house, stands waiting while he locks the front door, and then they wander down into the town, into the bustle and clamour of regatta.

# CHAPTER SEVENTEEN

Evie sees them as soon as she enters the bar at the Royal Castle: Mikey and Jason sitting together at the table by the window. She was amazed to get a call from Mikey suggesting that they should have coffee together; amazed and very pleased. Claude was out in the town and she was quite happy to enjoy an impromptu meeting at the Castle.

She waves, and Jason pushes back his chair and gets up.

'Well,' he says, pale eyes bright, 'what a turn-up for the books. Evelyn Drake, after all these years. Who'd have thought it?'

She offers her hand, which he barely touches, smiles at Mikey in his corner. She sees at once that Mikey is uncomfortable, wary, and she realizes that this isn't just a simple reconnection with the past.

'You've got drinks already,' she says, 'so I'll go and order myself some coffee.'

'I'll go,' Jason offers at once. 'You reacquaint yourself

with Mikey. I gather you've already met. Fate taking a hand, wouldn't you say?'

She doesn't quite know why his question should sound like a threat but she thanks him, says she'd like a cappuccino and sits down opposite Mikey.

'Thank you for inviting me,' she says. 'I didn't expect it. It's good to see you again.'

His eyes flick sideways, watching his father go to the bar.

'I told Dad we'd met,' he answers, 'and he thought it might be a good idea.'

He still looks unsure so she smiles at him.

'And so it is,' she says warmly.

She hates to see the shadow of anxiety in his dark blue eyes, the tense lines around the still-childish mouth, and she wonders how to help him to relax.

'Did you say that your aunt owns the flat you're staying in?'

He nods. 'My mum's sister. Aunt Liz. She says we can have it again at half term.'

'Well, that's good isn't it?'

Again that quick sideways flick of the eyes towards his father.

'I'd really like to come and Dad says we can as long as he can get time off from his new job at the university.'

'New job?'

'In the library. He used to be in a bookshop but it didn't work out for him. I think it was to do with Mum dying. You know?'

His turned-down mouth is tragic, his eyes miserable, and she nods.

'I know. Maybe this will be better for him. If you ever needed to, Mikey, you could phone me. Or write to me. The address is on the card.'

He stares at her and she looks steadily back at him, trying to communicate her concern without being too heavy or frightening him. Then Jason is with them again.

'Here we are,' he says. 'So. Making friends?'

The almost malicious brightness of his eyes, the tremor of his hand as he sets down the cup and saucer, register with Evie.

'Doesn't look like me, does he?' Jason goes on, sitting down. 'I'm like my dear mama. D'you remember my mama, Evie?'

'Yes,' she says calmly, thrusting down her instinctive fear. 'Yes, I remember Pat very well.'

Jason's smile widens. 'I thought you would. But Mikey looks like his grandfather, wouldn't you say?' He beams at her. 'Now, I'm very sure you remember *him*, Evie?'

She beams back at him, refusing to be frightened. 'Of course I do. We worked very closely together. And yes,' she smiles at Mikey, 'you do look like him. I noticed it at once. Do you share his interest in history?'

Mikey shakes his head. Evie can see that he is aware that some game is being played that he doesn't understand and she feels angry with Jason, but she will not let him control this meeting.

'But you like music and singing?'

Mikey nods, looking happier. 'Oh, yes. I love it.'

'Do you play an instrument?'

'The piano. A bit. I'm going to learn to play the organ.'

'But that's wonderful. Am I talking to a future King's Organ Scholar?'

He laughs, just as she intended him to, whilst Jason watches them almost speculatively, leaning back in his chair with one hand in his pocket whilst the other turns and turns his empty coffee cup. She leads the conversation around to regatta: asks which event Mikey has enjoyed most, which he's looking forward to. He tells her that he can't wait to see the Red Arrows and the fireworks tomorrow night, the last night of regatta, and she feels tremendous relief and pleasure as she watches his young face relax, his eyes shine with anticipation of the display.

'Well, you must come and visit me,' she says, putting down her cup, glancing at Jason. 'If there's not time before you go home then perhaps at half term?'

She feels that she must leave on this positive note, smiling warmly at Mikey, nodding in a friendly way at Jason, thanking him for the coffee. She goes out quickly, still confused by her mixed emotions: pleasure, relief, but still that deep-down tiny sliver of fear.


Jemima comes out of her office, hesitates at the end of Foss Street and turns down towards the Embankment where the 'waiters and waitresses' races are taking place, the competitors sprinting along carrying pints of ale. She laughs to see them as she dodges between the cheering onlookers, planning to grab a cup of coffee and a quick regatta moment before heading off to Dittisham. Benj is getting on so well with Jane that she's decided to leave them to it. Along the edge of the Embankment the crabbing competition is in full swing – eager children watched by encouraging parents resisting the urge to assist their offspring – and preparations are being made for the barrel-rolling competition.

Still smiling, Jemima turns towards the nearest stall selling coffee and comes face to face with Charlie.

'Oh,' she exclaims delightedly – just like that first day – and immediately feels an odd kind of constriction. This is the first time they've ever been completely alone.

He seems to understand at once; his smile is warm, full of pleasure.

'Time for coffee?' he asks, and she nods.

'I've left Benj with Jane,' she tells him. 'They were bonding so well I thought it was best just to let them get on with it. So I made them some coffee and decided to get a quick regatta fix before I go off to Dittisham.'

She hesitates while he orders the coffee, wondering if she should suggest that he might come with her. So far their friendship – she can't bring herself to call it anything else – has taken place within the framework of regatta, supported by the structure of their separate relationships with Benj and Evie and Claude. She tries to imagine how it might be, driving away from the town, alone together in her car; what pressure it might put on them. So far they have done nothing that might be destructive: there is no drama, here; no history.

He hands her the cardboard cup and they both turn away from the stall, standing close together but watching the races that continue along the Embankment, and suddenly she begins to laugh. He looks down at her, amused.

'Shall I guess?' he asks.

She nods. 'Go on, then. Bet you can't.'

'You're thinking "If this were a film, what would the soundtrack be?"'

She reaches out to give him a friendly punch and he dodges and ducks and just manages to save his coffee.

'I'm right, though, aren't I?'

She nods, still laughing, remembering the film game that Charlie and Benj play: one of them calling out the title of a film and the other having to hum the soundtrack. She's been able to join in with that one. She's a film addict, and it's been such fun.

Quite suddenly she doesn't feel like laughing any more. She sips her coffee, keeping her eyes fixed on the race, and feels the warmth of his shoulder as he stands close to her as if he is attempting to comfort her; to convey his understanding. She swallows coffee and tears, willing herself not to ask him to come with her to Dittisham.

'And who would we be?' he asks softly; rather sadly. 'Celia Johnson and Trevor Howard, only in reverse roles?'

'*Brief Encounter*,' she says quickly, as if they are playing the film game, trying to raise their spirits, and they both hum the Rachmaninov Second Piano Concerto theme tune.

He puts an arm around her shoulders and holds her closely for a moment, then he moves away slightly so as to take something out of his pocket.

'I was hoping I might see you,' he says. 'I just found this in the Shopping Village in the Marquee. It seemed right, somehow. Appropriate.'

She takes it: a small oblong of heavy smooth glass, which only just fits into the palm of her hand. It is a sea scene painted in strong, clean colours: stripes of turquoise, purple and blue across which a small white ship sails. Above the yacht, against the lighter blue of the sky, curve the wings of two white birds. The whole thing speaks of strength, simplicity, freedom: it is utterly beautiful.

He takes it from her and holds it up against the sun, so that colours are like jewels and the little scene is vivid with life, then gives it back to her.

'It's perfect,' she says.

She runs her thumb across it, unable to look at him, and suddenly she feels him tense beside her; the current between them is deflected, cut off.

'Evie,' he says. 'Hi. Have you been watching the race?'

He moves to stand between them so that Jemima has time to recover, to swipe the tears from her cheeks, and slip the glass into her bag. She swallows the last of her coffee, throws the cup into the bin beside the stall, and turns to smile at Evie.

'I'm dashing off to Dittisham,' she says. 'See you both later. Thanks for the coffee, Charlie.'

They look at each other and, just quickly, she grasps

his hand and holds it tightly, and then she turns and hurries away into the crowds.

Evie doesn't make the mistake of apologizing to him. He puts his cup in the bin and they walk away together, not hurrying, heading towards home.

'When are you going back, Charlie?' she asks him.

He breathes a deep sigh. 'On Sunday morning. Only one full day left. Ange is driving up after breakfast. Benj says he'll drive me to Exeter to rendezvous with them at the service station.'

'I shall be taking Claude to Totnes for the train,' she says. 'It goes just after eleven. I can take you on afterwards if you like.'

'Thanks,' he says. 'But I've said I'll be at Exeter by ten thirty. Ange wants to make an early start. Oh, by the way . . .'

He hesitates, looking awkward, diffident, and Evie wonders what new demand Ange has made.

'Spit it out,' she says lightly.

'Well, Ange was saying that it would be good to bring the girls down for half term.'

Her eyebrows shoot up, partly in dismay and partly with amusement: Ange is really raising the stakes.

'Really? Was she? Goodness. I can't remember the last time she brought the girls to Dartmouth. Well, well.'

'I know,' he says miserably. 'Look, I'm sorry, Evie. She's just got this silly bee in her bonnet about Benj and I keep telling her that it's none of our business but, well, you know what she's like.'

229

'Oh, I do,' agrees Evie. She isn't ready to tell Charlie about her new plan just yet. She's still in two minds about it, but she's not quite prepared to commit either. 'Well, let's see, shall we? We need to remember that it's Ben's home at the moment – or have you asked him already?'

'I did just mention it,' admits Charlie, looking even more miserable, 'and he was cool with it. Says it's a family house and so on.'

'Mmm,' says Evie thoughtfully, 'and so it is. Are you meeting him for lunch?'

'I said I'd see him in the pub for a pint after he's finished with Jemima's boss.'

'Well, I expect you'll find Claude there. In fact he's probably there now.'

'Bit early, isn't it? It's barely a quarter to twelve.'

'You know Claude. He says the sun is always over the yardarm somewhere. In fact I might join you all. Let's sit for a minute, shall we?'

They sit down on one of the benches in companionable silence and watch life on the busy river: the ferry edging out of Kingswear, yachts at their moorings, the guardship with its bunting fluttering.

Evie watches the passers-by: a couple attracts her attention. The woman is small and neatly dressed in tiny shorts and a halter top; her body is honed, polished, and stripped of every spare ounce of weight. Head down, she watches her bare legs as she walks, studying them as if amazed by their quick movement, their sharp bird-bones and smooth bronzed colour. Her man is bow-legged, bald; he wears baggy shorts and an unattractive vest. He struts importantly, chin thrust forward, lips puckered aggressively.

Evie studies them, wondering what it is that brought them together and keeps them together. Human relationships fascinate her. She thinks again about Jason and Mikey. At least there is a chance now of a reconciliation after all these years. It's clear that Jason is still antagonistic but she mustn't allow herself to become foolish about it; to imagine things.

'How did you manage, Evie?' asks Charlie after a moment. 'You and TDF?'

She doesn't pretend to misunderstand him. She puts Jason and Mikey out of her mind and concentrates on Charlie.

'By not wanting too much, I suppose. What we shared was very precious but completely separate from his life in London. Marianne was rather like Ange, Dartmouth wasn't really her scene except for occasional weekends with a little house party, but TDF had always spent time here. Oh, just a few days here and there, sometimes alone, sometimes with Claude, but he'd always done it so there was no particular change to his routine. I was busy working, and I'd never been used to a live-in relationship so that was no hardship either. I don't really know how it worked for TDF but I think like most men he was able to compartmentalize his life to adapt to it. Of course, it was hard sometimes; there are things you want to share with people you love, but you get on with it, don't you? And then we had twelve years together. That was an unexpected bonus.'

'And didn't you find that difficult? Adjusting to being together after all that time apart?'

'Sometimes. I was still working for the first eight years and TDF was busy modernizing the Merchant's House and redesigning the garden, so we still had a certain amount of independence. Oh, but it was great to have him here.' She turns to Charlie, smiling, close to tears. 'I really miss him, you know. I don't mean to sound tough and hard but we shouldn't have been doing it and we wanted to be certain that you and your mother were untouched by it. Of course, you'd already started work. I remember TDF saying that he'd rather have liked you to go to university but that Marianne was not keen.'

'I would have liked it,' admits Charlie. 'But I expect she was right. It seemed a bit silly when my future was already planned out and the job was there.'

And, thinks Evie, some pretty girl might have tempted you away from Ange.

She smiles at him. 'No chance to sow wild oats?'

He smiles back at her. 'None at all.'

'Well, make the most of this moment,' she says.

He stares at her, his smile fading, and she shakes her head.

'Sorry,' she says. 'That was totally out of order. I'm really sorry, Charlie. It was irresponsible. I've no excuses, except that I love you and I love to see you happy.'

'But . . . but I'm not sure I could handle things the way TDF did. He was so tough. So sure of himself. Oh, in a good way and all that, but I think the guilt would get to me, you see, and I don't have the courage just to walk away from Ange and the girls and my responsibilities in London. And I don't want to.' He smiles ruefully. 'Like most people I want my cake and to eat it, too, but I'm not sure it's possible.'

She watches him, not knowing what to say.

'Don't sound ashamed, for goodness' sake,' she says. 'I'm just so glad you've had this week.'

'Thanks, Evie. Thanks for that. And I love you too.'

She sits in silence, thinking of – and rejecting – things that she might say to him, and in the end she gets up.

'Come on,' she says. 'I'm going to buy you a drink.'


Once she is out of the town, Jemima pulls into the side of the road and takes the oblong of glass from her bag. It seems to her to be a symbol: the strength of the glass, the simplicity of the design, the freedom of the little boat and the two birds: her own little bit of sea.

She holds it up as he did, against the sunshine, tilting it to enjoy the richness of the colours. How will she manage without that adrenalin rush of seeing him, without the joy of being in his company? It will probably be easier for Charlie: he's going back home to his family, his work, his life in London. She knows that here she will be always looking for him, that she will see him everywhere: along the Embankment, around the Boat Float, walking up Foss Street; coming out of the Royal Castle with Claude; sitting across the table from Benj in Alf's with a newspaper and a cup of coffee. Charlie will be here for ever, caught like a fly in amber, in her memories of this regatta week.

'For goodness' sake,' she tells herself, 'you are such a drama queen. Get a grip.'

It was funny that down on the Embankment he guessed that she was imagining them both in some kind of film sequence, thinking of the soundtrack. Her old ma had always said that life would be so much easier if it were set to music; that we'd feel nobler if all our dreary little setbacks and emotions were lived to something dramatic like Brahms or Mahler, or heart-wrenchingly evocative like the voice of Nina Simone.

Despite herself, Jemima smiles. Frummie was quite right, though she can't quite imagine which composer would be the right one for this particular moment. She simply mustn't let herself dwell on the future: that way madness lies. Moment to moment is the way. She wishes she had Otto with her, sitting in the back, ears alert, hoping for a walk. At least, once regatta is over, he will be able to come in with her to the office again, to lie under her desk waiting for those trips out into the country, up on to the moor, to check out properties, welcome visitors, deal with any problems. She's not prepared to leave him up in the Park and Ride car park, however, so just this week he has to stay at home.

Jemima tries to concentrate on the positive side to the end of regatta but her gut lurches as she stares at her little piece of glass and sees Charlie in her mind's eye, holding it up to the sun, turning to smile down at her.

Cursing under her breath, she puts the glass away safely, switches on the engine and drives off towards Dittisham.

\*

They celebrate Ben's new project in the garden in the early evening once Jemima has arrived, walking across from the office to join them, up on the terrace where champagne is waiting, glasses set out.

It's best this way, thinks Claude. Tomorrow night, the last night of regatta, this would be too emotional. We can do all this this evening and tomorrow evening something else must happen. Ben and Charlie can take Jemima down to see the fireworks, have supper at the pub, anything rather than all sitting here knowing it's the last time, wondering where we'll be next year, and all that gut-wrenching stuff of saying goodbye.

We can laugh now, raising our glasses to Ben, telling him how great it is, all of us being a bit silly and emotional and over the top, and underneath each knowing what the others are really thinking and able to allow ourselves a little bit extra foolishness because tonight we have this excuse. Tomorrow it would be agony.

'To Ben,' he cries, as the champagne foams into the tall flutes.

'To Ben,' they all cry, raising their glasses.


I'm not sure I can bear it, thinks Evie. That look on Charlie's face is breaking my heart. And Jemima is being so amazing, so brave, and she looks so beautiful in her pretty long skirt and with her lovely fair hair all over the place. It's odd, really, that they seem like my children, these three. Dear Ben looking so pleased and proud but trying to disguise it. He's not used to being the centre of attention and he's really very touched that we're all so happy for him. And Charlie, pulling his leg and pretending his own heart isn't breaking, and my dear old Claude trying to make it special, buying the champagne and celebrating because it's the last night, really, and we all know it.

'To Ben,' she cries. 'Well done. Now you won't be able to leave us. What a lovely thought.' And she raises her glass to him.

Charlie grins at Benj and claps him on the shoulder, and all the while he wants to seize Jemima and tell her he loves her and say that they all belong here together: he and Benj and Jemima and Claude. And how, he wonders, can I ever go away and leave them? How is it to be done? And how can I ever behave naturally again with Ange and the girls and go back to my old life as if nothing has happened? And how am I going to get through this lovely supper that old Benj has planned for us. The last supper. Oh Christ . . .

'Congratulations, Benj,' says Charlie. 'Fantastic. Go on, my son!'

They're like my family, thinks Jemima. It's so weird. Like I've known them for ever, and I love them and I never want it to end. And this, really, is the end. Never mind the Red Arrows and the firework display and the rest of it. Regatta is ending here, tonight, in this magical garden with the smell of the lavender and the fizz of champagne, and yes, there should be music to go with this but whatever could live up to it? And I think I'm going to cry at any minute.

'To Benj,' she cries, 'and to the very best, wonderful, fantastic brochure we've ever seen. Hurrah!'

And any moment, thinks Benj, this is going to spiral completely out of control and I've got to get them all back on track. I love them, and it's wonderful, and agonizing. I wish old Charlie wasn't going back but however would it work out if he stayed? And if we drink much more without eating something then we'll all go right over the top and get maudlin and that would be utterly disastrous. Bless old Claude for thinking of champagne, and Evie for wanting me to stay. God, I am so lucky. But now I must do something. Take Jemima down to help me with the supper, while Charlie organizes the wine? Separate them just for a while and keep them busy? It just needs something to turn it around, but what? Something silly to take their minds off things. I know . . .

'Thanks,' he says. 'I shall do my best to make you proud of me. And now it's nearly suppertime. But first . . .' he holds up his glass, strikes a pose, and calls out: '*An Officer and a Gentleman.*'

There is a complete and surprised silence and then Jemima starts singing 'Up Where We Belong' in her clear voice and they all join in – Charlie's light tenor, Claude's croaky old bass, Evie's off-tune contralto – and the garden is full of music and laughter.

# PART TWO

# CHAPTER EIGHTEEN

It's still warm enough, up on the top terrace, to sit in the October sunshine with a mug of tea before the sun slips away behind the hill. Here in the garden there is a special kind of peace; of quiet waiting. Not the expectant longing for spring, waiting for life to burst from the frozen, sealed-in earth, but the contented satisfaction of something completed and the prospect of a well-earned rest. Pink and white cosmos and Japanese anemones, fragile and elegant, are still in flower in the border beneath the crab-apple tree, but most of its fruit has been picked and transformed into rosy jelly though a few scarlet globes remain on the highest branches, half hidden amongst the ivy that trails over the wall.

In between sips of her tea, Evie clips and prunes, sweeps up the crimson-tipped leaves of the acer japonicum. Tommy planted the acer, cherished it and watched over its growth, and, on an impulse, she picks up one of the leaves, lays it on the table and gently smooths it out: so delicate and miraculous. Carefully she puts it into her jacket pocket and then drinks some more tea, sitting down and breathing in the earthy scents of the garden: rich, ripe scents of the passing season. She thinks about Tommy, longing for him to come striding up through the garden, calling out to her, and she is stricken with the pain of loneliness.

Just recently, when she's come across to have supper with Ben, she's stayed overnight, sleeping in the bedroom she shared with Tommy; keeping a spare set of clothes and washing things just for those occasions. She looks forward to these evenings: Ben is a good and innovative cook, and sometimes Jemima joins them.

Evie sits, finishing her tea, one hand in her pocket unconsciously smoothing the tender acer leaf. Her companion, the blackbird, hops amongst the ivy, perches on a slender branch of a climbing rose and then flits away. Pale petals tremble and fall, drifting down to the dark, dank earth, but there are still a few buds on the prickly stems. Evie stands up and cuts one perfect bud; she wraps it carefully in a piece of tissue and puts it into her pocket with the acer leaf.

She feels Tommy's presence in the garden this afternoon. Memories flit in the long shadows and the warm sunshine, so that when her name is called, for one heart-stopping moment she imagines that it is Tommy who is coming up through the garden.

It's Ben, of course. He's enjoying working on the new brochure. It's a big job but he's still managing to keep up with his other work. Carrying a mug of tea, shouting a friendly greeting, he climbs up to the top terrace and stands the mug on the table.

'I guessed you'd be here,' he says. 'What a day. I've been out taking photographs of a cottage at Prawle Point. Gosh, it's really warm. Makes you forget all that rain, doesn't it?'

She's recovered, ready to listen to the events of his day, and to make plans for Claude's visit.

'I've had a thought,' he tells her. 'I've got a photoshoot in Salisbury on Wednesday and I wondered if Claude might like a lift down. I can go over to Winchester and pick him up when I've finished.'

'That's a brilliant idea,' Evie says. 'He was saying that he might have to drive this time, since he's coming for much longer than usual, but I'm sure he'd love a lift though it means that one of us might have to get him back to Winchester again. That shouldn't be a problem and it saves having to worry about the parking of an extra car. I'm sure he'll love having the company.'

'That's all good then.'

Ben sits at the table, legs stretched out, and breathes in the peace. Evie watches him; she longs suddenly to be able to confide in him, to say, 'How would you feel, Ben, if you knew that this house should be yours? That a miscarriage of justice deprived you of an inheritance?'

Instead, she says, 'How would you feel, Ben, if I were to suggest that I moved across here for the winter? I'm finding it a bit miserable in the afternoons and evenings down in the boathouse, and I'm getting a bit weary climbing up and down all those steps. What d'you think?'

There is no flicker of disappointment at the prospect of this intrusion, not even surprise in his face.

'I think it's a really good idea,' he says. 'I've told you that I think this house is much too big for one person. It's great when you come across for supper and then stay over. Why not? Apart from the fact that it's your house and you don't actually have to ask. But what about half term?'

'Oh, no.' She shakes her head. 'I'd wait until Charlie and Ange have gone and, anyway, I've got Claude staying until Christmas. No, I was thinking about after Christmas once Claude has gone back. Always so gloomy then.'

'I'm looking forward to Christmas,' he says. 'Listen. Why don't you and Claude stay over here for Christmas? It'll be much more fun than all the coming and going across the road. We'll get some logs for the drawing-room fire and have a tree.'

'It does sound rather fun,' she admits. 'I might take you up on that.'

There's a companionable little silence.

'It's a weird set-up, isn't it?' he says suddenly. 'Me living here and you across the road, and Charlie and Ange coming down again. And Claude. I suppose it's rather like a commune.'

Evie laughs; pleased at the idea. 'I suppose it is. But it works at the moment. Though I still feel it's rather a shame, having invited you to stay here, that we all do use it rather like a hotel.'

But Ben shakes his head, almost impatiently. 'No, no.

244

That's the whole point, you see. I love this house but I'm not sure I'd want the responsibility of it. Such a worry, isn't it? Must cost a fortune, keeping it in good nick. No, I just love having the chance to live in it, treat it like home, have people coming in and out, but not worrying about it all the time.'

She watches him thoughtfully. 'Is that really how you feel about it? I thought you loved it.'

'Oh, I do,' he says. 'I love it for all sorts of reasons. Because it's beautiful and there are lots of memories and it's part of the family. But I'd rather share it than own it. TDF must have spent a fortune on it when he did those alterations, and putting shower-rooms in a Grade II listed house must have been a nightmare. All those rules and regs.'

'It wasn't straightforward,' she agrees. She's still aware of Tommy's shade, as if he is close by, listening to them, encouraging her. She takes new courage.

'So,' she says, 'if I were to leave the house to you in my will, are you saying you wouldn't want it?'

He stares at her with such amazement that she bursts out laughing.

'You can't do that,' he says firmly, almost anxiously.

'Why not?' she counters. 'It's my house. I can do what I like with it.'

'Yes, but it's always come down on Charlie's side. It wouldn't be right at all.'

'Why not?' she asks again. 'Don't you think Charlie has enough?'

Ben looks uncomfortable. 'That's not the point. It's the whole tradition thing, isn't it? It's important to Charlie. Apart from anything else, he'd be hurt, wouldn't he? Why should you choose me over him? He's TDF's son.'

'But it might so easily have gone the other way, mightn't it?' she suggests recklessly. 'Suppose your great-grandfather had inherited instead of Charlie's?'

To her surprise, he bursts out laughing. 'Oh, that's easy,' he says. 'In that case there wouldn't have been anything left to inherit anyway. No, no.' He shakes his head. 'My side of the family would never have been the custodians that Charlie's were. They grafted and they deserve it. Let them keep it. I'll just enjoy the fruits of their labours for a little while.'

Another silence.

'Very well, then,' she says. 'I've got another idea. Supposing I leave the Merchant's House in trust to you for your lifetime and then, when you die, it would revert back to Charlie or to his estate?'

He stares at her, frowning. 'Could you do that?'

She shrugs. 'Why not?'

'So I could live here but Charlie would have it – or his children would – ultimately.'

'That's about it.'

He turns to look down across the garden to the house, as if he's never seen it before.

'Could it work, d'you think?' he asks at last.

'I don't see why not. They could all come and stay if you wanted them. It could still be a family house. You wouldn't be able to sell it or raise money against it but you could be here, enjoying it.'

'It sounds rather too good to be true,' he says at last.

'Of course,' she adds drily, 'I'll have to die first but meanwhile – here you are and here you can stay.'

'I don't think I quite know what to say.'

'Then don't say anything. And this is strictly between ourselves. I'm off. I'll phone Claude and make a plan about you picking him up. See you later.'

'Yes,' he says, almost mechanically. 'See you later.'

Back in the boathouse, in the dim, watery light of her big room, Evie walks across to the glass windows and gazes at the river. On the hill, Kingswear is still in sunshine: pretty houses and steep streets, crowding down to the marina with its dense thicket of masts.

She puts her hands in her pockets and her fingers encounter the rosebud and the acer leaf. She brings them out carefully.

*So*, she says silently to Tommy. *Did I do the right thing?*

Suddenly she remembers the etchings and how she'd planned to find new frames for them so that the two cartoons could be put back into the originals. She smooths the acer leaf between her fingers, puts it on the table and finds the cut-glass specimen vase for the rose. Then she goes into her study and takes down the two etchings from the wall. Putting them on her desk, she removes the pins and carefully edges the backing and the frames away.

As she puts the separate pieces out on the desk she sees that behind each of the etchings is a carefully folded sheet of blue air-mail paper. Picking one up, she unfolds it and stares at Tommy's tiny writing. There is a 2 at the top of the page so she picks up the other:

## 1

So this is my 'letter in a bottle', darling Evie. Probably madness but worth a try. If you're reading it then I am not around and you've probably decided to put these original frames back on the cartoons. I wonder why. Perhaps you want to rehang them? Perhaps someone's missed them? I know what a shock it will be to you when you find out that I've left the Merchant's House to you. I always wanted it to be there for you, Evie; your house, your home, for whenever you might need it, to live in it and be happy in it when the boathouse is a bit beyond you. That's what is most important to me and why I'm not just going to leave it in trust for you. It's no good discussing it with you. You'll refuse it, you'll say it belongs to Charlie, to the family. But it's your home, Evie. And after that, well, I have a feeling that somehow the future will reveal the solution but maybe I'm just passing the buck.

## 2

And maybe it's not you reading this, but someone down the years who doesn't know us. What an unsettling idea. When we sat on the top terrace on your birthday and you opened these little presents I thought of you at some future date taking them apart, removing the frames and finding my 'letter in a bottle'. I had a strong sense, then, that all would work together for good. Blessings, my darling, and thank you.

Evie holds the thin sheets of paper in her hand. They bring Tommy so near to her; she can hear his voice in the words. It's as if he has presided over the afternoon in the garden, and has confirmed the things she said to Ben, so that she is filled with relief and with confidence.

So this is why he left her the house: not so as to avoid taking a decision between Ben and Charlie but so that she might feel that the house is hers to move into, to live in, to look upon as her home. Still holding his letter she glances around her study; at the bookshelves, the cupboards, her desk with its laptop and its Anglepoise lamp. Now that it is no longer inhabited with the ghosts of her characters, the desk is bare of documents, lists and reference books. There is an odd kind of emptiness, an impersonal atmosphere. She leaves the etchings on her desk and takes Tommy's letter into the big room where she reads it again, thinking of him holding it, and then lays it down with the acer leaf.

She longs for him: for the touch and the smell of him; for the sound of his laugh and the sight of his eyes smiling into hers; his voice calling to her, 'What's the plan?'

Her heartache is intolerable, but she has a plan. The plan is that Claude is coming to stay, Charlie and Ange will be down for half term, and then there is Christmas.

Perhaps Ben is right to suggest that she and Claude should spend Christmas in the Merchant's House. It is something to plan for: the first step in making the move.

And there is Mikey. She's had two cards, both pretty watercolour sketches of Bristol scenes, from him; rather formal, informative up to a point, as if someone – Jason? – was looking over his shoulder: school is good, it's the rugby term, they're beginning rehearsals for a big choral Christmas concert in the cathedral. He put his home address at the top right-hand corner of the card so she replied to it, taking her tone from his: Dartmouth is very quiet after regatta, she'd taken a river-boat trip to Totnes, perhaps she'll see him at half term? The second card was along much the same lines, he was home on an exeat weekend, but added that they would be in Dartmouth for half term and were looking forward to seeing her and the boathouse.

Evie looks around the big room. She hopes that Mikey isn't just being polite, that he really would like to come here to see her again. It's odd how touched and pleased she was to receive these cards; that he took the trouble to write to her. It's as if – and she knows she's being foolish – as if she is being forgiven for her youthful indifference: for her selfishness in ignoring Pat's feelings and for her refusal to give financial help for Jason's school fees.

Russ and Tommy. They were alike in their ability to compartmentalize their emotions, in their enthusiasms and in their absolute respect for her own work. Perhaps it was because they were both older than her by a decade that they had the kind of confidence and experience that the men of her own age seemed to lack. Or perhaps it was – more simply – that she'd fallen in love.

The sun has disappeared, Kingswear sinks into shadow, and cold river-light trembles on the ceiling and the walls. It is time to light the lamps.

Ben picks up the mugs and stands in the garden, looking down towards the house, aware of the gathering twilight and the atmosphere of warmth and security between the high, sheltering walls. He goes down the wide shallow steps, carrying the mugs, trying to contain an up-welling of joy and excitement. He longs to share this amazing news with someone; to tell somebody that he has the right to stay here for all of his life. It is an extraordinary sensation.

When he walks into the kitchen he looks around him as if expecting that the room will look different; that this new sense of belonging will manifest itself in some different way. Yet everything remains comfortingly the same – nor would he wish anything to change: he would simply like to share this revelation with somebody special.

He rinses the cups and stands them beside the sink, thinking about Kirsty and what she would say if he could tell her. Suddenly he misses her: or rather he misses that old, easy intimacy of a long relationship, the ability to put his arms around someone and hug them, to share with them. Well, that's all over now: finished. He wishes that Laura would come walking in – 'Hi, Dad,' she'd say. 'How're you doing?' – but even then he couldn't tell her. Evie said that it must be between the two of them and that's how it will be. Oh, but it will be hard not to share this with Laura.

He remembers her visit a few weeks ago. Back from backpacking to Peru, and before setting off for Adelboden, she came down to see them all, making them laugh with stories of her adventures. She took over the attic room with her few possessions – 'I like to travel light, Dad,' – and told him, one evening at supper in the breakfast room, about Billy. Billy is the brother of a boy she's been at uni with: he's twenty-three and has spent several seasons working in Swiss ski resorts. He speaks fluent French and Italian and now he's got a catering job in one of the hotels.

'I know it's crazy,' she said, her brown eyes huge with love, 'but he's just, like, special. He's going to help me with my skiing. There's a group of us going out together so it's going to be amazing.'

Ben was filled with joy and fear, and a twinge of jealousy, that her eyes should shine so brightly for this unknown Billy.

'Perhaps,' he said diffidently, 'you could invite him down while you're here. He might like to see Dartmouth.'

She laughed, shaking her head, making a face. 'Don't worry, Dad, he's quite respectable but it's not really Billy's scene, meeting the rellies. Not just yet, anyway. Maybe when we get back.'

'Got a photo of him?' he asked hesitantly, not wanting to be pushy but needing to share with her.

She turned on her phone, got up and came around the table to stand beside him, scrolling through the images. He gazed at them: a tough, stocky, cheerful-looking fellow grinned back at him from different attitudes and locations.

'He looks fun,' he said at last, glancing up at her.

'Oh, he is,' she answered, her fixed eyes on Billy. 'He's . . . well, he's great. Perhaps I could bring him down after Christmas.'

'That would be fantastic.' Ben tried not to sound too keen, he didn't want to play the heavy father.

She looked down at him, her face bright with love, with joy, with all the expectation and optimism of youth, and he is seized with a whole range of emotions: delight, love, fear, anguish. She is so young: so hopeful and so confident.

'Be happy, sweetheart,' he said foolishly, and she bent and gave him a quick kiss, and then went back to her chair, talking about how she was going out with Claude the next morning on his scooter.

He let the moment pass. He didn't have to ask her to stay in touch – Laura is very good at texting and emailing – but his heart sank at the prospect of her absence. He was going to miss her random visits: those occasional weekends, those unexpected few days, here in the Merchant's House.

Now, remembering, the joy and gratitude bubbles up in him again. It might have been so different. He might have been living somewhere all alone, wondering how to plan his future. Instead he is here, living in the house he's loved all his life, with Evie across the road and dear old Claude down again soon. And then there's Jemima: they've had a lot of fun during these last few weeks. She's taken him to see some of the cottages so that he can take photographs for the brochure, they've had a few pub lunches and he's cooked supper for her and Evie. They don't talk about Charlie but his presence is almost visible with them. It's as if he is there, sharing the jokes, enjoying the jaunts across the moor or down to the coast. Sometimes it's frustrating but at least it prevents any misunderstandings and it allows a freedom within the friendship that is very precious to him.

Ben switches on the kettle: it's too early for a drink but he'll make some tea. He simply must do something to celebrate his extraordinary good fortune.


Jemima's mobile rings just as she leaves the office: Miranda.

'Hi,' Jemima says. 'No, it's OK to talk. I'm just on my way home. How're things?'

'It's just that I've got a bit of a problem with Maisie. No, she's fine but my mum's got people staying and Maisie's kicking up about staying with her on Saturday night. I suppose you couldn't help out, could you Mimes? I could bring her over on Saturday morning . . .'

Jemima thinks about it as Miranda continues to outline her weekend, remembering that she and Benj were going to meet up. It was a bit vague, but even so . . .

'Tell you what,' she says. 'Bring Maisie into Dartmouth and I'll meet you in Alf's. Eleven thirty-ish? No, it's fine, honestly.'

'She's being a right little madam just lately. Anyway, if you're sure?'

'Quite sure.'

'See you at Alf's then. Thanks, Mimes.'

Jemima thrusts her phone into her bag and stands for a minute, full of indecision. Part of her is irritated at giving in to Miranda; not that she and Benj had anything particular planned, but having a six-year-old around narrows the options. At the same time she knows it's difficult for Miranda to find reliable childcare at such short notice.

'Doesn't she have any other friends?' Benj asked once when something similar occurred and they'd had to postpone a visit to the cinema at Dartington.

'I think she's too busy,' Jemima answered tactfully, not wanting to tell him that Miranda's neediness tends to keep prospective friends at arm's length 'And she works antisocial hours. Her mother is very useful, of course, but she's elderly and not very strong so sometimes she can be demanding, too.'

Now, on an impulse, she walks back to the car, lets Otto out for a quick pee and then drives up to Southtown. Ben hasn't been in the office today but he might be at home. She's lucky: there are several parking spaces not far from the Merchant's House and there's a light shining out from the breakfast room. She parks, slides out, and crosses the road to bang on the front door.

Benj opens the door. 'Hi,' he says. 'Come in.' He hesitates. 'Did I know you were coming? I haven't forgotten something?'

'No,' she says. 'And I've got Otto. It's just I'm feeling cross and bitchy and stuff like that. Miranda wants me to have Maisie this Saturday and I know we were going to do something or other. And anyway, I just don't feel like it.'

He roars with laughter, opening the door wider. 'You poor old lambkin,' he says. 'Go and get Otto and come on in.'

She hurries back to the car, releases Otto, grabs her bag and they go in together, through to the breakfast room.

'I feel in a real old strop,' she admits, dumping her bag on a chair whilst Otto sniffs around and then drops down contentedly near the table. 'Oh, yes, please. A cup of tea would be great. Don't take any notice of me.' She frowns a little, studying him curiously. 'You're looking very chipper, though. Someone given you a present?'

He thinks about it, smiling to himself as if he knows a secret.

'Yeah. Actually, you could put it like that.' He pushes the mug of tea towards her. 'So what's this about Saturday?'

She's slightly hurt that he's not going to tell her his secret but she won't show it.

'Oh, it's just that I feel obliged to help out, even if I've got things organized, and then I get cross with myself for always giving in and saying "yes". Plus, it's more

256

difficult keeping a child entertained when the evenings draw in. Walking on the beach in the dark isn't so much fun, somehow.'

'But what's really the trouble?' he asks, wandering from the kitchen to the breakfast room, sitting at the table. 'It's not just Maisie, is it?'

She perches on the edge of the table, makes a face. 'I just didn't fancy going back to be on my own, I suppose. Doing the drive in the dark, deciding what to have for supper. All that stuff. I've just felt edgy all day.'

'Thinking about Charlie and Ange coming down for half term?'

She stares at him, almost affronted by this direct question.

'Probably,' she says reluctantly. 'Well, of course I am,' and at once she realizes that this is at the root of her low spirits. These few weeks with Charlie back in London she's been able to keep in control, to stay busy, to enjoy those jaunts with Benj and suppers with him and Evie. Now, as half term draws closer, the possibility of seeing Charlie again makes it so much more difficult to suppress her foolish hopefulness; the longing to see him.

'Anyway,' she says. 'Never mind that. What have you been doing to make you so cheerful?'

'I've been planning Christmas with Evie,' he says. 'You know Claude will be here, too? Well, I suggested that they both should stay here rather than us making sorties to and fro. Those stone steps can be lethal in the dark.'

'And did she agree?'

'Well, she did. She said she was wondering whether to move over for the winter anyway.'

Jemima feels an odd little pang: jealousy? Surely not. Yet she feels regret that these moments that she and Benj share so easily and casually might not be so readily available.

'Sounds very sensible,' she says. She can hear her voice sounding the least bit brittle and tries to warm it up. After all, she's very fond of Evie. 'It must get a bit lonely there all on her own.'

'Mmm. I told her that it's a big old house for one person so it was fine with me. Anyway, it's her house.'

He grins, almost laughs, and she stares at him, puzzled, almost irritated by his high spirits.

'So what about Saturday?' she asks, almost grumpily.

'Well, we'll start off at Alf's and then do a river trip up to Totnes. How about that? Maisie should enjoy that.'

'What about Otto?' She feels a perverse desire to put obstacles in his way.

Otto lifts his head; he watches them hopefully and his tail beats encouragingly. Benj leans down and strokes him, twiddles his ears.

'What about him? Doesn't Otto like Totnes?'

He looks up at her indignant face and begins to laugh. 'Sorry.' He holds up both hands in apology and then gets up. 'I'm being very tiresome and silly. Sorry.'

And suddenly he puts his arms around her and hugs her, and she holds him tightly for a moment before she draws away from him, pushing back her hair and feeling much calmer, but not quite knowing how to move on. She picks up her tea, half turned away from him, and hears him sit down again.

'So tell me about Otto,' he says. His voice is still slightly teasing. 'Does he get seasick? Or don't they allow dogs on the river-boat?'

Suddenly she begins to laugh, infected by whatever joy is bubbling out from him, and relaxing into it.

'Actually, I don't know,' she admits.

'Neither do I,' he says, 'but I know a man who does. Mr Google will have the answers.'

He pulls his laptop towards him and opens it and then stretches out an arm without looking at her.

'Stay for a bit,' he says. 'I'll make us some supper if you like.'

She pulls a chair close to his and sits beside him staring at the screen. He puts his arm casually across her shoulder and at last she is able to relax.


Mikey drops his rucksack on the floor and looks around the flat with satisfaction. It's great to be back here again though he almost wishes he could have come alone. Dad's in a bit of a weird mood, sort of hyper and slightly crazy, wanting to talk all the way down on the train about how they're going to get to know Evelyn Drake really well. Stuff like that. Mikey feels a bit uncomfortable about it, like when he was sending those cards Dad got for him: one before he went off to school and another during an exeat weekend. He wanted to write a card, he liked Evie, but it wasn't the same with Dad asking what he was writing, reminding him to tell her about this or that. He couldn't write what he really wanted to because Dad kept coming to peer over his shoulder and say silly things like, 'Mind you give her my love,' and then laughing, which made him feel embarrassed.

When they arrived at Totnes, Dad said they'd take a taxi to Dartmouth. 'Blow the expense,' he kept saying, taking a swig from his water bottle. 'You only live once.' The taxi driver gave Mikey a little friendly glance, like he was understanding how he felt but pitying him, and he hated it.

'You OK there?' Dad says, appearing in the doorway. 'I've unpacked the big case so I thought I'd go out and get some fish and chips. Shan't be long.'

Mikey feels disappointed. He wanted to walk around the town to see what it was like without regatta going on. It's still quite early, though. There will be time to go out after they've eaten.

He takes his mobile phone out of his pocket and looks at it. His aunt Liz gave it to him for his birthday.

'Time you had your own phone,' she said, 'but look after it and don't take it to school. No nonsense with it, Mikey, or I shall have it back. My number is in already, and Uncle Paul's, so if you ever need us or want to chat we'll be right there.'

It made him very slightly nervous when she said that; like she expected there to be some kind of emergency.

'You're a big boy now,' she said, 'and it's time you had a bit of responsibility.'

If he's honest he feels he's got quite enough responsibility with Dad's mood swings, making sure he's taking his happy pills, doing the shopping, but he doesn't say so to Aunt Liz. They're all missing Mum, he knows that, and Dad hasn't been too bad since he got the library job. Except for the last couple of weeks, when he wrote to say that he'd had a few days off: bad headaches, feeling a bit under the weather.

Mikey goes into the kitchen to get the knives and forks so as to lay the table. He wonders how long Dad will be. Sometimes he can be gone for quite a long time, even doing quick simple things. At least when he comes back from these sorties he's usually in a good mood. Mikey gives a great big sigh, like he's heaving off all his worries. He's back in Dartmouth and it's going to be great.

# CHAPTER NINETEEN

Ben is the first to arrive at Alf's on Saturday morning. He and Jemima arranged it so that he could meet Miranda who is curious about this new friend who works with Jemima.

'But don't let on about what I told you. You know? Maisie's father leaving them.'

Sitting under the awning in the autumn sunshine he thinks about Jemima; how it felt to hold her warm body in his arms. It somehow seemed a right and natural thing to do, just at that moment; to comfort her, a kind of celebration of his amazement and delight at Evie's suggestion, and a need to show his affection for her. He enjoyed the feel of her and the smell of her, though he'd realized how easy it might be to take advantage of her emotional state and he managed to pull himself together. Quickly, their easy companionship reasserted itself as they sat together at his laptop looking at various websites, trying to decide how Maisie might be entertained.

'Everything's a bit flat for her since regatta,' said Jemima, 'but I think the river trip would make too many demands on Otto.'

'I could have Otto,' he suggested, 'if it would help,' and had seen an odd expression flit across her face. It was rather as if she was disappointed that he wouldn't be one of the party and he was foolishly pleased.

'Let's start with lunch in Alf's,' she said. 'Then you can meet Miranda and we'll take it from there.'

So here he is – and here is Miranda, holding Maisie by the hand, scanning the tables and looking for Jemima. He recognizes them both from Stokeley Farm Shop, especially the child with her intent stare. She seems to remember him, too, waving suddenly and pulling Miranda forward.

He gets up, smiling at them, and Maisie calls, 'Hello!' as if they are old friends. Suddenly, he wonders if she's mistaken him for Charlie and if Jemima has told her friend about Charlie and how she and Maisie went to the dog show with him.

'I'm Ben Fortescue,' he says. 'Jemima should be here any moment.'

Miranda looks rather confused, clearly surprised that Maisie seems so friendly, but she shakes his outstretched hand and says, 'I'm Miranda. Hello. I've got a feeling I've seen you somewhere.'

He smiles at her, Jemima's voice in his ears: 'Don't mention Stokeley,' she has warned him. 'We work together, OK? I haven't told her how we met at Alf's or anything yet so you'll have to wing it if she remembers.'

'I wouldn't be surprised,' he says lightly. 'Would you like some coffee?'

She squints into the dark interior. 'Do they come to take your order or what?'

'You have to go to the counter. Shall I get it?'

She shakes her head. 'I'll go and see what they've got, thanks. Maisie, stay here with Ben.'

'I want a milkshake,' Maisie says. 'Or a Coke.'

'I'm sure you do,' says Miranda. 'I'll see.'

Maisie looks at Ben expectantly and he feels slightly nonplussed. He remembers Laura at this age: inquisitive, argumentative, stubborn. He thinks of several things to say, all of which seem rather pedestrian: 'Do you like school?' 'How old are you?' And all the while she watches him with this intent, slightly puzzled stare as if she knows something he doesn't. His relief when Jemima turns in off the pavement with Otto is huge and he gets up to greet her with such enthusiasm that she raises her eyebrows at him.

'I believe that Maisie thinks I'm Charlie,' he mutters in her ear and she makes a little face and murmurs, 'Oh shit,' and then she beams at Maisie and calls, 'Hello.'

Maisie is wriggling off her chair to stroke Otto, and Miranda is returning, so there is a general hubbub of greeting, then Ben sinks back into his chair, relieved that he can drink his coffee and leave it all to Jemima.

Maisie watches him. He looks like the man who took her to the dog show at regatta but there's something slightly different about him, though she can't think what it is. She also sees that Mummy is behaving a bit oddly too: laughing rather loudly, fiddling with her hair, showing off. That's what she'd say if Maisie was behaving like that: 'Stop showing off, Maisie,' she'd say. Cups of coffee arrive, and a milkshake, and now her mother is fussing a little bit, making Maisie sit up straight, even running her hand over Maisie's head and smiling at her: a specially sweet smile. It's as if she is saying, 'See what a nice Mummy I am,' and Maisie twitches away from her hand and kneels up on her chair even though she knows she's not allowed to. She can't see why Mummy is behaving like this and she feels anxious and cross with her for being silly.

She slurps her milkshake noisily and glances at Jemima, who is watching Mummy with a funny look on her face. She looks slightly surprised and even faintly annoyed, as if she is thinking the same thing: 'She's showing off.'

Then Jemima looks at Maisie, and grins at her, and suddenly Maisie feels much better. She gets off her chair again and crouches down to stroke Otto, who swipes at her chin with his tongue so that she laughs out loud. Jemima hands down a little biscuit to give to him, and Maisie and Otto sit contentedly together while he eats his biscuit and she leans against him and is happy.

Jemima is rather surprised by the way Miranda is coming on to Benj: surprised, amused, but at the same time just very faintly annoyed. It's silly, she tells herself, because

Benj is a free agent but nevertheless she feels the same reaction as when he told her that Evie would be spending the winter at the Merchant's House: a tiny stab of jealousy at the thought of anything coming between her and Benj's friendship. It's become very important to her to be able to meet up with him, drop in to see him, invite him over for a pint at the pub. There is no strain between them; they laugh a lot and have fun. Neither of them is looking for any kind of commitment: the break-up of his marriage is too recent and she is grateful for a relationship without all the drama of being physically and emotionally involved. Of course, just occasionally, it would almost be a relief to hop into bed with him but the brief satisfaction wouldn't be worth the risk. It would change the whole dynamic of their easy-going friendship.

She knows, however, that she would rather hate it were he to become involved with Miranda — but even as she thinks it Benj droops an eyelid at her across the table and at once she is comforted.

He's hot, Miranda is thinking. And I know I've seen him somewhere before. Fancy old Mimes keeping him dark. Not that there seems to be anything going on between them, really, so when she says he's a work friend she might be telling the truth . . . Even so. And she said he's getting divorced . . . I love the way his eyes crease up when he smiles. He's dead sexy. I can't believe Mimes doesn't fancy him. And he's really sweet with Maisie, but that's probably because, like he said, he's got a daughter and knows what they're like at this age . . . Gosh! It would be so good to have someone like Ben in my life. Just to be there. To look out for me and Maisie. I am just so fed up with being alone. Nobody to make me a cup of tea or pour me a drink when I'm tired, or to ask how my day has been . . . And I think he likes me. I'm really glad I wore these jeans with my boots . . . I wonder how I can make sure he's around when I pick Maisie up. I think Mimes said he lives in the town. Damn. I can't think how to organize that and now I've got to go . . . I wonder if he'll watch me walk out . . . OK, then. Time to go.

'Gosh,' Ben murmurs to Jemima as he watches Miranda leave. 'Am I just a vain, desperate middle-aged man or did she come on a bit strong?'

'Don't flatter yourself,' mutters Jemima. 'She's like that with all the chaps.'

'Really?' He's partly deflated and partly relieved.

Maisie, still sitting with Otto under the table, stares up at him. 'What are we going to do now?' she demands.

He stares back at her, wondering why he allowed himself to be involved in this jaunt. The few ideas he and Jemima had already come up with suddenly seem rather unexciting. Then he remembers a conversation with a girl in the office talking about the previous weekend and the need to amuse her two young children.

'We're going to the zoo,' he tells Maisie.

She scrambles up, her whole face alight with excitement. 'To the *zoo*?'

'Absolutely,' he says firmly. 'But no whining or fussing in the car. It's a bit of a drive.'

'I don't remember the zoo being an option,' murmurs Jemima, picking up Otto's lead. 'When did we decide about the zoo?'

He beams at her. 'Two minutes ago.'

'You're crazy,' she says, resigned.

'Yeah,' he agrees. 'But, hey, you're only young once.'

Jason sits at his table in the corner, watching them. He envies them their easy, friendly happiness. They look a jolly little family, with the child and the dog. The familiar jolt of anger seizes him: this is what it could have been like for him if life wasn't so unfair. First his poor mama with her disabilities and his father's weakness and betrayal, and his own disappointment at being denied a first-class education. Then his own health problems, and then Helena's death ripping his own life and Mikey's apart.

He can't quite bear to think of losing his job in the library: not quite yet. It doesn't seem real, and anyway he's made an appeal to the head of the department explaining that his wife's death is enough to make anyone 'unreliable' and 'difficult to work with' and whatever other things they'd wheeled in as an excuse to push him out.

He's quite sure they'll reconsider. Meanwhile he and Mikey need to cosy up to Evelyn Drake and make her see that it's pay-back time for all those hours of picking his father's brains, not to mention the misery she caused darling Mama. He'll get tough if he has to but he'll let Mikey soften her up first; he's just gone out to phone her on his new mobile which Aunt Liz has given him. Good old Liz is an absolute saint, just like her sister.

He feels tears threatening – but here is Mikey, coming in and looking around for him.

'Did you get her?' Jason asks eagerly. 'Did you make a date?'

Mikey nods, he looks a bit strained. 'She asked me for a cup of tea tomorrow afternoon.'

Jason fetches a great sigh of relief: game on.

'Great,' he says. 'Order yourself a Coke, why don't you? And see if there's anything you fancy for lunch.'

He feels generous, expansive, though funds are a bit short; but he can't worry about that just now. Everything will sort itself out given time.

# CHAPTER TWENTY

Travelling down for half term, Ange doesn't talk about Evie as she did on the previous journey, nor does she go on about the injustice of TDF's will and her worries that Ben might feel too much at home in the Merchant's House. This time she is thinking about Charlie. He's behaved oddly these last few weeks: not quite his usual affable, easy-going self. He's been slightly preoccupied, occasionally curt, and several times she's caught him looking at her with an assessing stare that makes her uncomfortable.

At first she worried that it might be to do with work, but everything was running smoothly, and then she wondered if he had a health problem he was hiding from her but his habits were unchanged, his appetite good. She even spoke to her mother about it — very lightly, of course — suggesting jokingly that he might be having a mid-life crisis, and her mother immediately asked if there could be a woman involved.

Of course Ange jumped on that one at once: Charlie, she said, was the last man in the world to be unfaithful. Her mother rather caustically replied that, never mind if he were the first or last man in the world, no man was immune to the flattery of women. Ange remained firm but she began to watch him when they were out with friends and she even – and of this she is rather ashamed – had a quick glance at the numbers in his mobile phone and checked his messages. There was nothing, of course. And, apart from the absent-mindedness and those curious side-long glances, there was nothing else to make her suspicious: no late nights home from the office, no unusual calls or unexplained absences. Her closest, oldest friend burst out laughing when Ange told her what her mother had said and had slightly hinted at her own fears of infidelity.

'You're kidding,' she said. 'Charlie? No chance. We've all had a try with Charlie. He's bomb-proof. It's just that middle-aged thing. It's not like you, Ange, to be so neurotic.'

She was comforted by this; reassured. Her friend's disbelief, the shrieks of laughter, confirmed her trust in Charlie. Nevertheless, there is something bothering him.

As they head into Dartmouth Ange shifts in her seat.

'I feel a bit of a fool, actually,' she says, 'arriving on our own. I mean it was supposed to be a half-term holiday with all four of us. Not just you and me.'

To her surprise she can hear in her voice a slight note of pleading: a requirement to be reassured. This is so unlike her. The truth is that Charlie's oddness has unnerved her slightly; it's never occurred to her that he

271

could unsettle her. His reactions have always been so predictable: he's such a calm, optimistic, laid-back man and so reliable with the children. Even when he's stressed or grumpy she knows it will be short-lived and she can make him feel guilty about it afterwards and exploit it. Lately, though, it's as if there's another Charlie existing alongside the husband and father she thought she knew so well. And yet it's all so formless, nothing she can really pin down, which makes it worse.

'I don't think it matters,' he's answering. 'I've explained to Evie and Benj that the girls had an offer they couldn't refuse. Or at least, if they had then none of our lives would be worth living.'

She listens to his voice and realizes what is missing: the familiar very slightly conciliatory note; that readiness to be jokey, to placate. He sounds as if he doesn't really give a damn whether she feels a fool or not; as if he is not actually thinking about her at all.

And if that is the case, thinks Ange, then who or what is he thinking about?

Charlie is thinking about Jemima, wondering if he will see her, and how he will react if he does. Benj has kept him in touch with an occasional phone call, telling him how she is and what they've been doing, so that he almost feels a part of it all. It's been difficult, just carrying on as if nothing has happened, trying to pretend that his life is the same as it was before regatta. Luckily he and Ange are both busy, of course. Ange has always worked part time on the marketing side of the business, and as MD he's got more than enough to occupy him. Yet now, when he's alone, he remembers Jemima; how she looked at him as if she recognized in him someone he hadn't known was there.

He drives down through Warfleet, into Southtown.

'Good,' he says. 'Benj has opened the garage door.'

Without thinking he reverses the car into the garage, as he always does when he comes down alone, and Ange doesn't protest. He only thinks of this once he's switched the engine off but the usual feelings of guilt, the need to apologize, are somehow absent.

'I'll bring the stuff in,' he says. 'Why don't you go and see if Benj has got the kettle on?'

He pulls out the holdalls and follows her in just as Benj comes out of the breakfast room.

'Hi,' he says. 'You made great time.'

Charlie notices that Benj is looking good: tanned and fit, and with a new confidence that somehow defines him more clearly. They exchange their usual hug and Benj smiles at Ange and asks her if she'd like some tea.

'Yes,' Ange says. 'Thanks, I'd like a cup of tea.'

And if Benj notices that she's not taking command as she usually does, he doesn't make any comment once she's gone upstairs; he merely raises his eyebrows at Charlie – who shrugs noncommittally.

'Tea would be good,' he says. 'So what's new?'

'Not much,' Benj says. 'I brought Claude back with me from a photo-shoot near Salisbury a few days ago, so he's with Evie. I'm sorry the girls couldn't make it.'

'Well, you know what it's like. They got this really good invite and they'd have just been slouching around and whingeing if we'd made them come with us.'

Benj laughs. 'Oh, yes. I know what it's like. They grow up so quick. One moment you're the centre of their little worlds and the next minute you're an embarrassment. At least Laura's over that now.'

'How is she?'

'She's good. She was down a few weeks ago before she went off on this chalet job in Adelboden.'

'Great. How's the brochure going?'

'That's good, too.'

Charlie watches him as he makes the tea, trying to decide what it is about old Benj that is different.

'Has the flat sold?' he asks. 'Any change there?'

'No to both of those,' says Benj, 'though there's lots of interest.' He doesn't seem too worried about it. 'You'll have to wait a little longer for your money, I'm afraid.'

'Oh, I didn't mean that. You know I didn't. I just wondered . . . You know . . .'

'Kirsty is very settled. We talk quite amicably. She's moved on.'

'And you?'

'Oh, I'm moving on, too.'

Not with Jemima, I hope, Charlie wants to say – but, of course, he can't. He wants to ask how she is, whether she has sent him a message, but Ange is coming down the stairs so he takes his mug of tea and goes to stare out of the window into the garden.

Behind him, Benj is offering Ange tea, saying that he was looking forward to seeing the girls. It's clear that Ange feels embarrassed about their absence. This is the second time she's said she's bringing other people who never actually materialize. Nevertheless, she still uses that slightly curt voice she adopts with Ben – as if he is some kind of tiresome dependant – though he takes it all in his stride.

'Laura went through a phase like that,' he says. 'We're all expecting it but it hurts a bit, doesn't it? She's coming down to Dartmouth for the New Year, which is fantastic. I very slightly hoped for Christmas but she'll be working.'

'I'll take this up,' Ange says, clearly uninterested in Laura's plans, 'and drink it while I'm unpacking.'

When she's gone, Benj looks at Charlie thoughtfully.

'Let's take ours up into the garden,' he suggests. 'It's still warm enough on an afternoon like this. And then I can tell you all the things you really want to hear about.'

How quiet the town is: the benches and shelters are empty and there is very little movement on the river. Claude stands with his hands in his pockets remembering regatta: the bump and grind of the music, the smell of frying, the children's voices. Today there is no bait for sale; the booths are closed. In the Royal Avenue Gardens bright leaves, scarlet and gold, crisp into old age in the slanting autumn sunshine.

He is glad to be back in Dartmouth, to be part of this odd little family group again. As he begins to stroll along the Embankment he is conscious of a sense of anticipation – and also apprehension – at the prospect of the arrival of Charlie and Ange. Claude reviews the new situation: Evie's plan to spend the winters at the Merchant House. He sees at once that this is a good idea.

'I couldn't bear to give the boathouse up,' she told him not long after he arrived. 'It's so glorious here in the summer. But I am beginning to rather dread the long winter afternoons and evenings. It seems a good compromise.'

And then she showed him TDF's letter.

'Crazy,' he said. 'Quite crazy! You might never have found it.'

'But he was right,' she said. 'Every time the Merchant's House was mentioned I'd completely stonewall it. It was Charlie's and that was an end of it. Now I feel differently. And I think he knew that one day I'd reframe the cartoons and find the letter. He was right about that, too, and the timing was perfect. It's given me courage.'

Claude snorts to himself. He hasn't got a lot of time for this mystical kind of stuff; on the other hand the timing *is* good. Ben is settled in the house, Evie can split her time between the two, and TDF's seal of approval has certainly given her confidence: enough confidence to leave the house in trust to Ben.

'I've changed my will,' she said. 'The house is left in trust to Ben for his lifetime and then reverts back to Charlie or his descendants. What d'you think?'

Claude thought it was an excellent plan, though he was obliged to hide a tiny flicker of disappointment that she had sorted it all out so thoroughly without consulting him. He was just the least bit hurt but then she went on to tell him how glad she was that he was here with her for Christmas.

'What d'you think of the idea that we should spend Christmas across the road?' she asked. 'I know Ben thinks it's cut and dried and he's thrilled about it, but do you think it's a good plan?'

And then they discussed it all, and she told him her anxieties about whether Ben was really comfortable about her spending the winter there, and he was soon back in the thick of it and feeling a part of it all again.

'I mean,' she said, 'it might be a bit inhibiting, mightn't it? Having me there? Supposing he wants to bring someone back?'

And then they began to laugh about the possible embarrassment inherent in such a situation and he suddenly asked after Jemima as if she might be relevant to that possibility.

'They are just such good friends,' Evie said contentedly. 'It's great to see them together and I'm so glad. I just wonder, though, what might happen with Charlie down again for half term.'

Remembering, Claude feels again the clutch of apprehension. What indeed?

'Has there been any contact?' he asked Evie.

She shook her head. 'As far as Ben knows, none at all. And I am certain that Jemima would have told him if there had been. Like I said, they are very close.'

'Have you seen her?'

'Oh, yes. Several times. She comes in sometimes after work or on a Saturday morning and we have long chats. I think she misses her sister. Or half-sister, rather. She used to live up on the moor but when her husband retired from the navy he bought a sailing school in Falmouth and then Jemima's sister sold up the house and moved down to be with him. Jemima usually spends her summer and Christmas holidays with them.'

'And she never mentions Charlie?'

'Only very occasionally. Sometimes it seems as if she's going to and then she draws back. She knows that I understand how she feels and I think it's almost enough for her. Talking doesn't always help.'

He felt a bit sceptical about that, remembering the full, frank exchange Evie and Jemima had on their first meeting, but then he realized that it was probably true. Evie was not a chattering, gossiping kind of person and, having established such a close relationship with Jemima, he could see that a continual raking up of the situation between her and Charlie would be fruitless.

'But she knows he's down this week?'

Evie nodded. 'Oh, yes. She knows. Actually, I asked her if she was going to stay clear since Ange is with him, but she smiled and said she'd take her chance. After all, she's here in the town most days. She can't simply take time off and disappear. Why should she?'

Claude feels another twinge of apprehension: he's not a man who enjoys drama and he doesn't want to see either

Charlie or Jemima hurt. He tries to comfort himself with the thought that it all might have been regatta madness, that were they to see each other again all that strong magic that surrounded them during that week would have disappeared.

He said as much to Evie and she smiled at him: it was a half-pitying, disbelieving kind of smile.

'You think so?' she asked.

He sighed irritably, feeling frustrated and helpless, but he didn't ask her what she meant. He doesn't want to know. Sometimes the practicality of women, their realism, frightens him to death. And then she told him about Mikey Dean, about his mother dying, and how she'd worked with his grandfather Russell. Mikey is down with his father for half term and has phoned to ask if he could come and see her.

'And you want me to make myself scarce?' Claude asked.

She hesitated for a moment. 'Just this first time,' she said at last. 'Do you mind? Just till we know each other a little better. Give us an hour and if he's still here when you get back, well, that's fine.'

Claude walks through the gardens towards the town, glancing at his watch. Charlie and Ange will be on their way; they might even now be here.

'It's epic,' Mikey says.

He stands on the balcony, his eyes wide with amazement and delight, whilst Evie watches him. He loves this place. He loves the town, though now there is none of the

279

bustle and excitement of regatta. But he loves the peaceful out-of-season vibe, too, the ever-present movement of the river, the boats rocking at their moorings. He utterly loves all of it. Briefly, he can take a step away from his anxieties about Dad, the gnawing sense of responsibility for him, his own grief and longing for Mum that colours everything he thinks and does: here all this is somehow contained. And Evie, though he doesn't understand why, is a part of it.

'I'm glad you approve,' she says. 'What do you like to drink, Mikey? Tea? Coffee? Elderflower cordial?'

'I drink tea,' he says, slightly self-consciously. She makes him feel grown-up; adult. A plate of cakes is already set on the little table on the balcony and now Evie goes back inside to make the tea. He wanders after her, looking around the huge, light-filled space, feeling surprisingly at ease. She doesn't fuss him or make him feel like a visitor; it's as if she's always known that one day he'd come strolling in.

'Be nice,' Dad said to him, before he set off. 'Talk about your grandfather and her books. Butter her up.'

Mikey felt surprisingly cross by that remark; as if he was going under false pretences.

'Why would I do that?' he asked, for once not bothering about whether he upset his father or not.

Dad just smiled; a kind of knowing, silly smile that made Mikey even more cross.

'Keep her sweet, that's all,' his father advised. 'You'll find out why soon enough.'

It made him feel uncomfortable, ill-at-ease to begin with, but Evie put it right. Now, as they sit at the little table on the balcony, she talks about Dartmouth, about his grandfather, how they worked together. He tells her a bit about school: the Carol Concert, which is to be televised; about Aunt Liz and Uncle Paul and his cousins who live in Taunton. And all the while he's watching the green-black water flowing just feet away, Kingswear on the hill opposite basking in the last of the sunshine, a big white yacht coming in under sail.

'It's awesome,' he tells her – and she smiles at him, offers him another cake and, for the first time since Mum died, he is aware of a sense of absolute peace and he is able to relax and feel safe.

# CHAPTER TWENTY-ONE

I t was a mistake to come, thinks Charlie the next morning, wandering with Ange into the town, pausing while she glances into shop and gallery windows. He is only half listening as she talks about Benj.

'He's definitely settled in,' she's saying, rather irritably, 'and now he's got this new work it'll make him feel even more secure.'

Charlie glances around the Boat Float, half longing to see Jemima, half dreading it. What would they say to each other? How would she look? He tries to imagine introducing her to Ange and his gut seems to shrink.

'What do you usually do when you're down?' Ange asks him, as they pause on the corner of Spithead, the familiar slightly discontented frown creasing her forehead.

It's rather difficult to answer this question in a way that will satisfy her: lazing about, breakfast in Alf's, going for a pint with Claude, supper with Evie. None of these things will be remotely attractive to Ange.

'Remember, I only ever come for a couple of nights,' he answers evasively, 'so there's not much time really. It was a pity you arranged to come for the whole week, wasn't it?'

Ange looks disconcerted and he knows exactly what she's thinking. At the time it seemed like a good plan to bring the girls and establish their rights in the Merchant's House, make Benj feel like a lodger, but now it's a rather different scene: a whole week with very little to do, amongst people she doesn't like much. She's been hoist with her own petard and he isn't feeling particularly sympathetic.

'I suppose we don't have to stay the whole week,' she says thoughtfully. 'We could go down and see Mummy for a few days.'

Just for one glorious moment he wonders if this could be a replay of the regatta week: maybe she'll suggest he stays on in Dartmouth.

'After all,' she's saying, 'you didn't see her in the summer and I know she'd be thrilled if we stayed for a few days. The Mayhews are down at their cottage for half term. They always enjoy a get-together. Maybe that would be more fun than just staying here for the whole week.'

Charlie's heart sinks. 'Maybe it would,' he says.

She looks more cheerful; suddenly her frown clears and she smiles at him, as if this new idea is bringing some kind of relief.

'I suggest we do that,' she says. 'What d'you think? I'll text Mummy and say we can drive down on Thursday after breakfast. Are you OK with that, darling?'

It's unlike Ange to use endearments and he is touched by guilt and frustration. It is crazy to want to see Jemima, to see her smiling at him: what can it possibly achieve except more heartbreak once she is gone? Ange is watching him with an odd expression: anxiety mingled with suspicion.

'Sounds fine,' he says quickly. 'Just fine. Phone your mum and see what she says. Shall we go and have a cup of coffee in Dukes?'

'Yes,' she says, cheerful again now at the prospect of Polzeath – and of Dukes: he knows she likes the deli. 'I need to dash into Boots, though, so you could go ahead and grab a table if you like.'

As he turns away, Charlie sees Jemima crossing the road. He stops quite still to stare at her, his heart jolting with a combination of joy and pain. She's with another woman and they are in animated conversation. Jemima, wearing a long corduroy skirt, leather boots and a short, smart wool jacket, is carrying a clipboard and they pause for a moment on the corner, referring to something on the board, serious now and intent on their discussion.

Charlie watches her, wondering if he can possibly stroll up and greet her; wondering what her reaction might be. Yet something prevents him: this is not quite the Jemima of regatta. This is a woman intent on her work, busy in her own life, amongst her own people and in the place she loves so much. It is inconceivable, at this moment, to imagine her in London, amongst his own set, a part of his life.

He tries to imagine how he might be able to have Jemima

in his life and can only see destruction, and yet she looks so familiar, so dear, so *necessary*. If life with her would be a betrayal of everyone and everything he loves, so does the prospect of life without her seem unbearably bleak.

Jemima parts from the woman and vanishes round the corner just as Ange comes out of Boots behind him.

'Still here?' she asks, surprised.

'I thought I'd wait for you,' he answers, and the look she gives him – friendly, pleased – makes him feel even more desperate.

'Come on then,' she says. 'Let's get some coffee.'

Jemima locks up the holiday flat in Anzac Street, makes a few more notes, and then heads back to the office. As she hesitates on the corner, she sees Charlie and a woman come out of Dukes. Her heart flips over at the sight of him, she gives a tiny gasp, but before she can study Ange too closely – she guesses that it must be Ange – a man approaches, calling out to Charlie, raising a hand in greeting. Jemima recognizes him as the owner of one of the small restaurants in Foss Street.

She watches as they greet each other, the man shaking Charlie's hand and slapping him affectionately on the shoulder, leaning to kiss Ange's cheek. Ange is a pretty woman with a smooth helmet of chestnut-coloured hair; not very tall and rather solid. She laughs, gesticulates, and suddenly turns to Charlie as if to ask him a question, and there is such easy intimacy as he bends towards her that Jemima's throat suddenly constricts with tears.

This is not the Charlie of regatta, the unattached man with no responsibilities – how easy it had been, during that magical week, to imagine him like that – this is Charlie the family man, with an established circle of friends, and a life in London.

She watches them, unconsciously pressing her hand to her heart, wondering how he would react if she were to stride over and greet him. Would his face change? Would he look embarrassed, shifty? She can't bear to take the risk. Yet this must be the pattern if she were to become part of his life. It is quite impossible to imagine Charlie giving up his life in London; abandoning Ange and his children to live here in Dartmouth, or in her tiny cottage. Even the thought of it is risible. So how can she possibly envisage any kind of life with him? Yet how can she manage, either, without that tiny glow of hope that's prevented her heart from breaking each time she thinks of him?

Charlie and Ange and the man are moving away towards the Boat Float and Jemima quickly crosses into Foss Street feeling utterly miserable and almost crashing into Benj as he comes striding towards her.

'Hey,' he says, catching her shoulders, peering down at her. 'Where's the fire? Are you OK?'

'Oh, Benj.' She clutches him, wanting to weep, to be silly. 'I've just seen Charlie and Ange.' She stares up at him. 'It was awful. They've just met a friend and they all look so . . . normal. What shall I do?'

He glances at his watch. 'Have you got another appointment?'

'Not till three o'clock. I was going to take Otto for a walk and grab something to eat on the way.'

He still holds her shoulders and now he gives her a little shake. 'This is going to happen, Mimes. You've got to learn to deal with it.'

She is grateful for his strength and common sense.

'I know,' she says. 'I know that. It was just this first time, I suppose. Seeing him like that, with Ange, and not like we all were during regatta. You know?'

'I know,' he says.

There is such compassion and affection in his face that she wants to clutch him even harder.

'Honestly, Benj,' she says. 'I am just a complete twit. Take no notice of me.'

'Tell you what,' he says. 'I've finished here for today. The car's in Mayor's Avenue car park. Let's go and have some lunch somewhere. Fetch Otto and I'll bring you both back to your car afterwards.'

She nods. 'I'll drop this stuff off.' She hesitates, feeling foolish. 'Sorry, I lost it. Thanks, Benj.'

He watches her go into the office, then glances back down the street lest Charlie and Ange are around. This is what he's been dreading ever since they arrived: that there would be some kind of accidental meeting, a confrontation that might give the game away. He gives a little sigh of relief that no harm has been done, but neither is there any kind of resolution.

He feels very lucky and very happy: he's coming to

terms with the divorce; Laura is loving her job – and Billy; Evie has given him a lifetime's use of the house, and he's enjoying all the different types of work that are coming his way. On top of it there is Jemima: he loves her yet he is not *in* love with her. He is happy with her and there are none of the insecurities, anxieties or responsibilities that are a part of passion and desire and wanting to possess.

He suspects that she feels the same. Of course there are odd moments when a purely physical need tempts him to think that it would be good to take her to bed, but he knows that it would change the whole dynamic between them and he also suspects that a brief moment of such relief would not be worth the loss of this other precious relationship.

Poor old Charlie, he thinks. No relief for him, but no compensation either. He wonders how Charlie will continue to make his visits to Dartmouth with the temptation of Jemima always before him. Because it must remain a temptation all the time she is unattached. There will always be the small voice questioning whether he would be happier, more fulfilled, if he were to give in and take the chance.

Jemima comes out of the office with Otto on his lead, glances anxiously down the street, and then grins at him.

'I'm ready,' she says. 'Let's go.'

He appreciates her courage, her determination not to give in to her emotions, and he folds her arm into his and hugs it to his side.

'Onward,' he says. 'It's a nice warm day. We'll go and sit outside at the Maltsters.'

Instinctively he guides her away from the main thoroughfare, crossing the little square that leads to the car park. They encourage Otto on to the back seat, and then Jemima climbs in and lets out a big breath.

'Phew,' she says, as he gets in beside her. 'I feel safe now. Silly, isn't it? I've got to do better than this, haven't I? I've got to learn to chill when Charlie's down.'

But as he drives along the Embankment, round the Boat Float and up the hill, Ben sees that she is peering out of the car window, her whole attention focused on the possibility of catching a glimpse of Charlie, of seeing him again.

Jason side-steps the couple, a tall dark man and a blonde woman that he thinks he's seen somewhere before, clutching each other in the middle of Foss Street, and makes his way towards the Boat Float to meet Mikey. He's had the call from Bristol about his job and he's heard that, though everyone is sorry for his bereavement, no allowances will be made. It's over: finished.

His heart flutters with an irregular beat, and his stomach churns so that he feels nauseous; his knees tremble. The bank is after him about his overdraft, and the mortgage company is threatening to repossess the flat. Now he has no job and nobody to help him. Life is so bloody unfair. He wants to scream and rage – and then he sees her: Evelyn Drake, across the Boat Float, with a short elderly guy.

Instinctively he steps into the shadow of the hedge,

watching her. He feels so weak, so angry, that he longs to rush round the Boat Float, grab her and fling her down into the water. At the same time he knows that she will save him. She must be made to see that it is time to make amends for betraying his mother, stealing from his father, and refusing to give him, Jason, the chance that would have made his life quite different. It's pay-back time.

He's shaking so much that he has to take the water bottle from his rucksack and have a quick gulp, and then another. Jason heaves a deep breath. That's a little better now. The drink has steadied him, calmed him down a bit. He watches Evelyn Drake and the man, who are now approaching him. He takes one last swig, thrusts the bottle back into his rucksack and steps out into their path. Their surprise makes him want to giggle; he feels very slightly unsteady but less disabled. He can hack this now.

'Hi,' he says to her. 'I was hoping I'd see you.'

'Hello, Jason,' she says, very cool, very collected, but he sees just that tiniest flicker of apprehension at the back of her eyes and he experiences a visceral jab of exultation; of power.

'You've spoken to Mikey,' he says. 'I expect he's told you about our troubles.'

'Yes,' she says.

She answers so calmly that he's taken by surprise. He assumed she'd ask him what troubles. After all, Mikey doesn't yet know Jason's lost his job. He doesn't know about the bank, or the mortgage company. The question was meant to wrong-foot her.

'He told me his mother has died,' she says. 'I am so sorry. Claude, this is Jason Dean.'

Claude says, 'Hello,' but Jason ignores him: Claude is negligible, totally unimportant.

'I don't mean that,' Jason says. 'That's only a part of it. It's time we had a serious chat.'

She raises her eyebrows with that same cool surprise, and suddenly he doesn't want to giggle any more. He wants to grab her by the neck and scream at her. She must see something of his reaction in his face because she takes an involuntary step back from him, just as the old guy steps forward protectively, and at that same moment Jason hears Mikey's voice calling to him.

'Hi, Dad. Where have you been?'

He glances round to see Mikey waving at him, then remembers he was supposed to meet him. This must wait; he can't do this with Mikey listening. Frustration grips him and panic takes possession.

'We'll speak soon,' he says to Evelyn Drake, and he elbows the old guy aside and hurries to meet Mikey.

# CHAPTER TWENTY-TWO

Back at the Merchant's House, leaving Charlie reading the newspaper in the breakfast room, Ange decides to have another little look around. The drawing-room has a much more lived-in look to it. A basket of logs stands beside the fireplace where a heap of ash bears witness to a fire. On a long low table a music system, with a pile of CDs beside it, is plugged in next to the sofa and a small pile of books are toppled together on the rug beside an armchair.

She bends to look at one of the CDs – Pergolesi's *Stabat Mater* sung by Emma Kirkby and James Bowman – and she raises her eyebrows though she doesn't quite know why she's surprised. What music does she expect Ben might enjoy?

She goes out and into the other bedroom and through to the little dressing-room: no sign of the cartoons anywhere. She resolves to speak to Evie, just to let her know that she hasn't forgotten, and wonders if there's anything more she can do to undermine Ben's sense of security. There is much more evidence this time that he is taking possession of the Merchant's House and, not only that, Ben himself seems to be more confident. The fact that he's lost his wife and his home doesn't seem to be having a negative effect on him. He is calm, even happy, and somehow unget-at-able. Her usual campaign – walking in, taking over, assuming ownership – doesn't seem to be achieving the required result. And now Evie and Claude are moving over to the Merchant's House for Christmas, meaning that when Charlie does his usual present exchange visit he will have to sleep up in the attic room.

'So what?' he asked when she challenged him about it. 'It's very nice up there. It's not a problem.'

She pauses outside the bedroom door, listening, then she nips quickly up to the next floor. Ben's bedroom is reasonably tidy, though he hasn't made his bed, and she opens his office door and glances round. There's the usual scatter of cameras and equipment, the laptop on the table – and then she gets a shock.

Hanging on the wall behind the desk are the cartoons. She does a quick count – and yes, there are seven of them. Evie must have given them to Ben and he's hung them up here in his room where nobody else will ever see them.

Ange is seized with fury. This, like nothing else, confirms Ben's growing sense of entitlement and Evie's partisanship. She hurries out and down the stairs, and then stands indecisively before she makes the second descent. Her instinct was to rush down to Charlie, to confront him with this proof of her fears, but suddenly she hesitates. Charlie is still in an odd mood and she is uncharacteristically reluctant to insist that he must take some action. She knows that he will shrug it off; say that it is unimportant. Instead she decides that she will confront Ben; ask him why he has appropriated the cartoons; or maybe she will ask Evie.

She descends the stairs and goes into the kitchen to make some tea.

The shadows are beginning to gather; lights glimmer out on the choppy water where the tide is running out, turning the boats at their moorings as if it would drag them all out towards the darkening sea.

Claude pours them each a drink whilst Evie is lighting the lamps and candles, though she resists drawing the curtains and pulling down the pretty blinds. She hates the dying of the light and is so grateful to have Claude with her, his bulky presence a defence against her fears and loneliness. Jason's confrontation has unnerved her. She's explained the little history to Claude, who is annoyed by Jason's behaviour and clearly anxious for her.

'You could report him for harassment,' he said, as they walked home together. 'The man's seriously unhinged. I think he'd been drinking.'

'I have to think about Mikey,' she said. 'I'm beginning to wonder if he should be on his own with Jason, but he has an aunt and uncle who must have seen that Jason is not well.'

'People like Jason can be very clever,' Claude said. 'Especially with his bereavement to sidetrack everyone. Did you see how his hands were shaking? It's not fair to the boy.'

'Let me think about it,' Evie said. 'I can't risk Jason imagining that Mikey and I are conspiring against him.'

She feels frightened, though; she remembers Jason's confrontational behaviour in the Royal Castle when she had tea with him and Mikey – and now this. But what should she do? With difficulty she pushes it to the back of her mind and changes the subject.

'Am I imagining it,' she asks Claude, 'or is there a slight change in our Ange? Do I detect the least touch of indecisiveness? And why?'

'It will be a miracle,' says Claude, putting Evie's glass on the low table in front of the sofa, 'if Charlie has managed to disguise the fact that he's fallen madly in love. Even Ange might pick up on it, though she probably won't guess what it is that's happened to him.'

'Do you find Charlie changed?' She sits down and curls her feet under her. 'He was very sweet with me, but of course he knows that I know. He's delighted that we're moving over to the house for Christmas.'

She's rather touched by Charlie's relief.

'I think it's a brilliant idea,' he said when she told him. 'And great for old Benj. I think he gets a bit lonely all on his own in the evenings. It's the obvious answer that you should all be together, and especially for Christmas. I only wish I could be here too.'

Then Ange came into the room and he talked about Christmas in London, what the girls were doing, but before the moment passed she asked him if he'd be coming down for his usual pre-Christmas visit.

'I hope you'll manage it,' she said, smiling at him, making certain Ange heard. 'Of course, Claude and I will have moved over by then but you'll be happy up in the attic room, won't you? Thank goodness TDF put in that shower and loo up there. Of course,' she added, glancing at Ange, still smiling, 'if you all decided to come you could use the boathouse. That would be lovely.'

Ange quickly disclaimed: she couldn't possibly get away so close up to Christmas – so much to do, the girls had so many invitations – but Charlie accepted just as quickly on his own behalf.

'Must do the annual Christmas present exchange,' he said cheerfully. 'It's a tradition, isn't it? Just two nights. Of course I shall come.' And he gave Evie a private, grateful glance.

Now, Claude throws the cushion on to the floor and sits down at the other end of the sofa. 'I'm sure he's pleased. I think he worries about you going up and down the steps in the dark. Poor old lad. I wouldn't be in his shoes for anything.'

Evie feels a little clutch of sadness when he says this: she loves Charlie so much and she grieves for him.

'He and Jemima must come to terms with it,' she says,

'one way or another. Lots of people fall in love and never tell. At least Jemima knows. They simply have to settle for those occasional moments of joy, like regatta. He's coming just before Christmas as usual. We must try to see that they have another moment then.'

'And you think that's wise?' Claude asks. 'It won't put too much strain on them? To be together without . . . you know?'

She smiles at him. 'It sounds odd, doesn't it, but if they can then these times might be like oases that they can draw strength from – or, of course, it might simply fade.'

'But you don't believe that?'

Evie shakes her head. 'How can I tell? It's not like some passing physical attraction. It's much more important, much more special. If they can deal with it without letting it destroy them it could be infinitely precious to them.'

'If you say so. But you think Ange might have guessed that something's up?'

'I'm just saying that she's a little less aggressive; a little more careful with Charlie. They came down to make sure Ben doesn't feel too secure, to assert their rights, but without the girls it isn't quite so effective and she's bored already. And, anyway, Ben has a new strength, which Ange can't possibly guess at. I just hope I've done the right thing. It's not real restitution – after all, the house will still go to Charlie and his descendants – but the crucial thing is that Ben will have the right to live there for all his life if he wants to.'

'And meanwhile you can use it just as TDF hoped you would? This won't make you feel differently about that?'

She shakes her head. 'Not at all. Well, it's perfect for me, isn't it? I'm not sure I would want to live in it alone and we can split the bills. It will be rather nice to have someone around during those drear winter months. Oh, I can see that there might be problems but nothing is perfect. What d'you think, Claude? Am I crazy?'

She watches him, anxious for his approval.

'It's certainly unusual,' he says at last, 'and some people would say that it might be fraught with difficulties, but knowing you and Ben as well as I do I think it's a very good arrangement. You'll get on each other's nerves sometimes but there's enough space to get away from each other, and anyway that's no different from ordinary family life. I'm lucky to have an annexe next door to my family but I am very aware that I need to respect their privacy and I have a horror about just walking in, or disturbing them at the wrong moment and seeing their faces drop. So now I tend to wait to be invited, or until they come round to see me, which rather takes the point off being close. In your case I think the good things outweigh the disadvantages. If it works you could rent out the boathouse next year as a winter let.'

'It just feels right,' Evie says, reassured by his reply. 'Christmas will be a good trial run.'

'So when do you plan to move over?'

Evie thinks about it. Now that Claude is with her she is in no particular hurry.

'Let's play it by ear,' she says at last. 'We'll give Ben a week or two to get over Charlie and Ange.'

'And you're not going to tell Charlie about this new plan about leaving the house in trust to Ben?'

'Not yet, though actually I think he'd welcome it. He'd know that the house was coming back to him at some point and I think he's fond enough of Ben to be pleased for him. I can't decide whether Ange will be content with knowing that her children will inherit it or would just make all our lives a misery. What do you think?'

He leans back in the corner of the sofa and gazes out at the reflections that jitter and tremble on the inky water.

'It would get it out into the open,' he says at last. 'It'll be tough for Ben living with her constant warfare and unable to speak out. After all, why not? It's your house. You know the truth about the inheritance so you aren't doing anything unfair. In fact, Charlie and Ange are lucky to be getting it at all. I agree it's a good way to deal with a very unsatisfactory situation but it might be sensible to be upfront about your will for Ben's sake.'

Evie takes a deep breath; in her heart she knows that Claude is right. Ben should be able to live in the house without the pressures that Ange will bring to bear on him. Evie can remember only too well, from her own experience of living in the Merchant's House with TDF, Ange's relentless campaign to make her feel like an outsider.

Now, thanks to TDF, she no longer feels like an outsider; legally the house is hers and she can go part-way in making the restitution TDF wanted without causing a family rift. Yet why should Ben have to put up with this ongoing campaign of Ange's if it isn't necessary?

'I'll think about it,' she promises. 'I think you're right and it would be better to have it out in the open. I just need the right moment to tell them.'

'Good,' Claude says. 'I'll drink to that and to Christmas in the Merchant's House,' and he raises his glass to her.


Mikey watches his father across the supper table. It's fish and chips again.

'Are you OK, Dad?' he asks.

Ever since Mikey saw him with Evie, Dad's been behaving very strangely. He refused to let Mikey go to say hello to Evie, dragged him into a little café for something to eat, and then they went back to the flat where Dad flung himself down on the sofa and dropped into a heavy sleep as suddenly as if he were falling off a cliff.

Mikey sat and watched him, feeling miserable and frightened. He missed his mum and wished he had someone to talk to; to share the responsibility of his father. He thought about Aunt Liz. Mum was her sister so she's gutted, too, and it seems unfair to worry her about Dad so Mikey always pretends that things are fine when he's with Aunt Liz, and somehow Dad's always on his best behaviour when she's around. Even so, he thought he might say something; tell her about these very odd moods. After all, Mum must have told her a bit about Dad's depression and the tablets he has to take. It's not a secret.

Mikey slipped out into the kitchen, keeping one eye on his father, and dug his mobile phone out of his pocket. Still watching, he sent a text to Aunt Liz.

*Worried about Dad. Think he's ill.*

He's still waiting for a reply though he's switched his mobile to silent in case Dad asks who the message is from or asks to see it. Ever since he came back from getting the fish and chips he's been a bit hyper and his breath smells of something strong. Mikey wonders if he's been into the pub for a drink.

'I'm fine,' he says now, staring at Mikey with oddly bright eyes, as if he's challenging him; daring him to question the fact. 'Why shouldn't I be?'

Mikey suddenly feels a little shot of anger thrill through him: it's not fair that he has to be so careful all the time in case Dad is upset. Why should he be the one always hiding his own sadness and pain?

'It's just you looked a bit odd on the Boat Float with Evie and that man,' he says. 'Right at the end I thought you were going to hit her.'

The oddest expression creeps over his father's face: a look compounded of amusement, complacency and hatred.

'So what?' he asks. 'She deserves it. Evelyn Drake ruined my mother's life and mine. Time she paid for it.'

Mikey's stomach curdles with fear; the fish and chips sit like a stone in his gut. Even so, he won't back down or try to soothe his father into a calmer state of mind. He's tired of doing that; he's had enough.

'I like her,' he says.

His father sneers at him. 'So did your grandfather. That was the trouble. Your grandfather liked her way too much. And she liked him.'

Mikey puts down his knife and fork and folds his hands tightly together under the table as if he is giving himself courage: bracing himself. He understands what Dad is saying – he's not a child, not a little boy – but even so, the words are a shock. It's as if Dad isn't really seeing him any more as Mikey but as another adult and he needs to prepare himself for what else he might tell him.

'It broke my mother's heart,' Dad is saying, 'but he didn't care and neither did she. He helped her with her research, she took everything he had to give and then she walked away.'

He begins to chuckle – a horrid sound that grates along Mikey's nerves – and his eyes look elsewhere as if he is seeing visions unknown to Mikey.

'This afternoon I would have liked to break her neck and chuck her in the water,' he says almost conversationally, 'but I'm going to give her the chance to make up for it.'

'How do you mean?' Mikey manages to keep his voice quiet and calm, even interested.

Dad glances at him as if he's surprised he needs to ask.

'Money, of course. She owes me. She broke my mother's heart, fleeced my father and cheated me out of a first-class education. Well, it's my turn now.'

His face changes again; he looks surly and tired and bleak. Mikey recognizes the look.

He draws a deep breath so that his voice will be steady and as he does so he feels his mobile vibrate in his pocket. He shoves his hand in quickly as if to muzzle it.

'Have you taken your tablets, Dad?' he asks gently but cheerfully, too, just like there's nothing wrong. 'How about some coffee?'

His father nods. He frowns as if he's puzzled, as if something is slipping away from him and he's trying to remember what it is. Mikey gets up, one hand still in his pocket, to find the happy pills. In the kitchen he quickly checks the little screen: a text from Aunt Liz. He pours a glass of water and carries it and the tablets in to his father, who swallows them back.

'Go and relax,' Mikey suggests. 'I'll clear up and make some coffee. There might be something on the telly.'

Still frowning, his father heaves himself off the chair, staggers to the sofa and slumps down. He looks exhausted. Mikey watches him for a moment and then goes back into the kitchen, fills the kettle and switches it on. Out of sight he scrolls down and finds the message.

*Can you phone me?*

Mikey glances through the half-open door. Dad is already falling asleep. He decides to take a chance and he sends back a text.

*Give me 10 minutes.*

He clears the table, piles the plates into the dishwasher,

makes the coffee. By the time he puts the mug on the little table beside the sofa his father is deeply asleep. Mikey stands looking down at him, his hand still holding his mobile, then he slips out and runs down the stairs.

Jason opens his eyes slowly. A strange spoked creature is crawling down the wall towards him and he stifles a scream of terror. Another glance shows him that this is simply a spider, its shadow magnified by the angle of the light on the table beside him, and he leans back, gasping with relief and feeling ashamed. It's that shot of Glenfiddich that's the cause of it. Perhaps it was two shots, but oh, the smooth, cool joy of the way it slid down his throat. He'd needed it after that scene with bloody Evelyn Drake, standing there mocking him, still making a fool out of him. He deserved a little treat and he simply wasn't able to resist as he stood there at the bar. Just the one wouldn't hurt while he was waiting for the fish and chips.

'No drink, Jay-bird,' Helena would say. 'Can't you see it's like poison to you? You don't need it.'

He leans forward, resting his aching head on his clammy hands and groans with the pain of his despair and longing for her. His troubles stand piled like an impenetrable brick wall, waiting to be confronted, but he can't face them. Jason looks at his watch: nearly midnight. Mikey must be in bed. He frowns, thinking about Mikey, trying to remember the conversation he had with him about Evelyn Drake but he can't recall it now. He's too tired and it's too late. Tomorrow will do: tomorrow he will deal with it all.

# CHAPTER TWENTY-THREE

Charlie doesn't particularly want to be in Alf's this morning with Ange. He's not sure that Alf's is really Ange's kind of place but she's suggested that they go for a coffee and now here they are, sitting under the awning, and every minute he's wondering whether Jemima will come strolling in with Otto.

He can't really concentrate on what Ange is saying and he's drinking his coffee quite quickly so that they can move on. Meanwhile he's trying to decide what would be the best *modus operandi* if Jemima were to arrive: to casually introduce her as a friend – or as Ben's friend? And how would Jemima react to a direct confrontation? He longs to see her – but not publicly like this with Ange beside him.

Even as he thinks about their first meeting, that expression on her face as she walked towards him through the regatta crowds, the impossible happens. Holding a woman's hand Maisie appears, coming in from the street eagerly as if she is looking for someone, and when she sees him her face lights up with pleasure and surprise.

'Hello!' she cries, and as she comes closer to him she beams at him. 'Charlie,' she says with enormous satisfaction. 'It's Charlie, Mummy.'

The woman is staring at him, frowning in confusion, and he can feel Ange beside him, stiff with suspicion. He begins to get to his feet, wondering what the hell he should do, when Maisie speaks again.

'You bought me an ice cream and we went to the dog show,' she reminds him. 'It wasn't Ben, it was you. You and Jemima had coffee and then we went to the dog show. I told you that it wasn't Ben, Mummy.'

The woman is looking at him with a mixture of apology and amazement.

'I really thought you were Ben,' she says. 'It's extraordinary.'

'Yes,' he says, trying to gloss over it, aware of Ange's growing annoyance. 'It wouldn't be the first time.'

'We liked the little fluffy ones, didn't we?' Maisie is saying. 'And Jemima liked the dog like Otto best.'

He stares down into the glowing little face. He could deny it – clearly Maisie's mother doesn't know whether it was he or Benj – but somehow he cannot lie to this child who looks so pleased to see him; who, somehow, has remembered him. It would be the denial of everything that happened to him during that regatta week.

'Yes,' he says. 'Yes, that's right.' He smiles at the

woman. 'I'm Charlie Fortescue, Ben's cousin, and this is my wife, Ange.'

'Hello,' she says. She smiles at Ange, who barely acknowledges her. 'I'm Miranda Weston and this is Maisie. She had such a lovely time with you and Jemima that morning.'

Even as she speaks he sees in her eyes a tiny flash of realization at what she's said and she glances quickly at Ange with a half-apologetic, half-curious smile. He knows she's wondering why Ange is so unresponsive and he stands awkwardly, undecided as to whether he should suggest that she and Maisie should join them.

The decision is made by Maisie who scrambles into the chair opposite so that Miranda hesitates, shrugs, and goes off to order drinks.

Charlie sits down; his legs feel shaky and he simply doesn't know what to do next.

Ange's voice is low, cool, and brittle as glass: 'Who is Jemima?'

Charlie tries to frame words that will not belittle Jemima whilst satisfying Ange. He feels miserable, uncomfortable and very nervous. Maisie smiles at him confidently, as if he is an old friend, and suddenly he decides to tell the truth, though maybe not all of it.

'I met Maisie and Jemima on the Embankment when we were down for regatta,' he says. 'Jemima thought I was Benj so we started on quite the wrong foot. It was funny, really, but she was so embarrassed that we bought Maisie an ice cream and watched the dog show.'

Ange is watching him with a kind of disbelieving contempt. When he's finished she simply repeats her question. 'Who is Jemima?' It's clear that all her instincts are working double time and Charlie begins to feel desperate.

'She's one of Benj's friends,' he says, almost irritably, as if he's assumed she knows that. 'It was Jemima who got him work with her holiday letting company. I told you, didn't I?'

He still feels as if he is denying Jemima, betraying her, and he cannot quite look Ange in the eye. Before he can think of anything else to reassure her, Maisie's voice chimes between them.

'Here she is. Here's Jemima,' and he swivels round in his chair to see Jemima strolling in from the pavement with Otto on his lead, and just behind them is Ben. Charlie wants to shout, to warn them, but all he can see is Jemima, who comes confidently in, smiling at him, at Maisie.

'Hi, Maisie,' she says. 'Well, this is fun. Hello, Charlie. And you must be Ange. Benj has told me so much about you,' and she stretches a hand across the table so that Ange can do nothing but take it.

Behind her Benj gives him a swift wink, slips his arm around Jemima's shoulders.

'Latte, Mimes?' he asks. 'Cappuccino?'

She smiles up at him. 'Cappuccino. Lots of chocolate on the top.'

He laughs. 'Would I forget the chocolate?'

For a brief moment, Charlie is taken in; they look so easy together. Then Miranda returns and there is a fuss about getting two more chairs and very slowly he relaxes just a little, his heartbeat slows, and he gives himself up to the pleasure of being with Jemima again, to watch the way she smiles and glows as she talks. He can tell that she's enjoying the situation, very slightly playing up to Benj, including Ange in the conversation as if she's delighted to meet her. Part of him wants to roar with laughter, part of him aches with the pain of it. When Miranda asks Ange a question, and she turns slightly to answer her, Jemima gives him one quick glance full of love, amusement, and that familiar deep-down knowing so that he is flooded with relief, with joy, and gratitude.

Ben watches the scene with a mix of horror and amusement. Jemima's text, that she planned to meet Miranda and Maisie in Alf's and did he want to join them, arrived moments after Charlie and Ange had left to go to Alf's for coffee.

He texted back and she came hurrying round from the office.

'Text her and change the plan,' he said anxiously. 'Oh my God, this is what I've been dreading,' but Jemima shook her head.

'Perhaps this is right,' she said quite calmly. 'It's going to happen sometime, Benj, isn't it? I'm not going into hiding each time Ange turns up. Why should I? Look, I don't intend to break up Charlie's marriage – I've made that decision – but I want to try to keep us all together. It might be too much to ask but I want to try. Of course, Miranda asked me to ask you along because she fancies you. She insisted on Alf's because she thought there was a chance she'd see you if I refused. Well, OK. Let's all go. Meet up in a big old muddly way. And, just for the purposes of verisimilitude, you and I can pretend that we're . . . well . . .'

She had the grace to look a little embarrassed and he helped her out.

'Slightly more than just good friends?'

'Something like that. It'll let Charlie off the hook if things are going wrong and it'll get Miranda off your back.'

He laughed at her. 'You're enjoying this, aren't you?'

'I want to see him, Benj. I just want to be with him for a few minutes and I know that I can do it if you'll go along with it. After all, Charlie won't be deceived and it will mean that Ange will just see me as a family friend. We can't afford for her to become suspicious.'

'OK,' he said, but he sent one more text as they set out together.

And now here he is, sitting beside Jemima, behaving in a very slightly lover-like way, which is clearly confusing Ange and irritating Miranda. Maisie is playing up to the crowd.

'I told you it wasn't Ben, Mummy,' she says to Miranda. 'I *told* you but you wouldn't believe me.'

And Jemima laughs, leaning a little into Ben, who has

his arm along the back of her chair, and says: 'Poor Charlie. We absolutely fell on him, demanding coffee and ice cream and dragging him to the dog show, and he was much too polite to protest.'

Ange's words drip like tiny splinters of ice on to Jemima's warmth. 'I wouldn't say they're that much alike. It seems quite odd to me. Why didn't you tell them, darling?' she adds, looking at Charlie, frowning at the foolishness of the story.

'Oh, I nearly did the same just now,' says Miranda, trying to draw the attention back to her, smiling at Ben. 'I thought he was Ben, too. You'll have to watch it, you know.'

She's trying to create a little something between them and he smiles at her simply out of gratitude that she's helping to allow this very sticky moment to pass as smoothly as possible. Then Charlie's eyes widen with surprise and Ben turns to see Claude and Evie standing behind them.

Jemima gives a little gasp. Ben grins down at her and leans to whisper in her ear.

'Reinforcements,' he murmurs.

Miranda watches with amazement as more of the family arrive and she begins to feel rather displaced. Maisie has suddenly disappeared under the table with Otto, overwhelmed by so many adults, and with the arrival of these two, Evie and Claude, whoever they are, Miranda is beginning to feel like a gatecrasher at a private party. Her plan to see Ben again isn't working out, and she doesn't like the way Mimes seems to have appropriated him. They weren't like this before, and Miranda feels cross with her old friend. She's expected a bit of loyalty here, especially after she told Mimes that she thought Ben was hot. In fact it's a bit embarrassing and she hopes that nothing has been said; that Ben hasn't guessed that she fancies him. It's really too bad that whenever she really likes someone everything seems to go wrong for her. Sitting here, feeling disconsolate, she suddenly sees all the attraction of emigrating to Australia: the excitement of a completely different life, new friends and the companionship of her own family all around her. It would be good to have the boys at hand when things went wrong; good for Maisie to grow up with her cousins and aunts and uncles. The idea of so much support fills Miranda with an extraordinary sense of relief. She looks around for Maisie but she's still under the table with Otto. In some way Miranda feels comforted: they will go to Australia for Christmas and maybe make plans for the future.

Ange feels angry, outnumbered, and her deepest instincts warn her that she is somehow being conned. When Evie and Claude arrive she feels her temper rising and, when Charlie gets to his feet to offer Evie his chair, she is ready for a fight.

'Extraordinary, isn't it?' she says coolly to Evie. 'Everyone turning up like this.'

'Oh, I don't know.' Evie looks around at the rather

noisy group. 'Alf's is like this, you know. We often all meet up quite by accident here. Great fun, don't you think?'

Ange has seen Evie kiss Jemima, smile at Maisie, and her instincts are even more confused. She decides to strike.

'I see you found the cartoons,' she said quietly. 'Did you know that Ben has them hanging in his studio? Not quite the thing, is it?'

'Isn't it?' counters Evie, frowning a little as if she is considering the idea. 'After all, they are the work of his great-great-grandfather. You might say that technically they belong to him. And I didn't "find" the cartoons, Ange. I told you that I had them in my study but that two of them were unframed.'

'Even so,' argues Ange, under cover of the conversation going on amongst the others, 'I don't think Ben should have them. I'll be honest with you, Evie. Even if the cartoons were done by his great-great-grandfather I still think they should hang in the main rooms. They belong to the family. To Charlie as well as Ben.'

'Actually,' answers Evie judicially, 'there's much truth in that statement. Though I wasn't going to mention it to you.'

Ange experiences a surge of triumph. At last Evie is admitting the truth.

'I think it would be unwise to hide anything,' she says. 'It would be a mistake for Ben to get the wrong idea.'

'Well, if you say so.' Evie looks regretful. 'But I'd like

you to keep this to yourself, Ange. TDF found some papers that imply that Ben's great-great-grandfather was also Charlie's great-great-grandfather. He was having an affair with his sister-in-law. That means that Charles and George were brothers, not cousins, and, George being the elder, under the law of entail the whole lot should have come down on his side. Charles was, in fact, illegitimate. The papers are quite clear. TDF was horrified but decided to say nothing at the time, though he hoped some kind of restitution might be made.'

Ange is seized with alarm and incredulity. Evie would hardly make up such things but how can they possibly be true? 'What nonsense,' she says angrily. 'What are these papers?'

'They were hidden in the back of the cartoons. I've still got them, of course, if you'd like to see them. I have no idea what could be made out of them. Worth a court case, d'you think? TDF decided – understandably since Charlie is his son and heir – to let sleeping dogs lie. I'm not sure Ben would agree with him. The decision is mine.'

Ange stares at Evie. Never has she disliked anyone so much.

'I don't believe you,' she says without conviction.

Evie laughs. 'Yes, you do. I can show you the papers but I rather hoped I wouldn't have to. I didn't want Charlie to know.'

'No,' says Ange quickly. 'No, he mustn't know.' She has a horrid vision of Charlie wanting to examine these papers, to take them seriously, and somehow make amends to Ben. 'Though,' she adds, 'I imagine they'd probably amount to nothing.'

'TDF was convinced they were truthful accounts,' says Evie quietly. 'I've decided not to tell Ben but it's why I am very happy to let him use the house, though it's nothing in terms of what he would have had if his great-grandfather had inherited.'

Ange is speechless. She wants to challenge Evie, to demand to see the evidence, but supposing it is all true? She feels frustrated, frightened. She stares at Charlie, who is talking to Miranda, at Ben and Jemima sitting side by side, and more and more she feels that she is the spectator at some play being staged for her benefit though she can't put her finger on the cause of her uneasiness.

'It's up to you, Ange,' Evie is murmuring. 'Any more silly fuss about Ben or the cartoons and I might show Charlie the papers. I promise you they make interesting reading and you're very hot on the laws of inheritance, aren't you, Ange?'

Ange pushes back her chair. 'I've got shopping to do,' she says. 'I'll see you later.'

She shakes her head at Charlie as if to say, 'Stay where you are. Leave me alone,' and stomps out into the sunshine.

Claude sees her go with relief. He's watched the whole thing and he knows, he just knows, that Evie is telling Ange about the papers. He can barely believe it. It's rather like the way Evie burst out with all her private feelings to Jemima at that very first meeting.

Never, he tells himself irritably, never will he understand women. All the conversations about secrecy and silence, the anxiety about letting Charlie or Ben know, and now here she is telling it all to Ange in the middle of bloody Alf's.

He watches anxiously, catching a few words here and there, seeing Ange's expressions of anger, disbelief, fear, and Evie's quiet relentlessness, and he feels quite weak with the enormity of it all.

Surely, he argues with himself, it cannot be right to hand Ange such weapons? She could destroy them all.

But at the same time, says a small voice, she would destroy herself.

Ange is pushing back her chair, getting up, giving a brief shake of the head to Charlie, and then she disappears. Evie glances up, catches Claude's eye and gives him a smile of pure mischief, and he stares back, trying to control his irritation.

Jemima watches Ange go and is immediately flooded with relief. Though it might appear that she is relaxed, enjoying herself, her gut is knotted with tension. She moves a little way away from Ben and bends down to talk to Maisie, who is under the table with Otto. She can't bring herself to look at Charlie; not quite yet. She waits for the moment, treasuring it, and then sits up straight again. He turns to look at her and she meets his eyes and connects with him again – and everything is good, so good – and suddenly she bursts out laughing as all the

stress and anxiety is finally released. Benj and Charlie
join in, and then Evie and finally Claude, until they are
all in fits of silly laughter, and the sight of Miranda's puzzled, almost indignant face sets Jemima off again until
she is nearly crying.

Evie sees Claude's irritation, she sees Jemima and Charlie reconnect, and she sees the expression of utter relief
on Ben's face. She simply can't stop laughing: the joy of
telling Ange has been like a shot of adrenalin. Her
instincts tell her that Ange will never spill the beans, she
has too much to lose – and anyway, the moment was just
so perfect. The sense of power was extraordinary and
dear old Claude's face an absolute picture: outrage, baf-
flement, utter disapproval. At the mere thought of it she
bursts out laughing again and Jemima joins in with her.
For a moment they are totally connected: two women
who have relied on their wits and their instincts to protect
people they love.

For a moment Evie forgets Miranda and the child
under the table. She looks at these four beloved people,
remembers how they gathered on the terrace in the garden at regatta, and raises her coffee cup to them with a
smile as if she is toasting them – and they lift their cups in
response.

# CHAPTER TWENTY-FOUR

Jason is sleeping late. Mikey creeps in several times to look at him but doesn't want to wake him. He stands at the door uncertainly, fingering the mobile phone in his pocket, thinking about what Aunt Liz has said.

'I'll come down,' she said at once. 'I'll get up early and drive down. Is it his depression getting worse, do you think, Mikey?'

'I don't know,' he answered miserably. 'I think he's drinking a bit. Mum always said he shouldn't because it was like poison for him, but I'm afraid of asking him.'

'I had no idea about this,' she said. 'Look, Mikey, I'll come down this evening,' but he'd been anxious about that.

'It's best to let him sleep now,' he told her. 'He's taken his medication and now he'll just crash. But why shall I say you're coming down, Aunt Liz? He'll think it's a bit odd, won't he? I don't want to say that I phoned you.'

'No, no, don't do that. Tell him I've got to get the flat

with a letting agent and I want to ask around locally to see who might be the best. If you're absolutely sure you're OK I'll get away early and be with you before lunch and I'll text when I leave so you'll have some idea. Jason can move into the other bed in your room and I'll stay overnight and then we'll all drive back together. I'll bring sheets and some food. Don't worry, Mikey, we'll get it sorted. You can stay the extra night here instead of there.'

Part of him is so relieved he feels quite weak but part of him is bracing up ready to tell Dad what's happening. Will he fuss about going back with Aunt Liz? He might not want to because it means losing two days of their holiday. Mikey feels sad about that but not sad enough to stay on with Dad on his own. He thinks anxiously about what might happen in Bristol between getting home and going back to school.

He can't get out of his head what Dad said about Evelyn Drake – or how he looked when he said he wanted to break her neck. It's always frightened him when Dad goes off on one but this was worse: not just the usual rage and anger and shouting but a kind of creepy madness.

He wishes Mum was here to take control. Before, it was like she and he were the adults and Dad was their child. Even when he was quite small she persuaded him to play this game, like they were taking care of Dad together.

'He's very sensitive,' she'd say. 'He feels things more than other people. We have to look after him, don't we?'

Sometimes Mikey didn't want to play the game, like when he had to go with Dad to post a letter or buy the newspaper.

'Take Mikey with you,' Mum would say, and Dad would look sullen, cross, as if he were being thwarted in some way. 'Go on, Mikey,' she'd tell him, nice and bright and jolly, as if she couldn't see Dad's expression. 'Go with Dad.'

She'd nod at him, make the little face that said: *Look after him*, and he'd take Dad's hand, smiling up at him as if it were fun, though fear fluttered in his insides. He had no idea why he was needed, back then, to shadow his father but now he's beginning to guess.

Mikey peers in again through the half-open bedroom door and sees that Jason is awake, lying flat on his back, staring at the ceiling: his face is closed and grim, and Mikey's heart sinks. He creeps away, makes some coffee, and carries it upstairs.

'I've made you some coffee, Dad,' he says. He keeps his voice cheerful, like there's nothing wrong, and puts the mug beside the bed on the little table. 'Aunt Liz phoned. She's coming down later today.'

Jason frowns as if he can't quite understand what Mikey is saying, and turns his head slowly on the pillow rather as if the movement hurts him. His pale eyes are cold, expressionless; scary.

'What d'you mean?'

Mikey stays by the door; he wishes that Aunt Liz were here already.

'It's something to do with letting the flat. She needs to come down and see someone about it. That's what she said.'

He decides not to mention the bit about them all going back together. Aunt Liz can deal with that. His father sits up slowly, still frowning, and picks up the mug.

'Do you want some toast?' Mikey asks. 'Or cornflakes?'

Jason shakes his head and Mikey slips away, glancing at his watch. With any luck Aunt Liz will be here soon.

By the time she arrives Jason is showered and dressed and ready for action. He's determined to be on good form for Liz but he still feels shaky and he has to be careful. She doesn't need to know, for instance, that he's lost his job: none of her business. It's a damned nuisance that she's here but, after all, it is her flat. Something is buzzing about at the back of his mind, something he needs to do, and he tries to remember what it is. This medication is doing his head in, that's the real trouble, and he simply has to stay in control. The bottles are hidden away in his rucksack but it's something else that's nagging away at him. Suddenly he remembers: Evelyn Drake, and his plan to get Mikey acquainted with her; to soften her up. He recalls meeting her by the Boat Float; he'd been angry about losing his job and probably said a few things he might regret. He curses inwardly: and now there's this plan to go back with Liz tomorrow which Mikey seems quite keen to do. Jason feels that things are slipping out of his control. The familiar sensations of panic and disablement edge in and he begins to need a bit of a boost: a little sip from his water bottle.

Liz is watching him, assessing him, and he smiles at her; not too cheerful, not too bright. He's a grieving widower and he's struggling a bit; that's perfectly reasonable. Helena told Liz about the depression way back when he was having a few difficulties holding down a job and she's always sympathetic, always concerned. Especially now, with Helena gone . . . Helena gone. Momentarily he's overwhelmed with terrible grief, just can't control it, and Liz sees his expression and touches his arm.

'It's hell, isn't it, Jay?' she says – and just for a minute it might be Helena standing there and he longs for Liz to put her arms round him as Helena would have done, to hold him, and stroke his hair and say, 'It'll be OK, Jay-bird.'

Instead she grips his arm for a minute, smiles at Mikey and says, 'Let's have tea. I've brought some cake with me.'

Jason pulls himself together, nods, but he has an idea. It's important that he doesn't let the Evelyn Drake plan slip. It's crucial.

'By the way,' he says to Mikey, very calm, very easy, 'you must be sure to pop round and say goodbye to Evie before we go. I told her that we'd be seeing her again so it would be the polite thing to do.'

Mikey looks surprised, gives a quick glance at his aunt Liz, who shrugs, slightly puzzled but unconcerned, as if it's none of her business.

'OK,' he says, rather warily. 'Like when?'

'After tea? You could phone her.'

Jason can only just control the panic, the need to make sure Mikey does what he's told. Evelyn Drake must be kept on side.

'OK,' Mikey says. 'I'll phone her after tea.'

Jason takes a deep breath, smiles at him. 'Good,' he says. 'Good boy. Need the loo, shan't be a sec.'

He slips into the bedroom, hauls the rucksack out of the wardrobe and takes a deep long swig from the water bottle. He dashes into the bathroom, flushes the lavatory, comes out again and draws another deep breath before he goes downstairs.

# CHAPTER TWENTY-FIVE

Ange turns up at the boathouse just before supper when Ben, Charlie and Claude are having a farewell drink in the pub.

'I wanted to be clear about things,' she says, coming in and putting her bag down on the table. 'I've been thinking about what you said, Evie. I shan't tell Charlie but I'd like to see those papers.'

Evie isn't really surprised. She guesses that Ange would be reluctant to give up her plan of campaign simply on Evie's word.

'Why not?' she answers calmly. 'Wait here and I'll get them.'

She goes to her study, takes the papers from the drawer in her desk and returns to the big room. Ange is still standing by the table and Evie doesn't ask her to sit or offer her coffee: this is not a social occasion. Evie takes the papers from the envelope and lays them carefully on the table.

'They're rather fragile,' she says. 'Please be careful with them. They are in the right chronological order.'

She watches as Ange searches for some spectacles in her bag, puts them on, picks up the papers rather gingerly and begins to read them. Almost immediately her expression changes from the familiar slightly disparaging look to one of intense concentration. She reads each page several times, completely absorbed, and Evie wonders what she might be thinking.

When she's finished Ange stands still for a moment before placing the papers on the table. Then she takes a deep breath and Evie observes that she is marshalling her resources; reassessing her position.

'Yes, I see,' she says, very cool, very possessed, taking off the spectacles and replacing them in her handbag. 'It's all rather hearsay, though, isn't it? It could never be proved that Charles was his son, not at this late date.'

'I suppose that Ben might want to give it a try, though,' answers Evie. 'Or Laura might?'

'Laura?' Ange stares at her, startled out of her careful composure.

Evie raises her eyebrows. 'Why not? She has just as much a claim and she might consider it well worth a legal battle. But it's not only about who wins or who loses so much as all the mess and muddle it involves. So destructive.'

'Are you threatening me, Evie?'

She laughs then, looking at Ange across the big table. 'I suppose I am. And this is the deal: that you stop treating the Merchant's House as yours and Charlie's. TDF left the house to me because he wanted me to be able to feel that it's my home, not because he couldn't decide whether to leave it to Ben as some kind of restitution, though he did feel guilty about that.'

'I still don't see why he should. He grafted all his life and so has Charlie. There probably wouldn't be much left of the estate if it had come down on Ben's side of the family. It would be utterly unfair to simply take it all away from Charlie and pass it over to Ben.'

'TDF agreed with that,' says Evie calmly. 'And so do I. But there is still a moral dimension. You are the one who preaches the inalienable rights of the law of inheritance, Ange. After all, if it is Ben's by rights then it doesn't matter what his ancestors might have done with it. So my decision is that Ben will be allowed the use of the Merchant's House during his lifetime, after which it returns to Charlie's estate.'

The expression on Ange's face morphs from wariness to relief.

'You mean it comes back to us – to Charlie – when Ben dies?'

Evie nods. 'Provided that during that time there will be no fuss and nonsense about it. My lawyer has those instructions. Your girls will get it all, Ange, and Laura will get nothing.'

'And you won't tell Charlie?'

'Not unless you persist with this tiresome campaign to make me and Ben feel like outsiders. You started this,

Ange, with your insistence on seeing the cartoons restored. The whole thing might have stayed a secret if you hadn't interfered. Well, now I've taken the necessary legal steps.'

Ange stares at her, unable to conceal her dislike. 'You could change your will at any time.'

Evie sighs, smiles. 'I could, couldn't I? But why should I? Ben will have his heart's desire and Charlie will inherit in the end. I love Charlie, Ange. I don't want him not only to lose his inheritance but also to find out that he's not quite who he thought he was. Yes, don't forget that aspect of it. I hope that Charlie will continue to visit us regularly and keep his connection at the Merchant's House and here in Dartmouth.'

It is clear to Evie that Ange is thinking it through, that her mind is doubling and redoubling to and fro, seeking for traps and pitfalls.

'Charlie's been behaving a little oddly,' she says, at last, reluctantly as though she hates to confide such an idea. 'Ever since he came back from regatta. Can you imagine why that might be?'

She's locked on to Jemima, Evie thinks, but she's not really sure. Ben's thrown her off the scent but her instincts are telling her that there's danger. I must completely scotch this once and for all.

'Well, of course I can,' Evie says, almost crossly. 'Can you really not see how angry it makes Charlie to see you treating Ben as if he's some sort of layabout squatter? Have you no idea how close those two are? OK, Charlie doesn't have a clue about the threat to his inheritance but he knows that he has a very great deal and Ben has very little. His marriage has broken up, his wife has been deceiving him, his home is being sold. Can't you see how happy it makes Charlie to think that Ben has a kind of sanctuary in the place he loves best? But because of your mean-mindedness it's constantly at risk. Can you really not see that, Ange? They had such a happy time once you'd gone off to Polzeath, just like the old days. Of course Charlie has been preoccupied. I expect that he's trying not to be disappointed in your grasping behaviour. Trying to decide how he'll cope if you actually succeed in driving Ben out. He loves Ben. Don't ever forget that. He's delighted that Ben is there and can relax while all this shit is going on in his life. But you won't let him be delighted, will you, Ange? So Charlie is divided in his loyalty between you and Ben. I'd be careful, if I were you.'

Ange flushes that unbecoming scarlet, as if she's been plunged in boiling water, and then, oddly, seems to relax a little; to look relieved, even. She doesn't notice that Evie is trembling from head to foot with the sheer adrenalin rush of speaking out at last; all her thoughts are inward.

'So Ben knows about your will?' Ange asks. 'Nobody else?'

'Ben knows, though I've pledged him to secrecy, and Claude knows everything. He's seen the papers.'

'*Claude?*'

328

Once again the ugly flush washes over her skin and Evie raises her eyebrows.

'Of course. Claude was TDF's oldest friend and now he's mine. He loves Charlie and Ben, and I needed someone I could trust. And, if I were you, I'd want to make certain that Charlie knows about my will, too, and knows that you are delighted with it. Then he can come down and stay with Ben, knowing that his cousin is secure but that the Merchant's House will come back to him eventually, and then I think you'll find he'll relax and be his old self.'

'But how can I tell him? He'll wonder how I know. After all, in the usual circumstances you'd be unlikely to confide in me, wouldn't you?'

Evie smiles at this thrust. 'That's true. I could tell him. I'd rather he knew and I think it would be a relief to Ben. But when?'

'Did I tell you that we're going down to Polzeath tomorrow morning?'

'Yes, I knew that. Well, let him come over to say good bye on his own and I'll tell him. You'll have to look surprised when he tells you. And pleased.'

Ange picks up her bag. 'I expect I'll manage.' She hesitates. 'I suppose I should thank you.'

'For what?'

'For leaving the Merchant's House to Charlie. You needn't have done that. You could have left it to Ben.'

'This seems the best solution. It gives Ben security for his lifetime and goes back to Charlie for his children. I would hate either of them to know about the papers.

I think it would be very destructive and achieve nothing. This way everybody wins and I can demonstrate my affection to them both. I'm sorry you had to know about the papers. It's hard keeping a secret from a husband.'

'I expect I'll manage,' Ange says again. 'I might not see you before we go so I'll say goodbye.'

'Shall we see you at Christmas?'

Ange shakes her head. 'It's just too busy around then for me and, anyway, it will be a bit of a squash if you and Claude are moving over.'

'You could use the boathouse.'

'No. Thanks, anyway. After all, Charlie always does the present drop on his own and it'll be nice for him to spend a few days with you all together.'

Evie is hardly able to conceal her surprise at this unexpected gesture of generosity and Ange smiles a rather wry and bitter smile.

'Well,' she says drily, 'I suppose I've got to start somewhere, haven't I? Goodbye, Evie. I'll send Charlie over as soon as he gets back from the pub.'

She goes out and Evie puts the papers away carefully and then sits down to wait for Charlie.

# CHAPTER TWENTY-SIX

Next morning, when Ben comes downstairs, his heart is full of grateful peace; how he loves this place. It's doubly wonderful now that Charlie knows about Evie's will.

'It's the perfect solution, Benj,' he said, as they sat in the drawing-room after supper whilst Ange was packing. It was a chill evening and Ben had lit the fire. 'So clever of Evie to think of it. We're all winners.'

'Even Ange?' Ben asked sceptically.

Charlie frowned; he looked puzzled. 'She's pleased,' he said. 'No, honestly. She can see that it's right for everyone. I must admit I was rather taken aback by her enthusiasm. I was so pleased that I kissed her.'

Ben laughed. 'Don't make it sound so unusual.'

'No, I didn't mean that. It was just so wonderful to be singing from the same hymn sheet for a change. I hate discord, Benj.'

'Me, too,' he said. He didn't add that it was one of the

bonuses of not being married any more. 'Pity she didn't suggest you could stay on, like at regatta.'

Charlie shrugged. 'I wish. It's been a bit of a week, hasn't it, but it's worked out surprisingly well in the end. That scene in Alf's aged me by about ten years. First Maisie walking in, then Jemima. I wasn't designed to live a double life.'

'We had it under control,' Ben said. 'Me and Mimes. It's a pity we couldn't all get together this time.'

'It's hell not being able to be in touch with her,' Charlie said, staring down into his empty coffee cup. 'But it's the only way I can hack it. We were able to have a brief talk together in Alf's, except that Miranda was there, and Maisie, of course. But Jemima seems to understand. I told her we were off tomorrow. It's weird how I feel, Benj. It sounds so selfish if I try to verbalize it. I want her in my life but on my own terms.'

'But doesn't she feel exactly the same way? If you can both hack it, why not?'

Charlie shook his head. 'I don't know. It just sounds bizarre.'

Ben watched him compassionately. 'Jemima doesn't want to live with you in London and you wouldn't last ten minutes down here. So you get together for a few days a few times each year. It's tough but it's been done before. Give it a go and see how it works. It might become easier, less dramatic, if you see what I mean.'

Charlie nodded. 'It's just this feeling that I'm being kind of unfaithful to Ange even though we're not having a physical relationship,' he says wretchedly. 'It feels like I'm cheating.'

'Well, you're just going to have to deal with it,' Ben told him brutally. 'If you continue to feel like that and you can't hack it then you'll just have to avoid seeing Jemima when you come down. But, hey, give it a chance. Why don't you take it a day at a time and see how it goes?'

Charlie gave a great sigh and smiled at him. 'Crazy, isn't it? Such a fuss. I'd better go and see how Ange is doing.'

Now, as he begins to prepare breakfast, Ben sympathizes with Charlie's dilemma. It is specious to say that because sex isn't involved Charlie isn't cheating on Ange, and he wonders how the relationship can possibly go forward between his cousin and Jemima; whether they will be able to contain it and bring it into a simpler kind of love. There are so many different kinds of love; so sad that any of it should be wasted.

He hears someone coming down the stairs, the sounds of bags being dumped down in the hall, Ange calling to Charlie to remember the coats in the hall cupboard. The holiday is over.

Jemima drives slowly. The autumn lanes are full of delights: a crown of pale honeysuckle trailing in the thorny hedgerow where scarlet rosehips cluster amongst the brambles; a few inquisitive bullocks trampling and jostling at a muddy farm gate; the delicate shining silk of a spider's web flung between bare twigs. A pheasant runs out from the ditch; it jinks from side to side in front of the car, and rockets upwards, screeching noisily. Fields glimpsed through gateways are a rich mosaic of colour: new-turned crimson from the plough and pale stubbly gold, just harvested. Black plastic-covered bales looking like giant cotton-reels are stacked against the hedges.

Jemima is aware of the autumn magic though, at a different level, she is trying to contain her excitement. This morning, soon, she will see Charlie. She's convinced herself that they will meet as they did before, by accident, by chance; just as they did at regatta, and when he gave her the little piece of glass. Ever since yesterday morning in Alf's she's been living on a high, remembering the look that passed between them, which has enabled her to push to the back of her mind the hopelessness she experienced when she saw him with Ange outside Dukes. Just for now he is again the Charlie of regatta, separate from Charlie the husband, the family man.

They managed to exchange a few words in Alf's, saying nothing, saying everything. He told her that they were leaving earlier than planned to go to Polzeath and at once she was seized with the hope that Ange might go alone again and leave him behind with his family.

As she drives she's persuaded herself that this has been the case and that somehow they will share a few precious hours together. She pulls into a gateway to check her mobile for a text from Benj but there is no signal and she wonders if she has the nerve simply to knock on the door of the Merchant's House. After all, since Alf's it's been established that she is Benj's friend. She has a few hours free so she'll throw it in the lap of the gods. If there's a parking place she'll take the chance, if not she'll park in the town and hope to bump into him.

And there is a space almost opposite the house. Her heart knocking about madly in her breast, her knees trembly, she puts the windows down a few inches for Otto and locks the car. Glancing each way, she crosses the road, and seizes the knocker.

Benj answers almost immediately, opening the door, gazing down at her as she waits there full of anticipation, beaming happily. He guesses straight away.

'He's gone,' he says.

She stares at him, her smile slowly crumpling into disbelief: 'Gone? What, gone already?'

He takes her arm, pulls her inside and slams the door behind them.

'I thought you knew,' he says, almost angrily. 'He said he told you they were going to Polzeath.'

She can scarcely answer him; her disappointment chokes her and the illusion of the bright morning folds gently, like a magician's coloured cardboard props, and collapses into dust and ashes.

'He did,' she says dully, 'but I didn't quite believe him. I didn't want to, I suppose. I thought he'd stay, like at regatta. And, anyway, I didn't realize they'd go so early.'

Benj leads her into the breakfast room and she stumbles along behind him as if she is suddenly old. He pushes her down on to a chair.

'Damn,' he says quietly. 'Damn and blast.'

She puts out a hand to him. 'Sorry, Benj,' she says. 'I'm such a fool. Don't be angry. I thought I was OK with it, I really did.'

'I'm not angry,' he answers, with weary exasperation. 'But do you realize how hard this is? First Charlie, then you. What the hell am I supposed to do?'

He kneels beside her and puts his arms round her, and she leans against him, too shocked to cry or complain.

'I was so sure, you see,' she mutters into his shoulder. 'I really believed he would be here.'

And then she does begin to cry: she weeps as if she will never stop. Her disillusionment is simply too much to bear, and Benj is so kind that it makes it even more difficult to pull herself together.

'Come on,' he says at last. 'I'm driving you home. We don't want Claude or Evie seeing you like this. I can get the bus back but we need to get you home. Give me your car keys.'

As they drive the familiar coast road she tries to control her tears, even to smile when Benj says, 'Get a grip, you're frightening Otto,' but she sees now how foolishly she'd hoped for some re-creation of regatta, some special magic that would materialize just for her and Charlie.

'Sorry,' she keeps saying, wiping her eyes. 'I'm really sorry, Benj. I thought I'd come to terms with it,' and he reaches out to hold her wrist tightly for a moment.

When they get indoors Benj fills the kettle whilst she

goes upstairs to wash her face and make repairs. She looks a complete mess; staring at herself in the little glass she is shocked by her shadowy, drowned eyes, her straggly hair streaking over her wet cheeks, and her grim, down-turned mouth.

I look old, she thinks. Old and haggy.

She tidies up, brushes her hair, and by the time she's finished, Benj has carried the coffee up to her little sitting-room with two glasses of red wine. Her heart swells with gratitude and affection for him and suddenly she remembers Evie saying: 'What a pity it isn't Ben.'

'The bottle was open and I thought it might help,' he says.

She sits beside him on the sofa, takes a sip of coffee and then picks up the glass: the mouthful of Merlot is smooth and delicious.

'I feel such a complete fool,' she tells him. 'It's like when I saw him in the town with Ange, isn't it? Every time I think I've got it under control it all starts up again. I'm really sorry to keep draining down on you, Benj.'

He slips an arm along her shoulders, gives her a hug. 'Stop saying sorry. It's OK. I just wish I could think of something helpful to say. I feel so damned helpless.'

'We both need you,' she says, leaning against him gratefully.

'What a hopeless pair you are.'

He smiles down at her, taking any sting from the words, and he looks and sounds so much like Charlie that when he kisses her she responds readily, almost with relief. This time neither of them draws back – and so it begins.

Mikey waits nervously outside Evie's door. Ever since he phoned, and they arranged to meet at the boathouse again, he's been wondering exactly what he should say: how he should explain this sudden change of plan. Now that he knows what his father thinks about Evie it's going to be almost impossible to be easy and relaxed with her.

'Be nice,' Dad said, just like he did before, and Mikey felt confused and angry. He wanted to shout, 'The other day you said you'd like to break her neck,' but he can't because of Aunt Liz and because he's beginning to be afraid of his father.

And here is Evie, opening the door and smiling at him.

'This is kind of you, Mikey,' she says. 'I'm so glad you've managed to dash over before you go.'

'My aunt's come down,' he says, following her inside, amazed again by the light and the reflections. 'She had to see someone about the flat so we're going back with her. We came on the train. We've got a car but it's old and a bit dodgy.'

He feels better now he's with her again but he still can't get his father's remarks out of his head.

'I'm glad your aunt is here,' she says. 'We wondered when we saw Jason whether he is quite well. He seemed very stressed.'

Mikey feels his face go hot and scarlet; he is ashamed and miserable.

'I think it's to do with Mum dying,' he mumbles. 'He has tablets for depression and sometimes he doesn't manage very well. That's why I phoned Aunt Liz because he was . . . well, like you said. That's why she came.'

'Jason doesn't like me very much,' says Evie, and he stares at her in surprise. 'Well, he doesn't, does he? Your grandfather and I were very close friends, perhaps too close, and your grandmother — Jason's mother — wasn't very happy about it. She was an invalid in a wheelchair and he probably still feels angry on her behalf.'

Mikey nods, still taken aback by Evie's honesty. 'He did say something about it.'

She looks so kind and understanding that he wants to tell her everything: about how Dad's always been like a child, needing looking after, how he rages and loses it. But it's being disloyal, which he knows is wrong.

'Sometimes,' she says, 'when people aren't well, or grieving like your father is, they need something or someone on which to project their anger and grief and pain. It gives all those emotions a different direction and it can be a huge relief. Probably, seeing me again after all these years, that's what's happened to Jason.'

Listening to her Mikey is filled with a sense of understanding. Since Mum died he's experienced all sorts of things: anger, fear, guilt, misery. It would be good, sometimes, to let it all out in a huge fit of rage.

He nods. 'I get that. Even so, I wish it wasn't you.'

She smiles. 'So do I,' she says cheerfully. 'Will you write to me, Mikey, and let me know how things are with you? From school this time, perhaps?'

And then he smiles too, and nods, because it's as if she really does understand what it's like and how Dad watched him write the letters.

'Good,' she says. 'Let's have something to eat and drink, shall we?'

Later he walks back to the flat with a greater sense of security, believing that he has a friend who is grown-up, responsible, and asks for nothing but his friendship.

'Come back and see us soon,' Evie said, and he promised that he would. Some instinct tells him that this place will always be special to him.

Mikey glances at his watch and hurries his pace; they want to be off before lunch. He takes one long last look across the Boat Float out towards the river and turns back into the town. The holiday is over.

# CHAPTER TWENTY-SEVEN

During these short late autumn days that topple down so quickly towards the end of the year, the best time in the garden is in the morning. Low sunshine slants across the roofs, dazzles on the water, touches the untidy mop-heads of the hydrangeas. Evie leans against the table and wraps cold hands around her mug of hot coffee: even on the coldest day, as long as there is a gleam of sunshine, she cannot resist the garden. She hears the blackbird rustling amongst the ivy, foraging along the wall, swooping down to peck up some crumbs she's provided for him. He has his gold-rimmed eye on the spring, protecting his familiar territory, which has provided such a perfect breeding site for his young.

As she looks around the quiet, sleeping garden, Evie finds it almost impossible to imagine it in blossom again, the borders full of colour, the scent of lavender drifting in the warm, still air. She and Claude have been happily settled in the Merchant's House for several weeks, adapting to the change of routines, enjoying the novelty: it's rather like being on holiday in familiar surroundings. After all, neither she nor Claude is a stranger to the Merchant's House.

It was odd at first, though, to be back here without Tommy; odd to be using their bedroom and half expecting to see him coming out of the shower or propped up against his pillows in bed, reading. To begin with it was very painful, as if she were coming to terms with losing him all over again, but gradually she grew used to it. There were so many good memories, small things she'd almost forgotten. He was always the first up – all those years of being early at the office – dragging on his dressing gown and going downstairs to make coffee. In the kitchen he'd switch on Radio 4 so that by the time he returned, carrying the tray, he was able to tell her various items of the day's news.

'Do I want to know?' she'd mutter, hardly awake, hauling herself upright. 'Can't it wait until after breakfast?'

He had an almost childlike fascination with disasters: tsunamis, hurricanes, floods. These terrible things gripped his imagination and occupied his mind.

'Appalling,' he'd say, sitting on the bottom of the bed, his face grave. 'Simply awful. All those poor souls. We'll need to get on to ShelterBox and see if they're doing anything about it.'

On sunny summer mornings he'd insist that she had her coffee up in the garden.

'Up you come. Up you come,' he'd say, as if she were a

recalcitrant horse, pulling back the bedcovers. 'It's a glorious morning. Much too good to be lazing in bed. You know you'll be glad when you're up there.'

And she usually was, though she was not by nature a lark; she was an owl: late to bed, late to rise. Before she moved into the Merchant's House with Tommy after they were married, it was during those deliciously lazy hours between waking and rising that she'd think about her day's work: plotting and planning, imagining scenes and conversations. Sometimes she did some work on her laptop before she got up; sometimes she'd make coffee and take it back to bed whilst she brooded on the story she was telling. Her life with Tommy changed things, she learned to adapt, and she never regretted those happy years with him.

She knows that Claude is remembering the past, too. They both are certain that Tommy would be pleased to see them all together here in his beloved Merchant's House, planning for Christmas. Charlie will be coming for two nights just before Christmas, but there has been no question of Ange or the girls accompanying him and Evie is relieved. She thinks that Ange has accepted Ben's rights to be here at the Merchant's House and, even if she had any suspicions about Jemima, that extraordinary encounter in Alf's went some way to allaying them.

Evie sips her coffee thoughtfully, thinking about Jemima and about Ben. Recently she has noticed a change – infinitesimal, carefully concealed, but a change – in their friendship: a new awareness flowing between them. There is something new, too, in the way that Jemima greets Evie: all the old affection, yes, but a new constraint as if Jemima fears a plunge into intimacy during one of their conversations. There is a brightness, lots of jokiness, a tendency to skitter away from more personal subjects. Evie watches this with interest — and anxiety: to her experienced eye Jemima looks like a woman who is having an affair. She remembers Jemima sitting on the balcony at the boathouse saying, 'I always say I'm mistress material.'

Ben, on the other hand, is quieter. There is a physical wellbeing about him yet he too is slightly cautious with Evie, lest he might reveal something he wishes to keep hidden. He makes no secret of the fact that he spends time with Jemima, and she still drops into the Merchant's House for a mid-morning cup of coffee or a cup of tea after work, but the old easiness between she and Ben has been replaced by something more knowing; a different level of intimacy that must be constantly monitored. The old innocence has vanished.

The blackbird swoops down to seize a crumb and Evie drinks the last of her coffee. She hears Claude calling to her from the house below and she goes down through the garden to meet him.

As Claude unpacks the shopping he gives thanks that Charlie is coming down by himself just before Christmas. Though Claude knows that Ange has never accompanied Charlie on the Christmas run there's always the fear of hearing that this year she's changed her mind.

344

It was a huge shock to Claude when Evie told him she showed Ange the papers from the cartoons.

'It was the only way to get her off our backs,' Evie said. 'I think you'll find everything will be easier now.'

'You make it sound like blackmail,' he grumbled, trying to imagine the scene between the two women.

'Oh, it is,' said Evie blithely. 'You see, she might have always thought that I'd invented them. There would have been that tiny doubt in her mind. So I showed them to her and told her how I'd left things in my will, whilst implying that it all depended on her behaving herself. She quite understood that, she's not an idiot, but she'll feel happier now that she knows that the Merchant's House will go back to her children eventually. Though she nearly had a fit when I told her that you'd read them.'

'You *told* her?'

'Of course. You're a kind of insurance policy. Don't be so pedestrian, Claude. You simply can't allow people like Ange to get away with things.'

'You are so ruthless,' he murmured.

She beamed at him. 'Yes,' she said. 'Good, isn't it?'

Now she comes into the kitchen, carrying her coffee mug, saying, 'Did you remember the *pains au choc*?'

'Looks like you've already had coffee without me,' he says, slightly aggrieved.

'Doesn't mean I can't have another,' she says. 'Not on ration, is it?' And she gives him a hug and says, 'I am so glad you're here, Claude. I was just sitting up on the terrace thinking about Ben and Jemima.'

'Yes,' he says rather glumly. He's been thinking about them too. He can no longer convince himself that everyone will be able to remain just good friends.

'Do you think they're sleeping together?' she asks, filling the kettle, switching it on – and as usual he's taken aback by her directness.

'They seem . . . furtive,' he replies reluctantly. 'No, not quite that, but it's like they know a secret that they're keeping from us.'

'Exactly,' Evie says, collecting mugs, spooning coffee into the cafetiere.

He watches her: she seems so matter-of-fact about it.

'Don't you mind?' he asks, almost indignantly. 'It was you who said that they should contain their feelings and keep them under control.'

'I didn't quite say that,' she answers. 'I said that if they could then their love might become a positive thing for them. And I was talking about Charlie and Jemima. Not Ben.'

'But where does this leave Charlie?' Claude asks crossly. 'I mean, if they're having an affair, how does this work now? Isn't Charlie going to be a bit put out to find that Ben's stolen a march on him?'

'The trouble is, he can't really complain, can he? He has his own life going on in London. Perhaps you were right when you said that Charlie wouldn't be able to cope with an affair and maybe Jemima has looked into the future and seen how bleak it might be, and that somehow she and Ben are comforting each other. Ben's had a bit of a tough rejection with Kirsty so they've turned to each other. It's understandable, isn't it?'

'Yes,' he says impatiently. 'Yes, I can see why it's happened, and I'm not judging them, but how does it go forward? Do we pretend nothing's going on? Does Ben tell Charlie? After all, Jemima and Ben are free agents. It doesn't have to be a secret. So why is it?'

Evie groans as she makes the coffee. 'It's not that simple, Claude.'

He gives a derisive snort: it never is. She can't help laughing at his exasperated expression.

'Well, it isn't, is it? She's in love with Charlie. You saw it yourself. We all know. How does she explain to us that she's going to bed with Ben?'

'OK, it's embarrassing, but I say again: where is it going to end?'

Evie shakes her head. 'I don't know but I'm worried about them. I was naïve to imagine that it might work out, I suppose.'

Claude is seized with a fresh anxiety but any words of comfort seem empty so he says instead: 'Well, pour the coffee. I'm dying of thirst after battling round M&S,' and he roots in the bag for the *pains au chocolat*.

Jemima and Ben are driving back from a pretty, thatched cottage near Thurlestone. Ben has taken photographs and Jemima has been making an inventory prior to it being taken on as a holiday let. Jemima drives; she knows these lanes, the back ways and the short cuts, and Ben has grown used to being a passenger, allowing himself to relax and his brain to freewheel.

It's odd, Ben thinks, that before half term, before that moment when Jemima arrived at the Merchant's House expecting to see Charlie, these jaunts were free of any constraint. Often it seemed that Charlie might have been with them; as if they were both happy to keep him included in their friendship, as part of the group. Now, the mere thought of him seems to fill the car with a silence that is difficult to break. It's as if they are both being unfaithful to him.

It's a ridiculous idea. Ben shifts in his seat, stares out beyond the small, neat, sloping fields to the glimmer of the distant sea. Jemima slips him a sideways glance as if she's read his thoughts, and he speaks quickly so as to deflect any suspicions she might have.

'Amazing, isn't it?' he says at random. 'Wherever you look it takes your breath away.'

'The cottage was sweet,' she says, diving into a gateway to allow a tractor to pass. 'Would you like to live in a little house like that?'

'No,' he answers at once, thinking of the grace and elegance of the Merchant's House. 'No, I'm not a cottage man. Too poky.'

Too late he thinks of her little cottage and there's a moment of silence whilst he tries to think of a way out. This new awkward dimension to their friendship immediately poses problems; doesn't allow the old ease of honesty.

Does his remark indicate that he wouldn't want to move in with her? Does it imply that at some point she might move in with him? He is filled with irritation and dismay. Nothing has changed – and everything has changed. Somehow on that first occasion, charged as it was with emotion, with the need to comfort, making love on Jemima's big old sofa had seemed a natural conclusion; their mood, the wine, all conspired towards this act. It was a long moment of relief, release, pleasure, before the world clamoured in again and there was the difficulty of moving apart, getting dressed, without knowing what might come next. He tried to take his attitude from her affectionate warm reaction but it was clear that they both felt slightly awkward, at a loss as to how to go forward. The old familiarity was gone but there was nothing to take its place.

'All those beams,' he says now, trying for a light touch. 'I'd have a permanent stoop. They must have been midgets in the old days.'

Jemima laughs, and somehow the tension breaks.

'Shall we have some lunch at Stokeley,' she asks, 'before we go back to the office? It's just about warm enough to sit outside so Otto can have a bit of a leg-stretch.'

'Good idea,' he agrees.

Jemima begins to talk about Maisie, about her next sleepover at the weekend, and Ben relaxes in his seat and tries to persuade himself that he is being oversensitive and that it will all work itself out.

\*

All the while though, as she talks, Jemima is aware of Benj's confusion. It matches her own. That first time was simple, arising as it did out of her sudden disappointed shock at Charlie's departure; Benj's readiness to console and comfort. It was later that the difficulties showed themselves. She guesses that Benj can see no way forward and is already regretting this impromptu love affair. And there *is* love between them, a very deep affection, but it is not the stuff of a long-term, full-on relationship. Jemima wonders whether Benj suspects he is being used as a substitute; whether he feels he is betraying Charlie. It's odd that she doesn't feel too badly about the physical side – she has no doubt that Charlie is sleeping with Ange – it's something much more important; something to do with the recognition they share, which is so crucial to her. Nothing can alter that, nor take it away. What *would* hurt would be Charlie's denial of it. It was reaffirmed briefly during that moment in Alf's and she'd counted on seeing him again, needing her fix so as to get her through the days ahead without him.

But there's something else here: the close relationship between Charlie and Benj that stretches back across their whole lives. How will Benj deal with what he might see as a betrayal? She would hate to be the instrument that might damage their affection for each other.

She turns off into the lane that leads to the farm shop, drives into the car park, manoeuvres the car into a space and switches off the engine.

'Come on,' she says cheerfully. 'Let's see what's on the lunch menu.'

# CHAPTER TWENTY-EIGHT

Evie crosses the road, opens the postbox fixed to the wall at the top of the steps and takes out her letters. She carries them down with her to the boathouse, lets herself in, throws the letters on the table and goes to open the sliding doors. She likes to come in on sunny mornings, to air the house, and to enjoy a moment of solitude.

Out on the balcony she pauses to look down-river but the wind is too cold to be able to stand for long and she comes back inside, glancing at the letters, shuffling them: two catalogues, a bank statement and another envelope, handwritten. She picks it up, filled with foreboding: the writing is familiar. This is the second letter that she's had from Jason and quickly she tears the envelope open and draws out the sheet of paper.

His writing is uneven, almost illegible, unlike his first missive, which was almost childlike in its style. She read it many times and remembers it now.

Dear Evelyn Drake,

I need money to get the car through its MOT. If I don't get it repaired I shan't be able to bring Mikey home for his exeat. The trains are very difficult and expensive. I know how fond you are of him and that you would want him to have a good time. Could you send me a cheque for four hundred and sixty-eight pounds?

Please help us.

Yours sincerely,

Jason Dean

She dithered over it, but somehow hadn't had the courage to show it to Claude. Of course, she knew how he would react – and she knew that she might be wise to listen to him as once she had listened to Tommy – but there was an element of authenticity about Jason's request: the sum was so precise. At last, she'd written the cheque and sent it to the flat in Bristol with a little note; just a few words: 'Here is the money, Jason. I'm glad to help on this occasion and I hope you both have a good exeat weekend. Evie.'

Now she spreads the latest letter flat on the table so as to read the scrawling, looping writing.

I've got a lot of problems, Evelyn Drake, and I really need help like thousands of pounds not just chickenfeed this time. I've got to pay the mortgage and I'm behind with all the bills. It's payback time. Jason.

Evie stares at it in dismay. She guesses that he was drunk when he wrote the letter but sober enough to address the envelope, find a stamp and post it. She puts it into her pocket, checks that the house is secure and climbs the steps to the road.

'I can't believe that you were crazy enough to send him money,' Claude says for the third or fourth time. He simply can't get over it. 'Honestly, Evie, what a bloody stupid thing to do. This is demanding money with menaces. You should report him.'

'Well, it's not quite menaces, is it, just saying that "it's payback time"?'

She looks defiant, guilty, and he wants to give her a good shake.

'Don't you see that with people like this there would be no end to it? And now you've sent him a cheque you've as good as admitted that he has some kind of claim.'

'I haven't,' she cries indignantly, though they both know she doesn't quite believe it. 'I merely helped to make sure that Mikey didn't suffer.'

Claude snorts contemptuously. 'And so where do you draw the line? When he can't pay the bills for heating? When the house is repossessed?'

'Oh, don't, Claude,' she says, suddenly looking worried. 'I know it was silly but I felt sorry for him.'

Claude experiences all the irritation that goes with suddenly feeling compassion for somebody with whom you're actually very cross, and he jams his hands into his pockets and closes his eyes for a moment.

'Look,' he says, drawing a deep breath. 'Look, I know you have ambivalent feelings about Jason. I understand about the guilt, I know you're very fond of Mikey, but you simply can't allow yourself to be blackmailed.'

'But what shall I do?' she asks miserably.

He stares across the table at her, his irritation evaporating.

'We'll compose a letter,' he says. 'We'll keep it short and firm but very clear.'

'I worry about Mikey. If things are really that bad . . .'

'Mikey is not your responsibility,' he says gently. 'He has an aunt and an uncle to watch out for him. Remember how you said he phoned them when he was worried about his father at half term and his aunt came straight down? They'll be keeping an eye. And if they can afford to buy a flat in Dartmouth they can't be too hard up. Jason must approach his own family if he's got financial problems.'

She nods but she doesn't look convinced and Claude feels frustration rising again.

'You know in your heart that what I say is true,' he tells her, 'or you would have shown me that first letter. You knew what I'd say and part of you knew that I'd be right.'

'Oh, don't be so sanctimonious,' she says crossly, and then they both burst out laughing.

'Well, it's true,' he says. 'Look at this.' He gestures at the letter. 'He'd been drinking, I'm sure of it. The same as when we saw him by the Boat Float.'

'I know,' she says anxiously. 'That's why I'm worrying about Mikey.'

Claude sighs. 'Well, write to the boy and ask how he is and if Aunt Liz is on the case. You'll know how to phrase it. Maybe you could ask for the aunt's address, though don't say why. Meanwhile we'll compose a letter to Jason straight away and get it posted. No good leaving any illusions in his mind.'

The sea rests placidly against the shore, each slight swell of its smooth surface lifting the tide just a little further to break in a gentle flurry of foam along the stony beach. A solitary fisherman sits hunched over his rod, basket open beside him, an ancient dog lying sleeping at his feet.

Jemima stands with her back to the sea, her eyes fixed skywards on the murmuration of starlings that forms and reforms in its fluid swooping flight as the flock returns to its roosts amongst the reed beds. The pale sky, luminous with the fading sunset, is reflected in the cloudy waters of the ley where mallard and coot huddle at the water's edge. Above, on the sheltering hills, gaunt trees, bare branches sketched in by charcoal, are outlined against the ploughed fields. There is no breath of wind.

Otto sits waiting, his eyes fixed on the fisherman's dog: friend or foe? The old dog doesn't move: he lies, head on paws, as patient as his master. Black-backed gulls, driven inland by the recent gales, are following a fishing boat, their raucous cries echoing back from steep cliffs and rocky coves. Jemima turns at last and walks on, heading towards her little cottage. She's finished work early today and the evening stretches ahead: first, a cup of tea by the fire; later, a friend coming to supper.

Maisie has had her last sleepover until she returns from Australia after Christmas and was absolutely incandescent with excitement at the prospect of the holiday.

'I have four cousins,' she told Jemima solemnly. 'Two of them are nearly my age, one's a girl and one's a boy, and there are two baby boys. *And*,' she added, having paused so as to give Jemima the opportunity to exclaim with amazement and delight at such good fortune, 'I have two uncles and two aunts.'

'Gosh!' Jemima said, suitably impressed. 'You are so lucky. I haven't got any uncles or aunts. Or cousins. I bet you can't wait to see them all again.'

She knows that Miranda's brothers and their families have made a few trips back to the UK in the last six years but Maisie can hardly remember them and, although they Skype, it's difficult for a six-year-old really to connect with people she doesn't know.

'You'll have to send me and Otto a postcard,' Jemima told her. 'Don't forget.'

And Maisie promised that she wouldn't forget, her small face glowing with the joy of expectation.

'She's out of her mind with it,' Miranda said as they walked along the beach. 'It's almost impossible to keep her calm until we go.'

But Jemima can tell that Miranda is excited, too; that

she can see the possibility of a whole new exciting life opening up before them both.

'So what about you, Mimes?' she asked. 'Are you sleeping with Ben?'

At first Jemima was completely taken aback; she had to remind herself that she and Miranda have these kind of conversations, that their friendship almost demands it. Of course, Miranda doesn't know the truth; she doesn't know about Charlie.

'Just once or twice,' she said casually. 'Nothing serious.'

Miranda raised her eyebrows. 'Why not serious?'

'Well.' Jemima cast about for an explanation. 'It doesn't have to be, does it?'

Miranda shrugged. 'I guess not, though I can't think of a good reason myself. I'd grab him with both hands.'

Well, we all know that, Jemima thought rather bitterly, but she forced herself to look amused, laid-back.

'You know me,' she said. 'I don't do serious. Anyway, I'm wondering about making a bit of a change.'

'What sort of change?'

What indeed?

'Well, there's a job going in the Truro office and I'm wondering whether to apply for it.' Was she? 'The same as I'm doing here but it would be a whole new area to explore. And my sister and her husband are in Falmouth, which would be good. I'm going down for Christmas so I might have a little look around at the renting scene.'

She listened to herself in surprise. Miranda looked surprised, too; almost affronted.

'Well, get you,' she said. 'And I thought you were well settled.'

Jemima laughed. 'If you can think about moving to Australia why shouldn't I think about moving to Cornwall?'

And then Maisie and Otto came running back and nothing more was said.

Now, Jemima lets herself in, checks that Otto has fresh water in his bowl, and pauses to look at Charlie's piece of glass that hangs at the window. Lit by the trembling sunset-light the little white boat appears to be dipping its way across the sapphire and turquoise waves, the two birds fluttering above it: strength, simplicity, freedom.

Soon Charlie will be back in Dartmouth. How will that work? Will they meet by accident? Manage a few hours together? One thing is certain: it can't be like regatta this time around. She feels confused: this little passage of love with Benj comforts her. With no contact, no word from Charlie, it's as if her precious memories of him are being kept alive by this intimacy. How can she resist it? Yet now, as Christmas draws closer, whenever she contemplates meeting Charlie within a family context she panics.

Otto is watching her hopefully, tail wagging, wondering if she's forgotten his dinner. She smooths his head, smiling at his anxious expression, murmuring to him. Most of the time he has dried food, very nutritious and healthy – she has to watch his weight – but occasionally he gets a tin of meat.

'Fast food tonight,' she tells him.

She spoons out the meat and the jelly, still talking to him.

'I do love Charlie, you see,' she murmurs to Otto, 'but then I love Benj, too, and Evie and Claude, which slightly complicates things.'

Otto watches her, ears cocked, alert. She puts his bowl down beside him and he sniffs at it with pleasure and begins to eat.

'Perhaps it's time for a change, Otto. Time to move on. How do you think you might like living in Cornwall? Should I apply for the job in Truro?'

Otto continues to eat but his tail wags politely as if to indicate that she still has his attention. He finishes his dinner, polishing the bowl with sweeps of his tongue so that the bowl jolts across the floor. Jemima bends to pick it up.

'Was it good?' she asks. She wonders how people who live alone manage without someone to talk to: a cat or a dog.

'I can't imagine not having someone around,' she said to Evie recently. 'Though usually I've had cats. They're a bit easier to cope with when I'm working. My last cat was utterly gorgeous. He was called MagnifiCat. He was a much better judge of character than I am. After he died I was distraught. I was just deciding to get another cat and then Otto came along and it was wonderful to have someone to talk to again, if you see what I mean. And so well behaved that he can come in the car with me and they don't mind having him in the office. Do you talk to yourself?'

'Sometimes,' Evie admitted. 'When I was writing I had

so much going on in my head that I never felt alone. So many characters, so many connections and ideas. It's rather lonely without them, especially once Tommy died, of course.'

'And all your characters have gone off and left you?'

Evie smiled. 'Something like that. Though just lately there's been so much excitement that I haven't had time to feel lonely.' She hesitated. 'We were wondering if you'd like to spend Christmas Day with us? Stay the night, perhaps?'

There was another tiny pause.

A few weeks ago, Jemima thought, I might have leaped at it. But now? How would it work? And why hasn't Benj mentioned it? Perhaps, now, he'd find it difficult. Perhaps he thinks I'd expect to share his room?

'That's so kind of you,' she answered warmly. 'The thing is, I always go to my sister in Falmouth for Christmas. It's become a kind of tradition, and her son and his family are coming down from London for it, too, so it's quite an occasion this year.'

'Well, there will be plenty of time for celebration,' Evie said easily. 'Charlie will be down for a couple of days just before.'

At once she panicked: how would she manage to be with Benj and Charlie, with Claude and Evie looking on? How would Benj manage? Evie's words brought the reality of the situation into sharp focus.

'I might be gone by then,' Jemima said quickly. 'I'm not sure . . .'

And Evie had looked at her so understandingly, so

lovingly, that Jemima longed to burst out with it all; to explain, but she couldn't frame the words and the moment passed.

That was the first time since this foolish little affair started that Jemima was forced to take a cold, hard look into the future and make a decision – and she acted instinctively: she would not be at the Merchant's House for Christmas.

Now, she puts Otto's bowl into the sink, pulls the curtains across the darkening windows, makes a mug of tea and goes upstairs to her little sitting-room with Otto at her heels. She switches on the lamps and lights her wood-burning stove, which begins to flicker cheerfully. She must prep the supper later but meanwhile she'll relax. She sits down on the sofa, pulls out Otto's rug and waits for him to clamber up beside her and settle comfortably with his head resting against her thigh.

Jemima picks up the remote, switches on the television, channel hops. Someone is singing 'Let It Snow!', and she drinks her tea, absent-mindedly stroking Otto and thinking about Charlie; how she first saw him at regatta, and that indescribable sensation of knowing and being known. Her little bit of glass is a symbol of all that he recognized in her: strength, simplicity, freedom. She closes her eyes, remembering his look of joy, his delight at their meeting. It was so important: so mysterious. Yet her connection through Benj, through Evie and Claude, is all she has of him. How can she bear to give it up?

# CHAPTER TWENTY-NINE

Jason drives carefully, warily, an eye on the rear-view mirror in case anyone saw him speeding earlier. He'd let his attention wander, just for a moment, and found he was doing eighty. Perhaps he ought to stop to have a cup of coffee but he just wants to get down to Dartmouth and ask Evelyn Drake what she means by sending such a bloody pompous letter.

The thought of the letter stiffens his arms in a little spasm of anger and sends the car in a swerve out into the fast lane. There is a blast of a horn, another car speeds past, its driver gesticulating angrily. Jason centres the car, trembling a bit, sweating slightly: he must concentrate. He's not going to get angry: he's not going to lose it. He just wants to see Evelyn Drake face to face and ask why she's been so bloody insulting. After all, she gave him the money for the car.

Jason chuckles to himself. It was a clever move that; picking a precise random sum sounded quite authentic – and she'd fallen for it, silly cow. Even so, he was surprised she coughed up; he hadn't expected it to be so easy. Shows she's got a guilty conscience, though. It was a mistake sending the second letter when he wasn't feeling at his best. He hadn't been so tactful; he'd been having a downer, the black dog was on him, and he'd gone a bit over the top. Even so, she owed him. He has to see her again and tell her how Mikey will be affected if she doesn't help out.

He takes a quick glance at his watch: not half past eleven yet. He made a good start immediately after the letter arrived, no second thoughts, so there's time to stop and have some coffee and perhaps something to eat. He's finding it a strain, to be honest, and he needs a rest.

Jason pulls into a motorway service station, parks the car, and goes to find refreshment.

Jemima and Ben are in Alf's when Laura phones. Ben hauls out his mobile, glances at the screen, makes an apologetic face at Jemima.

'It's Laura,' he tells her, and turns a little away. 'Hi, sweetheart,' he says. 'How's the snow?'

'It's great,' she says. Her voice is full of laughter, breathless with excitement, and he holds the phone more closely.

'You sound odd,' he tells her, half amused, half intrigued. 'What is it? Are you OK?'

'Yes. Yes, I'm very OK. Listen, Dad. Billy and I want to get engaged.'

'*What?*'

He's aware of Jemima watching him, her face puzzled and anxious. He stares back at her almost unseeingly, concentrating on Laura's bubbly, distant voice.

'I know. It's a bit sudden, isn't it? He says he should come home and make his number with you. What d'you think?'

Ben hardly knows what to say. 'Oh, sweetheart, that's wonderful. I'd love to meet him. We all would.'

He can hear her struggling to control her voice, to be more serious, and he guesses that Billy is there with her.

'Where are you, Dad?'

'I'm in Alf's with Jemima. Look, are you on your own?'

'No, Billy's with me. He says "hi". Listen. Another big shock. We were wondering if we could come home for Christmas? I mean to you at Dartmouth. Would it be OK with Evie? It's a bit of a cheek . . .'

'Of course you can come here,' he says quickly. 'Of course you can. This is your home, sweetheart.' And he blesses Evie in his heart that he can say these words with confidence.

'That's fab, Dad. Look, I'll phone again soon to make a proper plan. We'll check flights and things. It would just be the three days. If you're really sure?'

'Of course I'm sure.'

'Thanks, Dad. Love you lots.'

A click and her happy voice is cut off. Ben hesitates and then switches off his phone. He is in shock, wondering how he will deal with this new development in their lives and how Kirsty will feel about their coming to him for Christmas.

'Are you OK?' Jemima is asking him. 'It sounded rather exciting. Was it good news?'

He nods. 'Yes. She says that she and Billy are planning to get engaged and they want to come home for Christmas.'

'Oh, gosh,' says Jemima. 'Well, that's amazing. Do you like him?'

'I haven't met him but she told me quite a lot about him when she came down to see us,' he answers. 'She sounded just mad about him. She was . . . well, incandescent. You know what it's like at that age? A little group of them got taken on together at this skiing place in Switzerland. It's all such an adventure. Hard work but a chance to polish up on the skiing. You know the kind of thing? Billy, apparently, was looking forward to the catering side of it, too. He wants to be a master-chef.'

Ben remembers Laura's expression as she showed him the images of Billy on her phone – the joy and the hope – and he is filled with equal measures of happiness and anxiety. Is she ready for this big new step? Is he?

'Well, it all sounds wonderful,' Jemima says. 'Look, I've got to get back to the office . . . Do you still want to come over for supper this evening?'

'Yes, of course I do,' he reassures her, though he feels utterly distracted. 'I'll see you later,' and they get up together and go out into the cold, damp air. He kisses her quickly and heads down to the river, his whole mind concentrated on Laura, planning to come home with Billy for Christmas.

Claude is out in the town. He can't remember when he's enjoyed himself so much. Of course it's wonderful to be with his family at Christmas but he's always aware of his role of father and grandfather: that he mustn't take decisions without a great deal of consultation and that he is treated almost like a privileged, elderly guest.

In the Merchant's House there are no such boundaries. It is assumed that he will pull his weight, be constructive, take responsibility.

'I'll organize the tree,' he says – but then wonders if that is Ben's prerogative. He doesn't quite know what the form is; but then none of them does. Christmas has never been quite like this in the Merchant's House.

'Great idea,' says Ben. 'Where should it go? In the drawing-room?'

'Yes,' says Evie. 'TDF said there was always a tree in the drawing-room when he was growing up with the aunts so we kept up the tradition.'

'But it would be nice, too,' suggests Claude, 'if we had one in the breakfast room. In the window, so that people walking past can see it. Children will love it.'

This is greeted with such enthusiasm that he is gratified and takes the responsibility of the purchase of the trees upon himself. Now, as he wanders in Foss Street, studying the seasonal window displays, he thinks about what to buy Evie for Christmas. Very small presents, nothing extravagant, she says. It's a good rule but he would like to repay her for her generosity. Of course he's been contributing with food and wine and treats, but he still feels the need to mark this wonderful time he's spent in Dartmouth.

He decides that he might make it a present quite separate from Christmas; something just between the two of them. He peers into the Rowcroft Gallery: a little watercolour of some aspect of the town might be a good idea. Someone touches his shoulder and he turns to see Jemima.

'Choosing presents?' she asks, smiling at him.

He pretends to groan. 'Praying for inspiration.'

'I've just been having coffee with Benj,' she says. 'It seems as if Laura might be home for Christmas. That'll be fun, won't it? I'm on my way back to work. I must dash.'

She hurries away, turns into the office, and Claude continues to stand quite still, thinking about Laura and how she was when they saw her in the autumn. He's very fond of Laura: of her generation she's the one who is most like TDF and Charlie and Ben. She has inherited their brown eyes and dark hair, and their laid-back confidence. She went out on the scooter with him for a little jaunt to Stokeley, and on another day they all went on the river-boat to Totnes. She has that same grace that TDF had: the ability to share their own special qualities with those around them so that, briefly, those in their company feel blessed.

Laura, coming home for Christmas: this is wonderful news. He wonders if Evie knows yet. Perhaps Ben is telling her right now. Claude abandons the idea of buying a present and sets off along Foss Street, back to the Merchant's House.

'How exciting,' Evie is saying to Ben.

They stand together in the breakfast room whilst Ben tells her how Laura sounded, how taken aback he was, apologizing for agreeing that Laura and Billy can stay for Christmas without checking with her first.

'It'll be terrific fun,' she tells him. 'Stop worrying, Ben. We can fit them in one way or another.'

She is touched by his anxiety, his excitement, and she is filled with delight at the prospect of Laura's happiness. It's always wonderful to see two young people in love, planning a future together.

'It'll be a squash,' he says anxiously. 'Unless . . . I wonder if they're . . . well, you know?'

'Sharing a room?' She smiles at his discomfited expression. 'You'll have to ask.'

He looks so horrified that she bursts out laughing. 'You could simply offer them the boathouse, then they can sort it out for themselves.'

His relief is so palpable that she laughs even more.

'That's a good idea,' he says. 'If you're sure. Shall I do that?'

'Why not? They'll have more freedom. More space for Billy whilst he gets acquainted with us. And we can all get together here for meals and so on. Let's not panic about the details just yet. Send her a text or an email suggesting it, so that she and Billy can talk about it.'

'I'll do that,' he says. 'That's great, Evie. Thanks. It's good, isn't it?'

'Very good,' she says reassuringly, alert to the uncertainty in his voice. 'Laura's a sensible girl. She won't be bounced into anything she doesn't want to do.'

'No,' he says. He heaves a deep breath of relief. 'No, she won't. Though I don't know what Kirsty is going to say. Laura's very young to be engaged.'

'That's between Kirsty and Laura,' Evie says firmly. 'And Laura and Billy are no younger than you and Kirsty were. Stop worrying and just look forward to having your lovely daughter and her Billy home for Christmas. Ah. Here's Claude. Now you can tell him all about it while I organize the lunch. It's a bit too early for a drink to celebrate. We'll do that later.'

# CHAPTER THIRTY

Jason manages to find a space for the car on the Embankment, hitches his rucksack on to his shoulder and wanders out into the town. He hadn't expected Dartmouth to be so busy. He walks slowly, keeping his eyes open, looking out for Evelyn Drake or the old guy. He scarcely notices the lights and the decorations, he's just looking for her, hoping to take her unawares.

He walks around the streets, past the lighted windows, past the Royal Castle – but then he hesitates. One little drink won't hurt; it'll steady him, keep him calm. And she might be in there with the old guy having a late lunch. He goes in, takes a quick look round, remembering when he first saw her sitting by the window, but she's not there.

He goes to the bar and orders a small Scotch; just a single shot. Oh, it's good. Straight down in one go; there's nothing like it. He'll save the second for afterwards as a reward. As he walks out of the Castle, away from the Boat Float, he reminds himself of Mikey's description of the house and the address, and a few minutes later he's staring down, over the wall, at the boathouse.

Just for a moment he's distracted by the charm of the little cottages and the converted boathouses that cluster beside the river; the irregular roofscapes and the ancient walls. Then he climbs down the steep stone steps, crosses the paved pathway between the boathouse and its neighbour, and rings the bell.

There is no answer. He stands back, stares around him, at the blank windows of the neighbouring house, at the flowerpots standing along the wall, still containing the last of the summer blooms, decaying now in black, damp earth. The place is deserted. He rings the bell again, bangs on the door: still nothing. He feels his old enemies crowding in: panic, rage, despair – and he hears Helena whispering in his ear.

'Breathe, Jay-bird. Keep calm now.'

He takes a deep breath and thinks more clearly: he will go for a walk around and come back. He climbs the steps, pauses to catch his breath at the top, leaning for a moment on the wall. A tall dark man comes out of the elegant house opposite and strides away down the hill and Jason follows him more slowly.

It's a gloomy afternoon and already the wintry twilight is engulfing the town. The Christmas lights sparkle more brightly and once again he seeks comfort in the bar of the Royal Castle. It's warm here, with the log fire burning, and he sits quietly allowing the drink to comfort him. He's calm again, now; no stress. He'll go back soon and she'll be there and he'll reason with her and she'll see his point of view. He ought to get on with it, though. He doesn't want to be driving home in the pitch-dark.

He finishes his third whisky and with a huge effort he gets up again, hauls on his coat, picks up his rucksack and goes out into the chilly afternoon. Up the hill, he trudges – God, he feels tired, now – climbs down those steep, dangerous steps on trembling legs, and crosses to the front door.

Jason rings the bell, waits, hammers on the door. He stands staring at the house, willing her to answer him. There are no lights, no movement, and he wonders if she is hiding in there, looking out at him; watching him, mocking him.

'Open the bloody door,' he screams. 'Open it,' and he aims a kick at the solid, unyielding wood.

Still no answer, and suddenly he is washed with futility and despair. He begins to weep like a child, sobbing uncontrollably, lashing out, punching the air in his fury. Turning, he sees the earthenware pots standing against the wall, and he bends to pick one up. Its weight catches him off balance and as he swings the pot at the blank window he staggers so that it smashes against the wall instead and he is covered with dank wet earth. Beside himself with frustration he seizes another one but his feet slip on the mud and he lands on his knees, the pot breaking beneath him, a sharp earthen shard cutting into his face. The pain seems to sear his cheek, blaze in his head and explode into a violent ball of rage. He gets to his feet, trampling among the earth and the broken clay, so determined now to smash all the pots against the windows that he doesn't hear the voices or see the people looking over the wall and hurrying down the stone steps.

He is still screaming with the injustice of it all when his wrists are fastened behind him and he's carried away up the steps and put into the police car.

Ben dumps the shopping bag on the breakfast-room table and goes upstairs to the drawing-room. Evie is standing at the window.

'What's going on over the road?' he asks. 'Seems to be quite a lot of coming and going. Is everything OK?'

She turns round, grimacing at him with an almost amused despair.

'My neighbour has just been up to tell us that some drunk nutter has been smashing all her flowerpots. She came home to find him trampling around in the debris, having broken one of the boathouse windows in the process. The police have taken him off and Claude's down there helping to clear up and waiting for the glazier.'

'Bloody hell,' says Ben, going to the window to peer down. 'You didn't hear anything?'

Evie shakes her head. 'It's a long way down, and with all the windows shut and the radio on we didn't hear a thing. You can't see from here, either. You have to go and peer right over the wall. I went down with Claude and it's the most terrible mess. Lucky there wasn't more damage.'

'So who was it?'

Evie comes back into the room and sits down on the sofa. 'No idea. Some poor deranged soul with a grudge against flowerpots? Or perhaps it's a personal grudge against the Carters? It's lucky that they were out or he might have injured them.'

'You might have been injured, too, if he broke a window,' Ben points out. 'It's a good thing you were up here out of harm's way. Shall I go down and see if Claude needs a hand?'

'That would be kind,' she said. 'I came back to find someone who could make the window secure.'

'I'm off in a minute to have supper with Jemima,' he says, 'but I'll just check if Claude wants any help first.'

Evie watches him go. They've all had lunch, talked about Laura and Billy coming home for Christmas and Laura's engagement to this young man whom none of them has met. She senses the confusion that is going on in Ben's head and she feels a huge sympathy for him. She understands the muddle he is in about Jemima, guesses why the affair has started, but has grave doubts that it will survive. To begin with, Jemima is in love with Charlie, no matter how she might try to project that love on to Ben. And Ben is not ready for a relationship, he doesn't want any kind of commitment, but nor is he able to handle an affair with the same light-heartedness that Jemima will bring to it.

Evie wanders back to the window and stares down. She sees Ben come out of the door below her, cross the road and disappear out of sight down the steps, and then she looks across the rooftops to that glimpse of her own balcony.

The trouble was, she thinks, once I met Tommy nothing was ever quite the same again. And I think that's true for Jemima and for Charlie. Ben and Jemima are giving each other a kind of comfort but there's no future in it. Even if Claude and I weren't here it would make no difference. They're trapped now by their affection for each other. It needs something to break the pattern. But what?

# CHAPTER THIRTY-ONE

'*Love in the Afternoon*,' Jemima says later. 'Wasn't that the name of a book? Or, in this case it should be *Love in the Early Evening*.'

Ben, propped on one arm, looks down at her. 'And is it love?' he asks.

Immediately her smile fades; just for a moment she looks distressed, and he curses his clumsiness and rolls away from her warm, ample, generous body to sit on the edge of her bed. Nevertheless the question hangs between them.

Jemima shifts herself up on the pillows. 'Leurve,' she says, drawling out the word, trying to make a joke of it. 'How do you define it?'

He doesn't look at her as he hauls his shirt on and she puts a hand out and touches him lightly on the shoulder as if to reassure him.

'What are we doing, Mimes?' he asks, still with his back to her. 'What happens next?'

'Well, according to my personal experience,' her voice is still jokey, 'you tell me that you've got a wife or a girl-friend stashed away somewhere that you've discovered you can't manage without and suddenly it's "so long, and thanks for all the fish". You tell me, Benj. What happens next?'

'I don't know.' He stands up, pulling on the rest of his clothes. He doesn't know how to say, 'I do love you but I'm not in love with you.'

'What you're saying,' she suggests, 'is that it's tricky pretending to Evie and Claude that we're still just good mates, especially when we know that they've probably guessed exactly what's happening, and sooner or later we've got to go public. Or, on the other hand, we go back to being just good mates.'

'And could we do that?'

There is a silence and when he looks at her he is shocked by her expression. She looks as if he's hit her; wounded her in some way. His heart is wrenched with pain and remorse but he can't think of any way to take back the words or disguise their implicit meaning. Even as his mind tramples around in the debris of well-meaning phrases, she saves him.

'You're such a puritan, Benj,' she says lightly. 'Can't we just be having a good time?'

'I'm certainly having that,' he says warmly – almost too enthusiastically – trying to repair the earlier damage. 'It's just . . .'

Jemima moves quickly, swinging her legs out of bed,

talking about having a shower, forestalling any other tactless remark he might make, trying to draw them back from the edge of the precipice. He finishes dressing and goes downstairs where Otto greets him enthusiastically.

Ben crouches to speak to him, stroking his head, pulling his ears. He tries to convince himself that these few weeks have been like a sudden gift from the gods, an unexpected bonus, and he knows that Jemima has been happy to receive the gift and share it with him. Sex with Jemima is fun, light-hearted and very good. So why these fits of conscience, this requirement to look into the future?

He tries to imagine how he and Jemima might go forward asking nothing more than this, but he suspects that it can't happen without putting their relationship on a more formal footing. It's already becoming embarrassing pretending to Evie and Claude that nothing has changed; they're not stupid. And surely this very informal arrangement must undermine Jemima's relationship with them? Her old status as a close family friend is being damaged: the need for secrecy is corroding it. Perhaps he *is* a puritan but he's beginning to feel that he must acknowledge her as something more than his lover; beginning to feel they can never go back to that innocent friendship they once had. He tries to picture himself and Jemima coming down together for breakfast, casually facing Evie and Claude over the porridge and orange juice, and his heart quails; it is beyond imagining. And then there is Laura. How would he introduce Jemima to Laura? How would that work? And what about Charlie?

Ben winces, gives Otto a final pat and stands up. He tries to persuade himself that Charlie has made his choice and his choice is his wife and children and his friends. He can't have it both ways. Charlie walked away without even saying a proper goodbye to Jemima, leaving her unhappy and alone, and he, Ben, has been trying to comfort her.

So why does he feel so guilty about Charlie? So dissatisfied with himself? He thinks of their shared past and the affection they feel for each other; how Charlie has helped him financially from time to time. He remembers regatta and Charlie saying, 'I think I just fell in love, Benj.' Would he really be able to look Charlie in the eye and tell him that he and Jemima are lovers, and feel no twinge of guilt?

Ben hears the shower-room door open; he straightens up, takes a deep breath and prepares to be cheerful.


'So there we have it,' Jemima says to Otto, watching Benj drive away, her hand raised in farewell. 'I think that's what we might call the *coup de grâce*. Rather appropriate that it was actually *Death in the Afternoon* not *Love*. I think I've just finally blown it, Otto.'

It is beginning to rain and they go back inside. Suddenly she feels incredibly lonely; rootless. Yet she should be grateful that it's over. Of course she's grown used to being part of the family at the Merchant's House; of course she wanted to keep them all together, but her affair with Benj has put that very thing she longed for out of court and it's no good pretending any different. The dynamic has changed irrevocably. She isn't so easy and open with Evie or Claude, and it's much more difficult to be with Benj in their company – and impossible, now, to think of them all together with Charlie, as they were at regatta. She instinctively closes her eyes against the image of it. Now she can only imagine her and Charlie together away from his family, as they were when they first met on the Embankment, and the second time when he gave her the glass. Her embarrassment at the prospect of being with Charlie and Benj, and Claude and Evie, indicates just how necessary it is to step back: to finish the affair.

Nevertheless it is still humiliating when she remembers how Benj asked the question so quickly, almost eagerly: 'And could we do that?' as if he regretted even such a brief sharing of love. Going back, however, is out of the question, just as it's also impossible for her to imagine she and Benj living together, either here or in the Merchant's House. Especially not in the Merchant's House.

Jemima shakes her head impatiently at her own inconsistency. She knows that neither of them is ready to commit to a steady relationship. Benj's told her on numerous occasions how much he is enjoying his freedom; she knows that she is in love with Charlie. At the same time she's unreasonably hurt at how quickly Benj began to be uncomfortable within their new relationship that brought her physical comfort and relief.

She wonders just how guilty he's feeling about Charlie – but suddenly she can't bear to think about

Charlie. She doesn't want to admit how often, when she holds Benj in her arms, she makes believe that he is Charlie; how, once Benj has gone, she looks at her little piece of glass and feels as if her heart is just as brittle and vulnerable: simplicity, strength, freedom. Suddenly she fears that she's in danger of losing these very qualities that Charlie recognized and valued in her.

Her instinct is right: it's time to move on.

# CHAPTER THIRTY-TWO

The long, low, heavily beamed bar in the Royal Castle is a delightful place to be on this cold damp morning. The log fire is lit, the Christmas tree sparkles, and Evie sits by the fire watching people coming in, hugging each other, exchanging Christmas greetings. Presently she will go shopping but it is good to relax, to enjoy the atmosphere and see familiar faces.

She remembers how she sat here that evening just before regatta and saw Jason watching her from his seat in the corner. He's had a complete breakdown, Mikey's aunt Liz tells her, so it will be a long haul. Liz is a small, capable woman, horrified by what has happened. It was she who told them that it was Jason who smashed the window and the flowerpots; that he'd driven to Dartmouth to confront Evie and demand money and, being unable to find her, completely lost his fragile hold on sanity.

Evie still has a frisson of horror when she imagines Jason finding the boathouse empty and plunging about amongst the mud and broken pots, raging in his drunken impotence.

'Paul and I had no idea,' Liz said. 'I felt that I must come down to see you. We knew Jason suffered from depression, you see, but we hadn't realized it was getting so much worse. Mikey thought it was because he was missing Helena and we just accepted it. We didn't see Jason very often – Mikey usually comes to stay on his own – and he always sounded OK when I phoned. This is so terrible. I don't know how we can apologize enough. We'll pay for the damage, of course. We didn't know about the drink problem. He and Helena were always very close, very private, and with Mikey being away at school I suppose they were able to contain Jason's problems between them. When Helena died he was just completely devastated and I suppose he started drinking again to help him cope. I feel so guilty that I had no idea what was happening until Mikey told us at half term.'

Evie asked about Mikey; how he was managing.

'I promise you, you needn't worry about Mikey,' Liz told her. 'To be honest, I think it's been quite a relief for him to share the problem. It was a terrible burden for him. He'll live with us during the holidays, of course. Both my boys are very fond of him. They're at uni now but they come home quite often and there's plenty of room for Mikey.'

Jason, she said, became so violent when the police tried to restrain him that he was sectioned, and is being held in a secure unit whilst he has medical help and counselling, but in some strange way, she said, he seems almost happy; living in an odd world of his own, still in complete denial of his own behaviour. There is no strain, no stress; he doesn't have to compete to find or hold down a job, and it's as if he has withdrawn into himself whilst he comes to terms with Helena's death. He writes to Mikey as if they were having a perfectly normal period of separation and will soon be back together in the flat in Bristol, which is up for sale.

Evie sighs: she feels sad whenever she thinks about Jason. Her fear of him has vanished, replaced by compassion and a hope that one day he will be able to conquer his demons; be able to face life again and rebuild his relationship with Mikey.

Mikey has sent her two cards from school in the last few weeks describing his hectic life as a chorister in the run-up to Christmas; he hasn't mentioned Jason. He wrote that he and Aunt Liz are planning to come down for a few days in the new year and he's looking forward to seeing her and being in Dartmouth again.

Evie hopes that he will be in time to see the town decked in its Christmas spirit. She will introduce him to Claude and Ben and Jemima, and to the Merchant's House, and bring him here to the Castle and buy him some lunch. She will talk to him about his grandfather, and how they worked together, so that Russ will live again in his grandson's imagination and memory. It will be her own offering to the past; a gesture that might redeem her own unthinking indifference, which led to her affair with Russ and contributed to events that have come full circle. She knows that Tommy was right, his advice to refuse Russ's request was sensible and sound, but she feels a kind of gratitude that Mikey can be drawn into her life so as to complete its pattern. Tommy would approve.

The Royal Castle was one of Tommy's favourite places, a kind of home from home. They met here in those very early days, almost pretending surprise at seeing each other, getting over that first slightly awkward stage in any relationship. Later, he was always very apologetic about Christmas; that they couldn't be together. On the very rare occasions Marianne took it into her head to spend Christmas at the Merchant's House it made no difference. Generally, when the family came down from London, Evie made arrangements to go to stay with friends: it was safer that way. And when at last they were able to be together it seemed so strange, almost luxurious, to be free from any constraint, and sometimes quite challenging, so used was she to her independence. Tommy understood that. They moved casually, easily, between the two houses; giving each other space, allowing each other time to adapt.

God, I miss him, thinks Evie, smiling at an acquaintance, raising a hand in greeting. Thank God for Claude and Ben.

Yet, even though she is so grateful for their companionship, so glad that they are all together, she savours this moment of solitude. She knows that it is precisely because at any moment she can step back into that circle of friendship that she is enjoying it so much: she need not be alone. So she sits on, sipping her coffee slowly, enjoying the sense of being an onlooker. As she watches the people around her one or two ideas form at the edge of her consciousness;

several scenarios suggest themselves. Those familiar, though long absent, creative juices begin to move and flow within her and her stomach contracts with excitement. There is something new in the air, a different vibe, which connects her to the world of the imagination.

Evie takes a deep breath, sits back in her chair and opens herself up to it.

Jemima sits at her desk thinking about Benj. She thinks about the expression on his face when he told her about Laura, the love and the anxiety, and she knows even more certainly that it is right to finish their brief affair. More than that, she is beginning to feel the need to move, to change – to bolt.

She wonders why this need persists; keeps her on the edge, never wanting to put down roots. The price of freedom is loneliness, she knows that, but nevertheless she is driven to sit loose to the world. This summer and autumn has been a magical time but the sparkle is beginning to wear off. She has no future with Benj, and this is underlined by his behaviour when they talk about Laura; his absolute absorption with his daughter's future. And that is how it should be.

Perhaps if she and Benj had remained as friends she might still be able to be part of the family, but she can't turn back the clock. Once she'd believed that it could work, that somehow they could all be contained as a happy unit, but because of her own weakness that early, easy friendship has been done away with. She doesn't want to be left on the outside looking in, but nor she does she want to commit to something more demanding with Benj. She can see that there's some destructive element at work here, the same genetic element that drove her mother from lover to lover, but she can't bear just to become the faithful hanger-on; waiting for invitations to the Merchant's House, bumping into Charlie and Ange in the town.

She thinks about Charlie, about that heart stopping magic and deep-down recognition that flares between them, and she wonders longingly how it might have been if she and Charlie had met somewhere else, rather than in Dartmouth in the bosom of his family and the Merchant's House: in a café, perhaps, or in a bookshop. Jemima props her chin on her hands and imagines the scenario . . . Charlie would have been alone, having left Ange and the children on the beach at Polzeath whilst he visited some nearby town. Truro, perhaps . . .

On an impulse she leans forward, picks up the phone and dials the number of the Truro office.

'Hi,' she says. 'It's me, Jemima. Listen, Jane tells me you're losing a team manager . . . In February? OK. Look I'm coming down to Falmouth for Christmas so I'll pop in and see you . . . I know, I know. I *am* happy here but I've got itchy feet. Pastures new and all that . . . Great. I'll be in touch.'

She puts down the phone and draws a breath. She feels delightfully nervous, excited by the prospect of change, of challenges and new opportunities. Strength, simplicity and freedom: perhaps she can regain them after all.

# CHAPTER THIRTY-THREE

An hour after he sets out for Dartmouth, Charlie sends a text to Ben telling him that he'll be later than he hoped. The traffic is very heavy, there's been an accident on the M6 creating long tailbacks on the southbound carriageway, and by the time he gets through it he's running an hour later than he hoped.

It's funny, he thinks as he turns off the A38 at last, how he and Benj share this contentment when driving alone, listening to the radio, stopping whenever it feels right. Even being stuck in the traffic isn't really a problem with only oneself to worry about.

He can see that this is why the odd set-up down in Dartmouth works so well. Benj, Evie, Claude, are all people who are content to be alone, to be independent, and are prepared to allow each other space. Yet they enjoy the company and the friendship that they share; and Jemima is part of that picture: she fits in with them. He remembers meeting her on the Embankment at regatta, and he still feels the shock of it. There has never been anyone like her. How might it have been if she wasn't part of the Dartmouth set-up? If they'd met at a party, in a pub? Regatta was a one-off, a magical interlude, and during half term there was no opportunity to see her alone; just that brief exchange in Alf's. Even then, though, there was that vital connection, a sense of belonging, of being known, which he can't explain but for which he still yearns.

Funny that ever since that morning, Ange has been so . . . well, so much easier. Less sharp and abrasive and controlling. Of course, she's the same old organizing Ange, nothing will change that — and he doesn't particularly want it to — but there's a new gentleness that makes life very much easier all round and reminds him of the early days of their marriage. She was always a girl who knew her own mind, who liked to lead rather than follow, but back then their relationship was more relaxed. Of course, the births of the girls changed the balance: Ange has a strong maternal streak and the absolute need to be a perfect mother. She's worked hard bringing up the girls, keeping her hand in with the business. He has a lot to be grateful for, he knows that.

There's no doubt, though, that the news about Evie's will has put her mind at rest. If Ange is unhappy about the Merchant's House being left in trust to old Benj then she's hiding it pretty well. Knowing that it will eventually revert to the estate seems to have removed her terrible antagonism to Benj and to Evie, which was beginning to poison their lives. It's odd that the news should have quite such an effect but property means a lot to Ange and he's just grateful that she's happy now so that he can relax, too.

But he still doesn't quite know how to manage his feelings for Jemima. He can just about control them whilst he is in London, busy, occupied, but now he longs to see her alone, away from his family: on neutral territory. On an impulse he drives into the town, slides the car into a space in Victoria Road, gets out and walks towards the river. He turns into Foss Street, but it's not Jemima he sees coming towards him: it's Benj.

'Hi,' he says, and they exchange a brotherly hug. 'So here I am. How's everyone?'

'Great,' says Benj. 'Really good. I was just on my way home. You can give me a lift.'

Charlie hesitates and gives another hopeful glance along Foss Street, towards the office.

'No Jemima?' he asks almost diffidently, a bit jokily. 'Is she around today?'

'No,' Benj says, rather abruptly. 'She's already gone on holiday, I'm afraid.'

'Gone?' Charlie repeats. 'What, gone already?'

Ben stares at him. 'Yes, already.' His voice sounds odd. 'She always goes to her sister for Christmas.'

Charlie is silent. Yet, after all, what had he expected? That Jemima should sit around waiting for him to give her a few precious moments of his time? Even so, he is incredibly gutted and says so.

'And there's something else,' Ben adds gently. 'She's applied for a transfer to the Truro office so she'll be moving down sometime in the New Year. There's no doubt she'll get it.'

'Truro?' Charlie stands quite still, shocked.

'Evie and Claude don't know yet,' Benj warns him. 'She told me because I work with her and she knew I'd hear something about it, but she decided not to tell anyone else until after Christmas.'

'Did she say I could know? Did she ask you to tell me?'

'Actually, she did. She made a point of it. And she sent her love.'

And then, as they walk back to the car, Benj begins to tell him about Laura, and Charlie tries to pull himself together and concentrate; to enter into the joyful expectation of Laura's arrival with Billy for Christmas. He listens, offers words of congratulation on the prospect of their coming engagement, but just somewhere in the back of Charlie's mind a tiny flame of hope and excitement is flickering. Jemima wanted him to know that she would be moving to Truro, she sent her love to him – and Truro isn't very far from Polzeath.

Ben heaves an inward sigh of relief. The bad moment is over and he has survived it. Seeing Charlie walking towards him was a shock, even though he was expecting him. The real flesh-and-blood Charlie, hugging him, smiling at him, brought all kinds of emotions flooding up: affection, guilt, shame. When Charlie said, 'Gone? What, gone already?' Ben was reminded of Jemima turning up at the Merchant's House, asking the same question, and all that followed it. But Charlie's expression of terrible loss, so like Jemima's, somehow filled Ben with immense love and compassion for them both, which seemed to wash away any negative emotions. He remembers regatta: those suppers up on the terrace, the singing and the laughter, and Charlie's face when he said, 'I think I just fell in love, Benj'. He sees again Jemima's expression when she said, 'You'll tell Charlie I'm moving to Truro, won't you, Benj? Give him my love,' and Ben wonders if, somewhere in the future, there might be, for Jemima and Charlie, another time to laugh; a time to dance.

And now, as they drive home together, Charlie seems to have grown calm, even cheerful. He listens when Ben talks about Laura, and manages a joke, and by the time they arrive at the Merchant's House their old comradeship is restored and they are ready to celebrate Christmas with Evie and Claude.

'Stop fussing, Claude,' Evie is saying. 'The Christmas tree lights are here in a separate box. Those are just the decorations.'

Claude takes the string of lights carefully from the box she hands him, puts the plug in and switches on. The lights flicker and glow in their nest of plastic wire and he heaves a sigh of relief.

'Could have gone either way,' he says. 'Never can tell if they're going to work.'

'Ben or Charlie will have to put them on the tree,' says Evie. 'They've got nice long arms.'

Claude switches the lights off again and carefully disentangles them. Ben's idea that he and Charlie should decorate the tree is rather a good one. It will tide them over those first emotional moments of arrival, get Christmas under way, and begin these few precious days on a high note.

'I'll make some tea,' Evie is saying, 'and we'll cut the Christmas cake, shall we?'

'Good idea,' he says. 'And Ben's bought a CD of Christmas carols. He says he always has to have carols when he's decorating the tree. It's a throwback to when Laura was small and they did it together.'

There is a little silence.

'It's strange to think,' says Evie, 'that Laura and Billy will be here soon. We've never met him and he's to be her husband. One of the family.'

'Strange,' he agrees, 'but nice, too, don't you agree?'

'I do,' she says. 'Of course I do. It's just odd, isn't it? You make plans, get things sorted out in your head, and then wham! Between one minute and the next everything changes.'

'But that's the stuff of life,' he tells her. 'Stops us settling comfortably into ruts, stiffening into old age. The unexpected keeps us on our toes, ready for anything.'

She looks at him, half smiling then – unexpectedly – she puts her arms round him, hugging him tightly.

'You are a blessing, Claude,' she says, and she goes

downstairs. He hears voices calling and he knows that Charlie is here and that the party can begin. This will be the real Christmas for them. Of course, on Christmas Eve there will be Midnight Mass at St Saviour's and on Christmas morning they will have Buck's Fizz while they open presents and then they'll eat a long and delicious and probably a very late lunch and watch the Queen. But this is the real Christmas; these few special days with Charlie.

He checks the room: the fire is lit and there are sprays of holly fixed around the big ornately framed mirror above it. Meanwhile the tall tree waits in its painted tub, brightly wrapped presents piled on a chair beside it.

Evie comes into the drawing-room carrying a tray. Charlie follows with Ben, gives Claude a hug and then sees the tree.

'Wow!' he says. 'Now that's some tree. This is just like the old days. Are these the decorations? Benj says that you've kept them all these years, Evie, since when we were kids.'

'Of course we did,' she says. 'Remember, we used to have a tree, too. TDF loved his Christmas tree.'

Charlie kneels down by the box that contains the decorations and begins to unpack them.

'Look,' he says. 'I remember these painted glass ones. They're really old. They used to belong to the aunts. Oh, and look, here are those Victorian bells your mum gave us, Benj. Come on. You need to get the lights up first.'

'Hang on,' says Ben. 'I've got to put the carols on. Here we go.'

He presses the button on the CD player and the choristers' pure clear voices fill the room: 'O Little Town of Bethlehem'. Ben goes across to join Charlie, picking up the long string of lights and threading them carefully through the branches of the tall tree.

Evie begins to pour the tea, whilst Claude watches her and pushes the mugs around the low table in rotation for Evie to fill.

'Who made the cake?' he asks.

'Not I,' promises Evie. 'You can eat it quite safely knowing that Mr Marks or Mr Spencer is responsible. Ditto the Christmas pudding for tomorrow. Damn. I've forgotten the milk. How silly of me.'

'I'll get it,' says Claude. 'Don't worry.'

He's surprised at how emotional he feels, how lucky to be a part of it all. He's sad that Jemima isn't with them but, at the same time, as he and Evie agreed, it's probably the best thing all round that she's already gone to her family in Falmouth. She was certainly very cheerful when she came to say goodbye; very upbeat. This was a relief.

They were both anxious about how she and Ben and Charlie would have managed – if there would have been awkwardness and embarrassment – but as far as Claude can tell there is no constraint between the two cousins. They both seem determined to make the day a special one. He pauses in the kitchen so as to pull himself together, sees the jug of milk and carries it upstairs.

When he arrives back in the drawing-room, he stands at the door for a moment looking in. Evie is sitting forward at the low table, cutting the cake, whilst Ben, who is on tiptoe, precariously reaches to place a fragile bauble on one of the higher branches. Charlie kneels at his feet, sorting through the decorations, keeping up a running commentary on the history of each one.

The choir is still singing 'O Little Town of Bethlehem': they've reached Claude's favourite verse.

> Where Charity stands watching
> And Faith holds wide the door,
> The dark night wakes, the glory breaks,
> And Christmas comes once more.

Evie glances round, sees him standing there and smiles at him, and Claude closes the door behind him and goes in to join the party.

Fall in love with the next heartwarming and evocative
tale from Marcia Willett

# THE SONGBIRD

When Mattie invites her old friend Tim to stay in
one of her family cottages on the edge of Dartmoor,
she senses there is something he is not telling her,
as if he is holding on to a painful secret.

But as he gets to know the rest of the warm jumble
of family who live by the moor, Tim discovers that
everyone there has their own secrets. There is Charlotte,
a young navy wife struggling to bring up her son while
her husband is at sea; William, who guards a dark
past he cannot share with the others; and Mattie,
who has loved Tim in silence for years.

As Tim begins to open up, Mattie falls deeper in love.
And as summer warms the wild Dartmoor landscape,
new beginnings take root . . . But can fresh hopes
bloom where old secrets are buried?

Read on for an exclusive extract
from Marcia's next novel, out now

# CHAPTER ONE

All through the spring, early and late, the thrush sings in the ash tree below the cottage. It's the first thing he hears, when he comes carefully down the narrow precipitous staircase to make coffee, and the last thing, as he leans from the small window into the quiet luminous evening, unable to abandon the unearthly magic and get into bed.

There are no leaves yet on the trees. They hold up bare, misshapen arms and bony, twiggy fingers against a pale, translucent sky; yet he can never see the thrush hidden within these interlaced, fantastical patterns. He stands watching, seeing how the gardens tip down to the two fields – sown with barley, edged with thorn and ash – and across those fields to the lane beyond which curls and climbs up to the old farmhouse.

Tim's is the last in the terrace of cottages, converted from stables to provide accommodation for Victorian servants; modernized again more recently. The old stable-yard, flanked by two open-fronted barns where cars are parked, is separated from the courtyard behind the main house by a five-bar gate.

It is many years since Brockscombe was a working farmhouse. Bought by a naval captain with his prize money from the Napoleonic wars it has grown into a graceful family home, with white stucco and long sash windows, standing end-on to the lane and surrounded by fields sold long since to neighbouring farms.

Sometimes, when he's walking in the grounds, Tim thinks he sees ghostly figures waving at the upstairs windows – and his heart jumps with terror. But surely the ghosts are simply reflections: of racing clouds and the branches of the trees tossing in the wind? And why should he be afraid of ghosts? Is it because he fears he might soon be of their number: lost and alone, un-tethered from this friendly, familiar world?

It was Mattie who sent him to Brockscombe Farm. Pretty Mattie, with her honey-brown eyes and dark, curling hair.

'I'm leaving next month,' he told her as they made tea in the small kitchen of the London publishing house where they worked, she as a publicist, he in the marketing department. 'Taking a six-month sabbatical then moving on. I need somewhere to chill for a while. A cottage in the country but not too remote. Got any ideas?'

She looked at him thoughtfully, as if she could read his secret thoughts; suddenly he longed to tell her the whole truth but she asked no questions.

'You must go to Brockscombe,' she said. 'To Cousin Francis, William and Aunt Kat and Charlotte. It's perfect there for a sabbatical. Just west of Exeter.'

He laughed. The set-up sounded so odd. 'What's Brockscombe? Who are they, Cousin Francis, William and Aunt Kat and Charlotte?'

She laughed too. 'Brockscombe is a beautiful old Georgian farmhouse owned by Francis Courtney. He's in his eighties and he lives there on his own. He was an MP and now he's writing his memoirs. I'm not exactly sure how he's related to William and Aunt Kat but they are cousins and they share one of the cottages in the grounds. Charlotte is my big sister. She's married to William's son, Andy. He's in the navy, first lieutenant on a frigate based in Plymouth. Charlotte wasn't very impressed with the naval quarters on offer so they moved into the cottage next door to William and Aunt Kat last autumn just before she had baby Oliver, which is really good because Andy's ship will be at sea for the next few months so she's got lots of support. Kat's Andy's cousin, too, of course, but he always calls her Aunt Kat and now we all do. It's all a bit off the wall but great fun. You'd like them.'

'It certainly sounds . . . unusual.'

'There's another cottage,' she said. 'It was empty last time I was there. You'd be private. Up to a point.' She looked at him again, intently, consideringly. 'They won't be tiresome and nosy,' she assured him. 'Well, not much, anyway.'

They laughed again; it was so good for him to laugh, to ease the fear.

'I'd like to meet them,' he said.

'Well, I can arrange that. Would you rather go alone or shall we go down together and I'll introduce you?'

Once again fear chilled him, disabling him. 'I think that might be good. To go together. If you're sure?'

'Sure I'm sure,' she said casually. 'It's time I went down to Devon to see everyone. Let's make a plan to drive down, if you're happy to risk my old car.'

Cousin Francis, William, Charlotte and Aunt Kat: Mattie briefed him on the drive from London. So vivid were her word pictures that Tim was able to visualize them clearly as the M4 reeled away behind them. William, separated from his wife, Fiona, is in his middle fifties, an accountant: short, cheerful, with a tonsure of curly pepper-and-salt hair and bright blue eyes. Aunt Kat, in her early sixties, a former international ballet dancer and choreographer: tall, graceful, unconventional. Charlotte, just turned thirty-two, a web designer; energetic and capable, and determined to be the perfect mother to her baby, five-month-old Oliver, as well as looking after her and Andy's golden retriever, Wooster. Cousin Francis, thin, angular, tough, emerging from his lair from time to time to sit in the sunshine and have a chat. As she recalled past meetings, told anecdotes, described their idiosyncrasies, Mattie brought them so clearly to life for Tim that, when he finally met them, it was as if they were already old friends.

How easy she made it, how simple. Driving him down, booking him into a local pub as if she knew that he'd need his own space; introducing him to William and Charlotte and Aunt Kat, who welcomed him warmly and naturally. He was taken to meet Cousin Francis, a tall, frail but indomitable old man with a penetrating gaze, who agreed that Tim could take the cottage on a six-month shorthold tenancy. So it was arranged.

'Stay in touch, Tim,' Mattie said on his last day at the publishing house. It was almost a question. 'Charlotte will tell me how you are, of course, but it would be nice to know if it's really working for you.'

'Of course I will,' he answered. 'I'll email.'

Email was OK: he could manage that without committing himself too far.

Six weeks later he is here at Brockscombe: he loves the tranquillity, the extraordinary beauty of the old house, the stable-yard and the surrounding countryside. It is as if, at last, he has come home. He smiles wryly at the thought: rather late in the day.

'But better late than never,' he says to himself.

He's talked to himself quite a lot in the recent weeks, ever since that diagnosis of the very early stages of a rare degenerative disease; trying to stave off negative thoughts, anxiety, loneliness.

Now he has a plan. He has supplied himself with Ordnance Survey maps and he has begun to explore this wonderful county in which he so fortuitously finds himself. Sometimes his journeys take him across the moors, sometimes to the sea. Often he gets lost in the deep, secret lanes, but now he rises each morning with a sense of purpose, with a plan, to distract him from his fear. And now, for the first time in his life, he seems to have the family he's always longed for – thirty-two years too late.

Charlotte flips open her iPhone and reads Mattie's email:

'How are you all? Lovely pics of Ollie. He's gorgeous. Just showed them to everyone. Proud auntie. Don't forget to be nice to Tim. Everyone here sends love to him.'

Charlotte experiences a tiny spasm of irritation. She doesn't need to be told to be nice – to Tim or to anybody else – and especially not by her little sister. Anyway, she's glad Tim's around. It's fun to have someone of her own age to talk to sometimes, and he's very amusing though quiet and thoughtful, too.

'I don't know quite what's gone wrong for Tim,' Mattie told her, 'except that his relationship with his girlfriend broke up rather suddenly. He says he needs a new direction but he wants time to think about it.'

Charlotte checks on Oliver, fast asleep in his cot, shuts the door quietly and goes downstairs, twining up her long fair hair into its comb: an hour if she's lucky. She could do some more work on the website she's designing for a local hotel or she could catch up with the ironing. There's quite a pile but that's partly her own fault for volunteering to do William's for him this week.

'You are such a star,' Aunt Kat said, admiringly. 'As if you haven't got enough to do with darling Ollie and Wooster.'

But the thing is that she *likes* to be busy. It's better to wake up to a day full of different activities than to be gazing into emptiness. She said as much to Aunt Kat who answered that some people were perfectly happy simply gazing. Charlotte occasionally wonders what Aunt Kat does when she drives off in her little car, dashing here and there, but she doesn't ask. And Ollie adores Aunt Kat. Despite her lack of domesticity – 'Simply not a nurturer, darling,' – she is great with the baby.

Charlotte opens the front door and wanders out into the courtyard with Wooster at her heels. Last autumn she and Andy painted the old wooden tubs they found in the stables and planted them up with bulbs: snowdrops, daffodils, crocuses and tulips. Now, in the late March sunshine, the daffodils make puddles of golden light all amongst the flagstones and purple crocus glow against the surrounding grey stone walls. The big open-fronted barn to the north of the yard is empty except for her own little car, and a line of washing hangs in the sunshine in the south-facing barn where logs are stored.

Wooster wanders round the courtyard, lifts his leg half-heartedly against the gatepost, whilst Charlotte perches on a wooden bench and glances between the high stone walls, across the five-bar gate, to the big house: no noise, no movement.

'It seems rather a pity to think of your cousin Francis in there all on his own and you out here,' she said to William some months back. 'All that space going to waste. You and Aunt Kat would be company for him.'

She likes Francis, who often sits in the courtyard and chats to her, and who seems to understand the loneliness and responsibilities that go with being a naval wife.

William looked faintly uncomfortable – but she notices that he tends to edge away from discussions about Cousin Francis – muttered something about the old fellow being perfectly happy with his little team popping in to minister to his needs: Moira, the retired district nurse who checks him out each morning and evening, and drives him to any appointments, Stella, who cycles up from the little hamlet to clean and cook, and her husband, Rob, who keeps the grounds under control.

Even so, Charlotte feels there is a distinct lack of organization. The two cottages she and Tim now rent were empty for months after the elderly occupants, who also once worked for Cousin Francis, went to live with their younger families. If William and Aunt Kat moved into the house and the cottages were marketed properly there would be a good income to be had, and by the look of the house it could do with a facelift. Yet William and Kat seem content to let things ride. They live peacefully together, rather like an old married couple – though there is nothing old or married about Aunt Kat, or Irina Bulova as she is known professionally.

'She danced all over the world in all the leading roles,' Andy told Charlotte. 'And then she turned to choreography. She had a Polish lover who was a composer. He composed music specially for her – a kind of jazz ballet – and her work became iconic. He moved to New York and she went with him. He died very suddenly, very tragically, about two or three years ago and that's when she came home. She came here to recover. Dad adores her. We all do.'

And here she is, driving into the courtyard in her tiny car, waving to Charlotte, parking in the barn. The driver's door opens and a long elegant leg shoots out.

Every movement Kat makes is graceful, thinks Charlotte enviously. How does she manage it?

Tall, slender, her storm-cloud hair knotted casually, Aunt Kat emerges into the sunshine, her thin face alight with a wide smile.

'Time out?' she asks. 'Having a breather?'

She bends to murmur words of love and appreciation to Wooster whose tail thumps gently as he accepts her compliments with regal tolerance.

'I ought to be doing some work,' admits Charlotte, 'but I couldn't quite bring myself to go back inside.'

'Of course you couldn't.' Aunt Kat sits beside her, raising her face to the warm March sunshine, closing her eyes. 'Days like these are gifts from the gods. You should always seize them with gratitude.'

'Have you been shopping?' asks Charlotte idly. Foolish question: Aunt Kat never seems to do the ordinary, humdrum kind of shopping. One never sees her with carrier bags bursting with the rather dull necessities of life. A bunch of flowers, yes; a delightfully unusual toy for Oliver; a pretty piece of china. 'Found it in the market, darling. Couldn't resist.'

It is William who buys the bread, cheese, eggs, milk; plans the menus.

'He is a gastronomic retard,' Aunt Kat says cheerfully. 'Can't bear the least hint of anything spicy so it's best to let him do the cooking. Good prep school food.'

Charlotte glances sideways at Aunt Kat's lean body, long legs, and wonders if she eats anything at all.

'I went to see someone who wants me to do a talk,' Aunt Kat is answering, eyes still shut, her hand stroking Wooster's ears. 'At a ballet studio in Newton Abbot. Sweet of them to ask me.'

'You're still famous,' smiles Charlotte.

Aunt Kat opens her eyes and beams at her. 'For all the wrong reasons. All those lovers, dashing off to New York with Gyorgy, my choreography. I was always just a bit avantgarde. It wouldn't be remarkable now, of course.'

'You'll always be remarkable,' says Charlotte, still smiling. 'You can't help yourself. It's a gift.'

'Darling,' says Aunt Kat, clearly moved by this tribute. 'That's very sweet of you. I tell you what. I shall go inside and make us some coffee and bring it out and we'll drink it in the sunshine.'

'Oh, yes, please,' says Charlotte gratefully. William might choose the food but it is Aunt Kat who buys the coffee and it is seriously good. 'I'd love that.'

She, in turn, closes her eyes and relaxes. It is blissful to sit here with Wooster in the sun, in the rural silence, and anticipate Aunt Kat's coffee. The website can wait.

*

Kat makes coffee, whizzing the beans, setting out two pretty mugs and some milk for Charlotte. She chooses some biscuits and arranges them in a little dish. It's good for Charlotte to have a moment in the sunshine without the demands of Oliver or work. Kat smiles as she waits for the coffee machine. She likes to be Aunt Kat to Charlotte and Andy and Mattie – and Ollie as he gets older. This is her family. She's feeling stronger, happy, in love with life again, though she's beginning to miss her theatre friends, the world of dance. Just now, though, it's good to have Andy and Charlotte and the baby around – and now Tim. She loves to be with young people. It was right to come here, to William, to Brockscombe, after Gyorgy died. She couldn't bear the old haunts, the well-meaning sympathy of old friends. She needed change and peace in order to regroup: to mourn. It was wonderful to be with William again, after all these years, to be able to support him after the break-up with Fiona and the death of his mother. His father, Kat's uncle, died some years ago and her own father – a Polish fighter pilot – died whilst she was still a child. As children, she and William spent the summer holidays together and the bond between them is a strong one. They are happy here together, although there is always the uncertainty of the future: what happens to them all when Francis dies?

'I don't trust Francis' boys,' William would say.

'But surely they can't just throw us out,' Kat would answer.

William would snort. 'We're on six-month shorthold tenancies here. Nothing is certain.'

She'd jolly him along, as she always did, and they'd talk about having options, of looking for another house, though neither of them wants to break up this little family group. But now, as she makes the coffee, disquiet nibbles at the edges of her happiness. Could it really be possible that one day – even quite soon – they might all have to leave Brockscombe?

She thrusts the thought away, pours the coffee into a big pot and carries the tray outside to the courtyard, where Charlotte is waiting in the sunshine.

# Also by Marcia Willett

## Postcards from the Past

Siblings Billa and Ed share their beautiful old childhood home in Cornwall. With family and friends nearby, life is content. But when postcards start arriving from a sinister figure from their pasts, old memories are stirred. Why is he contacting them now? And what has he been hiding all these years?

## The Sea Garden

Jess is on her way to Devon to receive a painting award. Hosting her will be Kate and her family, and Jess is grateful for the warm welcome: Jess's own family fell apart years ago. But as they begin reminiscing, long-buried secrets are uncovered – but at what cost have they been kept hidden?

## The Christmas Angel

It's just after Christmas, and four-year-old Jakey is helping to put away the decorations. He hates seeing them disappear back into their boxes, especially the angel. But things are going to be different this year. His Cornish home is in danger of being sold, and everything is changing. Will his close-knit family unit still be together next Christmas?

### The Summer House

In a small wooden box, Matt's mother kept all his childhood memories. But something about the photos has always puzzled Matt — why does he not recognize anything? And where, in the photos, was his sister? Feeling that something has always been missing, Matt begins to discover the strange and tragic secret which has affected his whole life . . .

### The Prodigal Wife

Jolyon takes his new girlfriend Henrietta home to meet his extended family — but also to meet Marie, the mother who deserted him and his father many years ago, now seeking forgiveness. Henrietta, too, is still vulnerable from the break-up of her own parents' marriage, and unsure whether she can move on. Can a family ever be mended again?

### The Way We Were

In the middle of a snowstorm Tiggy arrives at the remote house on Bodmin Moor, pregnant and alone, and is welcomed by Julia into her warm and chaotic family. Nearly thirty years later, when Tiggy's son is about to become a father, the next generation discovers secrets from the past which must be uncovered . . .

### Memories of the Storm

Clio is staying at beautiful Bridge House with her godmother, Hester, reliving happy childhood memories. Jonah, visiting the area, chances upon the house where his mother stayed during the war. They don't yet know it, but their histories are inextricably linked. As the young couple become closer, Hester realizes they must know the truth, before it is too late . . .

### Echoes of the Dance

They were all there for different reasons, but all hoping the beauty of the Cornish countryside would bring them peace. At the house on the edge of Bodmin Moor, illusions are shattered, secrets are uncovered, and each of them discovers that in order to move forward they have to confront their pasts . . .

### The Golden Cup

Paradise: the house at the head of a sheltered Cornish valley where Honor Trevannion lives, surrounded by her family. But when a young American arrives bearing an old photograph and looking for a long-lost relation, Honor is inexplicably distressed. Increasingly troubled, she begs her granddaughter to find a cache of letters hidden for fifty years . . .

### The Birdcage

It was Felix whom they all adored, but while Lizzie longed for a father, Felix had other commitments: his wife and their son Piers, both living at beautiful Michaelgarth, on the edge of Exmoor. Many years later, when Lizzie meets Piers for the first time, she finds a family in trouble – and which needs her help to heal.

### The Children's Hour

Nest and Mina still live at Ottercombe, their beautiful childhood home in Devon. They came to the house before the war – and now they welcome their children and grandchildren. But when their sister Georgie, now frail and forgetful, comes to stay, the past returns too. For Georgie knows all their secrets, secrets which she wants to share . . .

### Indian Summer

For Kit, the quiet Devon village she visits every year is the perfect retreat. But this summer she arrives with a heart in turmoil and a secret from the past. As the summer unfolds, hidden truths are uncovered that will shatter the sleepy community. Some memories are best forgotten . . . Others won't ever go away.

*Do you love talking about your favourite books?*

From big tearjerkers to unforgettable love stories, to family dramas and feel-good chick lit, to something clever and thought-provoking, discover the very best **new fiction** around – and find your **next favourite read**.

See **new covers** before anyone else, and read **exclusive extracts** from the books everybody's talking about.

With plenty of **chat, gossip and news** about **the authors and stories you love**, you'll never be stuck for what to read next.

And with our **weekly giveaways**, you can **win** the latest laugh-out-loud romantic comedy or heart-breaking book club read before they hit the shops.

*Curl up with another good book today.*

Join the conversation at
**www.facebook.com/ThePageTurners**
And sign up to our free newsletter on
**www.transworldbooks.co.uk**